STARFIRE

NAOMI HUGHES

ISBN: 978-1-7363943-7-3

Ebook: 978-1-7363943-8-0

Cover art by: Amelia Buff

For all those living with disabilities—
visible or invisible,
mental, physical, emotional,
diagnosed, undiagnosed,
big enough to cause serious hardship
or so "minor" you don't think you're worth bothering over
(you're always worth bothering over):
I see you.

FOREWORD

The main character in this story has harm OCD, which is a real thing. It involves intrusive thoughts (scary/violent thoughts that seem to pop up out of the blue), along with a pervasive fear that the "bad thoughts" mean you are a bad person who is likely to carry out those violent actions in real life (not the case at all).

If you have symptoms similar to Per's, I encourage you to speak to a qualified mental health professional if at all possible. OCD sucks, but it's treatable! If you're curious about harm OCD or the many other subsets of obsessive-compulsive disorder, you can check out these sites for more information:

IntrusiveThoughts.org

Iocdf.org

Once, a sun fell into old-Earth:

fires of calamity, wave on wave,

unimaginable. Unsurvivable.

We fled into the solace of dark and empty space

But what we found was not dark. Not empty

but filled with a thousand eyes, ten thousand wings, monstrous teeth and

horrific light:

a cataclysm that breathes and shines, shines, shines.

We never should have left.

-

-Fragment of ancient poetry recovered from Pioneer Ship crash site

"Star dragons: the inevitable forest fires of the universe, decimating whole solar systems with their powers. Those who believe they exist call them an apocalypse. But what of seedling planets that might take root in their wake? What if they, like other apex predators, have a rightful role in the natural ecosystem of the universe?"

-Excerpt from the dissertation of Dr. Minerva Colton, since redacted

PROLOGUE

In my second-oldest memory, I'm seven years old.

I'm in an abandoned planetarium. The domed ceiling has long since deteriorated to a skeletal steel grid hung with strips of painted canvas: a tattered night sky emblazoned with stars. The fabric flutters in every gust of wind like tethered birds trying to break free. The real sky—an empty, claustrophobic expanse of blank white nothingness—is just a backdrop.

I came here to remember...something.

Anthem, the six-year-old who became my little sister last week, is zooming around with her arms outstretched in front of me. Her heavy stomps and flamboyant arm-flapping rattles the stage, which is little better than a deathtrap of rotted boards and rusted screws at this point. I tried to tell her to be careful—tried to insist she not even come with me in the first place when I ducked in here on my way back from my overwhelmingly large new school—but if I've learned one thing about Anthem, it's that she's not the careful type.

She swoops up the aisle where I'm crouched, my neck bent back as I stare at the faded stars. "Peregrine!" she whoops, using my brand-new name. "Come be a star dragon with me." She roars, opening her mouth wide and showing off the gap where she's already lost two teeth. Her dark bronze skin is streaked with dust that she has enthusiastically applied like face paint, and her long, wavy black hair is hopelessly snarled. When I don't answer at first, she flaps her arms with even more enthusiasm plus an exaggerated pleading expression.

There's nothing in me that wants to look away from the tattered stars overhead, but Anthem is asking me to play and I desperately want her to like me. She is a ferocious, feral girl who simultaneously terrifies and inspires me, and even though she and her parents made me an official member of their family last week, there's a part of me that's still scared they'll realize their mistake and drop me back off in the glint mine where I was found. So I oblige Anthem by getting up and traipsing to the center stage, where I stand atop the creaking floorboards and try not to imagine them collapsing.

"How do I play?" I ask.

"Just be a dragon," she says, flapping her arms again to demonstrate. She points up at the ceiling. "You can pick whichever star you want to hatch from. I'm from that blue supergiant over there." She motions grandly at a strip of fabric hanging from the far corner of the ceiling, which I'm pretty sure features Pluto from old-Earth's solar system rather than any actual star, not that I'm going to tell her that. "Then you just fly around and roar with me. Come on!"

I try stretching out my arms like hers, but it feels unnatural and wrong and I drop them back to my sides. Seeing my awkwardness, Anthem squints and tilts her head.

"Or you can be my victim instead," she says.

I peer at her, unsure if I like where this is going. "Your victim?"

"Yes. I'll swoop in and chase you and when I catch you, I'll breathe starfire and uncreate you. It'll be fun, you'll get to yell *lots*."

The forgotten memory I came here to find squirms at the back of my mind like a beehive poked with a stick. I tilt my head up to the fake stars and the real, blank sky beyond them. "I don't want to be uncreated." The words are rawer than I mean for them to be; I can't remember anything further back than the last month, but I know clearly that I am currently the happiest and luckiest that I've ever been. The thought of that being snatched away, transmuted like gold turning back to lead, is too much to bear.

Anthem drops her arms and furrows her brow. "It's just for pretend."

I swallow, suddenly struggling not to cry. The memory I'm groping for is floating slowly toward the surface of my mind and it's so *sad*, so terrible, that now I'm not sure I want to remember it at all. "No, it's not," I say.

Anthem stands helplessly in front of me, probably trying to think of how to make me feel better. If there was a bully taunting me she would punch them—which I know because that's happened twice this week already—and if one of the nameless adults from Child Well-being Services were pestering me with their endless questions then she would distract them. But whatever's wrong with me now is something neither of us knows how to ease.

Then her eyes light up with an idea. "We'll be creation dragons!" she proclaims.

I blink at her. Dragons—maybe-real, maybe-mythical creatures born in the hearts of stars—have only one power: uncreation. They are monsters, beautiful and horrendous and merciless. Everyone knows this. Except all at once, I want to pretend I don't.

Creation dragons. Yes. That is what I will be: a maker, not a destroyer. Not a monster. I spread my arms again and this time it feels right. The memory I was searching for flutters somewhere in my chest like a winged thing looking for a window, but the longer I play with Anthem, the more its urgency fades.

As the years go by, I return to the planetarium once a month, and then once a year, and then not at all. The memory evaporates into an ether whose scent I catch every so often, like smoke from a distant wildfire—but I always assume it's just some vague, unimportant recollection of my past life.

Until I turn seventeen, and the dreams start.

In my oldest memory, I am ancient and endless. My wings glow with the ethereal blue light of the star that hatched me. The black of space spans infinite all around me, a dark horizon I can rocket toward for a millennium and still never pass into. The light of a thousand suns spark everywhere and I could touch them all if I wanted, could sink into their gravity and swim through their fire. I am boundless. I am *free*.

And I am dying.

Chapter One

I don't usually put much stock in appearances, but I'm pretty sure the ship in front of me has to be a joke.

I glance at the boats moored at the docks beside it. They aren't beautiful by any stretch—everything in the Conglom, and probably the world, is mostly rust and sketchy welds by this point—but at least they look like proper ships. Barnacle-clogged hulls, tall steam stacks striped in the colors of their port cities, printed plastic mastheads in the shapes of mermaids with unrealistic curves. More than a few of the boats are listing to one side or the other like old soldiers dozing off during a night watch, but they still look mostly seaworthy.

I turn back to the vessel in front of me. It's a submarine. Most of it is lurking beneath the water, but judging by what I can make out from my spot on the main boardwalk, it's a wonder the thing can float at all. The plates of metal that make up its body are an odd cobalt blue and warped, joined together at seams that look entirely arbitrary. It's like one of those horror-movie dolls with stitched-up faces. It has its own plastic masthead jutting out from the front of its tower, too: a portly middle-aged man seated in a recliner with his feet up. He's wearing nothing but boxers and is clutching a beer can in his right hand. I crane my neck to read the letters printed in sloppy all-white capital letters on the hull below him: *The Shitty Clunker.*

This can't possibly be the right ship.

I hesitate for a second before I ease my ratty, patched-up bag off my shoulder and pull out a book. Though "book" might be a generous term; I've glued this thing together painstakingly over the course of years with my absolutely zero experience in book-making, and it shows. The pages are mismatched, some stolen from clunky textbooks, others lifted from antique fairytale collections. The margins are all filled with the tiny scrawl of my handwriting. I flip past star maps and poems and diagrams of scales to the end—the last entry, where I'd taped in a newspaper article.

Museum Receives Donation from "Star Slayer," the headline proclaims in bold font. Most of the article's space is devoted to gushing about the mysterious adventurer who researches dragons in hopes of finding and exterminating any that might still be lurking on the planet's surface. In the sole quote offered by the article, he claims to be pursuing a promising tip on a live, hibernating dragon. I glance past the first attached photo—a bowl full of fossilized fangs that may or may not have belonged to ancient star dragons that he's unearthed in the course of his research—and pause on the second one. It's a blurry, silhouetted shot of his face meant to protect his identity, set against a backdrop of seamed metal that looks an awful lot like a ship hull. I squint at the fuzzy letters painted on the hull in the far corner of the shot: *AV4220.*

Albergian vessel number 4220. As soon as I got ahold of this article last week, I used some of my precious energy allotment to get online and dig into the docking schedules of all the major ports. I set up pings to alert me if a ship bearing that identifier arrived anywhere nearby. The first and only notification came through just a few hours ago, leading me to this very bay.

I put the book away and look back up at the sub. *AV4220* is scrawled across its side. If my guess is correct—if the Star Slayer was posing in front of his own chartered ship and not some other random one—then he could be aboard *The Shitty Clunker* at this very moment. And if that's the case then I'm not going to leave empty handed, even if I have doubts—a *lot* of doubts—about his choice of vessel. I square my shoulders and step out onto the least rickety part of the dock.

And immediately almost get a face full of wrench for my troubles.

I dodge the flying tool just in time and it clanks forebodingly onto the main docks at my back, leaving a divot in the wood where it lands. "What the hell?" I demand, whirling around and searching warily for the wrench hurler.

A guy who looks maybe a year older than me is peering down from the shadows of the sub's tower, where the entry deck is. Only his head—mussed brown hair, face smudged with machine oil, sharp cheekbones—is poking up above the hatch. He's holding the handle of a screwdriver between his teeth. He shifts the tool to the other side of his mouth like it's a toothpick and calls down to me, "You're trespassing. Scram."

I spread my arms, bewildered and more than a little offended, to gesture at the dock and the algae-clogged brown water below. "This is a public dock."

"And that was a public wrench. Again I repeat: scram, before a public screwdriver messes up that pretty face."

I'm not quite sure how to respond to that—*you're one to talk about pretty faces, jackass* is what immediately comes to mind but that doesn't seem either wise or productive, so I settle for, "I have legitimate business here."

He sighs heavily and his head rises a little higher until his shoulders and torso are also visible above the hatch. His arms are bare and corded with enough muscle to make me both resentful and impressed, though I do everything I can to not let that show in my expression. I didn't come here to admire the scenery. I came here for answers about my dreams, which have been getting increasingly intense and detailed over the last few months. That foreboding sense that I'm dying is harder to shake with each successive morning, and lately I've even started slipping into daydreams of soaring through stars and rocketing into deep space during my classes, which is why I'm now dangerously close to flunking several of my senior projects. Even more unsettling than that, though, is the pain I've started waking up with—a ghostly, indistinct ache deep in my bones like a phantom limb I can't identify. The medic I went to couldn't turn up a cause for it, which should make me feel better but only makes me worry more. That's why I'm here. Whatever my dreams are, they've got something to do with star dragons, and no one knows more about dragons than the man aboard this sub.

I'm quiet for too long, considering all this, and the guy in front of me plucks the screwdriver out of his mouth and cocks his arm back to throw it.

"I'm here to see the Star Slayer," I say hastily. "I heard he was aboard this vessel. I want to join his crew for the next mission." It's an extreme measure—and one I still haven't gotten up the courage to ask my parents to approve—but if it gets me answers then it'll be worth it.

The guy rolls his eyes and tips his head back in exasperation, staring at the sky long enough to make me wonder if he's actually looking at something. I risk a glance upward. My heart catches for the barest second as it always does whenever I look up, like some gullible part of me expects to see stars flecked bright across a true night sky. Instead

I see what I always see: an eggshell-colored expanse of emptiness, like some cosmic entity has wrapped our planet in sheets of blank paper. The nearest star, which we call Sol after old-Earth's sun, is nothing but an indistinct blob of fuzzy yellow straining to shine through the Barrier.

A familiar claustrophobia envelops me at the sight. I still can't quite fathom how people can go about their lives beneath the Barrier, knowing there's a whole universe out there they'll never even see. How can anyone be happy with such a small life? Why doesn't everyone long to rip a hole in the sky the way I do—to leave this shell of a world behind, to swim out into the starlight of infinite possibilities? To be *free*?

I shake myself out of those thoughts, but the longing sticks with me. A lot of it comes from the intensifying dreams but a good portion of it is really just me wanting…I don't know. More. Something bigger, grander, than being trapped beneath an empty sky forever.

I pull my gaze back to the guy in the hatch. He's looking at me again, but this time his eyes are narrowed and a little bit too knowing, like he saw something I didn't meant to show him while I was looking up at the sky.

He whirls the screwdriver between his fingers, tosses it straight up into the air, catches it neatly and tucks it away into a pocket on his sleeveless shirt. Then he lifts the rest of the way up out of the hatch, revealing that he isn't standing on the exit ladder as I had assumed, but is instead sitting in some sort of retrofitted hoverchair. His feet are bare and completely clean, indicating he uses the hoverchair as his main form of transportation. Now that I can see more of him, I also realize he's older than I thought—twenty, maybe. University aged. Not that he looks anything like the Conglom's usual tight-laced, militaristic university students.

He reaches down to some levers on the side of the chair and flips two of them. The chair makes a *clank* reminiscent of the wrench hitting the deck earlier, and some sort of mechanism that looks like retractable landing gear extends from the bottom of his chair and attaches to the deck. "Magnets," he explains when he sees me looking. "Wouldn't do to fall overboard. The hover mechanism works like a charm most days but I'm the sort of guy who likes a safeguard or three."

I cast a doubtful eye over *The Shitty Clunker*, which looks like it eats safeguards for breakfast, but choose not to remark on it. Instead I ask, "So will you let me aboard? To see the Star Slayer?"

"Ugh, the fans that guy attracts," he mutters. "Look, he's not taking on any more crew members right now. What's your name, anyway?"

"Per."

"Pear, like the fruit?"

I give him a dead-eyed stare as he snickers. "*Per.* Short for Peregrine." It means *traveler*. My parents thought it was a good name to give the starry-eyed boy who was discovered lost in the glint mines. To be fair, my adoptive parents are amazing people. They just don't have the best naming sensibilities.

The guy on the sub raises an eyebrow. "Oh. That's actually a pretty decent name. I'm Z."

"Z, like the letter?" I say, adopting his own tone from a moment ago.

"Oh ho, he bites back!" Z crows. "Yeah, Z like the letter, genius."

"And you're...the ship's mechanic?" I hazard, eyeing the oil stains on his clothing and face.

"Mechanic, acting captain, and the chef too," he answers sourly, "now that our cook dumped us for a contract on one of those soulless floaters." He gestures at the rows of ships in the nearby bays.

"Acting captain?" I blurt, taken aback. Unless he really is one of the universities' star graduates in a very messy disguise, there's no way someone so young would be given the run of a ship. Even if said ship is *The Shitty Clunker.*

Z's voice sharpens whip-fast. "Regular captain is home on some business, sent me out to resupply. What's it to you?"

I hastily raise my hands in surrender. "Nothing at all. I'm sure you're doing a great job. Captain."

His eyes narrow. He gives me a long, steady stare. My palms start to sweat. "*Acting* captain," he grumbles after a minute.

"Right," I say tactfully, then shift from foot to foot, wondering how to get the conversation back on track without pissing him off further. "So...uh, the Star Slayer? I really do need to see him."

Z waves me off, not even looking at me now as he fiddles some more with the controls on his hoverchair. "I shall repeat myself: scram. He's not hiring. Go eat some fish and chips or polish your sense of righteous indignation or whatever it is pretty boys like you do with your free time."

I hide a grimace. I can't let him just shoo me away. "What about you?" I ask in a sudden burst of inspiration. "Are *you* hiring? You just said you're having to cover a bunch of jobs all on your own. If you let me come aboard for just the next leg of the Star Slayer's trip, I'll do whatever jobs you want me to do in the meantime."

He lifts his gaze and eyes me, considering. I hold my breath. "We *might* be able to work something out," he allows grudgingly at last. "We're only here to resupply for two more days, though, so if I do decide to take you on—which I'm not promising—you'd have to sign the journey-indenture contract before then. And my captain, she'd have to approve it too."

I nod quickly. Two days is a tight deadline for convincing my parents to let me go on a weeks-long jaunt in the middle of my senior year, but they've always been the open-minded sort, and I could probably convince them it's good life experience. I'll have a ton of schoolwork to make up for when I get back but at least I'll have the mental space to actually focus on it rather than my deep-space daydreams. Concentrating on calculus is a lot easier when you're not secretly worried that you might actually be dying, or that a maybe-mythical creature is somehow invading your brain and giving you the world's weirdest nightmares.

Z makes an exasperated noise. "Fine, I guess I can interview you or whatever." Before I have the chance to feel any relief at that lukewarm proclamation, he holds out a hand. "Now toss me that wrench."

I eye the tool that's still lying on the dock. "Is the wrench, uh, part of the interview?"

"No, idiot, it's part of me fixing this goddamn hatch so we won't implode and drown next time we submerge."

I'm a fan of not drowning, so I toss him the wrench. It arcs a good foot to the side of where I aimed it but he leans over and snatches it easily out of the air anyway, then uses it to bang on the inside of the hatch. "Rick!" he yells. "Get up here, got a fanboy who wants a contract!"

I wince—both at the noise and the fanboy comment—and mentally file the name *Rick* away. This must be the Star Slayer he's calling up to take part in my interview. Sure enough, after a minute a middle-aged Black man climbs out of the hatch, his back to me. He's wearing slacks that have been pressed to within an inch of their starched-crease life along with suspenders and, I see when he glances over at me, a purple bow tie. "I was under the impression we weren't taking anyone else on," he says. His tone is as crisp and tidy as his goatee. He looks more like a college professor than a would-be dragon slayer.

Z shifts in his hoverchair to reach something on the other side of the hatch with his wrench. "Yeah, well," he grunts, "this one was insistent. Star Slayer, meet bird boy." He waves at me with his free hand like he's swatting away a fly. I consider protesting *bird boy* but decide to pick my battles. "We can interview him on the way to the market. Soon as I'm done with this."

The Star Slayer nods at me, then shimmies out of the hatch—somehow managing to make shimmying look elegant in the process—and climbs down the ladder to the dock, turning to face me. He holds out a hand and I reach to shake it.

That's when I see the knives.

They're on a belt slung over his shoulder. Half a dozen of them. Small paring knife, forearm-sized hunting knife. A Bowie with a worn bone handle.

I rip my hand out of his grip and lean away from the weapons. My heartrate ticks upward. I tuck my hands in my pockets just in case they start shaking.

Rick frowns, looking puzzled but not alarmed at my reaction. He glances down at the knife belt. "Oh!" he says with a chuckle, his brow clearing. "Sorry, didn't mean to startle you. I'm a bit of a collector. I don't really use them for much of anything, but there's so much history in each of them."

I nod. My face twitches into what I hope is a polite smile even as my whole body locks up with the effort of holding myself in place. Rick doesn't seem to notice, since he launches into a lecture on the history of the Bowie while I try not to hyperventilate.

The knives are, what, three feet away? No distance at all. All I'd have to do is take two steps forward and reach out and close my fingers around a hilt, then I'd be armed. A veil of panic brushes over my thoughts as I realize that I'm looking directly at the knives—that I've broken one of my cardinal rules. Thoughts bubble to the surface of my mind, beading red and viscous like oil:

The give of flesh beneath a blade.

A mist of blood laced over cobalt metal.

The way Z and Rick would look at me if I stabbed them—shocked, betrayed, and then dead.

How many people are in that sub? Is there just the one entry and exit? If I go down that hatch, would they all be trapped inside as I went cabin to cabin and—

I snap myself down around the thought, imagine locking it in chains and throwing away the key. My heartbeat is thunder in my ears. My polite smile feels like a dead man's rictus.

"...discovered the Ancient Isles," Rick is saying. He's oblivious, smiling fondly as he taps one of the smaller knives. His words fade in and out of my awareness like a wavering radio signal. "All she had was this knife, stranded for forty-three days..."

My gaze is locked on Rick's face now, not on the knives, but they still sear the corner of my vision. *I am a good person*, I remind myself, a frantic edge to the thought. *I don't go around on willy-nilly stabbing sprees.* But then why did I have those thoughts the second I saw the knives? Good people don't have thoughts like horror movies playing in their brains.

Now Z is talking. "...do the trick," he says with an air of satisfaction, tucking his tools into the side of his seat. "Okay, I'm ready, let's get that market run slash-interview over with."

A wrenching helplessness grinds into me. I can't go with them. I can't be that close to weapons. I *can't*.

"Hello, bird boy?" Z calls. He's peering at me, but his expression is only quizzical, not confused or terrified. I can still pass for normal, I think bitterly. No one but me can see what's in my head, and thank the gods for that, or they would probably lock me away.

Maybe they should *lock me away,* I think to myself. The helplessness tightens its grip. I scramble for words. "Sorry. I, uh, I have to go to the bathroom. I'll...I'll catch up."

I need to get a job on this sub. I need to talk to Rick. This is my only lead to solving my dreams. Surely, *surely*, I'll be able to manage my awful thoughts long enough to pursue it. I just...need a break first.

"Seriously?" Z scoffs. He hits a button on his chair and it starts descending down the side of the sub next to the ladder. "Whatever, I guess. We're not waiting for you. You can find us in the market. Or not."

The weapons belt pulls at my gaze like it's a black hole. I think one last time about going with them, walking next to Rick in easy reach of those knives—and in response, another flood of red-saturated images blinks through my brain, even worse this time. An empty ribcage curled in on itself like the legs of a dying insect. Hair and skin splintered under my fingernails. The slip and slide of intestines.

I turn and flee.

Chapter Two

It was just a few months ago that I first found out I had OCD.

Obsessive-compulsive disorder has many subsets, said the handout Anthem slipped me. *One of the lesser known is harm OCD. This person typically has intrusive thoughts with violent content, and fears that the thoughts mean they are in actuality a violent person. They respond with compulsions (usually mental and invisible) meant to prove to themselves that they are not.*

Harm OCD. Such a simple term for such an agonizing thing. The handout was so short and matter-of-fact, like knowing what was wrong with me meant I would be magically cured of it.

I manage to restrain myself to a fast walk toward one of the nearby port annex buildings. There's a man arguing with a clerk about tariffs for giant eel catches, but other than that the place is empty. I quickly locate the bathroom, slip into a stall, put the toilet lid down and sit on it. Only then do I allow myself to drop the veneer of normality.

I bend over double and put my head in my hands, curling around the core of guilt and horror inside me. I retreat inside my mind. I replay the scene on the docks as if it's a football play I can fast forward and zoom in on and pause, and I go through it step by agonizing step, trying to recall exactly how far away the knives were and exactly how I felt when I accidentally looked at them. Was I tempted? Excited?

Turned on? I feel sick going over these checks, but they're necessary. I need to *know.* I need to know if I'm somehow a secret murderer just waiting for the right cue.

I need to know if I am good.

Thanks to the article I know that what I'm doing is a compulsion, an attempt to prove my obsessive fears wrong. I know that they don't actually make me or any of my would-be "victims" any safer. But knowing that doesn't make any difference at all.

I consider trying to slip into a daydream of space again to get away from my fears, but I've never had any success voluntarily calling those up. At least I know those dreams, whatever they are, aren't connected to my OCD. I'm never afraid or obsessive when I'm having them, just sad and full of longing for some distant, unreachable thing.

It takes a while—too long, long enough for Z and Rick to get halfway to the market district—but eventually, after replaying the scene enough times in my head, I begin to calm down. My heart, which has been skidding around in my chest like a juiced-up racehorse, starts to slow. I'm okay. I've managed to escape the thoughts coming true this time; if I keep being careful, keep a tight leash on myself and watch closely for any sign of bad intent, I can keep doing it. I *have* to keep doing it. There's no other option.

In the back of my mind, of course, I know that's not right. *People with OCD are among the most unlikely to ever actually perform acts of violence,* that article said. I know that my fears feature doing harm and being a bad person precisely because those are the most frightening things my brain can dredge up. But knowing that doesn't really help because there's always the chance I'm the exception to the rule, and the consequences of that are too terrible to bear.

I let out a long breath, lift my head out of my hands, and take in the details of my surroundings. I'm no stranger to breakdowns in public bathrooms by this point, but this has to be by far my grossest venue yet. Orange mold is creeping around the base of the toilet and the mushroom-colored grout is flaking away in chunks. The door's lock is rusted open. Anyone could've burst in on me and seen me utterly losing my shit. And not in the way people are supposed to lose their shit in bathrooms.

I stand and nudge the door open gingerly with my foot. It creaks a loud protest. I walk over to the sink and turn it on, washing my hands in the thin, grudging dribble of water. I glance in the mirror to make sure I look normal-ish. Shaggy wheat-blond hair, blue eyes, cheekbones that Mom likes to call "aristocratic." I look a little haunted to my own gaze but no one else would be able to tell the difference. Well—Anthem probably could. She's way too perceptive for her own good, which is probably why she's in training to be a counselor.

I dry my hands off and try to focus on what I need to do next. The market district is maybe a twenty-minute walk and it sounded like Z and Rick had a fair amount of perishables to purchase. If I hurry, I should still be able to catch them.

Checking my reflection one last time to ensure optimum normality-faking, I push open the restroom door and step out into the port office. Before I can get outside, though, my comm watch interrupts me with a sad burbling noise.

I glance down at my wrist. My watch's ancient rubber strap is in the last-gasp stage of disintegration, so I'm careful to move gingerly and not jostle it too much as I hold down the power button. I wince when I see the battery level—forty-eight percent. I've used up more than half of my weekly energy allotment already and it's only Tuesday. But the noise it just made means I've received a message marked as urgent, so I don't really have a choice but to use up another bit of energy to check it. A line of text flashes on the screen: *tell me your location so that I may come murder you.* Anthem has discovered my absence from school.

I flinch, quickly averting my eyes from the word *murder*—not a huge trigger in itself but still significant enough to try to avoid—and swipe in a return text that includes a location tag. *I'm fine, thanks for asking,* I send her as I keep moving down the docks.

The reply comes seconds later: *only until I find you, dickwad.*

I wince. *Stop worrying about me.*

A moment's delay, and then she replies: *Never.*

A twinge of regret fizzes through me. Anthem would be all for me having this little escapade if it didn't mean I was one step closer to having to repeat most of my classes. If that happens, she'll end up graduating alone and then go on to honors-track career placement alone, when we've always promised to get a posting together. And even with that possibility looming, I know she's only upset because I haven't told her why I'm suddenly so fixated—or at least, more fixated than usual—on star dragons, and she's worried about me.

I droop with guilt. *Sorry, sis. I'm running one quick errand then I'll be back in time for ancient lit.*

She sends back: *Does that errand have something to do with dragons? You realize you can do your weird scrapbook thing after school, right? Thus not flunking your senior year?*

Scrapbook—she means my cobbled-together collection of dragon intel, which I had the bad judgment to tell her about when I first started it. I sigh. *Sorry,* I repeat, since there's not really anything else I can say at this point.

I'm already on the uptrain. I'll wait at the station for you, Anthem sends, and then the blinking dot that signals her watch as being powered-up vanishes. She's gone dormant, effectively ensuring she gets the last word.

I grimace, turn off my own watch, and hurry through the door and toward the main port area. It's crowded here, with the dock workers and sailors clumping together in small groups as they hustle from their ships to the squat white port buildings and back again. Sheaves of paperwork rustle in their hands and the smell of old sweat and older fish billows out from them as they passed. I can pick out the veterans among them: they walk with rolling gaits, suspicion folded into their leathery, sunburnt expressions as they eye me.

I make it to the exit gates. The tall buildings of downtown are only a few blocks from here, draped in creaking scaffolding, sawing at the sky with the naked steel beams of abandoned construction. Even as I speed my steps, I keep one eye cast warily upward at the skyscrapers. Every few weeks someone gets nailed by falling debris.

I dodge bicycles, empty-eyed pedestrians, and a few cars driven by those rich enough to afford the skyrocketing price of the glint-based fuel they run on. A street vendor waves kabobs of mystery meat at me. Several people on the opposite sidewalk scream at each other over a box of spilled groceries. A slippery-looking man palms a wallet from someone's pocket and then vanishes into a deli that is somehow also a laundromat. Giant screens loom above the whole scene, bolted to the sides of the buildings, all of them as blank as the sky. I can't remember the last time I saw them turned on.

As I scan the streets for Z and Rick, I try to district myself from the thought of the knives by mentally running over potential arguments for convincing them to let me tag along on *The Shitty Clunker*. Judging by the sparse gossip available about the Star Slayer online, he's drawn to the star dragons because of their sensationalism, their aura of fairy-tale-villain power. He probably thinks he'd become a legend himself if he can find and slay one. Which is likely true. No one has ever uncovered concrete proof of them before, even though stories of star dragons are embedded in our oldest histories. When the Pioneer Ship carried the last human survivors to this small planet a thousand years ago, legend has it that the dragons nearly decimated them with starfire—mystical flames that have the power to uncreate anything they touch, not only killing people but wiping them from existence entirely, erasing even the memory of them. Many theorize that whole swaths of human history were lost because of their attacks.

Then the Barrier was erected. In a last-gasp effort to protect the settlers, the leaders of the Pioneer Ship used all that was left of the vessel's original power source to create an energy shield over the whole planet. It succeeded in keeping the dragons out. It also kept all the humans locked in, but no one besides me seems to mind all that much. Hypothetically, though, some dragons still would've been trapped down here when the Barrier went up. It's possible that one or maybe even a handful of them might still be somehow alive, hibernating or in cryo-sleep or something, even though any surviving dragons would eventually die anyway without the starlight they consume and convert to energy.

I turn a corner, following the flow of the city's main thoroughfare, and then—there! Rick is standing outside a vendor's stall, delicately eating a hot dog slathered in mustard and fried onions. Distantly, I catch Z's voice haggling with someone further into the market's maze of tents and stalls.

I pause for a slow count of one-two-three, mentally preparing myself. I am going to stand out of reach of the knives. I won't look at them, won't think about them. I won't hurt anyone with them. But so help me gods, I *am* going to talk to the Star Slayer.

I step forward. "Sir, Mr.—uh, Rick—can we talk now?"

He glances over and smiles at me, using a napkin to dab at his mouth. "Ah, there you are! What was your name again?"

"Peregrine Kent," I say, pleasant smile firmly fixed on my face, eyes watering with the effort of not looking at the knife belt. My hands are trembling a little but I curl them into fists and forge on. "I was hoping to secure a short-term indenture contract on board your ship. I have an interest in star dragons."

I lower my voice for the last sentence. The average person on the street couldn't care less about dragons, but there are some hardcore folks out there willing to do pretty extreme stuff for info on them.

"An interest, eh? Well, I usually do my investigations solo, but since Z vouched for you it's worth considering." My face must show my surprise at the thought of Z vouching for me, because he chuckles. "Don't let him fool you. He likes you well enough. Let me guess—he threw something at you, right?" I nod. "If it didn't hit you, that means he likes you. He's a wicked good aim."

"Oh," is all I can manage. I want to think more about what Rick's words might mean but I'm too distracted by the herculean effort of not looking at, or thinking about, the weapons slung over his chest.

"With that in mind," he goes on, "I'll ask you only two questions. First, what have you got to offer? It seems you'd be performing duties for the ship at large, which is more Z's department, but I understand you would also want to tag along with me. So: convince me you have something to contribute to my mission of finding a star dragon or at least authenticating their remains." He takes another bite of his hot dog and waits for my answer.

I scramble for something to tell him. I don't know when I'll get another opportunity like this, and I'm not sure what'll happen if the dreams continue getting harder to pull myself out of. "Dragon scales," I blurt out. "They...they glow. With stored solar energy. I think."

It's part of my dream: wings spanning out, shining with the otherworldly blue light of some alien star. I have no real reason to believe that detail or anything else in my dreams is real, except for the fact that they feel less like dreams and more like borrowed memories with every passing day.

The Star Slayer blinks, then gives me a long, considering once-over. He pulls a pair of thin wire glasses from his pocket and dons them, completing the professor look. "Dragon scales glow?" he muses. "I haven't heard that theory. Where did you get your info?" He pulls a little notepad and pen out of his pocket and scribbles something down.

"I, uh, have my sources."

He tucks the notepad away, finishes the last bite of his hot dog, then shakes his head. "Look, friend, if we ever come across a scale that glows, we'll know this info might be legitimate, but until then you could just be making this up and we have no way of knowing. But I can tell from that look on your face that you're one of the true believers, and I respect that. So I'll give you a pass on interview question number one. Here's the second and final one: why do you want to find a star dragon?"

As he folds up his napkin into neat squares and drops it into a nearby trash can, the words I wish I could say go leaden somewhere deep in my gut. I could tell him about my dreams, but even if he believed me, that's not the whole story. I want to see a dragon for reasons I can't articulate. I want to know if they really do shine with the light of the suns that birthed them: red dwarfs, white giants, blue supergiants. I want to know if their wings really are solar sails, whether they truly drink starlight and convert its energy to soar between the galaxies at the speed of light. I want to know that they aren't evil. If they aren't what people think they are, maybe I'm not what I fear I am.

At last, I settle on, "I want to understand them."

He taps his fingers on his thigh. "Hm. Seeking knowledge for knowledge's own sake. That's noble. I'll tell you what: I'll talk to Z about it, have him comm the captain, and see if we can't work something out. Come by the dock tomorrow morning and we'll let you know what we decide. I'll even tell him not to throw anything else at you."

I let out a shaky breath. That sounds like a win to me. My thoughts are already churning with dread as I think of spending an extended amount of time onboard a submarine knowing those knives are in there too, but I did what I came here to do. I'm going to get the answers I need.

Rick turns toward the market and I snap back to my senses, realizing I haven't thanked him yet. "I really appreciate—" I start to say, but before I can get out another word, all the screens bolted to the buildings blink on, emitting a loud static buzz.

As one, every person on the streets freezes and goes dead silent. Heads tilt up in confusion and wariness. Doors creak and jingle open and people come out of the shops and salons, craning their necks to get a better view. Someone curses and there's a clatter from further down the road as two rickshaws barely swerve in time to avoid each other, both drivers preoccupied with the screens as they brake. Nothing is showing on the screens yet, just the logo of the Conglom—a blue circle divided into eight slices, with each slice sporting the sigils of the separate city-states that make up our country. But as I watch, the logo dissolves and a woman's face fills the screen. She's got light brown skin and pin-straight black hair and she's wearing discreet silver earrings. Her hands are folded in front of her. They're clenched tightly enough to make her skin pale.

"This is an emergency broadcast," she says, and everyone inhales sharply. The last emergency broadcast was over a year ago when an earthquake brought down a stained-glass shale formation south of here. The shales are thin sheets of brittle, colorful rock that jut up from the ground at all angles like cities made of glass. They're beautiful and host diverse communities that welcome refugees and people from every country, but they're also incredibly dangerous places to live because the shale shatters like shrapnel during earthquakes. The emergency broadcast then hadn't even been to notify people about the event itself, but to warn of aftershocks set to strike other formations and cities nearby.

Which means whatever's spurring this new broadcast, it has to be big, and it has to be dangerous. The government wouldn't waste precious energy on anything else. My mind starts to circle, trying to figure out what's going on and how much trouble we're in.

"This broadcast will play three times in sequence and then end," the woman goes on. "If any further vital information is discovered, or any new directions are issued from the Council, another emergency broadcast will play. In the meantime, all citizens are urged to go to their homes or a nearby indoor shelter and remain there until further instructions are issued. All classes, religious services, and public events are cancelled effective immediately."

All the air on the street seems to evaporate like water on a hot stove. No one moves. It feels like no one is even breathing. The rickshaws and the handful of cars have all braked by now, and doors hang open as their passengers lean out to get a clearer look at the screens. A hypnotic sense of community thrums through us. Whatever's happening is going to affect us all, and none of us know exactly how yet. The moment expands, teetering, and then crashes forward with the broadcaster's next words:

"The Barrier has been breached."

Chapter Three

*B*reached. The word is so unexpected that it feels meaningless for a moment, like a beast too big and too close for me to fully discern. And then its meaning builds through me like a cresting wave, like bergs smashing against ships in the Icedrift Sea:

Someone—or some*thing*—has torn a hole in the sky.

The woman on the screens is still speaking. People around me are screaming now, some people yelling at them to shut up so they can hear while others just gape at the screens or the sky in disbelief. The sky looks normal from here: blandly eggshell-colored, a few low clouds drifting in from the ocean, the fuzzy blob of filtered sunlight creeping closer to the horizon. But somewhere out there, people are seeing the sky. Somewhere they're seeing stars.

I jerk my attention back to the screens. Earlier I wasn't breathing at all, but now my breaths are more like gasps. My hands tremble and I clench them into fists. I strain to hear the woman's next words.

"The location of the breach is over the town of White Pines in Albergia," she says. Next to me, the Star Slayer chokes in a sudden breath, but I can't tear my eyes from the broadcast to look at him. "The following footage is the only recording we have of the event, which began only minutes ago and is, as far as we know, still taking place. This footage has been verified by multiple sources."

The screen blacks out and then fills with a new feed. Images tumble one after the other: blank sky, snowy field, the black, grasping fingers of barren winter trees, and back again. Whoever recorded this on their watch was running. I can make out the person's frenzied breathing and their low, keening cries above the clamor on the street. The noise burrows into me. What was the person seeing, to make them sound that way?

The feed steadies. A face fills the screen, shot from a low angle; a man looking at the screen. He's sporting a scruffy beard and his eyes are an acidic green. His face is familiar but in the chaos of the moment it takes me a long second to place him. He's a rugby star. His smiling face adorns flags and posters and breakfast cereals. He isn't smiling now, though. His bright green eyes are glossy and blank with terror, and he's clenching his jaw so tightly that the tendons in his neck stand out. "Sweetheart," he whispers, his shaking voice mangling the endearment. "I love you. If I don't make it, just know that, okay? And—and tell someone, the Council, anyone, what's happening." He twists the watch around to show a snowy field and a ramshackle little building that looks like some sort of storage shed. Beyond it, through the branches of the black trees framing the shot, I can make out a small town full of brightly-painted homes. Jagged mountains yawn toward the sky behind it. This must be White Pines.

Behind the corner of the shed, something moves.

Scarlet light glitters against the snow. The hoarfrost on the trees catch the light, hold it, burn with it until the branches look gilded with melted rubies. There's no word for this shade of red. It's not a hue. It's not a degree of light or darkness, isn't a color that can be painted on canvas. It's unearthly. I know the second I look away, I'll forget exactly what it looked like, so I keep my eyes glued to the screen.

A three-toed talon slides out from behind the shed.

Gasps and cries go up from everyone around me. I can't speak; my lips are numb. My whole self, my whole world, has narrowed down to this moment: a star dragon stepping out onto the snow, glittering horned head following the talon, a rippling, streamlined, snakelike body emerging after that. The whole creature is about the size of a mastiff except longer. Its scales are like jewels held up to a candle, gleaming with that eerie liquid light. Its eyes are serpentine yellow with vertical slits for pupils. It snaps open its wings: two sets of them, one above each leg. I drink in the details. I am mesmerized beyond the reach of thought. Awe and terror fuse within me, not like metals melting together but like the reactions that happen inside a nuclear bomb. What's happening on that screen is consuming me. I couldn't tear my gaze away if I wanted to.

"They—they do glow," Rick exhales next to me.

A sharp scream rattles over the feed. I jump in surprise, jolted from my trance as the shed door slams open and a burly man in a parka stumbles out. "Help!" he shrieks, his eyes trained on the dragon as he wades through the knee-deep snow away from it. "Help me!" He scoops up a nearby fallen branch and hurls it at the dragon, who easily jerks its head sideways to avoid being struck.

The athlete wearing the watch sucks in a breath. "No, Mack, no, don't attack it, just *run*," he says, but his voice is nothing more than a shaky whisper and Mack doesn't hear.

The dragon leaps nimbly into the air and hovers there like a dragonfly, its wingbeats stirring the snow into an ice fog that dims the ruby light. It looks down at the shed and at the fleeing Mack. And then it opens its mouth, inhales sharply, and breathes out starfire.

The starfire isn't made of flames. It looks like the heartbeat of the sun: pure pearlescent light that shimmers with every color and no color at all. It makes no sound, but I hear it anyway—a noise more like sensation than anything audible. It's like the drop in your gut at the top of a roller coaster or the hollowness in your stomach when you wake up hungry, or the twinge in a broken bone that's healed wrong.

Or the strange ache of a phantom limb after a dream of flying through the stars.

The starfire cuts off. In its wake is left...nothing. Just an empty pit that reaches further than the recording can show, the dirt and snow carved neatly away at its edges. Something had been there a moment ago. I blink, searching for the memory, but only the vaguest shape of it comes. There was a structure there, I think, but I can't remember what it was. And I could swear I recall someone throwing something at the dragon—not the rugby star wearing the watch, but someone else. Someone who's no longer there. Even as I reach for the memory, it fades, like an afterimage dissolving away.

The watch's recording starts tumbling through a kaleidoscope of the empty sky, the trees, and snow again; the athlete is fleeing. A tiny square of ragged teal flits over the screen amongst the images—and everything in me stops existing for a single heartbeat.

The breach. That was the breach. That gleam of teal, it was the true sky. I strain forward, my neck beginning to ache from the awkward position as I stare up at the screens, but the Albergian feed cuts off and the broadcast blinks back to the woman's face. "This is an emergency broadcast," she says. It's looping, playing for the second time in the sequence, but I can't hear anything after her first sentence because everyone and everything around me is *roaring*.

Screams and shouted orders and mindless, braying panic fills the streets. Pedestrians are stampeding in all directions. Someone jostles past me. Another man shoulder checks me, sending me staggering to the side as he blows by. A toddler's wail competes with the sobbing of an older child as their father drags them across the street at a run. A car screeches as it peels out. Someone dodges out of the vehicle's path, and someone else bounces off its hood.

Beside me, Rick comes back to life. "Shit, shit, shit," he says in a low, reverent tone like it's a mantra, the profanity sounding alien in his cultured tone. "White Pines. Anywhere but White Pines." He yanks a wallet out of his pants pocket and steps in the path of the nearest rickshaw, tossing a wad of bills at the driver as he lunges into the seat hard enough to knock his glasses askew. "Go! The docks, fast as you can."

The driver, a bony woman with pale skin and freckles, is shaking her head vigorously. "No way!" she yells over the steadily-growing commotion. "Get your ass out of my rig, I'm going home!"

"The dragon is all the way in Albergia!" Rick shouts. "A thousand miles away! There's plenty of time to take me—"

"If one came through, more will too, and everyone knows it. Get out of my rig before you regret it." She reaches into her jacket and pulls out—

Oh, gods, a *gun*. She has a gun. I lunge away from it until my back is pressed against the damp brick wall of the clothing store behind me. I didn't touch it, did I? How close was I when she pulled it out? Do I feel any sort of temptation to reach out and grab for it, to use it? An image blinks into my thoughts: a mass shooting like the Conglom hasn't had in years, blood and bodies and carnage, no one left standing but me. So many people on this street. There are schoolkids huddled on the corner a block away. I couldn't hurt them. I'm not the sort of person who would hurt them. I'm not. I'm not. I'm not.

I'm gripping my head between my hands like I can squeeze the bad thoughts out. I have to get myself together. I don't have time for a breakdown, don't have time to analyze exactly how many inches the gun is from me and whether I might've accidentally touched it and what that might mean about me. A star dragon has torn through the Barrier and there is a hole in the sky and people are panicking in the streets, and Anthem is waiting for me at the uptrain station—where hundreds of people will soon be clamoring to get aboard and get to their homes. What if train service is suspended? What if people get violent? She's there because of me. If she gets hurt, that'll be because of me too.

But it makes no difference that the impossible has happened. It makes no difference that there's a crisis at hand and my sister could be in danger. I still can't stop the circling fears, and the longer I put off analyzing the moment the gun was pulled, the worse they'll get.

I have to get out of here. I have to get to Anthem. I can manage to put my compulsions off for that long. I have to.

"I'll pay you triple!" Rick is shouting now.

The woman hesitates. I force my hands away from my head, glue my eyes to Rick rather than the gun. "Wait," I croak. "Where are you going? The sub, my job, you—you said you'd be here two more days—"

The Star Slayer shakes his head frantically. "There's a real live star dragon out there just across the Icedrift Sea. If you want to go, this is your chance, but you've got to come with me *right now* or not at all."

I open and close my mouth, helpless. I need to go. Before, I wanted answers, but it's more than that now. That creature up there on the screen, it means *something* to me. I can feel it in my marrow, in my soul. It's the key that will unlock me. But I can't leave just up and leave my family in the middle of this chaos.

Rick sees the anguish in my eyes and knows my answer. He turns away, throwing his whole wallet at the woman's chest. She catches it with her free hand. "Take it all," he cries, "but let's *go*! Z, he's got family in White Pines, he won't wait for me!"

I inhale sharply and turn to scan for Z, who I'd completely forgotten in the mayhem. I heard his voice in the market a moment ago...there! A blur of silver careens around the corner next to the deli/laundromat, knocking two men aside like bowling pins in the process. Judging from the hoverchair's speed, Rick is right—Z won't wait.

I twist back around to Rick just as the rickshaw driver is tucking both the gun and the wallet away. "Fine!" she shouts, working furiously at the pedals. The rickshaw teeters as she swings out into the street, nearly hitting more than half a dozen sprinting pedestrians herself in the process.

And just like that, I'm alone.

I reel, sagging against the wall at my back. My fears are still clamoring for my attention and more join them with every passing second. The uproar on the street is nothing compared to the uproar in my head. I feel emptied out. Wrung dry. My dreams have literally come true, and I feel both elated and horrified. A part of me wonders if my wish to see a dragon somehow caused this to happen. I know it isn't possible, but I still feel the guilt, still wonder how many people are being hurt and killed by the creatures I wanted to see so badly.

I need to get to Anthem. I have to focus. I glance around, trying to get my bearings, trying to strategize the best route to the uptrain station from here—when a gunshot splits the air. I whirl around, thinking the rickshaw driver shot the Star Slayer after all, but the sound came from a different direction and it's swiftly answered by two more gunshots. The crowd of stampeding people parts to reveal two bodies in the middle of the street: one slumped over and still, one grasping his shoulder and holding a gun. Another man with a gun runs over and kicks away the injured man's weapon—which is swiftly absorbed by the crowd—and then pats him down, grabbing his wallet and a set of keys. Leaving the bodies behind him, he runs to a car whose door is hanging open, jams a stolen key in the ignition, and stomps on the accelerator. People dive out of the way, screaming.

The injured man shouts and tries to drag himself to his feet, lurching toward the unmoving man—his friend?—who is almost certainly dead. The crowd closes back over them like a river swallowing a dropped pebble. He'll be trampled within minutes.

Without thinking, I lunge into the crowd and fight my way toward him. Bodies jostle me. Something strikes me in the head. Several other people jab out with elbows or simply run in a blind panic, body checking me and shoving me back a few steps before I can shake them. I hunker down and keep going, driving through the mass like a linebacker. I'm not built like one, but I'm still decently strong—mostly as a result of going to our apartment's gym on a daily basis just in case all the advice to "exercise more and eat healthier" actually could cure my OCD (spoiler, it didn't)—that I make it through to the downed man without being trampled myself. I bend over, shove my arm under his unhurt shoulder, and haul him up. He staggers.

"My—my brother," he says, reaching toward the body that's already disappeared somewhere under the crush of people.

"I'm sorry, man, but we gotta get you out of here before you join him," I yell back.

He grits his teeth on a sob and nods, and together we stagger to the opposite sidewalk. I yank him toward me just in time to avoid an honest-to-gods *horse* galloping past us with a peace officer mounted on its back. I scan wildly for somewhere we'd be less likely to get introduced face-first to the pavement, and spot a glassed-in entry for the skyways. I hesitate—the skyways are rickety as hell and responsible for a lot of that falling debris I'd been watching out for earlier—but only a relatively small handful of people seem to be headed up those stairs, and the skyways lead straight past a med center a few blocks over.

I drag the injured man toward the entry. I have to wait for someone else to open the doors, then I squeeze past to wedge my shoulder against the handle long enough to laboriously pull the man through. That gets me yelled at when several people have to squirm past us to get inside, but I pay no attention. I have no idea how much blood a person can lose before they die but I'm worried this guy might be getting close. He was shot in the shoulder but blood has already fully drenched his shirt, soaked into his pants, and stained the entire left side of my shirt. His steps slow further as we climb the stairs.

Three flights up, the skyways—a series of glassed-in tunnels extending between buildings across most of downtown—finally yawn open before us. The unstable floor shudders beneath my feet as people sprint across it. A covey of startled pigeons explode away as one person climbs over a section of fallen ceiling. I carefully navigate through the debris and stay well away from the gaping holes in the walls where the glass panes have shattered or never been installed. I glance behind us to check our progress and see that we've left a trail of bloody footprints, smeared by the steps of the people running past us. I shiver and look away, knowing the image will be imprinted on my memory forever, knowing there will be hell to pay for all this, anxiety-wise, once I get somewhere safe enough to process it all.

I dare to glance out a busted window and see absolute mayhem on the streets below. There's at least half a dozen rickshaw wrecks and a crumpled, smoking car driven into a shopfront. Maybe twenty bodies are sprawled across the pavement and I try to convince myself they're just wounded but only a few of them are moving. Oh, gods, I can't even process what's happening right now. I let myself take a single look upward; the sky lays oppressive over us all, not a scrap of teal in sight even from this height. I pull the injured man forward faster.

We make it to the end of the skyways: an old banking tower. The med center is still down on street level the next building over. Everyone else is stampeding down the stairs in the almost-complete darkness, lit only by the dim glow from a few watch screens and the light that comes through the open door to the skyway. Panicked shouting and cries for help bounce off the close walls and dig into my brain. I shoulder through the current of bodies and decide to cross to the opposite side of the building to take the stairs down there. Otherwise, the guy I'm helping is likely to get trampled.

As soon as I get through the door to the building's interior, the screams go muffled and the darkness becomes complete. It's quiet enough for me to finally hear the way my heart is galloping in my chest, to feel the way my breaths ricochet around my rib cage. Everything in me—which is about 99% adrenaline at this point—pushes me to keep barreling forward, so I do.

I start moving, sliding my feet along the ground before I shift my weight because I can't tell if the floor might be rotted through in patches. The injured man is nearly dead weight now. His head is lolled on my shoulder and his breathing is getting more ragged by the second. "Stay with me, buddy," I say, jostling him, but he only moans.

My next footstep lands on something that tinkles and crunches: glass. I freeze, then carefully sweep my foot in a wide arc. More broken glass skitters under my shoes. I utter a low curse. They must've knocked the windows in when they boarded up this place and now there's broken glass strewn across the hallway that I need to cross, and I can't tell where it's safe to step or even if we're going in the right direction. I consider turning around, but I think I'm probably halfway across already and this guy has no time to lose.

I hesitate. I need to see, but it would use up most of my watch's remaining battery if I try to use it as a light, and who knows what other emergencies I might need it for on my way home. My hands clench and unclench as I debate. If only I had a flashlight, or a penlight, or *anything* that could shine—

Suddenly, an ethereal silver-blue light ripples across the floor like rolling fog. It catches in the dozens of glass shards splayed out in front of me and highlights them in sharp relief. I flinch, startled and then confused as I try to trace the source of the light. There's no one else around me and no windows or bulbs that I can see. Then the guy I'm helping staggers and nearly falls and I have to shift my grip quickly to keep him from collapsing—and that's when I see that my hand is glowing.

I gape. The silvery-blue light is coiling *through* my palm and fingers, lighting them up brightly from within as if there's a tiny supernova buried in my hand. My bones and veins are an insubstantial lace through it. The light feels somehow alive, pulsating and twinkling like distant stars on a summer night. And the color—the color is…indescribable. Otherworldly. I flounder for the name of the shade and come up empty.

Just like with the red dragon.

Goosebumps ripple over my skin. The hair on the back of my neck stands on end. I slam the door shut hard on that thought, lock it away to think about at some later point when I don't feel like I'll lose my mind if I consider it further. This is an emergency and I don't have time for…for whatever is happening to me. Everything is fine. There's an explanation I just haven't thought of yet. The man I'm helping moans again and spits out blood and I shake myself back into motion. Not knowing what else to do, I pick out a path through the glass shards and hurry toward the far stairwell, half feeling as if I'm trying to run away from the light, though of course it moves with me.

My breathing is a high wheeze in my ears by the time I reach the door. I lean my head against the chilly, dented metal for a second, trying to ground myself. The comparison to the red dragon's light squirms out from the place where I locked it away and bursts to the forefront of my thoughts again, relentless. I've been dreaming about dragons and now my hand is glowing like one. Or maybe I'm just going into shock. Maybe I'm hallucinating. I almost hope I am, because at least that would make *sense*.

I shake myself out of my thoughts. I do not understand why my hand is glowing, but I do know that it needs to quit before I go outside this dark hallway.

"Stop it," I whisper to myself and the light. "Just stop." I clench my hand and the light dissipates. I stare into the darkness for a long, hard moment, making sure it *stays* dark, then exhale a shuddering breath and push the door open. I box myself into the present moment, refuse to dedicate any more of my energy to trying to figure out the glowing. There'll be time to analyze it all later. Right now I have to stay focused or else the guy I'm helping could very well die.

There are people in this stairwell too, but not as many, and I'm able to jostle myself and the injured man down the steps and out into the street. I squint into the daylight and spot the med center across the street. Several people in scrubs are shouting at the front door, directing people in or away.

I half-drag the injured man toward them. Someone yells something about a code, and someone else says a sentence that includes "triage." I grab that man with my free hand, leaving a bloody imprint on the sleeve of his scrubs.

"This guy has been shot in the shoulder, he's lost a ton of blood," I told him. "Please, can you take him?"

The nurse gives the injured man a quick once-over and then, to my relief, guides him to a nearby gurney lined up against the wall. "I'll get him taken care of," he says, barely looking at me as he expertly lays the man down and snaps the gurney into place. "If you're family, come along. If not, you need to go. No extra space for bystanders, not with all the casualties coming in right now."

"I'm not family," is all I manage to get out before the nurse takes off at a near-run, wheeling the gurney into the center before him. He turns a corner and both of them vanish.

I turn away and stand still for a moment as I get my bearings, panting for breath. After I figure out my new route to the uptrain station, I take off down the street at a sprint, turning my watch on as I go. I send Anthem an urgent ping requesting her location and voice-text that I'm on my way to her.

Even though there's a part of me that wishes I were somewhere else right now—aboard *The Shitty Clunker* with the Star Slayer, on my way to that ragged square of the true sky. Is there any universe in which I could have dropped everything and gone with him? If that eerie light had shown up beforehand, would it have been enough to make me take him up on his offer?

I'll get to Albergia, I promise myself. *When I'm sure my family is safe, I'll get my answers. Somehow.*

To my left, the sound of shattering glass rings out. The emergency broadcast was barely ten minutes ago and the looting has already started. I duck around a man carrying a chest-sized safe and just barely dodge in time to avoid a pale woman who is bizarrely carrying a cage full of orange parrots. Other shops are already locking their doors and lowering the bars that cover the windows. The acrid tang of smoke begins to filter through the street. Someone's tipped over a trash can and set it ablaze.

My watch dings with messages from all three of my family members. Judging by the time stamps, they were sent right after the broadcasts. I must not have heard the earlier notifications over the clamor. I scan through them quickly.

Dad: *Where are you? Are you safe? Do I need to come get you?*

Mom: *If you get killed I will end whoever killed you and then kill you more for skipping school. Get home NOW.*

Anthem: *Got halfway to the station, saw broadcast, Mom called and made me turn around. Get home or I'm coming after you, dipshit.*

I go dizzy with relief. Anthem isn't at the station, which means she's a hell of a lot safer than I am at the moment. From the tone of Mom and Anthem's texts, though, they're genuinely terrified for me. The more scared they get, the stronger their threats tend to be. Insults are their love language.

I send a group text to them all: *I'm okay. Headed home fast as I can.* I don't want them to worry, so I set my watch to send all three of them a location ping every few minutes to keep them updated even though it'll drain my battery like nobody's business. Then I plunge back into the streets.

The crowds haven't thinned any. They seem to be moving in waves—workers and shopkeepers trying to get home, parents trying to get to their kids' schools and then trying to get their kids home, looters looting and other people still standing and staring in empty-eyed shock at the blank screens. Normally it's a ten-minute ride on the elevated trains to get home from here, but if I have to walk *and* fight against this sort of current the whole way it could take ten times that long.

It's only maybe fifteen minutes, though, before an ancient rust-bucket of a car fishtails around a corner and screeches to a stop next to me, leaving trails of smoking black rubber on the road behind it. The door flings open and the driver—a girl with dark bronze skin, wavy black hair that could star in shampoo commercials, and dark brown eyes that snap with even more righteous fury than usual—glares at me. "Get in, loser!" she yells, and I obediently dive for the passenger seat and buckle up before slamming the door shut and then locking it for good measure.

"Anthem," I pant, "how in the names of all the lost gods did you get a *car*? Tell me you didn't steal it."

My sister spins the wheel around with flair, her long fingers dancing over it like a pianist playing a beloved tune. Anthem has a thing for cars even though—or maybe especially because—we could never in a million years afford one. "Okay," she says with a one-shouldered shrug, not taking her eyes off the road, "I didn't steal it."

I level a look at her. She doesn't even glance back, too busy playing a relatively gentle game of bumper cars with the panicking pedestrians, nudging them out of the way as she taps the fuel pedal in fits and starts. "Mrs. Kowalski wasn't using it," she says, referencing our elderly and more-than-a-little crotchety neighbor from three doors down.

"You stole a car from an old lady?"

"Her whole family is already home and safe. She doesn't need it right now. I borrowed it, that's all. I swear I'll even wash it myself when we're done." Anthem glances at me then and lets out a sharp curse, snatching up my left hand with one of hers. "And apparently I'll need to get the inside detailed too, holy baby *Jesus*, Per, that better not be your blood!"

I glance down at the seat, where the tattered faux leather now sports smeared bloodstains, and wince. "It's not. A guy got shot and I helped him to the med center."

"Thus risking life and limb to rescue a total stranger? Yeah, sounds like you." She snorts and shakes her head in exasperation, then gives me a longer measuring look. "Are you okay?"

There's something unquantifiable in her voice, something only I am ever able to hear. She's not asking after my physical health. She knows in at least a general way how much that emergency broadcast would have meant to me, and she also knows—is the *only* one who knows—about my harm OCD and its myriad triggers, nearly all of which have been tripped within the last half-hour.

I avoid her gaze. "I'm fine."

"And I call bullshit. You're not fine."

"Okay, I'm not fine, but I don't want to talk about it." The compulsion to ruminate, to analyze all of the awful things that have happened and how much involvement I'd had in them and exactly what I'd been feeling and thinking when they'd happened, is going to overwhelm me soon. I can feel it like a ticking time bomb in my mind. If I talk about it in any more depth right now, I'll explode.

And also, I don't want Anthem to know or guess the exact sort of images that went through my head. She knows I have violent intrusive thoughts but I will never tell her the details of them. It's bad enough this horror show has to live in my head. I'm not going to put it in anyone else's, too.

"Can we just go home?" I ask quietly.

But Anthem is a fixer, and an irritable one at that, and there's no way she's letting me off that easy. She slaps a hand against the steering wheel. "Damn it, Per, when are you ever going to quit running from your shit and confront it? If you would just work through this stuff—"

"I feel like the *middle of the dragon apocalypse* is not the time for working through my hang-ups," I say tersely, bracing myself against the dashboard as she stomps on the gas and whips around a corner.

"They're more than hang-ups and you know it!" she says, managing to gesture sharply at me while also giving the finger to a pedestrian who's now trying to kick the driver's side door in. She accelerates more and the guy gives up. She glances back at me. "You're the whole reason I'm taking a psych internship, buddy, and I'm going to use those skills on you if it's the last thing I do."

Only Anthem could turn therapy into a threat. I really, really can't talk about any of this with her right now, so I play my trump card. "And what does your supervisor think of that plan?"

I know about Anthem's evaluation from last semester. The supervisor recommended she extend the internship for another full quarter—a probation, basically. No idea why, but I'm betting it's something to do with her aggressive bedside manner.

She glares at me, then makes a face and returns her attention to the road. "Maybe the middle of the dragon apocalypse isn't the time for working through my hang-ups either," she concedes in a mutter. Then she glances back at me. "But look—you know I've got your back, right? No matter what. That's all I'm trying to say."

Something within me curls up and dies a little. I should be the one having *her* back. I don't want to be the fragile one in this relationship. She's my little sister, and every day it feels like I need her more, and like I'm failing her more because of it.

"I know," I reply, looking out the window.

I need to find that star dragon. I need to see the sky. I can't explain to Anthem why, but I *know* it would solve everything.

I just have to figure out how to get to Albergia without *The Shitty Clunker*.

Chapter Four

M om and Dad are waiting for us when we pull into the garage. Dad's hauling three suitcases stacked on top of each other and Mom's sporting a ratty backpack on each arm and a scowl to end all scowls as she taps in a message on her watch. Indy, our giant black-and-tan dog, is on a frayed leash that's been tied around Dad's waist.

"Uh oh," Anthem says, summing up the situation neatly.

Mom looks up from her watch as we pull in. Anthem's hands freeze on the wheel as if Mom's gaze is a tractor beam reeling us in against our will. The car putters to a gentle stop and Anthem puts it in park. "Back me up?" she says under her breath to me.

I mentally gird my loins. "Yep."

Mom marches over to us, each step emphasized by the staccato beat of her cheery yellow high heels. She comes to my side first, pulls open the door, grasps my head between her hands and kisses my forehead forcefully. Her curly, bright ginger hair swings over her shoulders and surrounds me with the smell of her: strawberries and mint and the safety of childhood. "I love you," she says, emphasizing each word. "I am so relieved you're okay. Killing you later is still on the agenda."

"Fair enough," I say. "It's thanks to Anthem I'm okay at all, though. It's all due to her quick thinking—"

"—and masterful getaway skills," Anthem interjects.

"And masterful getaway skills," I add loyally, "that I'm home safe."

Mom doesn't buy it. She lifts her tractor-beam gaze to Anthem. "*Your* punishment is that Dad gets to drive all the way to the cabin while you sit in the back with Indy."

"*What?*" we both say at once. Indy, hearing her name and surmising she's been summoned, lunges against the leash and nearly bowls Dad over as she drags him toward the car. She reaches the driver's side window, jumps up, and begins licking it furiously, trying to get through to Anthem and me.

Mom straightens and tosses the backpacks she's toting toward the rear of the car, where they sag against a tire. Then she leans back toward us and says in a whisper, "Mrs. Kowalski is watching from the stairwell so I have to sound harsh, but I'm proud of you, girl." She sticks her hand in the car below the dash to give Anthem a surreptitious fist bump. Then, louder, she says, "I am so disappointed in you. How dare you steal a car to go and save your brother from a mob? What sort of person does that?" In a whisper: "A good one. And you *almost* got away with it."

I peer cautiously around the door. Mrs. Kowalski is indeed standing in the shadows of the stairwell, her pruny mouth puckered up, gaze skewering us. She inherited this car from her landowner dad and it's her pride and joy even though she's only driven it a handful of times.

Another rust-bucket car pulls into the garage, and Mom squeezes herself against our vehicle to make room for it to slide past. Several bicycles and a rickshaw that looks like it's been through a war enter after it. Their riders all abandon them at the base of the stairs as they race up to their apartments. The wheels on one of the bikes keep spinning in the air, the broken spokes emitting a wheezing death rattle as they scrape against the frame.

"What do you mean, 'the cabin'? Are you re-stealing the car from Mrs. Kowalski to drive us somewhere?" Anthem asks as Dad pulls Indy sideways so he can open the trunk and load the suitcases and backpacks in.

Mom motions at her watch. "We now own this car and Mrs. Kowalski's family cabin; I just sent off the digital signatures for the contracts. We've already loaded up your backpacks and the suitcases with everything we can take. We're leaving for the cabin right now."

I gape at her. "What—Where did we get that sort of money?" There's no way we could afford any property beyond our apartment, especially not anything on acreage. Mrs. Kowalski's cabin is barely worthy of the name, covered in spiderwebs with a leaky roof and questionable well water, but it's got a ten-acre lot on the shore a good two hundred miles to the south of here.

Two hundred miles further from the dragon. Two hundred miles further from the hole in the sky. Which is, of course, exactly the point. I can see Mom and Dad's logic; the city is already in turmoil and it's only been an hour since the emergency broadcast. It won't take much more pressure for the place to turn into a powder keg and we don't have the sort of resources we'd need to deal with that for very long. I recall the looters I saw on the way here, the man who got shot for his car keys. I shudder and turn my thoughts quickly away, back to my new problem of escaping a remote cabin on the beach to get to Albergia while also making sure my family is safe and has everything they need to be fine without me.

Mom draws a deep inhale through her nose and then answers my question. "We traded her the apartment."

"What?" Anthem yelps. Dad closes the trunk, comes around to open the driver's side door, and motions at Anthem to move to the back. She climbs over the seat, still staring at Mom as she waits for an answer.

"We made an executive decision," Mom said. "This is not the sort of place we want to be trapped if things get worse. If we're out by ourselves at the cabin, at least we've got firewood and a stove for heat and cooking, well water to drink—after it's *thoroughly* boiled, I'm pretty sure there're fifty types of parasites in there—and your father can fish for food."

"Your father cannot fish for food." Dad speaks for the first time, arching one of his thick black eyebrows at Anthem via the rearview mirror. He's got a pencil nub stuck behind his ear, half-buried in his wavy black hair. His dark bronze skin is a match for Anthem's but that's where their similarities end. Where Anthem is tall and lean and ferocious, Dad is short, rumpled, and thoughtful. He runs an antique bookstore—the source of most of my stolen scrapbook pages. It's a tiny hole-in-the-wall place that he loves more than anything besides us, so his being willing to leave it now makes this whole catastrophe seem suddenly more real and personal than ever.

"*I* will fish for food," Mom amends without missing a beat. "Just as soon as I watch an instructional cast on how one fishes for food."

Dad finally unties the leash around his waist and lets Indy in the car. She barks joyfully and uses his lap as a launching pad to scramble into the backseat, swiping her tongue across my face on her way. I give her a distracted rub between the ears and don't bother to wipe the slobber off. There's worse than that caked all over my clothes and skin already. Mom's laser beam eyes have already spotted the bloodstains, scanned me for injuries, and concluded I'm okay. I'm sure she'll question me later though—an interrogation I'm not looking forward to at all. She'll be proud of me for helping the injured guy, of course, but I would rather do just about anything other than rehash it all in front of her. I'll have to lie about why I snuck downtown in the first place, lie about how I freaked out over Rick's knives and the rickshaw driver's gun, and lie about how I plan to utterly lose my shit once again the very second I manage to get somewhere secure and alone. And now, thanks to my mysterious little glowstick trick, I'll have to lie to them about that too. I hate lying to my parents. I'm beyond lucky to have them and I love them a stupidly ridiculous amount, which is why I can't bear to see their horrified expressions if I dared to tell them all my secrets. I don't want them to think of me differently. And, gods help me, I couldn't stand it if they were *afraid* of me. If they don't have faith in who I am, there's no way I can either.

"What about school?" Anthem is saying now. "And my internship at the psych center, and all my *friends*? I can't just abandon them in the middle of this! And what about the bookstore, and your job, Mom?" Mom teaches ballroom dance to rich people, which is the sort of career that only exists in a big city.

Mom jerks her head at me to move to the backseat. I do, quietly, even though I'm silently panicking about all the turns this situation is taking. "Everything's cancelled until further notice," she says. "Once the situation is dealt with, we can come back to our lives here."

Anthem continues protesting, bringing up the fact that it took years of work to afford our apartment in the first place and there's no way Mrs. Kowalski will trade it back, but the argument stalls out as we ease from the garage onto the clogged street. In the few minutes we've been inside, the city has gone from scattered panic to full-on apocalypse. A fire has started somewhere down in the decrepit old subway tunnels and heavy, acrid black smoke is boiling up through the grates and the roped-off stations, flowing over the street like a layer of toxic fog. Cars blast through it, some of them swerving madly around people and obstacles, others plowing right through. All of us duck when a battered shopping cart ricochets off the fender of a delivery truck and skids into my window. Its cargo of canned goods crack against the car, pop-pop-pop like artillery fire.

Dad silently pushes the button to lock the doors, then another button to recirculate the air inside the car. Then he steps on the gas.

None of us speak as we jolt and shudder our way toward the freeway. The smoke eddies up to our windows, clearing long enough to give us glimpses at the chaos outside: a group of kids standing on the roof of a school, climbing one by one through the broken window of the temple next door. A smashed fire hydrant geysering twenty feet high. A line of peace officers in riot gear, carrying traffic cones and rolls of spiked wire, apparently planning to block off roads. Beneath it all wends the symphony of chaos: sobbing, screams, sirens, and the occasional punctuation of gunshots.

Indy is no longer excited about the impromptu car ride. She's curled into a furry, shivering ball wedged between mine and Anthem's feet. She whines softly, the sound blending with our own shaky breathing.

Dad glances back at us and then says something under his breath to Mom. She extracts one hand finger by finger from her armrest, leaving half-moon indents in the upholstery in the process, and taps on her watch. The opening strains of a waltz swell around us, the music's classic one-two-three beat almost blocking out the crack of gunfire.

We're maybe a mile from the freeway when the first person tries to steal the car.

It's a man. Middle-aged, heavyset, balding, he looks a bit like *The Shitty Clunker's* masthead. Instead of a beer can, he's holding a hockey stick, and it leaves a spiderweb of cracks when it comes down on our windshield.

He lifts it for a second blow. Dad slams on the gas. The man drops the stick and tries to throw himself in front of the car to block us, but Dad swerves and the man glances off the side of the hood. He tumbles into the fog of smoke and vanishes in our wake. I hold my breath as I twist in my seat to look back. Surely we didn't hurt him. He's got to be okay, maybe just bruised. But we've already careened onto the on-ramp and I can't make much out through the smoke anyway. I clamp my jaw against a protest and tuck this new guilt away with all the rest. Silently, I promise myself that I'll analyze the hell out of it as soon as we make it safely to the cabin.

We merge onto the freeway and Dad revs the engine. Three pot-holed lanes open up. The sounds of screams and gunshots fade, and after a minute, Mom turns off the music. The buzz of silence fills the car. It's just as surreal as the waltz.

"We're going to need supplies." Anthem's voice cracks in the silence. Her eyes are bright and a little bit glassy, but her spine is ramrod-straight. "Dog food. Nonperishables."

Dad glances at us in the rearview mirror. Somehow his voice sounds calm and only a little bit strained. "There's a market a few hours out. I've stopped there before on my way to a supplier's shop. They should have enough to get us through until...for a while."

"Have any more dragons come through the breach?" I blurt before I think better of it. I tense as soon as the words are out. What sort of person am I, to hope I might get to see a star dragon in the middle of a catastrophe of their own making? I can't help it, though.

Mom powers up her watch and quickly browses through news sites. "They're calling the breach event 'Starfall,'" she reports. "I don't see anything about any more dragons yet, or—or the...town. The one where it landed." Her brow creases. "I can't remember what town it was."

"Its name, it had something to do with…the woods?" Dad tries, his brow wrinkling as he steers around an exceptionally deep pothole. None of the highways this far out have been kept up very well. Black stripes of tar snake across the road in a half-hearted attempt to patch up damage from earthquakes and age, and several of the bridges we pass over groan and sway in an alarming way. Dad is driving extra cautiously, unwilling to risk a flat tire even though it's making the already-long journey crawl by.

"No, something to do with a color," Anthem replies, but she looks equally confused.

I reach into my own memory. The woman on the emergency broadcast said the name of the city, I'm sure of it. And Rick said it too—said that Z had family there. I can remember every other detail of the day in dazzling, terrible clarity. Why can't I remember this?

And then I recall that there was another detail that seemed to fade from memory as soon as I'd seen it: the person or structure that had been in the place of that pit before the dragon had burned it out of existence with starfire. A leaden horror sinks through me as I remember the legends about what exactly starfire does. I quickly power up my watch to test my theory. I download the video from the emergency broadcast and swipe through it, pausing on the spot where the man—Mack, of course that was his name, but even as I think it, it starts to fade again—throws a branch at the dragon. Then I rewind it to listen to the broadcaster call the town White Pines. Again, the name dissipates like ether as soon as it enters my mind.

"We can't remember the name of the city because it must have been uncreated," I say hoarsely. "It's gone. Wiped out of existence by starfire." Which apparently left nothing at all in its wake except the ghost of a memory and any recordings that had been made, and even when we watched those we couldn't hold the names or details in our heads for longer than a second or two.

Mom twists around in her seat, her mouth open as if she's about to say something, but nothing comes out for a long moment. Finally, she sags back. "Jesus," she mutters, running a hand over her face. "I thought these monsters were supposed to be myths."

Dad reaches out with his free hand and entwines his fingers through hers, and they cling to each other for a long time.

The sunlight is a smear of bland, early-evening amber through the Barrier when we slow to a stop. I sit up and blink away the remnants of a space daydream, wincing at the leftover ache in my spine and surreptitiously checking to make sure Mom and Dad haven't noticed anything off about me. They're focused on the road, though. There's a line of cars ahead of us, bright orange traffic cones narrowing three lanes to one. Peace officers move from car to car talking to the drivers. A bunch of vehicles are doing U-turns and creeping down an overgrown side road that disappears into the woods to the west. Apprehension curdles in the pit of my stomach.

A cop strides over to us. Dad rolls down his window, filling the car with the smell of warm tar, and then rests his hands on the steering wheel to keep them in plain view. The cop starts talking before Dad can get a word in.

"The bridge ahead is out," he reports. "If you want to keep going south, you'll have to divert to that side road to get to F-94, take the bridge over there."

Mom tenses. "How long will that take?"

"All night, with this traffic," he says shortly, then starts heading to the next car.

We all look at each other. "Do we have enough gas?" I ask.

"To get to the cabin, *and* for the return trip?" Anthem stresses.

Dad peers at the gas gauge and fiddles with the pencil behind his ear. "Probably not. But the market is only maybe a mile past this roadblock, before the bridge. I bet these other folks don't even realize it's there. We could walk over, get supplies and gas before we go on."

"Excellent point, dear," Mom says, and starts to open her door.

"We can't leave the car," I interject, sitting up straight. Most of these people in the line, they aren't any less panicked than the hockey-stick guy back in the city. They're just lucky enough to already have vehicles to make their getaways in. But if they run out of fuel or have engine problems, there's very little to stop them from stealing our car or siphoning gas from it while we're out resupplying. I doubt the peace officers would even notice.

Mom closes her door as quickly as she'd opened it. "Another excellent point," she says. "New plan: Per and I will stay with the car and glower firmly at anyone who approaches. You two go get the gas and supplies."

Dad nods. "I pity anyone caught in your glower, love." He kisses her, then gets out of the car and opens Anthem's door. The two of them head off past the roadblock. Mom watches them go, sliding to the driver's side and turning the engine off to save gas.

As Anthem and Dad vanish into the tree line, Mom muses, "Per, baby. Do you know the first person who's going to be caught in my glower?"

I freeze like a rabbit scenting a bobcat.

"Yep," she confirms, meeting my gaze in the rearview mirror. "It's you. Now that your little corroboration buddy—that would be your darling sister Anthem, who is chock-full of bullshit and bravado, a fact I normally find delightful but which is right now unhelpful—now that she's gone, you're going to tell me what the hell you were doing skipping school to go downtown this morning."

I frantically piece together a plausible half-truth while also trying to remember what degree of eye contact people make when they're telling the full truth. I immediately start sweating at the effort. "I was interviewing the crew of a submarine," I tell her. "For Mr. Gunner's class. He gives extra credit for in-person interviews and I wanted to make up some of the points I lost on the last test."

Her eyebrows inch upward. "The points you lost on the last test."

Crap. She hadn't known I flunked it. At least, not until I just told her. "Uh, right. Yes. And this crew, their missions cover the same topic as unit four in modern tech class. So I...decided to interview them."

"You decided to interview them," she repeats flatly.

Oh, crap. She's doing that thing where she echoes whatever I say and lets me panic-chatter in response. I'm practically interrogating myself for her.

"Yes," I answer, and force myself to not say anything else as she eyes me in the mirror. She stares me down like she can suck out my soul for examination through sheer psychic willpower. I slink down in my seat a little.

After a long, long moment, she prompts, "And you had to skip school without permission to do this because..."

"I didn't find out they were in port until the last second. It was a snap decision."

"You don't make snap decisions."

"I do when I'm desperate." The words slip out and I can't reel them back in.

She turns around fully to look at me, her brow wrinkling as her expression goes from pissed off to concerned. "Per, why would you be desperate? What's going on with you lately? Talk to me. Seriously. I'm on your side."

Something cracks in my chest at her support. Would she offer it so easily if she really could examine my soul? If I tell her about my dreams, my scrapbook, or even just my OCD, would she understand? A surge of longing rises at the back of my throat: all the words I want to say to her, the truths that have been eating at me like acid.

But...earlier, she called the dragons monsters. I have their dreams, and now I have their glow, too—and I keep wanting to see one, keep being fascinated by them, even though I know they've wiped out at least one city and everyone in it. Even now, I'm counting the hours until I can be alone so I can investigate how I might get to hole in the sky.

If I tell her the truth, she'll either love me and forbid me to go, or be too frightened for me to stay. I'm too much of a coward to find out which is true and I can't stomach either option anyway.

"I'm okay," I tell her at last. "Just...senior stuff, you know? Trying to figure out my future. If there even is a future anymore now."

She shakes her head—her bullshit-o-meter is way too good to take my words at face value—but lets the matter drop. We wait together in silence until Dad and Anthem return. Deep sepia twilight is coating the woods by then and the car line has backed up out of sight, honking and yells filling the air.

Dad squints in the blaze of headlights and motions at us to pop the trunk. He's got a bag of dog food slung over each shoulder and Anthem's carrying a gas can along with at least a dozen plastic bags of groceries. There's something hanging over her shoulder, too, but I can't make it out.

"I got a hatchet for firewood," she calls as soon as she's near enough, ostensibly just reporting in but in actuality warning me of the weapon I'm about to share the car with. I tense up as she circles to the trunk to stow the hatchet out of sight before she and Dad arrange the other supplies wherever it'll fit between us all. Dad tops off the tank with the gas can, then we join the long line of cars snaking down the side road.

The officer was right. The trip is a long, painfully slow crawl, and I'm too wound-up and anxious to fall asleep until we reach the next freeway over and finally speed back up. It's nearly dawn by then. All of us spend the following day taking turns driving—Anthem is so tired and frazzled she doesn't even look like she's enjoying her time behind the wheel—while the others doze. We get a flat tire around noon and Dad changes it out for our single spare while the rest of us eat a tense lunch of baked beans from the can. A few people stop and offer to "help," and we politely run them off before they can knock us out and steal our car.

We make it back on the road. Hours pass. We check our watches for updates; the only thing on the news is story after story of chaos, riots, and panic.

In the last leg of our drive, Mom reports that an official shelter-in-place order has gone out worldwide. All travel is shut down as of tonight. Highways will be blockaded at all exits, there's no train service anywhere, and all ships have to return to their home ports immediately except for Albergian vessels carrying refugees to safety over the next few days. Even the Council's hovercrafts are grounded. Dad steps on the gas and we pull into the cabin's rocky driveway just after dark, barely in time to avoid the order's enforcement.

Pebbles crunch under the tires and ping off the undercarriage. The cabin is a ramshackle building that reminds me of a child's toy set, logs glued together helter-skelter and then abandoned before the project was completed. The ocean behind it is a vast dark swath. I look out across the sea and feel lost. I look at the sky, and feel trapped.

Anthem turns to me and wrinkles her nose. "I would claim first shower," she says loud enough for Mom and Dad to hear, "but I think Per needs it more than me. Preferably a very *long* shower with a lot of soap."

I shoot her a grateful look. She's covering for me, buying me time to analyze alone without interruption. Anthem twists her mouth ruefully in response—she doesn't like "enabling me" and says I'd be much better off in the long run if I tried to not do my compulsions, but she's willing to go along with it for now.

We head into the house. I take off my shoes to avoid tracking in any crusted blood and make a beeline for the bathroom. The tub has orange and black stains and I'm pretty sure an enormous spider is lurking behind one of the broken tiles, but it doesn't matter. I turn on the water and a weak sprinkle sprays from the showerhead, probably coming from a reservoir that I'll need to refill with well water later.

Once the shower is on and I can't hear anything but droplets raining onto tile, I stand in the middle of the bathroom, barefoot and cradling a bloodstained shoe in each hand, while I stare fixedly at the sink and finally comb through my memories of all the terrible thoughts I had yesterday, all the weapons I saw and how I felt when I saw them, and what I can glean about my true nature based on those things.

My saving grace ends up being the memory of how I rushed to save the injured man. No matter how many times I dissect that memory, I come to the same conclusion: I did it instinctively, unthinkingly. That has to mean that the person I am in my deepest self, the one who shows up when there's no time to think, only to react, is someone who runs to help people and not to hurt them. There's still doubt—there's *always* doubt—but that conclusion is enough to finally allow me to do the things I need to do: take the world's fastest shower to scrub off the day-old blood, dump my clothes and shoes in the washer with all the detergent we can spare, and start researching ways I might get to Albergia amid a shelter-in-place order.

I huddle in the bed I've claimed and pull the ratty, scratchy blanket up to my waist. The faint noise of a hushed conversation filters under the door: Mom and Dad talking to each other about all the worries they don't want us to overhear. I try to tune it out as I power my watch up. I start to navigate to the travel sites but then hesitate before swiping in a search string for the Star Slayer instead. There are far more results for him than ever before—compilations of his newly-validated findings, gossip casters speculating about his true identity, people in the comments clamoring for him to slay the dragon in Albergia like he's meant to be the savior of humankind or something. If he was barely internet famous before, he's getting his full five minutes of fame now. The person with the most up-to-date reports on him is "Check-It Chessie," some formerly low-level gossip caster who's managed to dig up the same intel as I did—that he's chartered *The Shitty Clunker.* Judging from her pic she's not that much older than me, sporting silver-and-gold streaked hair and an old-timey explorer's hat along with a self-important smirk. Her latest post is a mysterious message saying she's "in the field" and will have a huge new story about dragons to break soon. I set my watch to send me an alert when she posts anything, just in case it's useful.

Then I spend an extra few precious percentage points of my battery digging for news on Z. I find out that *The Shitty Clunker* docked in Albergia as a refugee-bearing ship about an hour ago, but there's no news about whether its acting captain is okay or if he's managed to find whatever family he has there. I tell myself I barely even met the guy and I have way bigger problems, but I still can't tear myself away from my search until my watch beeps a battery warning.

I sigh and navigate away to the travel sites. After a few minutes of browsing them I come to the conclusion that a boat is my best, perhaps only, bet. They've all been ordered to moor indefinitely at their home ports, but Albergian ships are allowed to sail freely in order to ferry refugees away from the tear in the sky. If I can somehow manage to get back to the Conglom's main port, maybe I can catch a ride on one that's headed there to pick up a load of people. But even as I try to find the sailing schedules on my watch, I hesitate. What would my parents think? And Anthem—can I really leave her behind like this? She'd be furious, and they would all worry about me. Especially since I'm not sure when or even if I would be able to return.

I resist looking at my hands. They aren't glowing, and there's no part of me that wants to check to see if they might glow again on command, because if I try it and they do that means I will no longer be able to pretend, even to myself, that something unthinkable isn't happening to me.

I bite my lip and glance around. My door is closed and locked and the curtains are drawn. After another moment's hesitation, I get up and stuff a towel over the door crack and then get back in bed and pull the covers over myself. Am I really doing this? I'm really doing this. Oh, gods.

I squeeze my eyes shut. I take a deep breath, hold it, and think, *shine.*

A blistering heat rolls through me like a storm spilling over a desert horizon, all lightning and ozone. In seconds it has billowed through every bit of me—but rather than feeling like I've been pulled beneath a disastrous current, I feel...buoyant. Like I might drift away from myself at any moment. Terror slams through me at the sensation, at the loss of control. Then the backs of my eyelids go from inky blackness to red, and the odd buoyancy grows until I curl my hands in the sheets to tether myself to the world, heart pounding in terror and confusion. A noise escapes my throat and I screw my eyes shut tighter. I barely stop myself from burrowing beneath my pillow and pretending absolutely nothing is happening.

I have to see. I have to know.

I suck in a shuddering breath and crack open one eye, an act of bravery that I immediately regret, because *my hand is shining* and it's utterly foreign and unnatural and somehow familiar at the same time, and all the more terrible for it. Even worse—it's beautiful. Silvery blue threads of light knit together and pull apart beneath my skin, slowly spiraling around the center of my palm like the tides of a galaxy. It's hypnotic.

Despair ropes through me, adding an extra edge to my panic. It's real. Whatever this is, it's actually happening, and it *doesn't make any sense.* Have the dragons somehow infected me with this light, with my dreams? What other symptoms might show up next?

Then something about the light catches my attention, and I tilt my head, trying to place what's different about it. It takes me a moment to realize that it's flickering slightly, like a split-second power interruption dimming a light bulb. I'm almost positive it wasn't doing that last time. And actually, it seems a little dimmer overall too.

Drawing in a shuddering breath that feels like it scorches my lungs, I shake out my hand and clench it into a fist. The light disappears.

Indy is staring at me from her spot on the floor, her own head tilted, looking puzzled and curious and not at all like I've done anything terrifyingly unnatural. The panic that's been buzzing in my chest grows tendrils and starts creeping through me, vein by vein. My breathing accelerates. I feel like I'm losing control of myself—both because of the light, and in the way I always feel like I'm losing control during a panic attack.

There is something wrong with me. Even more than what was *already* wrong with me. The dragons are vicious, unthinking, murderous. Everyone says so. Sharing this type of light with them—what does it mean about me?

I shove myself off the bed and grab my bag. I thrust my hand blindly into it and feel the soft, worn edges of my scrapbook. I yank it out and flip it open. I've spent years building this, sometimes because I was curious, sometimes because I felt desperate and compelled to prove...something. That I'm not like the star dragons? Or that I *am* like them, maybe, that they're not evil at all, just a natural part of the universal ecosystem.

Something in the back of my mind whispers that I can't possibly believe that anymore, not now that they're senselessly attacking our planet, but I push it aside with the strength of desperation and look down at the page I've opened the book to. It's an excerpt from a doctoral thesis, a statement from some researcher whose name I can never remember that talks about dragons being just like other apex predators—simply filling a spot in the food chain. It calms me a little, and I flip to another page, seeking more reassurance.

This one is a fairytale, one of the lesser-known, really old ones. Anthem found it for me ages ago in one of Dad's antique books locked in a glass case at his store. I couldn't tear out the page in a book like that, so I copied it over word for word instead. I scan through it again now.

Come close, and I will show you the heart of a dragon, it starts. My shuddering breaths even out the tiniest bit at the comforting familiarity of the line that I've read so many times, and I keep going:

No, child, not a trophy. Not a slain thing. The heart of this dragon is full of light and its eyes are full of stars. It follows in the wake of its brethren, its kindred who lay waste to worlds, and it cups the nothingness that's left behind in its wings and shapes it into something new.

Shush, child. Don't tell me what's not possible. Listen close and I'll tell you.

One night long ago, the Pioneer Ship carried its precious cargo of the last few thousand humans into the Great Darkness of barren space. Some children were gathered at one of the bow windows, playing a listless game as they waited for the ship's fuel to run out. A small girl glanced out into the emptiness and realized, all at once, that it was not empty. Here's what she saw:

Far off in the darkness was a shape. It had two great wings, a tail large enough to spear a moon, and glittering eyes like suns that turned toward her. As the girl watched, the dragon exhaled. Its breath was not starfire, though, not those horrendous flames of destruction. Instead, what formed before its vast muzzle was a newborn planet. Oceans condensed on its surface, steaming as they settled. The dragon's breath cradled the new world and shaped it like a potter at her wheel. As it continued forming, as the dragon's eyes turned once again to the Pioneer Ship, the watching girl realized what the planet was: a gift. The star dragon was making them a new home.

Her heart trembling in wonder, she put her palm to the cold window. Her breath fogged on the glass. By the time she wiped it away with her sleeve, the Pioneer Ship had fired its missiles.

The girl pounded at the window in helpless horror as the missiles struck the creation dragon, as the still-forming world before it shattered like an ornament. The captain and the Council and the elders had spotted the creature, had made their assumptions about its nature, and had attacked it, as men attack all things they don't understand. They battled with the dragon and won their victory against it, and the girl was the only one who saw the truth—that humanity won not because they were stronger, but because the dragon did not wish to harm them.

And here my tale ends: with humanity commending themselves on vanquishing a bloodthirsty foe, not noticing the crushed bits of their new home among the debris.

By the time I finish the story, my heartrate has settled, but not by much. I still don't have any answers. Or even any idea how to go about finding answers beyond the vague goal of getting to the hole in the sky. But at least I'm not full-out panicking anymore, which is something, I guess. This story always has an odd effect on me—it's tragic to think of a newborn planet being wiped out because of humanity's rash decisions, but at the same time, the concept of a creation dragon is a beautiful one. If only that creature had been among the dragons who'd come to our world instead of only the starfire-wielding ones, maybe there could have been some sort of peace between our species. Maybe I could get my questions answered without the fear of being wiped from existence in the process.

Indy climbs up on me then, nosing me insistently until I lay down and make space for her atop the covers. I keep one hand atop my book's cover and bury the other in the thick fur at the ruff of Indy's neck, taking comfort from her warmth and nearness. It still takes me a long time to fall asleep, and when I do, I'm plunged into my dream.

The deep of space opens around me. I blaze a path through it, spiraling around worlds no one has named. The dust of nebulas glides over my wings. My scales cast a glow across the universe. I am free.

And then I am not.

I am trapped. The dark around me is not the depths of space, but the crushing weight of a single world. The sky is papered over. The starlight fades from my scales and drains out of my blood. The universe is closed to me. I mourn it and no one hears.

Time passes. Before, it flew, but now it crawls.

I will die far from the stars, and alone.

I wake with a gasp at dawn, jerking so violently that I knock Indy off the bed. She grumbles and curls up on the ratty rug but I barely even notice. The phantom-limb ache is permeating every bit of me from the inside out, marrow to skin, and I can't shake that horrific feeling of being entombed. And the *loneliness.* Oh, gods. For a few long moments I can't do anything but bury my face in my pillow and try not to sob.

It takes maybe ten minutes before I regain composure, and longer than that for the ache to fade into a dull, distant throbbing. I sit up and drag in a breath. What the hell was that? My dreams have never been that detailed before, or that emotional. It felt like a memory—or like a call for help that no one can hear but me. I glance down at the scrapbook that's still lying on my covers, painted now with a weak wash of pinkish light from the sunrise over the ocean. Maybe the nightmare was a stress dream, a reaction to the terrible events of Starfall plus the fairytale I read before I fell asleep last night. It's a logical assumption but it doesn't ring true. I get up and get dressed and try to put both the dream and the story out of my mind, which of course doesn't work at all.

Later that day, the rolling blackouts start. I'm bringing Indy in from a jog along the beach when the lamp next to the couch goes out. Anthem, who'd been scrolling through social media to check on her many friends, glances up and tries to flick the lamp back on. Nothing happens. I flip the wall switch for the main light. Nothing again. Dad checks his watch. The Council has initiated emergency power measures. Apparently everyone is using too much power to try to communicate with their loved ones and follow the news updates, and with the worldwide glint shortage, the energy companies are struggling to keep up. We've been put on a six-hour blackout rotation.

Dad turns his watch off and looks at us all. "We need to keep our watches off from here on out, limit our news checks to perhaps twice per day. If blackouts have already started it means we aren't guaranteed our weekly energy allotment for communications. We may have to make do with the charges we've got currently for a while. How much percentage does everyone have left? I've got seventy-nine."

"Sixty," Mom says, grimacing.

"Fifty-two," Anthem answers, then when Mom raises her brow, she flings her hands up defensively. "What, you expect me to just abandon my friends without a word? I had to text them! And I had to message the psych center to put my internship on official hold, just in case they wanted to be jerks and punish me for vanishing during a crisis."

Dad allows that with a nod, then turns to me.

I look away and mumble, "Fifteen percent."

Anthem gives me a look. She knows, or at least guesses, that I've been researching travel routes and playing and replaying that video of the broadcast, pausing on shots of the dragon and that ragged square of teal sky. She doesn't know about my dreams or the whole I-might-be-dying thing, but she does know about my sudden fascination with dragons, and my longstanding desire to see the sky.

"Per!" Mom says sharply. "Seriously? Who have *you* been texting?" She hears the emphasis and winces. "I didn't mean it like that, kiddo, I'm sorry," she says hastily. She's right, though—I don't have any friends close enough to check up on, which is by my own design. More people I care about means more people I worry about.

I don't say anything to dissuade her of her assumption that my battery is drained because I've been keeping up with friends, though. I just promise to keep it powered down according to Dad's new schedule, and no one says anything else about it.

We try to occupy ourselves with fixing the house up for the rest of the day. We're in that weird crisis space where the initial jolt of adrenaline-fueled terror has passed, and now there's just quiet uncertainty stretching out like a string of melted taffy. It'll break soon, but we don't know how or when, and it makes us all exhausted.

My OCD gets steadily worse as a result. Intrusive thoughts strike out of nowhere. I use pruning shears to clear up the overgrown garden and imagine snipping fingers rather than weeds. I pour food in Indy's bowl and think of her choking to death. When I look out at the green algae bloom on the ocean I think of blood coating the water instead, dark and oily like a slick on the waves. It makes me sick, disgusted with myself and frustrated that I have to focus so much energy on combatting my own brain. Part of me wishes I'd taken up Anthem's offer to introduce me to a counselor a few weeks back. The rest of me plans ways to get to the Conglom port and then to the hole in the sky.

We work on the house. We eat the few cans and bags of food that Mom packed. When the power returns we check the news and find a new video: Albergian soldiers with machine guns and energy weapons advancing on the dragon. Bullets bounce off its hide like rubber. Energy bolts do absolutely nothing. It breathes starfire over the small army and obliterates a huge swath of it. Feeling sick, we turn the video off.

Mom marches to the closet, extracts a battered fishing pole from its depth, and turns to us with her chin held high. "Who wants to fish?" she says in an iron tone that means everyone is going to fish.

Dad takes the ever-present pencil out from behind his ear and twiddles it between his fingers, which is his only tell that he's worried. "I believe it traditionally only takes one person to fish, dear," he says mildly.

She narrows her eyes. "Not when one person is fishing, one person is scouting for the best fishing locations, and someone else is looking for other edible sea life like kelp or..." She casts around for some other edible form of sea life.

"Oysters?" Dad offers.

"Oysters!" she echoes triumphantly.

"What about the fourth person?" I dare to ask.

"Moral support and dog caretaking," she proclaims, and that's that.

We troop down to the beach. Mom and Dad lag behind, and when I look back, I see they're clinging to each other's hands again. Something rueful and bittersweet nudges at me. I'm glad they have each other, and I'd like to think I could have something like that bond with another person someday—except I never will, because I'd always be afraid there's a possibility I might wake up in the middle of the night and murder him.

The thought and the emotion it carries hits me right in the core of my stomach like a sucker punch. I stop short, sand spraying across my shoes. I will never be with anyone. I've thought it before, but never so clearly and with such certainty. Suddenly, I want to sit down right here on the beach and cry, but I can't, because that would alert my family to the fact that something is terribly wrong with me.

I force my lungs to expand. Force my feet to move forward again. Assemble something like a smile on my face. My family is already dealing with a shit-ton of trauma right now. I can't add to it by dropping all my own problems on them too. I can deal with this myself. It's what I've always done.

"Here we are!" Mom announces unnecessarily when we reach the shore. She shoves the end of the fishing rod into the sand and "invests" a minute of her watch's energy on looking up an instructional fishing cast. Dad peers out at the ocean as if he can see anything past the foamy, algae-laden waves, and Anthem mutters curses as she wades through the surf and drags her fingers through the rocky sand to search for oysters. Which I'm pretty sure don't live in the sand.

Mom finishes the video and attempts to wield the fishing pole. "Six o'clock, twelve o'clock," she mutters as she swipes the pole from position to position, winding up for her cast. "Hold the butt with the left hand...release the button thingie with the right."

Anthem glances up with a smirk, then looks at me with one eyebrow raised to see if I'm going to fulfill my marching orders as moral support. I straighten up and try to infuse my voice with normality. "Go, Mom!" I shout, cupping my hands over my mouth. "Hold that butt!"

She shoots me a thin-lipped glare that means she's trying not to laugh. Anthem has no such compunction and chortles loudly. I manage an almost-genuine chuckle. Indy, hearing the sounds of merriment, capitalizes on it by wiggling up to me to present her belly for rubs. I fulfill my other assigned duty by petting her while Mom hooks a beer can, a piece of driftwood, and her own shoe in sequence. She hops on one foot, cursing as she nearly turns her ankle on the rocks while she tries to extract the hook from her bright yellow pump. Anthem glances up again, cueing me.

"A bold fashion choice to wear high heels on the beach," I say to Mom from the boulder where I've perched. "You pull it off so well."

She manages to unhook the shoe, which is now utterly ruined, and lobs it at me. I dodge it. "I'm a *ballroom dancing instructor,* dammit!" she says, laughter in her voice. "I don't own anything *but* heels!"

I try to smile again. Damn, I wish this was real—wish I actually felt the gritty, determined humor of this little family gathering in the midst of the apocalypse. Instead, it feels like a bubble that encompasses everyone but me.

Mom minces gingerly across the rocks, one foot now bare, to cast her line again. Dad leaves his post to go over to her and takes off his beat-up loafers, offering them up without comment. She looks at him with gooey eyes and then pulls him in for a kiss.

My smile gets the tiniest bit more real. Anthem doesn't even have to cue me for this one. "Gross!" I call to my parents. "I'm not offering moral support for that." Mom waves me off without breaking the kiss.

Anthem lets out a whoop and charges over to us, holding something in her cupped hands. "I found an oyster-clam-shellfish thing!" she shouts, grinning. "Now, how do I open it?"

The tiny shellfish is barely as long as her little finger, but she's beaming with pride, and no one ruins her delight by pointing out it'll provide maybe twenty calories to whoever eats it while the rest of us have a big old plate of starvation for dinner. Or at least that's what I'm guessing will happen based on the fishing skills Mom's displayed thus far.

Dad pulls out a handful of the sundry items he always has in his pockets: gum, two more pencils, cracker crumbs, and a small chipped pocketknife. I suddenly find the pebbles beneath me utterly fascinating while Anthem takes the knife and pulls its blade out with a little *schick.*

Come on, idiot, don't ruin the moment for them, I order myself sternly. It'll be over in a second and then the knife will vanish into

Dad's pocket and we can go back to having at least some degree of fun while distracting ourselves from the world's current catastrophe.

But then Anthem yelps, and my gaze shoots up to her. She's turned toward the ocean. The oyster-thing has fallen forgotten to the ground, along with the knife. An eerie, otherworldly bluish-violet light paints her expression in lines of disbelief and awe and horror. Mom and Dad are frozen too, staring in the same direction. I follow their gazes.

A star dragon is arcing across the sky like a meteor plunging to the earth.

It's massive, far bigger than the first dragon, and it gleams with a blue-purple light that throws everything on the beach into stark relief even though the creature is skating across the distant horizon. Jet-black shadows peel away from my family members and splash themselves up the shoreline meter after meter, sharp-edged and lurid. The dragon is so fast that it pulls a streak of blue behind it like flames from a jet engine. It paints the underside of the Barrier with a brief but dazzling light: the first time I've ever seen the sky colored anything but eggshell. And then it's gone, vanished beyond the horizon to the east, taking its light and its planet-ending sense of awe with it.

"In the house," Dad manages to say, his voice scraped thin. "Everyone, back in the house."

As if that'll protect us. As if anything could. But even as I think it, I find myself straining toward the beach, stepping out into the surf, peering in the direction the dragon came from.

North. Albergia. It slipped through the hole in the sky and soared into my world, and I want nothing more than to follow it back out into the stars. The longing erupts in me and melts into my blood, fuses with my bones. But then I glance over at Anthem and see the way she's looking at me: like I'm already lost to her. Like she's already started mourning me. She doesn't know all my secrets but she knows enough to guess how much the sight of the dragon has pulled at me. As I look at her, I realize I can't leave her. I can't leave any of them. Even if it means the slow suffocation of my own soul. Even if it means never, ever getting answers about what's happening to me.

"Come on," I tell her, my voice only a little hoarse. "Let's get inside."

She nods, looking cautiously relieved, and leans down to pick up the knife—and that's when I see it.

She's cut herself.

A thin trickle of blood is smeared across the base of her thumb and my whole self zooms in on it: the way it follows the lines on her palm like a tiny river delta, the splatter pattern it makes on a pebble when a drop falls to the ground, the red thumbprint standing out starkly on the oyster shell.

Just like that, panic roars over me. Images surge through my mind one after another: me driving that knife into her stomach. Her blood spattering over my own hands, warm and then cooling, a brand-new sticky delta oozing over the rocks. And worst of all, the expression on her face when her faith in me is shattered. When she realizes she should have been afraid of me all along. When she finally sees me for what I truly am: evil.

I stumble back, Indy barking and nipping at my heels in confusion. I've always been terrified of having an intrusive thought about a family member, but I've never actually had one happen before. It's so much worse than I ever feared. So much more visceral—as if it's already happened, over and done with, and my hands are still sticky with blood. On a normal day, maybe I would have a panic attack, do some compulsions, and eventually manage to convince myself everything would be okay. Not today, though. Not after Starfall, not after how bad my OCD's been lately, and definitely not after the dragon light and dreams that seem to be slowly hijacking my mind and body.

My gaze meets Anthem's again and I don't know what she sees in my expression, but it makes her stiffen with wariness. Not of me, but about what I'm going to do next—because she can guess what fear just shot through my head and how much it affected me, and she knows I'll do *anything* to stop that fear from coming true.

And she's right. I will do anything. I will protect her from me even if it means leaving her behind.

Tonight, I'm going to steal the car, and then I'm going to Albergia.

CHAPTER FIVE

D ad shutters the windows and Mom locks the doors. They check the news. Three more dragons, including the one we saw, have come through the hole and landed in several different countries. We discover more details we can't hold in our memories for longer than a second or two: the shape of the mountain range at our western border. What the president of the Saskrin nation looks like. The name of the Ancient Isle's capital city.

The car keys are still lying forgotten on the table. I mark their position and then go to bed early. I don't sleep. Instead I mentally retrace the route we took on the highway and backroad to get here, look up alternate routes on my swiftly-dying watch, and try to pinpoint exactly how much gas is left in the tank. It doesn't matter if I run out halfway there though. I'll abandon the car and walk the rest of the way to the port if I have to.

I pack. It takes about thirty seconds. I don't put any food in because I won't take anything Mom and Dad and Anthem—and Indy, for that matter—might need.

I dig around until I find a crumpled book report in the bottom of my bag. I use the back of it to write a note. It's short and to the point, because what can I really say to make them understand that I'm doing this, at least in part, for their own good? They'll be better off without me. As for me, I won't have to worry about hurting the people I love anymore. Maybe once I get my answers I'll be strong enough to come back to them. Maybe then the dreams and the light, and the increasingly awful intrusive thoughts, will stop.

Should I feel brave? I don't. Deep down this feels more like an act of cowardice than one of protection or self-sacrifice, but it doesn't matter. I'm going anyway.

I'm sorry, I finally scribble. *I know you won't understand but I have to go. I'll try to get word to you that I'm safe, for as long as I can make my watch battery last. Take care of each other. I love you.*

It's a feeble note, a pathetic goodbye message, but it's the best I can do.

I lay down on the bed and wait for midnight.

I doze a little. I dream once again of blazing a trail through the stars like I'm a winged creature myself, making my own light, not trapped in my own human brain. The dream and my sleep are both shallow, though, and part of me is still aware of my surroundings—and aware that I need to get up. I wake to silent darkness and ease off the bed, slinging my bag over one shoulder. It's time.

I nudge the bedroom door open and glance out. The door to the room Anthem has claimed is firmly shut. Mom and Dad are curled up together in a nest of blankets by the back door—the door closest to the beach—as if to protect us from anything that might enter. I don't see Indy, which means she must be in Anthem's room. That's a relief. It means she won't wake everyone up with her curiosity as I tiptoe through the cabin in the middle of the night, and it also means I won't have to say goodbye to her.

I scoop up the keys, careful not to make a sound, and leave the note in their place. I silently unlock the door and ease it open. It creaks a little. Dad snores and rolls over but doesn't move after that. I twist the doorknob's lock back and then slowly, quietly shut it behind me. The little *snick* of it engaging is the only sign that I've left.

I turn and exhale into the chilly night air. The car is parked a few meters away—hopefully far enough that it won't wake Mom and Dad when it starts. I unlock it, slide into the driver's seat, and make sure to turn the headlights off before I start the engine. As soon as it rumbles to life, I back out onto the road fast so I won't have to see whether Mom and Dad wake up and come out and see me leaving them.

And then I drive.

The car has about three-quarters of a tank of gas. Enough, I think, to make it back to the port if I take F-94 the whole way and avoid the downed bridge we ran across. And then what? The sailing schedules I looked up earlier were out of date, scrambled up. The whole world has been thrown into chaos and no one can keep track of which refugee-bearing ships are where. But I'm positive there will be at least one Albergian vessel at the Conglom port. There has to be. I'll stow away on it if I need to, though I hope I can barter for passage, or maybe indenture myself to a job onboard during the journey like I was going to with *The Shitty Clunker*. I'll figure it out when I get there. For now, I focus all my attention on the drive: avoiding potholes, crossing bridges, searching for roadblocks. I come across a few but not a single one is manned. They're all just orange and white striped portable barriers, easily to nudge aside as I drive through. Some of them are even lying on the ground in splinters already—victims to other panicked drivers, no doubt. I run across a few other vehicles and a good number of bikes and rickshaws headed south, but don't see anyone else going north. Every so often I catch the gleam of distant headlights in my rearview mirror, and once even the flash of a patrol car's warning lights, but I speed up and no one stops me.

The fuel gauge is hovering over E and the sun is a yellowish smudge overhead by the time I reach the city. It looks like a ghost town. I can feel gazes digging into my back, a sensation that raises the hairs on my neck, but I see very few actual people. All of the clamor from a few days ago is gone. Abandoned bikes and debris lay discarded in the street, doors are barred, and windows are smashed. A portion of a skyway has crashed to the ground and blocked off an entire street that I have to route around. There are more than a few body-shaped lumps lying in alleyways that I look away from quickly. The smell is awful; between the bodies and the trash that has been piling up ever since Starfall, I wonder how anyone can bear to stay here. I think of Mrs. Kowalski and our other neighbors and hope they're okay.

As I pull up to the port, my watch warbles with an urgent message. Mom and Dad will have woken up by now and seen my note, found the car missing. Do they think I'm selfish for stealing it, for robbing them of their only means of transportation, of escape? Something in my chest wrenches and I don't check the text. I wish there was a way to get the car back to them after I'm gone, but I know someone will steal it the second I'm out of sight.

I throw the car into park, grab my bag, and practically lunge out onto the pavement before I can waver in my decision. I march toward the docks, already scanning the ships moored there. Several of the bays have soldiers or armed security guarding them—probably from looters—but none of those ships sport the Albergian sigil anyway, which means they're grounded and useless to me.

And then my gaze lands on the last bay in the row. A submarine is docked there. A submarine with a mid-forties, reclining, beer-holding masthead.

The Shitty Clunker is back.

I hesitate, staring at it. On the surface this seems to be extraordinary luck. I already have an in with the sub's crew, and I know they're almost certainly going to be heading back to Albergia—for the dragons, if not for the sake of picking up more refugees. But therein lies the problem, too. The Star Slayer will still want to slay a dragon. And I'm having a dragon's dreams, and my hand glows like their scales. What will he do if he finds out? He doesn't seem like the sort of guy who would murder or experiment on a teenager, but catastrophes make people desperate enough to do things they'd never consider otherwise.

But if I join Z's crew, I wouldn't technically be allying with the Star Slayer, who's just a passenger. He might not even be onboard anymore. And if he is, I can tell him I don't want to tag along for his mission after all—that I want to get to Albergia to find some friends, or something—and then I can just avoid him the whole trip. Or maybe try to casually chat with him, see if he has any info that might help me figure out my dreams without making him suspicious. My supply of chill is low at the best of times, so the "casual chatting" plan probably isn't my best bet, but I'll just have to see how things go.

My fingers tighten on the strap of my backpack and I stride forward. I keep my eyes glued on *The Shitty Clunker*, feeling the suspicious glares of all the guards heavy on my back. One of them, a pale middle-aged guy so sunburnt he might as well be a cooked lobster, stops me at the end of the dock. "Where you goin'?" he demands, his heavy accent placing him as being from the Conglom's southernmost city-states. His pale green eyes are sharp as he fingers something under the side of his jacket. A gun?

I keep my gaze up and regulate my breathing even as I take what I hope is a subtle step back. "I've got a job on that sub," I tell him.

His brow arches. "Then why ain't I seen you before?"

"It's a new job."

He tugs his jacket aside and I see the gleam of black plastic. It *is* a gun. Everything in me wants to run but I grit my teeth and stand still, unexpected anger flaring up at the compulsion to avoid the gun. I'm not letting my OCD cost me this, too.

"I don't believe you," he says. "You know what I think? I think you're a thief. What you got in that bag?"

"Nothing. Just clothes. My stuff. The usual." I'm sweating now. I've come all this way; it can't end here, as simply as this.

"Let's see it," he says, holding out one hand, keeping the other on the gun. I start to swing the backpack down when a new but familiar voice calls out from behind me.

"Chester, leave him alone, will you?"

I spin around. Z is behind me, his hoverchair zipping from the port up the dock toward us at an unsafe clip. He looks...awful. His brown hair is even more mussed than the last time I saw him and he seems to have tried to take a bath in machine oil judging from the amount of splatters on his clothes, but it's his eyes that make the real difference. They look hooded. Haunted.

He has family, the Star Slayer said when he saw where the dragon landed. I wonder if he still does.

Z slows to a stop next to us. He raises one lazy, sardonic eyebrow at me, seems to dismiss me entirely, and then turns a glare on Chester. "I don't pay you to harass my employees."

My heart leaps. He's covering for me. And, I think, hiring me?

Chester glares back and leans forward a little, easily looming over the seated Z. "You don't pay me at all."

Z lays a hand on his heart, a mockery of affront. I notice he's got some sort of fabric looped around his palm and secured with medical tape—a makeshift bandage. He must've hurt himself since we last met.

"I let you eat with my own crew," he says to Chester. "I cooked your lunch with my own hands."

"That's punishment, not payment," Chester grumbles, but drops his hand away from his gun. "What's he been hired to do? You said you weren't takin' anyone new onboard. Cause if you are, you know I need to hitch a ride to the shales to see my folks—"

A muscle in Z's jaw feathers. "No one is hitching any rides."

"You got to stop by the shales anyway!" Chester protests, scratching at a patch of peeling skin. "I've been guarding your dock out of the goodness of my heart for hours, and you won't even let me come along for one stop?"

Now the muscle is ticking. I watch it, fascinated, wondering if Z does jaw workouts or something. Normal people don't have facial muscles that defined, do they?

Z takes a deep breath, looking like he would pray for patience if he were the praying sort. Which I strongly doubt. "The shales are a pit stop. The fewer people I have to drop off there, the quicker I get back to Albergia."

Chester spits on the ground. "You so eager to go home to your own death, *captain*? You should stay where it's safe before no one can remember you either."

The look on Z's face is stark, shocked, like he's been sucker punched. I don't quite understand whatever personal impact Chester's words have on Z—but what I do understand is that look on Z's face, and I realize suddenly that I very much do not like it. I step forward and intervene. "Nowhere is safe," I say, keeping my voice level even though I'd like to yell at Chester. "And I'm not here to make trouble."

"Found it anyway," Chester grumbles.

"Fine. You can come along, but only to the shales, Chester," Z grits out between his teeth. "Just shut up and get on board. We prep to launch in half an hour."

A frown wrinkles Chester's face. "Already? Just got here coupla hours ago, didn't you?"

"I don't pay you to make obvious observations."

"You don't pay me at all," Chester says, but wastes no time in scurrying up the ladder and vanishing down the hatch, not bothering to wait and see if Z needs any help getting his hoverchair up.

"Thanks," I say awkwardly as Z nudges a lever on his armrest, zooming forward toward the ladder.

"Don't thank me," he says sharply. "I've got no idea why you want to go to Albergia and I don't care. I just need a cook, that's all. I was bad enough at cooking when I had two good hands—I don't intend to try it with one." He waves his bandaged palm. "Come on. I'll show you where the galley is."

He engages the landing gear things again and this time they come out from the back of his chair, clamping onto the sub to either side of the ladder. His chair emits a low buzz as the magnets haul him upward.

"That thing is pretty handy," I remark.

One corner of his mouth lifts a little. "Built her myself," he says proudly, stroking the side of the chair like it's a pet. He reaches the top of the ladder and the magnets smoothly shift to the bottom of the chair to carry him toward the hatch. His voice drifts down: "Get a move on, bird boy."

I eye the dock in front of me. I remember Rick's knives shining in his belt just a meter or so in front of where I'm standing now, between me and the ladder. I feel the panic begin to build as I consider walking past it. I make a decision.

I am going to get on this sub.

I do. I go fast, skirting as wide as I can around the spot, not pausing to let myself think, and although my anxiety ticks upward I don't lose control of myself. Maybe because the knives aren't actually here this time. *Or maybe,* I hear Anthem's voice say in my mind, *it's because "bad thoughts" don't make* you *bad, and real people don't actually just "snap" and go on stabbing sprees, and you have always been a good person. Idiot.*

My eyes sting at the thought of her. I take a deep breath and lean out to grab the ladder, then start climbing. I reach the top and pull myself up onto the tower's deck only a little shakily. I peer back down at the dock, feeling a weird mix of nerves and euphoria now that I've managed to get through this one small fear, then I step over to the railing at the front of the tower. "Can I ask you something I've been wondering ever since that day we met?" I ask Z.

He shoots me a wary look. "If I say no, will that stop you?"

Ignoring him, I gesture at the side of the tower below us. "What's up with the masthead?"

He blinks and then snorts a laugh. "I thought you were gonna ask what happened to me," he says. I frown, confused, until he gestures at his chair.

"Oh. No. That seems rude."

"That doesn't stop most people," he mutters. "They want a juicy tragedy, not a boring bike accident followed by a botched surgery." He shrugs then and motions at the masthead below us. "That's based on an old friend of the family. Joe Hank, and yes, he was exactly as hick as his name sounds. But he was also a great guy and we thought hey, it isn't fair for pretty girls to get all the mastheads, let's make things a little more equitable." He smirks. "We may also have been drunk the night we were designing it."

"Who's *we*?" I ask as he unlatches his landing gear magnet things and maneuvers his chair into the hatch. Only after I ask the question do I realize the full impact of his statement. He helped design the masthead. Did he help design the entire ship? How could someone as relatively young as him have been involved in such a project? And this ship looks *ancient*—how old was he when he was getting drunk and designing mastheads?

A line furrows between his brow like he's confused or trying to remember something. Then his expression shuts down, the haunted look returning. "Lunch is at one," he says. "I just took on a hell of a lot of vegetables so I hope you know what to do with those." Then the chair lowers and he vanishes into the sub.

I follow him down. The inside of *The Shitty Clunker* is just as ugly as the outside, but with a well-loved quality, like a much-read book held together with twine and tape. A burst of tinny classical piano music warbles over the intercom. It startles me for a moment, as with Z being the captain or acting captain or whatever I'd sort of expected to hear trash-rock or something with a lot of screaming guitars and curse words, but this music is actually kinda nice. Tattered band posters paper the cobalt metal walls, covered up here and there by glossy new pictures: still shots taken from the vids of the star dragons. I spot the original small ruby dragon, a fuzzy distant shot of the massive blue one, and pixelated close-ups of two horse-sized orangeish dragons. I grimace. This must mean the Rick and his people are still onboard.

I turn away from the pictures and follow Z deeper into *The Shitty Clunker*, where I catch sight of a narrow room filled with rows of bunks through one of the round porthole doors. Many of the bunks are empty, but some are shielded by tattered curtains or hanging beads, and one particularly messy bottom bunk is smudged with a few spots of machine oil and has old sword-and-sorcery novels and tools scattered across it. Easy to guess who that one belongs to.

"Galley's down here," Z shouts. He's in front of a porthole with a ladder hooked onto it leading downward. Before I can react, he twiddles a switch on his hoverchair that makes it lift up to the porthole's height, then he zooms through and drops like a rock. A little alarmed, I quickly follow and stick my head out to look down the ladder just in time to see his hoverchair bob to a gentle stop at its usual hovering height a foot off the floor below. Apparently he doesn't need to engage his landing gear when there's no risk of falling overboard.

I slide down the ladder after him and follow him through a corridor into what must be the galley. It's as small as our old apartment's kitchen: just a single long oven with four burners set into the top of it opposite a line of chest freezers and a fridge. The room ends in a meagerly-filled pantry. I step into it and poke gingerly at a sagging bag of flour. "How many people do I have to feed?" I ask, already wondering how I'm going to make these supplies stretch to supply the entire crew. At least it's only a single-day journey to Albergia. Although the stop at the shales might add another day or two, depending on which formation we're travelling to.

"About half a dozen crew members plus four refugees left now," he answers. "All the rest of the refugees chose to disembark here and make their way further south."

Surprised, I turn to look at him again. "I'd think a sub this size would require more people to run it."

He shrugs. "Nah. If things go south I could probably even run it on my lonesome. It runs on pure glint, barely takes a few gallons for a day's journey. We built this thing to be efficient as hell." He bangs an affectionate fist against the warped cobalt wall. I eye it doubtfully when it creaks under the minor blow.

"Are you sure this thing is still seaworthy with all those dents and dings and warps?" I venture. "I though submarine hulls were supposed to be smooth so they don't, you know, crack under the pressure and drown everyone."

He maneuvers his chair back toward the door, already ready to leave. "If it's good enough for the Pioneer Ship, it's good enough for *The Shitty Clunker.*"

Well, I can't just let him say *that* and then leave. "Wait, what? This is the same type of metal that the Pioneer Ship used?"

"It's metal salvaged from the actual Pioneer Ship itself," he corrects. "Stronger than anything we can build nowadays while still having some flex. It creaks like a mother when we dive but the pressure hasn't cracked it yet." He continues out the door, like that's a totally normal piece of info to drop on your way out of a conversation.

"I thought the Pioneer Ship was in some kind of museum?" I call after him.

"It was," he shouts back over his shoulder, already halfway down the hall. "We salvaged it when they shut the place down for budget cuts a few years back. Now go figure out what to make for lunch, bird boy, and then you can pick a bunk."

I step back into the galley, staring at the warped blue wall. I place my palm against it reverently. This metal has been in space. Starlight has shone on it. I smile softly as I trace my fingers over its dents—put there by asteroids? Dragons? Rocky landings on other worlds?—and a small spark of wholly unexpected joy kindles in me.

After a minute, I force myself to stop admiring the wall and investigate the food supplies. I find a ton of vegetables in the fridge along with a carton of eggs nearing their expiration date. There's some meat in there, too, and much more in the freezers, but not a lot else. A few big bags of flour, some sugar, yeast, beans, and jars of gelatinous brown goop that's labeled as beef base. I step back and ponder the ingredients. Mom's never been much of a cook but Dad always enjoyed it, and I've helped him make dinner more than a few times. I could probably throw together some flatbread from this stuff. Roast some meat and veggies to serve with it. Z hasn't stocked the proper spices but I can make do. I check the time: ten o'clock in the morning. Z said we'd be diving in half an hour—less time than that, now—and that lunch would be at one. Plenty of time to find my bunk, get settled in, and bring myself to check Mom and Dad's message. Or maybe the text was from Anthem. A lump forms in my throat as I step into the hallway. I know they'll all be much more worried and hurt than angry, which only makes this harder. But I can't just ignore them. They deserve to know I'm safe, at the very least.

As I climb the ladder to head back toward the bunkroom, I keep a wary eye out for Rick. At this point I'd prefer to avoid him but I doubt I'll be able to manage that for the entire trip. Maybe I should prepare some small-talk topics just in case I do get into a conversation with him. He'll remember me from when we met, of course, but hopefully he still assumes I'm just a regular, true-believer fanboy.

I'm so focused on looking out for the Star Slayer that when I spot someone else already in the bunkroom, the only thing I register at first is that it's not him. I'm already letting out a breath of relief by the time I realize it's someone much, much worse.

"It's about time," Anthem says, glaring at me with her arms crossed. "Get in here and close the door. We have some things to discuss."

Chapter Six

I gape at my sister. I'm so shocked that I don't even panic for a full three seconds as my mouth moves and no words come out.

She raises one eyebrow. "You look like a fish when you make that face," she observes coolly.

I'm finally jarred into motion. I grab the wheel on the porthole and use it to slam the door shut, then march over, snag her arm, and tug her up off the bunk where she's sitting.

"Hey!" she protests, her eyes bright like flares now. She's *furious*. And—upset. I see the sheen of tears and the set of her mouth, but there's no time to try to calm her down. The sub dives in what, ten minutes now, headed straight for a glacial nation full of dragons, and *my sister is onboard.*

"You have to leave," I tell her.

"Let go of me this second," she hisses.

I don't. I try to tug her toward the exit. But as I anticipated—which is why I didn't leave the porthole open—she digs her heels in and refuses to move. "You're hurting me," she says sharply, and I drop her arm like it's burned me and take a long step back.

"I'm sorry," I say, raising my hands, worriedly peering at her arm to make sure she's okay. "But you can't—Anthem, you don't understand."

She swipes a hand across her eyes, bright and angry and betrayed. "You're right. I don't understand. You were just going to leave, Per," she says, the words ragged, every syllable a drop of poison. "Going to steal the car and go investigate your precious dragons by yourself. You were going to abandon me."

"I left to protect you!"

"Bullshit," she replies, stabbing a finger to emphasize the word. "You left because you were afraid."

I turn away and scrub a hand through my hair, feeling lost and strung out, pulled in too many directions at once. I remember feeling like I was committing an act of cowardice when I left the cabin, and flinch. "Maybe," I allow, my voice cracking. "Maybe that too."

She crosses her arms and stares at me. "Come back with me."

"I can't do that." Then a thought occurs that probably should've come to mind earlier. "Wait—how did you even get here?"

"I saw the look on your face at the beach," she accuses. "I didn't want to think you would do something this stupid, but I hid outside the cabin to keep watch anyway. And lo and behold, what should happen but you sneak out, steal the car, and drive off before I can even yell at you?"

She didn't answer my question. My eyes get a little wider with apprehension. "Anthem. How did you get here?"

She makes a motion like she's shooing a gnat away. "It doesn't matter! I jogged to the town down the beach, flirted with an officer, and stole her patrol car, okay? And then I followed you, and now here we are right back at the port where you snuck off to at Starfall. You're going to Albergia, aren't you?"

"You *stole* a *patrol car*?" I yelp, then quickly lower my voice even though it's shaking now. "Anthem, that's—a *felony*, you could go to jail! You could've been shot! How could you do something so dangerous?"

"The same reason you claim to have left us," she says, her voice low and fierce. "Because you're family, and I won't let you get hurt." She swallows and visibly tries to gather herself. "Per, don't you realize that it's going to hurt all of us much more if you die in the middle of this dragon quest, or OCD quest, or whatever it is that you're doing? If you get uncreated, if I'm left with nothing but a wisp of a memory and a brother who never existed, don't you think that's a hell of a lot scarier to me than the one-in-a-million chance that you might actually be a secretly evil serial killer?"

I cover my face with my hands. This is a disaster. "You don't understand."

"What's there to understand? I know your OCD has been getting bad, but that doesn't mean you run away from your only support system! I can *help* you, Per. And so could Mom and Dad, if you would just tell them the truth."

"This isn't about my OCD!" I shout, but my voice catches because I'm not sure how true that is.

She crosses her arms tightly across her chest. "Then tell me what it *is* about! You and me, we've helped each other through everything else our whole lives long. Don't you think I would help you with whatever you're going through now?"

How long until the sub dives and she's stuck here? I've got to get her back on solid land, back to the cabin, back to relative safety. I don't know what to say to make her go. "I just...I need to get to the sky, Anthem."

The words seem to reverberate within me: the first time I've said such a thing aloud. I immediately wish I could take them back. Not because they're untrue, but because they're terribly, powerfully true, and I don't fully know *why*.

She stares at me in silence for a full two seconds. "What?" she says at last.

"I need to get—"

She holds up a hand to cut me off. "I don't need it repeated. I need it explained. Why the hell would you be trying to get to the sky?"

How am I supposed to explain something I don't really understand myself? I can *feel* the stars out there, can feel the ache and thrum of them planting hooks in my chest and reeling me in toward them. All my life, the sky has been papered over, and no one except me has seemed to care all that much—but there's a deep-down part of me that wants *out*, and that teal hole in the Barrier is one step closer to that. Even more urgent, but just as hard to explain, is the fact that I need to get answers about my dreams and the dragon-like light before the feeling that I'm dying escalates into me actually dying. "I just...there are questions that I have to get answered," I say at last.

Anthem takes a deep breath like she's trying really hard to be patient. "And you're willing to leave us all behind for those answers? Willing to potentially be uncreated?"

I spread my hands in silent appeal, unable to give her the reply she's seeking.

Anthem lifts her chin. "Fine. Then I'm coming with you."

I gape at her. "It's too dangerous!"

"And it's completely safe for you?" She scoffs.

I shake my head and press my hands to my eyes. "Nowhere is safe," I say with a choked laugh, remembering my words to Chester and Z earlier. And it's true. Whatever is happening to me, I know by this point that it's not going to stop on its own. It's like my OCD: the problem is inside me, which means there's no running from it. I can't solve my mental illness but at least I have a shot at solving this, and seeing the stars in the bargain.

Fingers wraps around my wrists, pulling my hands away from my face. Anthem is glaring at me steadily but something in the quality of her glare has changed. It's less anger and betrayal and more calculation now. "This has something to do with your interest in dragons, something more than just wanting to know about them. What aren't you telling me?"

I flinch. She sees it and presses the advantage, stalking forward and backing me up towards the nearest wall of bunks.

"You've been interested in dragons forever, but you started getting way serious about it earlier this year," she says. "*Long* before Starfall. Cutting class to follow leads, going to dangerous parts of the city on your own. Did you...what, did you somehow know they were going to get through the Barrier, or something? Did you get entangled in some government coverup thing and now you're on the run?"

Her words are relentless, hail pummeling me in a storm with no shelter in sight. "What? No! I swear, I'm not 'entangled' in anything."

She steps closer. The rail of one of the lower bunks is digging into my calves now, and the back of my head bumps into the upper bunk. "Then why would you risk all of this?" she demands, advancing until she's uncomfortably close. She's a little shorter than me but she still somehow manages to loom. "What could possibly be so shocking, so terrible, that you would leave your own family and go out on a potentially-deadly quest to see the goddamn *sky*?"

Something within me fractures and desperation and recklessness flood out through the cracks, fusing together to make something altogether more dangerous. I fling up my hands between us and cry out, "*This is!*"

Liquid sapphire-silver light blasts into the room like a supernova from both my hands. It's only that bright for a second before it sputters and dims, but it's enough to temporarily blind me. When I blink away the spots I see that Anthem is no longer standing in front of me. She is pressed against the wall opposite, fingers splayed flat against the metal like she's trying to phase through it, and her pupils have contracted so tightly they're barely a pinpoint swimming in deep brown. Her chest rises and falls rapidly. There is an expression on her face I've never seen before—shock and horror and something else—and it's *terrifying*, like watching a sinkhole yawn open under your childhood home and swallow up everything that ever made you who you are.

Desperate to wipe that look off her face, I step forward and reach for her. She lets out an inarticulate cry, flinches away, and throws up one hand in front of her like she's warding off a blow. My whole body freezes.

Anthem is afraid of me.

I start to hold out my hands palm-up in surrender but then think better of it and tuck them behind my back, out of view. "Anthem," I say, my voice strangled. "I would never hurt you. I will *never* hurt you."

She lowers her arm and stares at me. Her breath is still coming in pants but her pupils begin to dilate slowly. We stare at each other from opposite sides of the narrow room for a long moment, and then my knees give out and I fall to sit on the bottom bunk behind me. I pull up my legs and wrap my arms around them and start shivering like I'm buried in a snowbank. When the torment of watching Anthem be afraid of me gets too great, I grit out, "Say s-something."

Her breathing has started to slow a little, but her hand is still slightly raised like she might have to defend herself. The sight is a pile driver to my gut all over again. Then she sucks in a huge breath and bends over double with her hands on her knees like she's just run a marathon, or like she thinks she might throw up. "Holy shit," she says in a trembling voice.

"Agreed," I say through clattering teeth.

"Holy *shit*," she says more effusively, sounding a little more like her old self now. "That was...that was..."

"The same light as dragons have," I finish for her, because I don't want to hear her say it. Another tremor grinds through me. Is this shock? Stress? Flat-out terror? Whatever, it's not helping matters at all, but I can't make it quit.

She inches away from the wall toward me. "What—how—what?"

I choke on a laugh, feeling slightly hysterical. I've made Anthem speechless. That's a first.

She frowns sharply and moves forward more. "Stop laughing and start talking, dipshit."

The sinkhole feeling eases a little. She's insulting me, which means she still cares about me. "I...I started having dreams last spring," I confess, and as I continue talking, my shivering slows down. "Weird, intense dreams about flying in space, seeing real stars all around me, having these amazing glowing wings."

Her eyes narrow. "Wait. Spring, as in before Starfall. You were having dreams about glowing dragon wings *before* Starfall? How could you have known that they'd glow?"

I shake my head, suppressing another semi-hysterical laugh. Words bubble up out of me and I can't stop them. I've been keeping these truths at arm's length, too afraid of what they mean to let myself think about them much, but now all my defenses are down and I can't hide them anymore—not from Anthem, or from myself. "I couldn't have known. No one could've. The dreams kept getting more and more intense, and I started, like, almost blacking out and having them during the day too. And every time I wake up, I have this awful, bone-deep certainty that I'm dying. It *hurts*, Anthem. More and more every day, every time I wake up. I'm starting to be afraid that I really am dying—that this is some kind of warning or signal or something. That's why I've been researching star dragons so much. That, and I feel this…I don't know, connection to them. It's hard to explain, but I *know* that seeing them up-close and alive will help solve whatever's happening to me."

She's been inching closer the whole time I was speaking, that terrible fear on her face easing into caution—which I still can't stand to see—and now she sits down at the other end of the same bunk. Miserable, I keep my eyes on my knees.

"That…doesn't sound like it's part of your OCD," she says at last.

"It's not. It feels totally different. Lucky me, my brain gets to torture me in *two* completely different ways."

"And—and the light?" she asks, her voice going airless as she shapes the last word, like she can't quite bear to say it aloud. "What is that?"

I shake my head. "I have no idea. When I was helping that guy during Starfall, I had to go through this dark corridor and there was a bunch of glass I couldn't see. I was wishing I had a light, and my hand…did that."

She blows out a long breath. "That's creepy as hell, Per. I mean—I *know* you would never hurt me. And obviously you're not a star dragon so it's not like you could uncreate me or anything anyway. But that light, it's…it does something to me. Something visceral. Same as when I saw that blue dragon from the beach but like doubled."

I close my eyes. "I'm sorry."

"You didn't choose for any of this to happen to you," she says, her voice sharp now. "You don't have anything to be sorry for."

"I could've blinded you!"

"But you didn't. And even if you had you wouldn't have done it on purpose."

"But what if I did?" I press, and it's like poking at a bruise but I can't stop. "I shot that light at you without even thinking. It was instinctive, and it hurt and scared you. I *instinctively* hurt and scared you. What if that means I lost control, that I—that I *wanted* to hurt you deep down, and it's only sheer luck I don't have enough juice or power or whatever to actually blind you—"

She picks up a nearby pillow and whacks me in the face with it, hard enough to snap me out of the panic spiral I was about to fall into. "Now that *does* sound like your OCD. Do you want reassurance?"

She always asks that first because reassurance-seeking is a compulsion too. She keeps telling me it doesn't do me any good, that I should try to be more comfortable with uncertainty instead of working so hard to be positive that I'm definitely a good person, but I can't help it. Right now, I very desperately need to hear that I am okay. I grit my teeth and nod.

"You're a good person," she says firmly, "idiot. You didn't 'shoot' light at me, you were just trying to answer my questions in a very melodramatic, Peregrine sort of way."

"I'm not melodramatic," I mutter, but feel the tiniest bit better. She just snorts.

The sub shudders beneath us and I hear distant shouts from the crew. *The Shitty Clunker* is about to submerge. This is my last chance to get my sister off the ship. "Will you go now? You understand why I'm here, why this is necessary. Whether or not I'm actually dying, something undeniably very creepy is happening to me and I need to do this to figure out why, but you don't. Please, go back to the cabin."

She straightens her spine, throws her shoulders back, and lifts her chin: Anthem's battle stance. She flings her words out like they're a gauntlet thrown down. "Stop telling me to leave you. I won't. I am going to help you figure out what's happening to you and why, because creepy light or no creepy light, you are my brother and you are *not* dying on me."

And that's it: Anthem's decision. She will not leave me. Nothing I say or do now could ever convince her to go. Fear hollows out a home in my chest.

I hesitate, not quite looking at her full on. "Are you still afraid of me?" I manage.

She's sitting about a foot away from me now. She doesn't scoot closer and throw an arm around me or punch me in the shoulder like she would've yesterday, but she doesn't move away, either. "I know you would never hurt anyone," she says, which isn't exactly an answer. "It's just...it's gonna take me a sec to wrap my head around this, that's all. Can you give me a little time?"

"Yes." The word is a barb in my throat but I force it out anyway. I feel like the foundations of my whole world are shaking beneath me. Not even Starfall itself can compare to this: my sister, knowing me and afraid of me.

She nods, looking resolute. "Good." She glances at me sideways and sees my expression. "Stop looking that way. I'm gonna fix you, Per. I promise."

"You can't fix everything."

"Watch me."

I let out a breath, feeling both frustrated and affectionate—a comfortingly familiar emotion when it comes to my little sister. I don't bother arguing with her though, in part because I desperately hope she's right.

"Anything else I should know in the meantime?" she asks. I'm not sure if the words are wry or pointed or both.

"The Star Slayer," I tell her. "I'm pretty sure he's still onboard."

Her brow furrows and she stares at the bunk across from us like she wants to interrogate it. "And…what would he do if he found out about your shining thing?"

I lift my shoulders. "I have no idea. Toss me off onto the nearest 'berg to freeze to death? Put me in a cage and experiment on me? Turn me over to the government so *they* can experiment on me?"

"Like hell he will," she snarls, sounding more like her old self.

I start to reply, but a rustling noise startles me before I can speak. Something beneath the bed makes a low, sad moaning sound.

A very familiar sad moaning sound.

My eyes widen. "Anthem," I say, "tell me you didn't."

The intensity in her eyes dims a bit and she winces with…is that sheepishness? I'm not sure I've ever seen such a thing on her face before. "I, um, may have brought an unintentional traveling companion."

I bend down to look under the bed between my knees. Two big brown eyes stare back at me and a black-and-brown tail thumps hopefully. I sit back up. "You brought *Indy?*"

She winces. "I didn't mean to. She wouldn't stop barking, and the officer was starting to get suspicious. I had to let her get in the patrol car with me before she got me caught."

"Anthem."

She rubs her forehead. "Honestly, I thought I'd just get you to turn around and go right back home before we got a mile down the road," she admits.

"Why didn't you try to stop me, then?"

"You *left us*. I wanted to know why. I guessed you wouldn't tell me, so I decided I would find out for myself."

"You could have at least messaged me."

"I sort of used the last of my battery messaging my friends. One of those new dragons landed in Josefina's city. I had to make sure she's okay."

I groan. Indy edges partway out from beneath the bed, checking to see if we're done yelling at each other. She's never been one for conflict.

The sub rumbles ominously again under my feet again then, reminding me that we only have a minute or two before we dive and lose all signal. "I need to text Mom and Dad," I say heavily.

"Yeah. You should do that," Anthem says, wincing a little. She knows just how bad this is going to be.

I power up my watch. My fingers hovering over the messaging home screen as I try to figure out what to say to my parents. They've sent me multiple messages, each one more panicky than the last as they realized Anthem was gone too. My heart dips. I am the worst son in the history of sons, but there's no turning back now. I quickly type in a message.

Am okay. Anthem and Indy followed me and I didn't realize till just now. We're on a ship—I didn't want to tell them I was on a submarine that looked like it could crack open at the slightest current—*headed north. I would say don't worry but I know you will. I really am sorry. I didn't mean to drag Anthem into this.*

I send it and wait, holding my breath until my watch chimes with an answering text, which takes a grand total of about eight seconds. The reply is from Dad.

I don't understand, son. Why can't you tell us where you are and why you left? Whatever is wrong, we'll solve it as a family. If you're in trouble we will protect you. Come home. Bring your little sister home.

My heart twists painfully. *I swear I will keep Anthem safe,* I reply. *We're setting off now—have to go in a sec. I just wanted to let you know we're okay. Will check in again soon as I can. Anthem's battery is dead.*

Mom's watch comes online. *Why would you do this?* is all she types in, and it just about kills me.

Nothing to do with either of you, I manage to reply. *I can't explain right now. Just know we love you and we'll be back as soon as we can.* My watch blinks an alert. I have ten percent left, and I need to preserve battery for when I have signal again at the shales.

That's not enough, Mom says. *Come home now. Come home.*

My vision blurs. I scrub a hand over my eyes and power my watch down. Anthem and I sit in silence while Indy whaps her tail tentatively on the floor and pokes my shin with her nose. I reach down and pet her.

The sub shudders and groans again. Something scrapes against the hull with an ungodly noise. We've cast off. Just like that, my journey to the stars has officially begun.

I stand up. "I'm supposed to go make lunch," I tell her heavily. "What will you...what are you going to do, now that you're here?"

She's looking past me toward the door. "Um," she says, and clears her throat. "Probably introduce myself to that guy."

My heart stutters and I whirl around. Z is in the doorway and he's glaring straight at my sister.

"Who the hell are you, and what are you doing on my ship?"

Chapter Seven

My heart skips a beat. Z looks *pissed*. I panic for a second, wondering how much he might have seen and heard, then realize the sound of the sub diving must've covered up the noise of him opening the door. That means he can't have overheard any of our earlier conversation or seen my light.

I step in front of Anthem. "She's just a refugee headed to the shales," I try before she can speak.

His gaze shoots to mine. "Try lying to me again and see what happens," he dares.

Anthem stands up and pushes me out of the way. "I'm his sister. Nice to meet you." She smiles shyly and looks at him through her eyelashes, even managing to blush a little, but he's immune.

"You brought your *sister?*" he demands, incredulous as he turns back to me. Indy, hearing the sounds of conflict brewing once again, scrambles all the way back under the bunk. Z catches the movement and his expression somehow becomes even more incredulous, which I wouldn't have thought possible a moment ago. "What the hell is that?"

"That's Indy," I say, struggling to stay calm. We've already dived. It's not like he can make them walk the plank or anything. I'd like to think he would resurface and put them both out on the docks right now so Anthem can go home safely, but it has to be a lot of hassle to resurface and dive again, which means he'd be more likely to dump them at the shales. I can't let that happen. "She can...she can guard the sub," I offer, nodding at Indy. Or rather, the spot where only the tip of Indy's nose is sticking out.

He looks at me, then at Indy. He bends down from the waist and extends a hand, whistling. "Here, puppy," he says, his tone changing like flipping a switch. He sounds gentle and—gods help me, *sweet*?—as he rubs his fingers together to lure Indy out. "Who's a good girl?" Indy, the traitor, immediately bounds out from under the bed and wriggles up to him on her belly, letting him scratch her ears without compunction. Her tongue lolls with delight. Z looks up at me and raises that sardonic eyebrow. "Uh huh," he says, voice thick with skepticism. "She's downright vicious."

Anthem puts her hands on her hips, dropping the helpless-maiden act. "Look, whatever Per is here for, I'll help with that. We only want to get to—"

"Albergia, yeah, I know." He sits up straight. Indy jumps into his lap like it's perfectly natural and he gives a little *oof* at her weight but doesn't shove her off. She rapturously breathes dog breath in his face. He looks over the top of her head, somehow managing to continue looking pissed even while he resumes scratching Indy's ears. "Just because I let bird boy here indenture himself as a cook doesn't mean I need two of you. And this beast of a dog weighs a ton—I don't even want to know how much of my food she'll eat, not to mention the problem of where it'll wind up once it comes out the other end." He glowers at Indy. She licks his face. "Is there anything else you're useful for, sister-of-Peregrine?"

"My name is Anthem. And I'm training as a counselor. Although it's sort of illegal for me to practice therapy without a license. Also there's the fact that I'm currently on probation."

"So, you're *not* useful for anything else." He sighs, sounding deeply tired as he nudges Indy off his lap. She lands on the floor with an ungraceful plop and hops onto a nearby bunk to sulk. "Well, lucky for you, we've already dived and I'm in a hurry. You're not worth the hassle of surfacing to offload at the moment. I'll figure out some other way you can make it up to me."

She inhales sharply. "What exactly are you implying? If you think I'm going to let you—"

He rolls his eyes and waves at her dismissively. "Down, girl. That's not what I meant. You're not my type anyway."

Anthem isn't appeased. "Damn straight," she snarls.

Meanwhile, I'm still tense as hell—he didn't say he wouldn't drop Anthem at the shales, just that he wouldn't resurface here and slow down his trip. I've got to find some way to convince him to let her stay; the shales are way too dangerous of a place for her to be stranded, especially since earthquakes have been hitting more frequently all over lately.

Someone shouts from down the hall. Z leans back in his chair to glance out and then scrubs a hand through his hair, his jaw tensing. "Sonar's on the fritz," he mutters, then slices a finger at Anthem. "You, Melody or Annie or whatever—"

"*Anthem*," she growls, "and for the record you're not my type either. I like girls. And sometimes guys, if they're not absolute assholes. So you see how you wouldn't qualify."

He doesn't even respond to that. "Anthem, then—go find something to clean."

"Why, because I'm a girl and therefore I must automatically be good at cleaning?"

"Because, and I can't emphasize this enough, *you are a stowaway.*" He flaps his hands at her. "Shoo. Clean. Everyone's got to earn their keep on my ship and this is where you start." Then he glances at Indy. "As for that one, how about I take her to visit the refugee family? They're staying in the captain's suite. They have little kids who could probably use a friendly dog to hang out with for a bit." He waits for our answer and we both nod—me eagerly, hoping that Indy might win us all some points, and Anthem begrudgingly.

Someone shouts at him from down the corridor again. He leans his head back into the hallway and shouts, "I'm coming, jackass, hold your horses!" He sighs deeply and steeples his fingers, looking back at us. "One last thing. What I came here to tell you in the first place. In about an hour we'll be entering the Icedrift Sea—international waters. It's full of 'bergs along with the occasional giant eel. Bergs are easy, we can just steer around 'em or crash right through the smaller ones, but if we spark the interest of an eel we'll have to run quiet. I've got the sonar hooked up to the main generator; if we ping any big critters it'll automatically turn everything off except the blue emergency lights, which are a wavelength the eels can't see." He jerks his head at a bare, blue-shaded light bulb dangling from the ceiling of the bunkroom. "So if everything goes blue, shut up and stay shut up until the lights come back on. Unless you want to end your life in a digestive tract."

With that, he fiddles with a switch to manipulate his chair's hovering height so he can hop it back over the porthole's raised threshold. He whistles for Indy, who bounds over toward him and only remembers to stop and look at us for permission when she's already at the door. "Go on, girl," I tell her.

"I'll have the family bring her to the galley at lunch for you to pick up," Z says. "Come on, you ridiculous beast of a dog, follow me." Indy trots along happily after him as he zips down the corridor. I glance out to make sure she doesn't get distracted and run off. When they're nearly out of sight around the corner, I spot Z covertly drop a hand down to pet her again, and I realize for the first time that the haunted look on his face has eased a bit. Hoping that means he'll be more likely to let her and Anthem stay, I step quietly back inside and close the door again.

I glance at Anthem. "That could've gone worse?" I venture.

She snorts, finally meeting my eyes. She glances away quickly but at least it's a start. "Your captain is a dick," she mutters.

"He's not *my* captain."

She raises a brow, looking remarkably like Z wearing the same expression. "Sure he's not." She sits down then, grabs the backpack I'd dropped by the door earlier, and starts rifling through it.

"Hey, that's my stuff," I protest.

"I'm taking inventory of what we've got to work with. I didn't pack anything, remember?" She upends my bag on a bunk and quickly sorts through the detritus of my clothing, water bottle, and the torn remnants of the old school report. "Well, this is all useless," she says critically, using a pencil to poke through my things like they might be radioactive. "No food, no tools, not even a can of pepper spray."

"You know how I feel about weapons. Even defensive ones. And I didn't want to take anything you and Mom and Dad might need."

She sighs, scoops everything up and stuffs it unceremoniously back in the bag. "Okay," she says. "What's the game plan now?"

I turn away, looking at the wall opposite. It's easier to have this conversation with her if I don't have to see her expression. "I suppose the main thing I need for now is to keep off the Star Slayer's radar during the trip. His name is Rick, by the way."

"Okay. What do we need to do to make sure he doesn't find out about...?" She gestures vaguely in my direction, not quite looking at me either.

"Well...for a start, I need to know who reports to him. I have no idea who on this ship is part of Z's crew and who's travelling with Rick."

"It sounds like you need a spy," she muses, her voice thoughtful with a spark of intrigue. "A spy who can charm people into giving up their intel...and, if they're pretty, perhaps their digits too."

I roll my eyes but my heart lightens at her tone. I risk turning back around to look at her and see that she's attempting a smile. It's not her real smile—which is wolfish and slightly scary—but I can tell she's trying, so I do too. "You have no battery left, remember? Getting digits won't do you much good," I tell her. "Also I think all of us sleep in this room together except for the family in the captain's quarters, so it's not like there's going to be many opportunities for romance."

"There are *always* opportunities for romance. And what about you, what's your plan? What are you going to be doing during the trip?"

I smile weakly. "Alternating between cooking and freaking out? With maybe a little hyperventilation thrown in here and there to spice things up."

She flings the pencil at me. It bounces off my chest and skitters across the floor. "Pessimist."

"Realist."

"Whatever."

I sigh and tilt my head back and then confess the thing that I know I'm going to have to do now. "I think I should try to befriend Z. If the Star Slayer does figure out the truth and tries to trap me or experiment on me or something, then we'll need allies on our side. The captain of the ship, or acting captain or whatever he is, is the best one we could have."

I do not like this plan. I don't like the idea of intentionally trying to get close to *anyone*, but especially Z. If I get close to him just because I need to manipulate him, I'll feel guilty, and if I end up actually liking him—which, if I'm honest, has already happened—then he'll be one more person I've got to worry about hurting. I came here in part to ensure I wouldn't be putting anyone I care about in danger and instead I may have just made the whole situation worse.

I try not to think about the memory of the blood on Anthem's hand, but the aftershocks of those images are still churning in the back of my head. I was able to sort of blank out my mind during the trip up here, and there's been enough going on since then to keep my horror mostly at bay—but the second I slow down, I know my anxiety will swallow me up again. I worry that it's going to be a very long night of panic attacks and analyzing: do these new thoughts mean I'm getting closer to actually becoming violent, or just that my OCD gets worse under stress? How can I ensure that Anthem stays safe from me now that we're stuck in close quarters together?

Weirdly, though, my anxiety baseline isn't quite as bad here as it was back in the cabin. I actually feel *less* trapped and claustrophobic in this relatively compressed space than I do under the empty sky. Maybe it's the Pioneer Ship's metal lulling me, or maybe just the knowledge that I'm on my way to finally get answers.

"That's not a bad idea," Anthem says, then nods decisively. "Okay. I'll go snoop around while I pretend to clean."

"Please actually clean," I interrupt. "If you don't make yourself useful, Z might dump you at the shales where we're stopping next before we get to Albergia."

She frowns. "Why are we stopping at the shales?"

"I think the refugees have family there. That's where they wanted to disembark."

"Fine then, I'll 'actually clean,'" she says, using air quotes, which isn't reassuring. "Meanwhile, you do your chef thing—with as little freaking out and hyperventilation as you can manage—and try to make friends with Z. With everyone else, just be chill."

I am not a chill person. I have exactly zero chill. Still, I make myself nod, because what else can I do? I've got to keep her and myself safe as best I can.

She juts her chin at me on her way out the door. "Be safe. *Bird boy.*" Her smirk is a hesitant thing, more a question than an expression, and I answer it with a smile that falls the second she's gone.

The shaking starts again then. I have to sit down, brace my back against the wall, and do the most complex mental math problems I can think of for a solid five minutes before I've distracted myself enough for the trembling to stop. I still haven't managed to convince myself that everything is going to be okay, but it's time to make lunch, so I force myself to get up and find my way back to the galley.

My first job is relocating all the knives. They're just lying there in the cabinet, a drawer full of death, shiny and nightmare-inducing. I rummage through the other cabinets until I find a few kitchen towels and then I drop the towels over the knives one by one, scooping the resulting bundles up gingerly, depositing them in a big empty bucket stuffed in the very back of the pantry and being careful not to look directly at them in the process. Then I do the same thing with the blender and food processor blades, along with some sort of long skewer thing that looks like it might be a meat-stabbing implement. I'm frustrated with myself the whole time, as usual, because I know how ridiculous it is to hide knives in a bucket but I can't risk *not* doing it. When I'm done I put the bucket's lid back on tightly enough that opening it again might take a pry bar. I stand back and look at it. I feel like I've created some sort of weird killer cache, but at least this way I can cook without constantly worrying that I'll mindlessly reach in the wrong door, touch a knife, and go on a murder binge. As for the bucket, I'll just have to hope no one finds it till after I'm gone, or I'll have some hard explanations to make.

I get to work. The flatbread dough is first, and the work is easy and calming. While the dough rises, I take inventory of the meat and vegetables. I can use ground beef easily enough, but none of the vegetables are pre-sliced, and I can't chop tomatoes and peppers with my bare hands. I rummage carefully through the drawers until I find some meat shears. They're not sharp enough to qualify for the death bucket but they're still sharp enough to make me nauseous. I'm not sure I can even make myself touch them.

An acrid anger rises in me suddenly. No. I'm not going to do this. I am not going to be beaten by a pair of goddamn fancy scissors, not after everything else I've been through today. I get a stroke of inspiration and grab a permanent marker I found earlier, scrawling *meat shears* on the handle. It's a silly thing but it eases my fears a bit, as if labeling them as a tool will make them definitely not a weapon. I still have to wrap a kitchen towel through the finger loops so I'm not actually touching any part of it, but I manage to use the shears to sloppily cut the veggies and get them all sizzling in the pans.

I finish grilling the flatbread and get the whole meal laid out on a dozen tin plates, plus a big bowl of ground beef and naan scraps for Indy. By the time I stand back to admire my handiwork I am thoroughly exhausted. I spent most of last night driving and now my seemingly endless reservoir of nervous energy is nearly drained. As the crew starts trickling in to grab their food, I contemplate just going straight to my bunk to sleep, but I'm foiled by my own need to make allies. Anthem is already hard at work, rotating from table to table as she effortlessly chats up the crew members.

I grab my plate and step out of the galley and then freeze like a deer caught in a clearing full of wolves. There are half a dozen tables before me, each with one or two people sitting around them, and almost everyone is a stranger to me: a pair of middle-aged women who look like they might be sisters, a twentysomething person with a riot of curly red hair and a they/them pronoun pin, and one of those leathery old-sailor type guys who could be fifty or eighty. I spot Chester scratching at his peeling sunburn but I definitely don't want to be stuck trying to make conversation with him. Standing here with my plate and trying to surreptitiously choose a table without looking like I'm trying to choose a table—I'm getting flashbacks to being the new kid in the high school cafeteria all over again. Then I spot the family with little kids seated in the corner, both of the pale, generously-freckled children hiding under the table with Indy as they giggle and feed her pieces of their flatbread. The tension in my shoulders ease. I can sit with them. At least with Indy there I'll have a buffer and something to talk about if things get awkward. Which they usually do when I'm trying to make small talk with strangers. I start to walk toward them, but then hear a surprised shout from my right. I turn and freeze yet again.

Rick is sitting at a table no more than three feet away. He's wearing red suspenders, leather loafers, and an honest-to-gods tweed jacket. He's smiling and waving at me enthusiastically, beckoning me to sit with him.

He's not wearing his knife belt today, thank the gods—but something in my chest feels like it's retreating, curling up tight like a threatened armadillo anyway. Though I knew he was likely to still be onboard, there was a big part of me that hoped I was wrong, that he'd disembarked already. But here he is, smiling at me and waving me over to his table. Will he get suspicious if I refuse? It's too late to pretend I don't see him. I glance over at Anthem and see that she's looking back at me, putting off strong "don't be an idiot" vibes. *Be chill*, she said earlier. The Star Slayer isn't likely to suspect anything unless I act suspicious. And he doesn't look all that dangerous at the moment—more like a college professor than a would-be fairytale knight out to slay dragons and perhaps also anyone showing tangentially dragon-related traits.

I grip my plate tighter and make my way to his table. "Hi," I make myself say woodenly, standing next to the table. There's only one other person sitting with him, a girl a few years older than me with brown skin and a head full of bouncy, tight black curls. She had been talking to him in a low, intent voice a moment ago, but she goes quiet and sits back in her chair, looking frustrated as I approach. I shrink in on myself a little more.

"Hey, kid!" Rick says to me with a grin. "This food you cooked is absolutely delicious. Especially compared to the, shall we say, *lesser* fare that Z tends to serve us. I'm pleased to see you joined up after all!"

A familiar voice calls out from behind us: "He joined my crew, not yours, Star Slayer, so don't get any ideas." It's Z. He's carrying a plate with one hand, a cup with the other, and is nudging the controls to his hoverchair with an elbow. He's somehow also managing to shoot Rick a dark look at the same time. My gaze bounces between the two of them as the Star Slayer's smile falters and he tilts his head in reluctant acknowledgement. What's going on here, some sort of rivalry between these two? Before I can try to figure it out, Z drops his plate with a clatter at the tables across from ours, then stares up at me. "You sitting down, or you just gonna hover there?"

"Oh. Right." I slide into the seat opposite Rick and set my food down, then make myself scoop up a forkful of the sauteed vegetables and meat even though I don't have much of an appetite. The surly-looking girl at the table transfers her glare from Rick to Z, who completely ignores her as he goes to work on his food, mechanically shoveling it in without pausing to taste it.

Rick catches my eye again and tilts his head at the girl. "This is Lexie, by the way. My daughter. She's the onboard medic." Even though I can tell there's tension between the two of them, I don't miss the trace of pride in his tone. The girl juts her chin in greeting and then goes back to ignoring me.

"I'm Per," I say to Lexie. "Short for Peregrine."

No response. Rick's smile grows a little more forced but he keeps his gaze on me. "Peregrine—that's right, I remember now," he says to me. "I couldn't recall if you'd introduced yourself before, what with...everything that happened. I'm Rick Malley. Nice to officially meet you."

Lexie turns around in her seat then, her jaw clenched and her eyes flashing. "Seriously?" she says to her father. "You're just going to act like everything is fine and normal?"

"Lexie," Rick warns, but she slashes a hand through the air at him.

"Don't *Lexie* me. This is ridiculous. And dangerous. If you won't talk to him, maybe I will."

"Uh," I say, thinking at first that I must be the *him* she's referring to, "what's dangerous? Do you mean my sister stowing away? I'm sorry, I didn't—"

"She's talking about me, not you," Z interrupts. His mussed hair is splayed over his eyes, his fork suspended halfway to his plate as he twists around from his table to look at us. He gestures at her with the utensil. "You got a complaint you wanna register, Lex?"

The flatbread I just took a bite of turns to a hard lump in my throat. I swallow with difficulty, trying to figure out how I can extract myself from whatever argument is brewing here. Before I can make a move, though, Lexie leans toward Z, her palms flat on the table. "Yeah, I do," she snaps. "Here's my complaint: what sort of a captain goes around letting his crew—"

Z drops the fork. It hits his tray like the peal of a bell. Silence ripples out around us as everyone turns to look. Z is wearing the same expression as earlier at the docks, like he's been sucker punched, all the air knocked out of him. His hands slowly curl into fists—not like he's going to hit something, more like he's grasping for something to hold onto. He leans toward Lexie, whose eyes have gone wide with surprise and, I think, regret.

"I am not. The goddamned. *Captain.*" He stares her down for a long moment and then shakes his head. "You know what? I'll eat on the go today. I'm supposed to check on the sonar again anyway." He sweeps up his fork and tray. Then, with a flick at the controls of his hoverchair, he whirls away and is out of the room before anyone can counter him.

I stare at the table, where a few sauteed peppers have fallen off his tray. I desperately want to make an excuse and flee in the opposite direction of wherever the sonar is, but if I'm going to try to make Z into an ally, I need to know more about him. Also...I have to admit, at least to myself, that I'm a little worried about him. "Is he okay?" I ask Rick at last.

Rick sighs. "I don't really know anymore. This was his first mission as acting captain," he explains. "It was supposed to be an easy resupply, a bit of on-the-job training. Everything's gone a bit sideways now, though, and I think he was feeling the pressure even before that."

Lexie, who's still looking at the doorway Z disappeared through, mutters, "That's no excuse."

"That's a bit harsh," Rick protests, but she forges on.

"*Dad.* Do you not get it? These aren't some overeager fangirls trying to corner you. These are soldiers. There's a *warrant* out for you, dammit!"

My eyebrows lift at that. Lexie catches sight of whatever look is on my face and ropes me into their argument. "Peregrine," she says, latching onto my name like she's pouncing on prey, "you can provide an unbiased opinion."

"Lexie," Rick cautions, but she waves him off and leans toward me. Her eyes are a dark, earthy brown, so intense they pin me in place.

"With all that's happened, the Conglom army and what's left of the Albergian forces all want a piece of Dad—they think he's got some secret knowledge about how to kill a star dragon."

A bolt of heat and shock cracks through me. My gut reaction to the news is something like dismay only more powerful, which is confusing—this should be good news. I set my fork down. "Really?"

"So now he's on every government watchlist that exists. Thanks to some stupid caster girl and her internet infodump, they know he's on this ship. It's only a matter of time before she digs up a description of what he looks like, too. The people who've interviewed him before, seen him, they were all sworn to secrecy, but it's not like they'll hold to that now."

"Wait—caster girl, you said?" I dig through my memory, trying to figure out why that's ringing a bell. Then I remember one of the sites I saw when I was looking for news about *The Shitty Clunker* after Starfall. There'd been that one girl, the caster who'd discovered the Star Slayer had chartered this sub. "Check-It Chessie?" I ask, recalling her name. "Is that who you mean?"

"Indeed," Rick says ruefully. "In the past I've not been well-known enough for such an exposé to matter, but after Starfall, well… her follower count has grown exponentially, and apparently includes some military higher-ups. And now she's been dropping hints that she's going to put out some big story about how star dragons can be killed, and she's crediting me for the knowledge."

Lexie is still zeroed in on me. "Now pretty much every government on the planet wants a piece of him, and whether or not he has the information they want, they'll do whatever they have to do to try to get it out of him."

I flounder, my breathing starting to accelerate. Something nudges my hand: Indy. She's left the family to come over and check on me. I pet her gratefully and the feel of her soft, familiar fur helps ground me.

"So tell me," Lexie says, "if my dad knew some intel that would get the soldiers off his case, wouldn't you think he should tell it to them and save his own hide? Whether or not the *acting captain* wants him to?"

So this is the source of tension between these two and Z, is my first thought. Then the meaning of her words hits home. Is she seriously asking me if I think the Star Slayer should tell the government how to kill star dragons? "I…don't know," I say, even as everything in me screams *no.*

Lexie throws up her hands and snatches her plate, standing. "Whatever. Dad, just please think about it, okay?" Without waiting for an answer, she stalks over to the trash and dumps her plate, then heads out the door.

Rick is rubbing his forehead. "I apologize for that. I'm embarrassed you had to get caught in the middle of a family argument. I'd actually better go after her. Thank you for sitting with me, however briefly."

"Do you really know how to kill star dragons?" I demand before I can stop myself. I've got my fork in a death grip now, the fingers on my other hand wound tightly through Indy's fur.

He stands up and grimaces a smile at me. "As Z said, you're part of his crew, not mine, so I can't share Star Slayer secrets with you. But I hope you find whatever you're looking for on this trip, kid. Be safe." He nods at me, straightens his tweed jacket, and follows after his daughter.

I stare after him for a long time, trying to process everything he's said, picking apart each word and examining every phrase for hidden meaning. If he does know how to kill a dragon, could that be why he's heading back to Albergia—to test out his theory on the original ruby-colored dragon, or on the next dragon that comes through the breach? I need more information, but I have no way of getting it. I'll have to wait until I can meet with Anthem again tonight and see if she got any intel that might help me understand what's going on.

A loud clatter breaks me out of my daze. I jump and make an undignified sound, turning to find the source of the clatter: a tray dropping down at the spot opposite me. It's already been scraped clean, barely a trace of pepper sauce left on it, but some sort of unfamiliar, grayish muffin-type things are leaning drunkenly against each other in one corner.

I raise my eyes. Z—the apparent owner of the muffin tray—casually backhands the nearest chair and sends it skidding a few feet away. His hoverchair takes its place across from me. Without comment, he grabs one of the muffin things and tosses it to my side of the table, where it lands with a solid clunk.

I blink at him, mystified, then glance around. Apparently I was so lost in my thoughts that I didn't notice lunch was over; everyone else is gone, even Indy, just the distant hum of fading hallway chatter marking the crew's presence. If I crane my neck I can make out their dirty trays cresting the top of the sink. I glance down at my own tray, which is still almost completely full and stone-cold by now. The muffin Z threw at me sags against it like a waterlogged sailor trying to climb aboard a life raft.

"What's…this?" I dare to ask, examining the muffin. At least I think that's what it's meant to be. It smells oversweet, like fruit dangerously close to rotting, and there are big, soggy gray chunks littered throughout it.

"A banana muffin," Z says, taking a big bite out of his. He wears a grim, determined expression as he chews it. And keeps on chewing it. He grabs the water canteen from his tray and slams back a gulp of it like a shot of hard liquor, apparently trying to wash the muffin down.

"Okay," I say. "Why is there one on my plate?" I don't mean to be rude, but I feel like it's best to be as clear as possible when it comes to Z. He's a bit hard to read at the best of times.

He levels a raised eyebrow at me. "Because your plate is still full of untouched lunch and you look like a starving abandoned puppy sitting over here by yourself."

Unsure whether I should feel offended or touched, I gingerly pick up the muffin. "So you're…feeding me?"

"It would be criminal not to. Crew neglect. I'm responsible for everyone on board, you know."

Now it's my turn to raise an eyebrow. "I don't see you feeding banana muffins to anyone else."

"Only had the two of them left."

"Right. One for abandoned, starving me…and one for you," I say, turning my raised eyebrow to the muffin sitting on his plate with a single bite taken out of it, and then back to Z, who's now chugging his water and looking like he has no intention of taking any further bites from this Franken-muffin that I'm guessing he made himself. He doesn't seem hungry at all, and he definitely doesn't look like he actually wants to eat the muffin on his tray. He could've just dropped mine off and left. Instead, he stays at his spot opposite me, his eyes narrowing in challenge as he very deliberately lifts his muffin and takes another bite out of it, martyr-like.

My lips twitch but I try not to smile. Stubborn and surly as he's acting, it's actually kind of sweet—him noticing that I haven't eaten, and trying to feed me, and sitting with me while he feeds me. I lift my own muffin up and take a bite, trying not to look too closely at it as I do. I immediately have to choke back on a gag reflex. The thing manages to be somehow slimy and hard as a rock at the same time, and it tastes like he might've accidentally used salt instead of sugar.

Z wordlessly slides his canteen across the table toward me. There could actually be hard liquor in there for all I know but I scoop it up anyway, my eyes watering as I gulp it, forcing the muffin down my throat. The liquid turns out to be water, clear and sweet, and it does the trick. I come up for air after a minute and squint at Z, panting. "Thanks," I manage.

His lips curve up a bit and he looks pleased, though he quickly shuffles his expression back into a scowl. Something in my chest flutters a little and I try to squash the feeling before he senses it. I need him to be my ally. I do *not* need to have a crush on him. That is a bad idea for so many reasons.

I look at him for a long moment, not knowing how to continue the conversation, if that's even what this is. "So," Z says at last, "you gonna tell me now why you're trying to get yourself uncreated in Albergia?"

My heart pops into top gear but I try not to let it show. "I thought you said you didn't care why we were going."

"Maybe I do care." He hurls the words at me like a challenge. Apparently he lobs all declarations of potential affection, whether they're in the form of tools or words. "Don't you?"

I make a rueful noise despite myself. "You have no idea how much I care about literally everything," I mutter, and take another bite of the muffin before I remember how gods-awful it is. Eyes watering, I chug more water to chase it.

"But you're still going."

I nod, internally scrambling to remember what excuse Anthem and I had agreed to use if anyone tried to pry into our business onboard, but he cuts me off with a sharp motion. "Don't bother lying to me. Maybe I don't care after all," he says, shaking his head, mouth thinning out. He grabs his tray and starts moving his hoverchair away. I search wildly for something to say, some way to keep him talking to me and maybe-liking me, but from the set of his expression he's done with this conversation.

"Z," I say anyway.

He doesn't stop. "What?"

I flounder. "Uh...thanks for the muffin...thing."

His expression eases and he smiles at me a little—not a smirk, but an actual, honest-to-gods smile, barely there but undeniable—over his shoulder. "Muffin thing? Are you insulting my cooking?" he drawls.

"Never," I say, and force myself to take another chomp.

The smile grows just a touch. He lifts a hand for me to toss him his canteen, which I do, after taking another gulp and screwing the cap back on. "Don't think this means you're off my shit list," he says, sounding serious. "You still brought a stowaway on my ship. And I doubt very much that she's doing any actual cleaning to make up for it."

I hem and haw. He mutters and shakes his head, stows his canteen in the side of his chair, and vanishes into the hallway.

I stand up and start toward the kitchen, feeling like I've dodged a bullet but also sort of wishing the bullet would come back and talk to me more. I hesitate as I hold the tray over the trash and then grab the remainder of the muffin and eat it before throwing everything else away.

As I place my tray in the sink, a wave of exhaustion and all-too-familiar dread washes over me. I sway a little; I've been through way too much today on way too little sleep. I consider forcing myself to do the dishes now just in case keeping a clean kitchen will help me stay on Z's good side, but in the end my feet carry me to the door. I'm so strung out and apprehensive and exhausted that I can no longer think straight; I need to find a bed before I curl up right on the floor and shut down, my brain simply giving in under the weight of everything that's happened. I trudge to the bunkroom, locate a bed that looks mostly unused, and pass out on it.

My last conscious thought as I'm pulled beneath the current of sleep is that whatever mixed feelings I might have for Z, both he and the Star Slayer are hiding something—and my life might just depend on finding out what.

Chapter Eight

I wake up to someone flicking my ear. I rocket up out of bed, smash my forehead on the frame of the bunk above me, and then promptly bang my shin against the siderail of my own bunk. I clap one hand over each injury and try to calm my galloping heart rate as I glare at the offending flicker of ears.

Z smirks back at me, completely unaffected by my glare. "Skittish," he comments in a quiet tone that's thick with amusement.

My initial panic has now fully subsided into irritation. I look for something to throw at him but nothing is readily at hand, and my disloyal guard canine merely grumbles at the disruption and dog-spreads to absorb the newly freed blanket space.

"What do you want?" I mutter, squinting as I try to orient myself. The narrow bunkroom is dark, with only the dim glow of the hallway lights to illuminate the snoring lumps of people scattered across the bunks. I pick out Anthem's form on the bunk across from mine. She's sprawled out and snoring loudly, and I know from a lifetime of experience that it would take an earthquake to wake her in this state. I'm not sure if I'm glad or disappointed that I haven't had the chance to talk to her again since my revelation.

"Time to earn your keep," Z whispers back, and jerks his head at the door.

"I thought cooking was what earned my keep," I mumble, but then I remember my dual missions to befriend him and convince him to let Anthem stay, so I drag myself out from under the covers and reluctantly follow him into the hallway. I'm still dressed in the clothing I wore to lunch earlier today—or is it yesterday now? It feels like it must be past midnight—and so is Z. As we move into the hallway, though, I see that his clothing is newly anointed with a fresh spatter of machine oil and is also sporting an array of tiny holes across his left shoulder. Angry red skin shows through the holes like he got splashed with some sort of acid.

"What happened to you?" I ask, yawning.

He's got a screwdriver in his left hand and he whirls it around his fingers like a gunslinger practicing for a shootout. "Me and the glint tank got in a bit of a fight."

"Who won?"

"Yet to be determined."

He leads me down a narrow side corridor I haven't been in yet. When he navigates through a porthole and his hoverchair scrapes the frame, I realize belatedly that the rest of the ship has corridors and doorways that are plenty wide enough for his chair to fit down with ease. But then, if he helped design this ship, it makes sense that he would make it as accessible as he could.

He notices me looking at the black mark the scrape left on the side of the hoverchair and polishes it away with his sleeve. He makes a sour face. "I usually go down the wider main corridor but Lexie was in there pacing and muttering earlier, and I don't want to risk running into her if she's still up. I'm not her favorite person at the moment."

"Why? Did you flick her ear too?"

"Is that a euphemism? If it is, no, and if it isn't, also no. We've just had some...disagreements."

I remember my lunch conversation with the Star Slayer and jolt to sudden full wakefulness. "Because of the warrant thing with her dad?" I venture.

"Eh, something like that," he answers vaguely, then motions at me with the screwdriver, pointing to a large porthole ahead. In the room beyond, a dim but somehow soothing silvery light glows. "In here, come on."

"What exactly did you bring me—" I start, and then my words wither up and die when I step into the room.

It's the control room. It has to be, with all the panels full of screens laid out before me, but those aren't what holds my attention. It's the window that does that. It spans the whole front part of the room, ten feet wide, and the silvery light that's illuminating the room is coming through it from outside. We're gliding through some sort of coral formation. The structures grow from cracks in the ocean floor, spiraling upward for what must be dozens of stories, pulsing with a dim glow that feels like a heartbeat. The light illuminates the darts of bright scales as fish flash past. Tiny plankton with miniscule shells that gleam like distant stars drift slowly by, parting like a curtain as we slide through the deep. The sight plants hooks in me and pulls until I am unspooled. I don't realize I've moved to the window until I see my palm laid flat against the glass, white with pressure as if I'm trying to squeeze my atoms through it and into the sparkling endlessness stretching out beyond.

"It's something, isn't it?" Z says from behind me.

I suck in a breath. I wind myself back in, tuck my longing away, and retract my hand—but there's still a lump in my throat. "It is," I say, turning to Z. He's not looking at me, though. He's staring out the window past me, and on his face I see what must've been in my own expression a moment ago. He looks unguarded, vulnerable, reverent.

It's almost painful to watch. It doesn't strip away that haunted expression he's been wearing but only emphasizes it: the hollows under his eyes, the gaunt curve at his cheekbones, the emptiness that echoes in his gaze. Then his eyes slide to mine and he registers that he's been seen. He retracts himself as smoothly as I did a moment ago, tucking everything away beneath a smirk and a raised eyebrow.

"I didn't bring you here to gawp at fish," he says, nudging the joystick on his chair. "I'm doing some repairs on the glint tank and I need someone who can watch the readouts while I work. I tried doing it without a spotter and, well," he gestures at the holes in his shirt and the angry red skin beneath. "Glint is corrosive and it burns like hell if you get splashed, and I've already met my weekly quota of injuries." He glares at the bandage that's still wrapped loosely around one of his hands.

I stand in the spot where he waves me to, in front of what looks like a supply closet. He pulls at the handle. Nothing happens. He whacks it expertly with the butt of the screwdriver and the latch pops open. Inside is what looks like an ancient water heater tank hooked to a maze of tubes and pipes. He gestures at a little screen hooked onto the front of it. "This is the thing to keep an eye on," he says. "If the temperature readout gets into the orange levels, pull me out. If it turns off entirely, run."

"This is starting to sound like it's not a great idea," I remark. "Can you not call in an expert to fix it at the next stop?"

He braces his hands on the armrests and lifts himself up out of the chair with a grimace. One hand flat on the wall, he steps toward the tank with the slow, careful steps of a person in pain, his expression flat and determined. When he reaches the closet he sinks down to lay on his back and then wedges himself underneath the tank like he's working on a car. "I am the expert," he says, his voice muffled.

An ominous clanking noise ensues. "What does the readout say?" he demands.

I eye it. "Uh, some letters and numbers. The temperature readout is still green."

"What are the letters and numbers?"

I read them off and he grunts. "Okay. Not bad so far."

I stand there in silence for several more minutes as the readout doesn't change. "You know, you probably could've used your watch for this," I say idly. "Set up an app to connect to the readout and alert you via voice when it changes."

"But that would rob me of the pleasure of your company," he says with a wink. I mean, I can't see whether he's actually winking since his whole upper torso is out of view, but judging from his tone he's definitely winking. I'm in the process of convincing myself it's not a good idea to flirt back when he goes on: "Anyway, I don't wear a watch, so that nixes that." Something creaks beneath the tank and I spot the flash of his screwdriver turning.

"You don't use a watch?" I ask, surprised. There are some non-techs who prefer to live off the grid, but they're mostly older folks, and judging from all the displays and screens we're surrounded by as well as his hoverchair, Z is very much pro-tech.

"The chair uses my entire weekly allotment of energy," he says, his tone losing all traces of flirtation and going bitter instead. "Or did you think the government made exceptions for the disabled?"

"Oh. Wow. That sucks." I think for a second. "But then what about the glint you use to power the sub? How can you—or anyone—afford that? Didn't the Conglom government start buying up all the glint surplus when the shortage started a few years back?"

He sticks a hand out from under the tank to wave at me impatiently. "Go get the multitool out of my chair," he orders. "Yeah, they bought up all the shortage, which is why we sneak up on their facilities and siphon a little off the top of their storage tanks. They never even notice. Well, they definitely notice, but they don't know it's us who's doing it. Yet. Probably."

I gape at the spot where his legs are sticking out. "*What?* You steal from the *government?* That's a good way to get disappeared." Conglom and Albergian citizens have a lot of constitutional rights, but glint thievery is as bad as stealing a horse in old-Earth's old west days. There's often not even a trial, just a quiet "accident" for those suspected of the crime.

"Multitool," he reminds me irately, and I belatedly move toward his chair and inspect it for anything that looks like a multitool. "Yeah," he goes on, "they're not too fond of it, but like I said, they haven't caught me yet. It probably helps that I used to be their university's star cadet—I know how they operate, their code rotations, all that shit."

Huh. So my first impression of him was right; he *had* been a university student. "Did you get kicked out?" I say, then immediately attempt to reel the words back in, hearing how blunt they sounded. "I mean, not that you seem like—I just meant—"

He snorts, sounding amused. His screwdriver rattles against something metal under the tank. "Nah, it's cool. I actually didn't get kicked out. I was on track to graduate early to the navy's command track, before I became a...well, let's say a 'conscientious objector.'"

"Objecting to what?" There was an awful lot to choose from, based on my own limited knowledge of how the Conglom military does business.

"Eh, you know. Stuff and shit."

Vague as ever. "So you dropped out?"

"The military doesn't exactly let its cadets 'drop out.' Technically I've been AWOL for a year or so."

Mildly alarmed at this, I look up from where I've been poking at his hoverchair. "AWOL? Isn't that punishable by, like, court martial or military prison, or hanging or something?"

"Why, Peregrine dear, is that worry I hear in your voice? Are you concerned for my safety?"

I roll my eyes but also flush a little. "Don't flatter yourself, I worry about literally everyone. And sometimes inanimate objects too if it's a slow day."

I return to poking at the chair until I spot the seams and almost invisible inset handle for some sort of storage compartment. I run my fingers along it and it pops open. Inside is a virtual magpie's nest of tools, a handful of colorful broken shale rocks with sharp edges, and a flask that smells suspiciously alcoholic. "Aren't you underage?" I ask, rooting gingerly through the tools for something that looks "multi."

He makes a distracted noise. "What, the whiskey? That's not mine. It's—" He cuts off suddenly, whatever he was going to say cleanly amputated, the rest of the sentence left hanging without it. "Where's that multitool?" he snaps after a second, his tone closed-off now.

"What does a multitool even look like?" I ask, exasperated.

"It's like a giant pocketknife."

I freeze and then snatch my hand back out of the tool nest. A hard pebble of panic lodges behind my breastbone and I try to breathe around it. "Uh," I try. "You might have to come out here and find it."

He curses. "Are you kidding? Did you not see how much trouble it was for me to get under here in the first place? It's in there, you just gotta look harder."

I glance around frantically for a towel, an oil rag, a jacket, anything I might be able to use to bundle up the multitool the way I did with the kitchen knives, but there's nothing. I peer back into the storage compartment and finally spot what has to be the multitool. It's nearly a foot long and bristling with different-sized blades and hooks and scissors and screw heads. There's no way I can touch it. The situation is too dangerous—Z is stuck under the glint tank with no quick way out. He can't even see me. He's completely vulnerable. Why would he allow himself to be so vulnerable with a practical stranger? Why would he trust me? He shouldn't. I don't trust myself.

"What's the holdup?" he demands irritably.

I spot a folded-up piece of magazine paper tucked in the side of the compartment and exhale shakily with relief. I grab it and use it to pick up the multitool—then pause, suddenly struck by the realization that what I'm doing is not actually protecting anyone at all. Why do I feel better wrapping a knife in paper, or a towel for that matter? It's not like I couldn't still stab somebody if I really wanted to. All it does—all any of my compulsions do—is provide a false sense of security. And the more I do them, the more I feel like I *have* to do them.

It's a disturbing train of thought that I'm certain will keep me awake later, but for now I try to shove it out of my mind and focus on what I'm doing. I set the multitool on the ground and nudge it toward Z's questing hand with my shoe. "About time," he grumbles, pulling it underneath the tank with him.

I cast around for the thread of our earlier conversation. I'm still supposed to win him over for both my sake and Anthem's, plus I don't want him to suspect anything's off with me. "If it's so risky to get the glint you need to travel, why chance it? Where do you need to go?"

"*Where* do I need to *go*?" He makes a disgusted noise. "I don't need to go anywhere. I just need to go. There's a whole world out there—and a whole universe up there, now. Why would anyone *not* want to go?"

I'm silent, struck by the echo of my own thoughts. I'd believed I was the only one with that longing eating away at my soul.

The multitool clatters as Z drops it and picks his screwdriver back up. The readout on the tank changes. "It's saying 'code 544B' now," I tell him.

"Damn, damn, damn," he mutters. His movements turn hurried as he wrenches the screwdriver around. The temperature readout slowly creeps toward orange. "How about now?"

"No, that made it worse."

"I don't think it likes you."

"I'm not the one screwing around with its innards."

"You're enabling me. You share the blame." Something clinks. The readout falls back into green. The code vanishes, replaced by the prior combination of letters and numbers.

I breathe out a relieved sigh and relay the news. "Does that mean it's fixed?"

"It wasn't broken in the first place. Well, not until I just almost broke it, anyway."

I frown. "If it wasn't broken then why are you under there at all?"

"I've been meaning to replace one of the pipes back here for a year and never got around to it. Figured now was as good a time as any." He grabs onto the bottom of the tank and uses it to shove himself out of the closet. He sits up, looks down at his hands—which are smeared with oil—and then shrugs, wiping them on his shirt.

I make a skeptical face. "Now, in the middle of the night when everyone who could help you is asleep and we're creeping through the Icedrift Sea, is as good a time as any?"

"An acting captain's work is never done." His tone is arch and mocking but his face doesn't match it as he leverages himself up and makes his slow, painful-looking way back to his chair. The light from the shimmering coral is fading as we exit the formations, leaving just a trace of silvery glow that highlights that haunted look in his eyes. He glances up at me. "Couldn't sleep," he admits. "Hit the lights, would you? It'll be pitch black in a second now that we're out of the coral."

As he eases back into his chair, I go to the wall and search for anything that looks like a light switch. I tentatively flick a few of them but nothing happens.

"I said, hit the lights," Z repeats irately.

"I'm trying. Which one is it?"

He zips over to me, slaps my hand out of the way, and flicks the exact same switch I tried a second ago. Nothing happens again. He frowns. "It shouldn't do that unless—" He cuts off, his gaze jerking to mine, and that's when I realize that it's not pitch black in here as he predicted, and neither is the room illuminated by the silvery glow of the coral any longer. Instead, his face is painted in hues of navy and azure.

The blue bulb dangling overhead has blinked on.

As one, we turn in slow motion to the window. For three long heartbeats, it shows nothing, not even the curtain of plankton or the remnants of the coral's shine. Then a zigzag of pearlescent lightning bends across the curvature of something massive that's hovering only a few meters outside the sub. The lightning sparks again a second later, illuminating the overhang of a hooked jaw, the edges of bladelike scales.

A giant eel.

I can't see all of it. It's too big and too close. But I can see enough to know it's at least as large as the sub. Bolts of pearly electricity zip up and down the length of its sinuous body as it investigates us.

Z's eyes slide to me. He slowly lifts a finger to his lips, signaling me to silence. The haunted look is gone. The smirk and arched eyebrow are gone. He looks serious. He looks *scared*. He flicks a switch on the side of his chair and its low hum dies as it sinks to the ground, powered down. Then, slowly, Z braces his hands on the armrests and pushes himself up out of his chair once again. I widen my eyes, trying to wordlessly ask what the hell he's doing risking a fall at this moment when silence is so obviously key, but he just grimaces and braces himself on a nearby panel as he steps laboriously back toward the closet.

I have no idea what he's doing, but I have to hope that he does, so I hold my breath and move over to him and stand awkwardly at his side, wondering how to communicate that I can help him if he needs me to. He glances up, spots me, and slings an arm around my shoulder without wasting a second. I help him over to the closet, where he slides down beneath the tank again and picks up the dropped multitool. It scrapes lightly against the floor. We both freeze. The lightning arcing across the eel outside speeds up and multiplies, flitting across its body in a net of electricity. Some branches of it are starting to arc outward toward us. I'm not sure what'll happen if that electric current nails us but I know it can't be good.

Something metallic squeaks and clinks lightly as Z does whatever he's doing beneath the tank. My hands curl into fists as I watch the scales and lightning outside begin to move faster, vanish, and then appear again. It's circling us. Or maybe there's more than one out there. Z finishes his task and extends a hand toward me. I clasp his wrist and pull him out and up, but we don't walk back to the chair. He doesn't let go of me, either, but only loosens his grip enough for his hand to slide down my wrist and to my own hand. His palm is warm and square and callused and in other circumstances I would be either thrilled or apprehensive as hell or, more likely, both, but right now all either of us can do is stand motionless and watch the monster.

It pauses. The lightning seems to roll over it like thunder rippling over a prairie, smooth and hypnotic. It eases closer and then further away. Then, at last, the electric zigzags vanish entirely and it's gone. The backwash from its exit makes the sub rock slightly, pitching me into Z and nearly knocking us both off our feet. We right ourselves silently—breaking our grips on each other in the process—and wait without comment until the lights turn back on.

I squint and blink, blinded. Z lets out a long, shaky breath. "Well," he says eloquently, "shit." He slides to the floor and sits there staring at nothing for a long moment.

"Are you okay? And also, what did you do?" I ask, moving carefully toward the window and peering out for any sign of the creature. "Under the tank, I mean. Did you do something to make it leave?"

He's still focused on something faraway. "I must've accidentally loosened the offload pipe earlier," he says faintly. "In case of emergency, it's supposed to dump our glint into the ocean. But it's an emergency measure only because eels are attracted to glint. They're like sharks—they can smell the tiniest trace of it in the water."

"And when you loosened the pipe earlier," I realize, "you accidentally dumped some of the glint into the ocean."

He rakes a hand through his hair, making it even messier than normal. "Yeah. Didn't realize it till the monster appeared though. We're lucky I managed to fix it quick enough that it decided it wasn't worth the trouble of frying us." He doesn't look celebratory, though. He puts a hand on the wall at his side and runs his fingers across the cobalt metal, lingering on the divots and warps. "I could've lost her," he says quietly then, and I begin to realize just how much the ship means to him.

Intending to give him a moment of privacy, I turn away. Something crinkles under my foot. I glance down and see the magazine paper I found in his chair's storage compartment. I pick it up and glance over it, meaning to stick it straight back where it came from, but my eyes snag on the picture in the upper right corner. It's Z, looking nearly a decade younger and grinning like he's won the lottery. Standing next to his chair is a woman who looks an awful lot like an older version of him: dark hair thrown into a messy bun, face wearing a scowl belied by the sparkle in her eyes. *Mother-Son Duo to Repurpose Pioneer Ship Remains,* proclaims the headline.

I should stop reading, I realize. Z kept this hidden in a private storage compartment and I should respect that. But the text and my own curiosity pull my eyes downward, and I read on despite myself.

Museum curator Dr. Minerva Colton and her son, Honors Graduate prize winner Zeus "Z" Colton, confirmed today that they put in the winning bid for the majority of the Pioneer Ship's physical materials.

When asked how she could afford the purchase, Dr. Colton revealed that she traded her full share of the Museum of Origins—a hugely successful educational foundation of which she was a founding member.

Dr. Colton has not yet publicly stated what she intends to use the materials for, saying only that she has a "restoration project" in mind.

That's it. The whole story is three short paragraphs. I read it again, frowning. Something is off about the article, but I can't quite figure out what.

"It's the name," says Z from behind me. I flinch and turn guiltily. He's standing again, leaning heavily on the wall, his eyes dark as he looks at the magazine page I'm holding. "That's what's throwing you off. That's what you can't quite hold in your mind. Tell me, because I can't remember either," he says, his voice cracking, "what is my mother's name?"

I stare back at him, caught in his gaze. I can't for the life of me remember the name or the image of the woman in the article, but his gaze is pinning me in place and I can't glance down to read it again. I'd thought earlier that he looked haunted. Now I know who the ghost is.

He has family in Albergia. Not anymore.

He looks away. The moment snaps like a frayed thread, and he suddenly just looks tired again. "Bring me my chair and get lost," he says wearily.

Mutely, I flip the switch he used earlier to power the chair down and then push it forward until he can sit in it. Then, as ordered, I flee.

Chapter Nine

There's no more sleep to be had for me that night. I don't even attempt to lay down again. Instead, I search the sub until I find another window—this one facing up just behind the tower—and then I sit beneath it and wrap myself in the feeling of the sea. It's dark out there now but the star-like plankton are still present even if I can't see them. This room has screens similar to the main control room I was just in, but they're dusty and cluttered with junk: a mop bucket, a tin cup, a few yellowing notebooks, and two dogeared fantasy novels tucked under a console. This must be some sort of auxiliary control room.

Huddled against the wall with the beautiful, crushing depths of the ocean skimming past overhead, I finally let myself feel the anxiety that I've been bottling up all day. I'd managed to hold off most of my usual compulsions to analyze and ruminate on what triggered me and what it means about my nature but I can't do it anymore. I *need* to figure myself out. I need to know that no matter what is going on in my head, I am good.

I want so badly to be good.

So I go through the last day in my mind, picking apart my motivations and responses and emotions, playing out all the worst-case scenarios. I sink into the shame and guilt of what people would think if they could see my thoughts, of what sort of person those thoughts make me, and of knowing that this is all my OCD but not being strong enough to just...make it stop.

I spend what feels like hours effectively paralyzed by my spiraling fear before I hear quiet footsteps in the hallway. They pause at the porthole to this room and then move toward me before I feel the warmth of another presence as someone sinks down to sit at my side. "I told you," Anthem says, "as little freaking out as you can manage."

I huff. "This *is* as little freaking out as I can manage."

"You okay?"

I lift one shoulder, even though she can't see it in the darkness. I am not okay. I'm starting to suspect I'll never be okay. But what right do *I* have to not be okay? "Sure," I say, but my voice sounds lifeless even to my own ears. I hesitate but have to ask then: "Are *you* okay?"

"Oh, not at all," she says with a snort. "I am super not okay. But I'm rolling with it."

My heart twists. I tuck my hands between my knees. "I'm sorry."

"And that's twice now you've apologized for—what, exactly?"

"Not telling you the truth earlier. Telling you the truth now. Scaring you."

"Ugh," she mutters, "you're an idiot. Show me the light again."

It's a command, not a question, as is typical with my sister. I lift one hand and think, *shine*. My skin goes translucent. My bones are dark lines and my veins indistinct rivers, a map I don't know how to read. The light is even dimmer this time, not even bright enough to light up the entire room.

I risk a glance at Anthem. Her mouth is a thin pale line, her eyes thrown into sharp shadow by the underlighting. She is still afraid of me.

Everything in me wrenches and I close my fist, putting out the light. "I'm—" I start, but she lands a light backhand on my ear before I can finish. "Ow," I protest.

"You were going to say sorry again," she accuses.

"I *am* sorry." I duck away in case she tries to whack me again.

"Turn the glow back on," she orders, like I'm a human flashlight. I comply but look away so I won't have to see her fear. "This," she says, poking a finger into the palm of my hand nearly hard enough to bruise, "*is scary.* It is scary because the ancient, unevolved lizard part of my brain screams DANGER in big bold letters when I see it, even though the more evolved part of me knows that you're not going to hurt me. I can't control my lizard brain. Lizard brains gonna lizard. It's just what they do."

"So you're saying you can't help being afraid of me—that you'll always be afraid of me now?" I ask, hopelessness burrowing into me.

"No, dumbass. I'm saying my fear is not your fault. I *know* who you are, and if my lizard brain disagrees with that, it can suck my—"

"Anthem," I say with a cough, "can you please say whatever you're trying to say more clearly?" I glance over at her. Her eyebrows are dark, defiant slashes, even though fear still lingers in the set of her mouth.

She sighs. "Okay. Yes, I am afraid of you, but it won't last forever. That's why I wanted to see the light again. The more often I see it and feel scared of it and *nothing bad happens,* the less my lizard brain will correlate you with danger. Soon, this glow won't mean imminent death. It'll mean my brother, Peregrine, who just happens to be a human glowworm. And then everything will be fine."

I stare at her, speechless for a long moment. When I manage to speak all I can get out is: "*Glowworm?*"

She shrugs. "Whatever. This lizard-brain stuff is solid science—and, by the way, it's also what the therapy for your OCD would be based on, if you ever go in for treatment."

I shift, uncomfortable, but I can't deny that I'm curious—and also that my OCD has become more exhausting than ever lately. "What do you mean?" I ask tentatively.

She turns toward me a little too eagerly, and I realize I've stepped right into her well-meaning trap. "It's called exposure and response prevention therapy. Basically, you lean into your fears instead of trying to escape them or prove them wrong, and eventually you habituate—your brain learns it doesn't have to respond to intrusive thoughts with panic."

Anxiety wells up in me at that idea. "I thought the point of therapy was to make me stop having awful thoughts."

"No, the point of therapy is to teach your mind to not freak out about the awful thoughts."

"But I'd keep on having them."

"Yeah. *Everyone*, or at least almost everyone, has random weird or scary thoughts that pop up out of nowhere at times. It's just, your OCD means you tend to react to them more strongly, notice them more and freak out about them more. It's that reaction, not the thoughts themselves, that are causing a problem."

"What would therapy even look like, then?"

I feel, rather than hear, her inhale deeply before she responds. "In your case," she says with a forced casualness that informs me I'm not going to like whatever she's about to say, "it would involve things like touching knives, or carrying around a piece of paper that says 'Peregrine is a murderer,' or listening to crime casts without trying to figure out whether you're capable of committing those crimes too. You get exposed to your fear, then you prevent your usual response to it.

Thus teaching your lizard brain to not be terrified every time you get an intrusive thought."

I rub my brow with my free hand. "Well, that all sounds like a nightmare."

"Yeah, that's what I thought you'd say. Look—therapy is hard work but I've seen it change lives. And there's medication that can help a lot too."

Tentatively, I try to imagine it: my life as a person in remission from OCD. Still having bad thoughts but not freaked out over them. I can barely wrap my mind around it. Such a life feels not only impossible but wrong. If I have terrible, violent thoughts and I *don't* worry about them, wouldn't that mean I'm the type of person who isn't bothered by violence? And if I let myself be that type of person, doesn't that mean I'd be *more* likely to do terrible things? I need to worry about my violent thoughts. Worrying about them is what keeps me, and the people around me, safe.

But Anthem just said that everyone has intrusive thoughts sometimes. And logically I know that the vast majority of people don't go around killing others on a whim.

"Okay," I say at last. "I'll think about it. But I can't promise anything more than that."

She slits her eyes at me. "You can do better than that, Per. Come on. If you'd try to solve your problem instead of—" She cuts off, but it's too late. I can already hear the words hanging between us: *instead of whining about it. Instead of letting your OCD walk all over you. Instead of making me cover for you all the time.* She wouldn't actually say any of those things, not in such a mean way, but I know it's at least partly how she feels.

Usually I'd beat myself up about how draining I must be as a family member, but something inside me feels different now—here in the belly of the repurposed Pioneer Ship, on my way to seek out a star dragon. I sit up a little straighter. "My OCD is definitely a problem, but it's *my* problem," I tell her. "It's not your responsibility to fix me."

Her shoulders go rigid. "You sound just like Dr. Hernandez," she says, exasperated, then immediately looks like she wishes she could suck the words back in.

"Dr. Hernandez?" I ask, not about to let her off that easily.

I watch her debate with herself for a moment before she sighs and her shoulders drop. "My supervisor at the psych center," she admits with a grimace. "She's the one who put me on probation for an extra term. Because, and I quote, 'Anthem's bedside manner needs improvement.'"

"Ah," I say, trying to be tactful but also dying of curiosity. Sensing it, Anthem rolls her eyes and humors me.

"Apparently in Dr. Hernandez's opinion I don't do enough gentle guiding and hand-holding for patients. Instead I 'prod and browbeat them into making therapeutic progress'."

I bridle a little. I mean, Anthem definitely does a lot of prodding and browbeating, but no one except family is allowed to call her on it as far as I'm concerned. "That wasn't cool of her."

Anthem fiddles with a strand of her hair. "I guess she's not exactly wrong," she confesses after a moment. "And I *do* want to do better. I want to help people, not, like, try to bend them to my will or whatever."

My heart hurts a little at her raw tone. "You aren't trying to bend people to your will," I assure her. "You're not manipulative. You just very forcefully believe that everything and everyone can be fixed if they do what they're supposed to. Which isn't always the case, you know?"

She slumps against the wall, looking lost in the dim silver-blue light emanating from my hand. "Right, I get that, it's just...it feels like giving up if I know how a situation can be improved and I don't do everything I can to improve it. I don't know how to not be me, you know?"

"Yeah," I say, heartfelt. "I do know."

She gives me a rueful sideways smile and then sits up straighter, visibly recalibrating herself. "Anyway. We have more important things to talk about than my bedside manner. First, does it drain your solar energy or your glowworm juice or whatever to keep that light on?"

I hesitate—I feel like this whole fixing-people topic might merit more discussion, since it seems to be eating at her—but decide to let her change the subject. I flex my hand and consider her question. "I'm not sure. I don't know how it works or even why I've got it, but I don't feel drained or weaker after I use it. It just...slowly gets dimmer."

"Hmm. So theoretically, if you left it on for a while, maybe it would just go away? Maybe we could solve the whole problem by just doing nothing?"

My instinctive reaction to that is immediate, not to mention concerning. "I don't think it works that way. The dimming feels like—a warning. A countdown." I grimace as I try to articulate the foreboding that's brewing deep within me. "The light will go out eventually, but I think that's when something bad will happen. And my dreams aren't getting weaker, they're intensifying, so just waiting things out wouldn't work on that anyway."

"Well, damn," Anthem says, crossing her arms and peering into the darkness as she thinks. "Okay. So the dimming isn't a product of you using the light—you could hypothetically use it as much as you want and it would get dimmer at the same rate. This is one of those rare times I wish I was a science major. I could calculate your lumen output or whatever and track how fast the light is deteriorating, and then we could extrapolate our deadline from that."

"I bet Z could do all that," I note, though I feel queasy just thinking about telling him what's happening to me. It was hard enough coming clean with Anthem, a family member who has supported me through tons of shit in the past. I can't imagine how much higher the stakes would feel with a relative stranger/maybe-ally/potential crush like Z.

Apparently Anthem agrees, because she whirls around and sticks a finger in my face. "No way, absolutely not, we are *not* telling him about any of this! That guy is shady as hell and trusting him is our absolute last resort. You're not gonna spill your guts to some rando just because you have a crush on his cheekbones."

I flush. "I don't have a crush on his cheekbones," I mutter.

The seriousness fades out of Anthem's expression and one corner of her mouth twitches. "On other parts of him, then?" she says coyly.

I shove her in the shoulder with my non-glowing hand, relieved to see she doesn't flinch this time. "Shut up and tell me what you found out about the crew yesterday."

She sits up straighter and preens. "Happily. I have done some truly magnificent spywork and I expect you to fully appreciate it."

By the time we're finished, I feel like I know way too much about all the dirty details of the crew members' lives—except for Z, of course, who apparently refused to engage in small talk of any variety with Anthem. Most of the other details she got is inconsequential stuff, like how the middle-aged women (who are indeed sisters) are both sleeping with the same guy in the Conglom port and haven't realized it yet, or how the young person with the riot of red hair dreams of being a concert cellist, or the fact that Rick had indeed been an actual professor for an educational foundation in Albergia. Only a few of the details Anthem gleaned seem relevant.

"There's some sort of beef between Z and Rick—or rather, Lexie is upset about some beef between them even though the two of them just seem more, like, mildly concerned about whatever it is."

I fill her in on the warrant and potential dragon-killing-intel situation. "That's what it's got to do with, I bet," I say.

Her brows knit together in speculation. "Could you tell if he was for real? If he truly knows how to kill a dragon?"

"He wouldn't say. He said I was part of Z's crew, not his, and he couldn't give me Star Slayer secrets. But...I'm worried that we might be going to Albergia so Rick can test out whatever theory he's got on how dragons can be slain."

I wince. It feels like a betrayal to worry for the dragons' sake when they've done so much damage already, but killing them feels *wrong*. They're not true predators—they eat starlight, not people. I prefer to think they're meant to keep the balance of nature, to clear away old, empty star systems and galaxies so that new ones can be born. Whatever they're doing down here, I desperately want to believe they have some sort of reason for it.

Anthem hisses out a breath. "Everyone I talked to got super squirrely about the Star Slayer stuff—no one would talk to me about any of it. Which crew they were on, how long the Star Slayer had been aboard, whether he's a temporary passenger or a regular customer. I wonder if they've all signed some sort of non-disclosure contract or something."

"So I should basically stay clear of everyone just in case."

"Except for Z," she pointed out. "He's the only one who *definitely* isn't on the Star Slayer's crew. Just taking his money for passage, as far as I can tell. Are you making any progress on getting him on our side?"

"I think so? It's hard to tell," I admit, and give her a broad sketch of what happened overnight.

She's gaping at me when I'm done. "There was a *giant electric eel* about to *eat us whole*, and you didn't wake me up?"

"To be fair, I don't think it was going to eat us. Just electrocute us. Probably."

"That's so much better," she says with full snark. "If it happens again, do not let me die in my sleep. There are several pretty people on board, and I would much rather die kissing one of them." She aggressively pulls her hair back, wrapping it around itself at the back of her head until she's turned it into some sort of messy bun-nest thing. "Moving on. I'm up this early because Z very rudely came into the bunkroom and yelled at everyone to rustle up their own breakfast from the galley because we're landing at the shales pretty soon now. He wants us in and out as fast as possible. And he gave me an assignment to 'earn my keep' since apparently he's of the opinion that my cleaning is not up to scratch. Which may be fair since I did little to no actual cleaning."

I frown. I'm relieved that Z has apparently decided to let her stay on for the next leg of the trip, but I'm leery of any assignment in the shales. "What does he want you to do?"

She grins slyly. "Tail Lexie. Apparently she's planning to disembark even though she has no real reason to, and I guess he's suspicious about what she's up to. I'm supposed to follow her and report back. Prepare yourself for more magnificent spywork."

"I'm coming with you." It's not like I'll be able to offer much protection from falling shale—which accounts for hundreds of fatalities in the settlements each year—but there's no way I'm staying here twiddling my thumbs while she's potentially risking her life to help me.

"Yeah, Z actually guessed you would say that," Anthem replies. "He said to tell you, and I quote, 'Be careful.'" She nudges me with her shoulder, an amiable, easy contact that feels like a minor miracle with everything that's happened between us lately. "I think he likes you. Maybe you're doing better on the ally-making front than you give yourself credit for."

"I don't know about that," I mutter, but turn away guiltily. Whether or not Z and I could be genuine friends or romantically involved or anything else if the world were a different place and I was a different person, nothing like that is possible now. It was already harrowing enough to worry that I might lose control of myself and stab him while he was stuck under the glint tank. The more I like him, or anyone, the more mental torture I add to my daily regimen of waking nightmares. I wish I could just win him over without letting myself care about him in return, but apparently I'm not built that way.

"Hmm," is all Anthem says, looking at me like she can see my thoughts. "In any case, we'd better get going. Lexie was already hovering by the tower exit when I came this way. She'll probably bolt the second we surface." She tilts her head at my still-glowing hand, her gaze flicking quickly to it and then away, still uncomfortable but not quite as fearful as earlier. "Better turn that off for now."

I extinguish the glow and my skin goes back to normal. I feel a pang at its loss. I flex my fingers and stuff my hand into my pocket so I won't have to look at it. "Anthem," I say as she's almost to the door. "Thank you. For...for everything."

She turns and glances back at me, barely visible in the dim lights coming from the main hallway around the corner. "You would do the same for me," she says.

I would do anything for her. I duck my head and follow her out.

Everyone is gathered at the base of the tower ladder already, many with fruit or leftover flatbread in hand. Z spots me and tosses an apple in my direction. I fumble to catch it before it gives me a black eye. I recall Rick saying that you could tell whether Z likes you based on if the tools he throws hit you or not, and wonder if the same is true of fruit.

"Indy is staying onboard," Z says to me. "There's too much fallen shale out there that would cut her paws." Before I can respond, he raises his voice to address everyone. "I've set the surfacing protocols and I'm going to be headed back to the control room in a second to initiate them. We'll be at the docks in under twenty minutes. You all have your assignments." He nods at the two middle-aged women, who are bracketing the refugee family like they're their bodyguards, then at the redhead and Rick, who are carrying a large insulated crate between them that must be for resupplying purposes. Chester isn't carrying anything at all, and Z just gives him a brief, sour look. "Anyone who's going on to Albergia with me—Peregrine, Anthem, Rick, and Lexie—needs to be back onboard within two hours or I will leave you behind. Everyone else, good luck on your journeys, see you around, till we meet again, et cetera." The old sailor guy jerks a nod and the redhead smiles at Z. No one else reacts except to eye the hatch at the top of the ladder, as if we're all at the starting line for a race and waiting for the signal to go.

Anthem speaks up then. "Why the rush? Are we slated to move more refugees?"

"There are no more refugees coming out of Albergia," Z says grimly, and there's a moment of silence as we absorb what that means. Before Anthem can follow up with any more questions Z is already turning his chair to head back to the control room.

And then there's nothing to do but wait.

Sunrises have always been graceless, lackluster things. The sky pales from charcoal to stormy gray to off-white, the blurry sun drifts above the Barrier like an egg yolk sliding across a pan, and then it is officially daytime and that's that. So when the tower hatch opens and I step out onto the wet deck, I am caught so off-guard by what sunrise in the shales looks like that I stand frozen at the top of the ladder for a full twenty seconds as I try to comprehend the glory laid out before me.

The stained-glass shales aren't actually glass at all, but a type of rock so thin it's nearly transparent. Earthquakes push new slabs of it up from deep beneath the sediment at the same time as they send old ones shattering to bits and raining down on whoever happens to be taking refuge below. The shale is incredibly strong but also very brittle, and when it breaks, it has a dangerous tendency to snap into knifelike shrapnel. All of this I know from news reports and the documentaries they make us watch in school. But here are the things I did not know until now:

The way dawn looks through jagged towers of emerald and amethyst, opal and amber and aquamarine. How the shale formations become enormous lenses, focusing and filtering the sun's bleary rays until they cast not shadows but jeweled light over everything below. Through their alchemy the ocean is turned from brackish brown to dazzling fractals of color, making an endlessly shifting geometry out of the rippling waves.

Then Lexie jostles past me with a "*Move,* jackass," that makes me stumble and grab the railing, and the spell is unceremoniously broken.

"Huh," is all Anthem says when she tops the ladder next, but the arch of her eyebrows says she's impressed. "I guess now I get why people would live in a place that can kill them."

Rick is next. He straightens his bow tie—yes, he is wearing a bow tie, and it is a cheery lime green color that somehow still looks dapper and not ridiculous on him—and casts me an apologetic look. "You'll have to forgive Lexie her rudeness," he says under his breath. "Hopefully, this touch of shore leave might provide the fresh perspective she needs."

I nod mutely and start down the tower's ladder after Anthem and Lexie. The rest of the crew and the refugee family follow. The little kids look awed and frightened and overwhelmed, so on a whim I hand one of them my apple, which I have no appetite for anyway. "I bet you could trade this for a new toy," I whisper to the girl. Her face brightens and she nods a thank you, then they scuttle away after their parents, who are searching the port for their relatives.

Anthem nudges me and casts a meaningful glance at Lexie, who is already almost out of sight down the docks. Wherever she's going, she's in a hurry, and she apparently has a specific destination in mind. We move after her. Anthem keeps her in sight while I continue taking in the scenery unfolding around me. An endless array of people bustles past me in all different shades of clothes and skin and hair—pale, freckled Albergians, Ancient Isle wayfarers with long jet-black braids and elegant coats, Pthuli tribesmen and women with delicate white tattoos filigreed across their ebony-shaded collarbones. There are also quite a few people who identify with their old-Earth ancestors. I spot the flash of brightly-colored kimonos, women wearing saris with red or black *bindis* on their foreheads, and people with rich mahogany skin and stretched earlobes. The languages are a stew of clipped northern Conglom consonants and the slow, liquid drawl of the southeast and many other accents and dialects I can't identify. The only thing that all of these people have in common is the fear in their eyes when they dare to glance at the sky. The realization dulls the edges of my wonder and I pull my gaze back to Anthem.

We weave past stalls where vendors hawk their wares, including shoes made from woven seaweed, clever little wind-up toys, and shelves full of tiny tinkling bottles. The smell of saffron and sage drifts through the air like incense. Spices, medicine, clothing, food: everything the people here need to survive, except true safety. I crane my neck. The shales loom overhead, but not like a threat—more like a cathedral ceiling, lofty and elegant and protective. I dare to run my fingers along a citrine-colored shale. It feels cool and just slightly textured under my hand, and has the same sort of calming effect that I get from petting Indy. It's weird, I thought I'd be fighting panic the whole time I was out here, worrying that Anthem would get nailed by falling shale, but my anxiety isn't quite as bad as I feared. Here in this place, I feel...not safe, exactly, but connected?

My watch warbles its urgent-message notification then, startling me, and I pull my hand away from the shale to power it up fully. My heart sinks as I watch message after message come through from Mom and Dad now that I've got enough signal to receive them. There are a few other notifications in there as well that I missed while we were at sea: a ping from one of Anthem's friends, a notice from my homeroom teacher that classes are indefinitely cancelled—and a notification that Check-It Chessie has uploaded a new post to her site. I glance at that last one quickly. It looks like she uploaded a short new message just after *The Shitty Clunker* left the Conglom, telling her audience that she was working on something huge and to stay tuned for an "epic story" that would air on her cast on a specific date—today's date, I realize. I frown, wondering what she's up to, but there's no other information and I don't have the battery to investigate further anyway.

"Anthem," I say. "I've got to call Mom and Dad."

She grimaces but nods, keeping her gaze on the path. "Yeah, go ahead. I've got eyes on the target—looks like she's ordering food from a stall not too far up."

I hide my smile. *Eyes on the target?* She's enjoying this whole spy thing a little too much. But my smile fades quickly as I navigate to Mom's icon and touch it, initiating a videocall to her.

She picks up instantly. Her face crumples with relief when she sees me. She claps one hand over her mouth, her shoulders shaking. Tears sheen her eyes.

I want to curl into myself and drop through a hole in the earth. I have never before seen my mother undone, and now she is, and it's because of me. "We're all okay," I tell her first, my voice hoarse.

Dad's face crowds into the frame. His brow is creased with worry and the lines around his mouth have deepened, making him look haggard and wan and a decade older than the last time I saw him. He doesn't say anything, just stares at me like he's memorizing my face, then lets out a long, quiet exhale. "Anthem," he says then. "We need to see Anthem too."

Ahead of me, Anthem winces when she overhears his words but then throws her shoulders back and marches over to me, giving the screen a sharp nod. The second she sees them, though, her face crumples just like Mom's did. "I'm sorry," she says. "I'm sorry. I didn't think things through, I should've told you I was worried instead of stealing a patrol car, I should've—"

"You stole a patrol car?" Mom asks, her voice managing to sound dangerous even though it's choked with tears.

Anthem winces. "Yeah? For a good cause?"

Mom looks like she's about to say something she'll regret, so Dad steps in. "There is no cause good enough for stealing a patrol car," he says firmly.

"This is my fault," I cut in. "Don't blame Anthem. She's done nothing but watch out for me."

Dad holds up a hand. "There will be blame plenty enough for all of us later. How much battery do you have left?"

I check it. "Eight percent."

"And how much longer do you anticipate this journey going on before you return?"

Anthem and I don't look at each other. "I'm not exactly sure," I hedge.

"Please," Mom says, her voice ragged now. "Please tell us where you're going. Please tell us why you left. Whatever it is, we can take it. We just want to *understand.*"

While I try yet again to disappear through a hole in the ground, Anthem comes to my rescue. "It's not something we can discuss over an open line," she says, and I'm suddenly pathetically grateful for her love of spy lingo.

Dad closes his eyes and inhales. "Regardless, we need to make a plan so your mother and I can keep abreast of the situation. Is it safe to say your journey will take at least a few more days?"

I nod mutely.

"Then let's set up a time for you to check in at least once a day. Sunrise, Conglom time?"

I hesitate. "We don't have signal at sea, and there's...at least one more leg of our trip." Gods, I hate this. I hate lying to them. "We have to go now. But I swear, we'll be in contact as often as we have signal."

Mom and Dad trade a look. Mom heaves in a shuddering breath and her expression firms. Dad turns back to the screen. "So you won't come back? And you can't guarantee that you'll check in on a regular basis?" I shake my head mutely. "Then," he says heavily, "we will have to come and find you."

I freeze. Anthem and I trade wide-eyed looks. "*What*?" I demand, just as Anthem says, "But we took the car!"

"Shut up," Mom orders. For the first time I register that there's a bridge over her shoulder, in the background of the shot. I can't make out much of it, but it looks an awful lot like the bridge we crossed on the way to the cabin, the same one I crossed in the opposite direction on my way back to the port.

"Wait. Where are you? You're still at the cabin, right?" I demand. A few people around me turn and frown. My voice is too loud. I don't care.

Mom glares daggers at me even as she scrubs her sleeve across her face. "We're on our way to the port. You found a ship? Well, so will we." The screen tilts a little and I see the rusty frame of an old bicycle.

"You're—you're riding *bikes* all the way to the port?" Anthem demands.

"No way, you have to stay off the roads, people are crazy right now and there's the lockdown—" I'm saying at the same time.

"You want us off the roads? You want us in lockdown? Then come back," Mom says fiercely. "Otherwise, we are coming to save you and then we will *end you*."

"I'll help her," Dad vows from somewhere offscreen.

"You don't even know where you're going!" I say.

The frame tilts to show Dad's face again. He raises an eyebrow coolly. "So far I've heard at least three languages in the background on this call," he notes. "And the lighting is odd, colorful. I'm guessing you're in one of the stained-glass shale settlements."

"No we're not," Anthem blusters, shading my watch with her hands to block out our surroundings.

Dad is relentless, though. He pulls the pencil nub out from behind his ear and scribbles something on...did he seriously take a *notepad* with him on whatever cross-country bike trip of doom my parents have embarked on? I choke back a semi-hysterical laugh.

"Based on the amount of travel time you must've spent before you sent us that first message," Dad muses, "it's most likely you did, indeed, depart from the main Conglom port."

"Wait," I say. "Wait. A minute ago when you were crying, when you were begging us to schedule check-ins—were you trying to *trick us* into telling you where we were?"

"No need to trick you when your dad knows math," Mom replies, managing to sound smug, angry, and worried all at the same time.

Dad goes on scribbling and musing, ignoring us all. "Judging by the time that's passed since then while you were onboard whatever ship you stowed away on—"

"We didn't stow away!" Anthem protests.

"*I* didn't stow away," I can't help muttering.

"—and accounting for the varying potential speed of the ships that are registered as refugee-bearing, which are the only ones allowed to sail right now, then..." He finishes his calculations with a flourish. "There is only one settlement directly reachable by ship that fits the bill. So. We know where you are, and we're coming to get you."

"But we're only here for two hours! Please, Dad, Mom, just go back to the cabin—"

Mom swings the watch around so that her furious face fills the whole screen. "And sit around and wring our hands and do nothing while we wait for our kids, *and our dog,* to finish whatever hope-fully-not-deadly quest they've decided to set out on while the *literal world is potentially ending*?"

"Please," I try one last time, at a complete loss for how to handle this situation that is spiraling so far out of my control. "I need to know you're safe. I can't—I can't do what I need to do unless I know you're safe."

Mom smiles, a fierce baring of her teeth. "Then you know exactly how we feel."

I have no response to that.

"Save your battery," she says, triumphant. "We'll see you soon." And with that, the screen goes blank.

"Damn it," I curse. "She even got the gods-damned last word in." I whirl to Anthem. "What are we going to do?"

Anthem is mute and wide-eyed. She shakes her head slowly.

"We can't go back," I say helplessly. "*I* can't go back. Not until I figure all this out."

"I go where you go," Anthem says, but she still looks as dazed as I feel.

I scrub a hand through my hair. "Then...then I guess we just have to hurry. And hope that they get a flat tire." And that they don't get robbed, beaten, or killed while on the road. Oh, gods. I squeeze my eyes shut.

"How long do you think it'll take them to get to the port?" Anthem asks.

I throw a hand in the air. "I don't know! I got a D in geometry!"

She frowns. "Is that even the type of math you'd use to measure speed and distances and velocity or whatever?"

"I have no idea! Which only illustrates my point!" My anxiety is slowly ticking into full-blown panic territory.

She holds out her hands like she's trying to calm a wild animal. "Okay. Chill. There's nothing we can do to slow them down anyway. We just have to focus on our part of things, take one step at a time. Focus on one task at a time."

I inhale as much air as I can suck into my lungs and let it out slowly. "Yeah. Okay."

"So our next task is..." Anthem prompts, then we both jerk upright.

"Crap," I say, spinning around and searching the maze of market stalls ahead. "Crap, crap. Where'd Lexie go?"

"Shh!" Anthem hisses. "Don't say her name! You might as well hang a sign around your neck saying 'hey, we're stalking you!'"

"We're not stalking her!"

"Yeah, *now* we're not!"

I remember that Lexie wore her tightly-curled black hair in a short pouf tied with a red ribbon today, so I scan the people around us for that color and spot it a few vendor stalls away. "Is that her?" I ask, squinting and craning my neck to try to make out the person beyond the racks of dried fruit.

Anthem stands on her tiptoes and edges sideways to get a better view. "Yeah," she says, blowing out a relieved breath. "Good catch. Looks like...she's meeting with someone. Huh—guess Z was right about her being up to something. Think it's a lovers' rendezvous?"

I take a few steps sideways and peer at the figures behind the fruit stall until Anthem rolls her eyes. "Stop being so obvious," she hisses, but I don't answer because there's something familiar about the person Lexie is talking to. It's a girl. She's wearing a worn brown hat and a backpack that has the legs of some sort of long tripod contraption sticking out of it—but it's not until she leans over to look at Lexie's watch and her gold-and-silver-streaked hair slips out from beneath her hat that I realize where I've seen her before. Or rather, where I've seen her pic.

At the top of a gossip cast site. Right above a headline screaming *Star Slayer on Albergian Submarine!* "That's Check-It Chessie," I whisper, horror blooming slow inside me. Check-It Chessie, with millions of brand-new info-hungry followers including military members, is meeting with Lexie, who thinks her dad should tell everyone how star dragons can be killed. Right after Chessie just told her audience that she was about to break an epic story.

Suddenly, I have a terrible feeling that I know exactly what it is.

CHAPTER TEN

An emotion flushes through my veins and propels me forward. It's the dismay I felt earlier upon learning there might be a way to kill the dragons, but times ten. I don't stop to wonder why my reaction is so strong, and I don't pause to remind myself that I should be playing it cool so no one suspects me. I don't think at all. I just act. I barely hear Anthem's loud, confused whisper as she tries to call me back. "Chessie," I call loudly as I stride toward her.

Chessie jumps and whirls around, wary. "What?" she says, scanning me over, probably thinking I'm some sort of fanboy who recognized her.

Lexie is staring at me, shock and guilt rippling over her face until her expression settles on anger. "What the hell?" she demands. "Did you *follow* me?"

"Technically I followed you," Anthem says, stepping a little in front of me and folding her arms. She whispers to me, "What exactly are you doing, genius? This wasn't the assignment."

"Wait," Chessie says, sticking up a hand to ward us off. "Lexie, do you know these folks?" Without waiting for an answer, she turns back to us, eagerness lighting her expression. "Do you guys know the fake Star Slayer too? Or even better, the *real* one? I could totally use some extra interviews. You know, talk about what he's like, if you feel betrayed now that his secret's out, all that jazz." Without waiting for an answer, she slings her backpack off and pulls out the tripod device, which seems to be some sort of expensive camera.

I open my mouth and then stall out. *Real* Star Slayer? My gaze cuts to Lexie, who is clenching her jaw stubbornly but also not meeting my gaze. "What do you mean?" I ask cautiously.

Chessie grins, glancing up from the tripod. "You can watch the full reveal on my channel later today with everyone else."

Lexie's brow furrows. "Wait, you said you were only going to funnel this intel to your military contacts."

"Funnel what intel?" I say, too loudly, but Chessie is ignoring me as she checks her watch.

"There we go, the vid finally came through," she says with a triumphant grin aimed at Lexie. "Thanks, girl. You've been a big help. I'll be sure to give you a credit at the end of my cast."

"Please don't," Lexie says, tight-lipped.

Anthem has had enough. She barges into the middle of our little stand-off and throws out her arms like she's breaking up a fight. "All right, that's it," she declares. "If you guys don't tell me what is going on in the next three seconds, I swear to the gods, Lexie, I will call Z and see if *he* can deduce what you're up to." It's a bluff, and also the exact wrong thing to say. Lexie's eyes snap with fury and she leans forward, hands curling into fists.

"Go ahead," she snarls, "call that bastard. Tell him as of today, everyone will know his dirty little secret."

"*What* secret?" I demand. "Is this something to do about the warrant on your dad? Lexie, whatever your reasons, please don't let Chessie air anything about how to kill dragons. It's not—it could—it could put more people in danger," I say, floundering for a believable reason for not wanting the creatures dead and gone like everyone else.

"Too late," Chessie says with an exasperated eyeroll as she screws the camera into its holder at the top of the tripod. "I've already uploaded the footage to my cloud, and I'll be posting it to my cast in a few hours. Soon everyone will know the Star Slayer's true identity *and* how to get rid of the dragons. And even that's just a teaser. I've got a story planned that'll blow the top off everything everyone thinks they know about...well, everything."

My mouth goes dry. Something in my chest pulls taut with anxiety. My gaze flits to Lexie and she stares back, challenging and guilty. I should follow up on that very foreboding *blow the top off everything* statement, but my mind is snagged on what Chessie said just before that. "What do you mean, the Star Slayer's true identity?"

Chessie puts out a hand, still fiddling with the camera. "Whoa, whoa, guys, hold on just another minute, save the drama till I can get this rolling."

Lexie juts her chin out, defiant, ignoring Chessie to glare at me. "She means the *real* Star Slayer. My dad might be willing to take hits for him, pretend to be him for interviews and to keep the military off his back, but I'm not. If there's a warrant out for the arrest of the Star Slayer, then they should be going after the right guy."

I can feel my breath rattling around in my chest. There's a strange buzzing in my ears. If Rick isn't the Star Slayer, isn't the biggest threat to me onboard *The Shitty Clunker*...then who is?

"Who's the right guy?" I ask.

Lexie starts to shake her head but Anthem is already in motion. She steps toward Lexie, moving like she intends to commit violence, and Lexie stands firm at first but wavers and starts to backpedal as she gets closer.

"Anthem," I say, grabbing my sister's wrist to hold her back. She looks furious but I know her too well; I know the line of her shoulders, that tilt of her head, the tightness in her eyes that says she's scared. We thought we knew the threat to me and now there's a new one, and we have no plan to deal with it. Our earlier conversation with Mom and Dad already put her on rocky ground emotionally and now she's discovered that the person she thought she could help protect me from isn't even the right person.

Anthem lets me pull her to a stop but leans in toward Lexie. "Show us whatever footage you have," she orders, "*right now.* Or I swear to the gods, Lexie, I will call your dad and tell him exactly what you're doing. I have to guess you're leaking this info against his wishes, right? Because otherwise you wouldn't have to leak it at all. Wouldn't have to sneak off the sub and give him that bullshit about taking 'shore leave' to clear your head."

"Hey!" Chessie protests, stepping away from the tripod to grab at the back of Anthem's shirt. Anthem bats her off without looking. "This is an exclusive! Don't you dare show her that footage, Lexie, or you can forget about getting credit in my cast!"

Lexie gives Chessie an incredulous look. "Are you serious? You think I'm doing this for the recognition? All I want is to protect my dad! And apparently I'm the only one trying to do that." She snaps up her wrist and jabs her finger at her watch, queueing up what looks like the start of a recording. "You want to see the bastard who's willing to throw Dad under the bus to keep his own secret? Be my guest." She flings out her wrist toward us as the video starts playing.

My world narrows to a tiny two-inch screen. I lean in to watch.

It shows a star dragon—the original melted-ruby one, the one that's the size of a tiger but still decimated an entire town and a huge swath of the Albergian army. It's skimming over the surface of what looks like one of the country's carved-glacier cities. The background is all whites and blues and beautiful sculpted ice formations, and in the corner of the screen I can just make out the deep blue-green color of the far northern Icedrift Sea. The dragon's wings dip and angle and hover, coordinating as it moves in a slow and perfectly straight line, breathing starfire down on everything beneath it. The pearlescent shimmer of uncreation is beautiful, enthralling. I can't look away. It doesn't drill down into the ice, doesn't explode the glacier or boil the sea below. Everything it touches is simply...gone.

Then, from the corner of the screen, a glint of something sharp and amethyst-colored flies toward the dragon. It's tumbling end over end in a perfect arc like a thrown dagger, but even with as fast as it's moving, I see enough of it to recognize the material: a shard of stained-glass shale about the size of my forearm.

The dragon spots the incoming shard. Its blast of starfire jerks upward, toward the screen. It makes a noise and its wings begin to move in a rush as it rears backward. But the path of the shale rock is unerring. It strikes the creature straight in its eye—

And the dragon explodes into a burst of starfire.

I stumble back from the recording. Horror tightens a net over me. On the screen, the starfire clears. The dragon is gone. Dead. *The dragon is dead.* My dreams blink through my mind: flying free through space, diving into the black horizon of the universe, dipping wings into the fires in the hearts of stars. I imagine all of that awe, all of that history—an ancient, sentient force of nature—gone in the blink of an eye. It feels *wrong*.

The screen wobbles and turns. Whoever is recording—a woman, I think—lets out a whoop, a sound that's hoarse with disbelieving joy. Then the screen focuses on the person who threw the shard. His hand is still outstretched. A line of blood is etched across his palm. His eyes are empty, haunted, shocked. His messy brown hair is flecked with snow. His hoverchair is crusted with frost.

Z is the Star Slayer.

Z has killed a dragon.

Z has *lied to me.*

I jerk backwards, away from Lexie's watch. I cover my mouth with my hand. My foot knocks against the corner of a vendor's stall and I trip, landing on my knees. Dimly, I register Anthem saying something in an alarmed tone, but she might as well be speaking another language.

Z's mother was uncreated by a dragon. He has nothing left of her except an article with a picture he can't keep in his head and a name he can't remember. The story unfolds in my mind like origami, perfect and terrible: Z headed straight home to Albergia when Starfall happened, only to find his home gone, his mother gone, his whole life wiped from existence like it doesn't even matter. He sees the armies march. Later, no one can remember them either. Bullets bounce off scales. Missiles have no effect. The dragon seems invulnerable, but Z has been researching dragons for years as the Star Slayer and he has a theory. He decides to try it out.

I remember the broken pieces of shale in his chair's storage compartment. I remember what Rick said of Z when I first met him: *He's a wicked good aim.* In my head, I see the amethyst shale gleam again and again as it spins into the dragon's eye.

And I've been trying as hard as I can to make him my ally. I considered telling him about my light. *I trusted him,* and it turns out he's the one I should have been worried about all along.

Panic is a freight train thundering through my head and I am tied to its tracks. My mind frantically searches for a way to make this revelation untrue, to make Z innocent, to make him what I believed him to be and not a liar and my potential enemy. I was worried enough when I thought kindly-professor Rick was the Star Slayer, that he was the one with the potential to trap or experiment on or kill me if he discovered my secrets—but Z is infinitely more dangerous. Z has lost his mother, every scrap of her, to the star dragons. He's grieving and haunted and angry. If he thinks I've been actively hiding something dragon-related from him, or worse, that I've got some sort of nefarious agenda aboard his ship... I don't know what he'll do to me. I don't know what he'll do to Anthem, if she tries to defend me from him, which she will. We are in so much more danger than we thought. And it's not like we can just stay in the settlement and let the sub go on without us. The countdown is on, the clock to—I don't know, something terrible—is ticking, and I need to get to Albergia before time runs out. Before my parents put themselves in even more danger for my sake. All my choices are wreathed in danger, and if I choose wrong, the people I care about could pay the price.

I reach out blindly for something, anything, to ground me. My fingers brush against the shale formation at my back. Something invisible jolts from it to me, or maybe from me to it, like static electricity.

The air above the settlement cracks open, and a dragon snaps into existence a hundred feet over my head.

Its scales shine with the rippling amber light of a brown dwarf star. Its stiffly extended wings are so bright they're nearly impossible to look at, with snaps of energy sizzling through them like veins. The dragon hangs motionless in the air for a second that seems to stretch into eternity. But it has traveled here at the speed of light using the energy of stars to power its solar-sail wings, and when that second is over, the sonic boom it has dragged behind itself like a kite string finally catches up.

The sound is so loud it's not a sound at all; it's a force, a hammer blow to the chest, a splintering of bone against bone. It scoops up shale shards and booths and people and me, flinging us all outward in an expanding ring of destruction. I tumble with no sense of direction. I land against something hard with a crack that makes me wonder if my spine is broken.

I open my eyes. The blank-paper sky stares back at me, indifferent. Skin and clothing and screams blur past me as the people who can stagger to their feet and flee. A metallic shrieking noise shivers through the air. I manage to focus my eyes on the towering shales above. They've gone crooked, their top halves sitting at jaunty angles like disjointed skeletons. As I watch, those top halves all begin sliding slowly sideways. The shockwave has split them neatly a hundred feet off the ground, and when their slow tilt turns to inescapable plummeting, they will fill the settlement with billions of billions of knifelike shards that will impale anyone trapped beneath them.

Anthem. Anthem. *Anthem.*

I try to get up to look for her but I haven't quite regained the ability to move my body correctly yet. My head flops to the side. More limbs and clothing and faces and screaming jolt past me, a blur of doomed humanity. My heart is not racing. It is thudding—a hard, slow, almost painful beat like a bass line in my chest.

And my hands…my hands are glowing. They're radiating with dim but undeniably otherworldly light, a blue-white hue that doesn't quite match any color humankind can create.

My heart thuds again, almost unbearable in its immense pressure.

I find that I can move. Oxygen floods my lungs and I gulp it down greedily, rolling to my side. *Anthem.* I turn my head to look for her and spot the dragon instead. It's about the size of *The Shitty Clunker,* larger than the ruby dragon but far smaller than the enormous blue one. Its golden-brown scales gleam like winter stars, its alien eyes slitted with emotion and intelligence. Its sinuous body curves like a sea snake cutting through a current, its deft wings working independently to keep it hovering in place.

It inhales.

"No," I choke out. I shove myself up. "No. Don't. *Please, don't.*"

But it either can't hear me or doesn't care. It breathes out starfire, and the pearled light of uncreation burns cleanly through the wreckage of a dozen vendor stalls barely a few yards away from me. The slowly-tilting shale towers refract the starfire, and jeweled light strobes over the ground like we're all caught inside a kaleidoscope: citrine, sapphire, topaz.

I stagger forward. I have to make it understand. If I could just get to it, if I could just find some way to communicate with it, I could send it away. I could make it stop. What good does my light do me if it can't do this? *Shine,* I think, and the glow in my hands spreads out across my body. Maybe I can at least make the dragon pause if it sees me. I take another stumbling step toward it as it swivels its head, cleanly sweeping its starfire across a group of fleeing people whose details evaporate from my memory the second their bodies dissolve.

Then I spot Anthem, and with her, Chessie. They're cast in the golden starlight like creatures trapped in amber, blood-flecked gashes rent through their clothing and skin. Anthem's cheek and ear are bleeding. Her hair hangs wild as she stares up at the dragon, at the shales, at the end of everything.

Then, like she's sensed me, she turns and our gazes lock. Fear floods her face like some tangible dam has broken within her. She takes a step away. Not from the dragon breathing out starfire above. From *me.*

I look down at myself. I'm still glowing, every square inch of skin burnished in the blue-white of some alien star. It pulses in time with the beat of some ancient song I can almost recognize. I did this to try to communicate with the creature above. To stop it. To save Anthem.

You don't have to be afraid of me, I want to cry out, but haven't I always wondered whether she ought to be?

Someone screams. I tear my gaze away from Anthem and see Chessie. She's staring straight at me, her eyes wide, mouth gaping. She's fumbling at the top of the tripod next to her. The camera. She's pulling it off the stand, turning it toward me. She's going to record me. In the midst of the chaos, the running and screaming and dying, this should be the furthest concern from both our minds, but terror grows roots in me anyway. She has seen me. She has seen my secret, and I cannot take it back, and if she records it then everyone will know there's something wrong with me. Including my parents. Including the armies. Including—

Including Z. The Star Slayer.

Fear lashes through me, igniting me, and I launch myself forward. Anthem is quicker, though. She follows my gaze, spots the camera, snatches it away and throws it on the ground and drives her heel into it. Chessie protests but Anthem just shoves her, hard. "RUN!" she snarls, and they do. I follow as they stagger-sprint-fall through the kaleidoscope of color and uncreation, dodging bits of shale that have already begun to splinter off, weaving between fleeing people and leaping over bodies. Some of those bodies are still moving, some of them are reaching out for help, but I can't stop, I can't I can't *I can't,* because Anthem is ahead of me and so, suddenly, is the dragon.

Its claw-tipped talons rake effortless gaping chasms in the ground. Its now-closed muzzle lifts like it's scenting the air. Its wings flare above it and beside it, blocking out the empty sky and filling every-thing, *everything,* with the dazzling light of the star that hatched it. Every part of me stretches toward it: the call of open space, the black horizon of the universe, the splash and span of endless suns.

The dragon looks at me.

The dragon *sees me.* Sees my otherworldly glow, sees my human form, and *knows...*something. I can't grasp what that something is but I watch it come together in the creature's eyes like a black hole collapsing in on itself.

It opens its mouth and inhales. I know a moment of distilled terror. My sister's words ring in my mind: *it's going to hurt all of us much more if you die...if I'm left with nothing but a wisp of a memory and a brother who never existed.* I pray she's wrong but I know she's right. Z is proof—the rust in his voice when he asked for his mother's name, the haunted look in his eyes when he tried to remember building the sub with her. Even if Anthem's mind can't remember me, even if Mom and Dad can't recall the boy they found in a glint mine, a sliver of me will still lodge in their souls and they will know the shape of me from the hole I leave behind—and it will hurt them. I want to weep. Even in nonexistence, I still hurt them.

The dragon reaches the height of its inhale. It bends its neck downward. Its nostrils flare and its maw begins to gape open.

Something sails through the air and hits it on the muzzle. A warped chunk of wood. The dragon jerks, exhales a surprised burst of regular air, and moves its gaze from me to the person who threw the missile: my sister, arms outflung, eyes wild with terror and courage as she distracts a star dragon to save me.

The dragon's pupils turn to thin onyx slits. Its lips ripple into an outraged growl. It inhales again, and starfire begins bubbling up into its throat like a liquid. I have perhaps three seconds to make a choice. I don't need even that long.

I fling myself forward. I tackle Anthem at waist height and she flies sideways. She ricochets into Chessie and they both tumble into the wall of one of the few nearby buildings made of actual bricks and wood: an embassy of some sort, with a bright blue-and-green banner hanging from a pole on the roof. Chessie hits the wall head-first with a crack and then goes limp like a rag doll, entangling Anthem in a mess of skewed limbs as my sister tries to fight her way free. Her eyes are wide with panic and she's shouting something I can't hear. A shard of splintered emerald shale crashes to the ground beside her, narrowly missing her leg.

I am now the only one standing in the path of the starfire. I don't have time to leap out of the way, so I hurtle forward instead—toward the dragon, toward the starfire I can see roiling over its tongue and teeth and flooding toward me. If I can just touch the dragon, if I can somehow make it understand all of the things I don't even understand myself, maybe I can still save everyone.

But I'm not fast enough to outrace starfire, and with a terrible silence, the brilliance of uncreation veils me.

It is light and sound and the absence of both. It is the grand, echoing emptiness of unlimited potential. It is a supernova burning the universe to cinders to make way for seedling planets. It is an ancient, holy unmaking—and it does not unmake me. Instead the pearled starfire whispers across my skin, communicating with the light inside me even though my human brain can't comprehend the language. I can sense the emotion of it, though. Something like wonder. Something like joy. Something like purpose, fulfilled.

And then I am submerged into my dream.

Unfettered wonders tucked into the folds of endless space. A wilderness of stars, an ever-changing glory of primordial beauty. It belongs to me and I belong to it. I fan my wings in the light of a foreign sun and am at peace.

Until I am trapped. Buried beneath an impossible weight, no more flying, no more space, no more suns. I struggle at first but my blood is draining of its starlight and I must sleep to survive.

Years creep by. Decades. Centuries. A millennium.

I am dying. And I am so very alone.

The weight that crushes down on my body gets heavier and heavier, and I know I will never be able to free myself of it. I have survived a thousand years here, but I will survive only another decade or so before I perish—before I explode in a blast of starfire, uncreating my own body and anything and everything around me. And there is so very much life around me.

I do not want to be a destroyer. I am meant to be a creator. My kind is rare among star dragons; I have never met another. If I perish, my abilities will too, and then who will mold the universe? Who will follow in the wake of my kin and seed the emptiness they leave behind with planets, with nebulae, with the cosmic dust that will someday compress into a star and hatch a new dragonling?

If I am going to die, I do not want to leave only destruction in my wake, and I don't want to die alone.

I am a creator, so I create.

I have just enough energy left for this: molding a body in a shape like that of the humans who keep me trapped here. I let creation choose its own course, let it flow how it wants because I haven't the strength to direct it; making takes far more energy than unmaking. When it finishes, I see that I have made a boy. He is young and pale-skinned with hair like a golden sun, and although there is not yet any life or consciousness in him, I can already see the stars in his eyes.

In my eyes.

This vessel is my last chance. I cannot survive in my current form, but maybe, just maybe, I can find a way to get back to the stars if I walk among the humans as one of their own. And if I do die, at least now I won't be alone, and at least I will have done everything I can to save them.

I breathe myself into the boy.

My body and soul separate. My body goes into a deeper sleep than ever before, one it will never wake from unless it receives an influx of starlight within the next decade. My soul slips free of it and fills up the empty human vessel before me. This brain is so different, so alien, that it cannot hold my memories or knowledge. But it can hold what's most important: a longing to find the stars.

I open my eyes, and am human.

I crash back into my body. I am tumbling through the air surrounded by pearlescent starfire. I am saturated in the joy and wonder and purpose of the amber dragon before me, but just one thin layer beneath that are my own emotions, and I know that when they break through that crust they will snap me like kindling because I have just finally, finally solved the riddle of me, and oh gods, I wish I hadn't. Images blink through my mind, jackrabbit-quick:

The glow of silver-blue wings against the black of space.

The weight of a world pinning me beneath an empty sky.

A boy with stars in his eyes and the soul of a dragon. My eyes. My soul.

I know now why I can't remember anything from before I was seven years old. It's because I was never six or five or four. I was never born at all. This body—me, Peregrine Kent, brother and son—is mine, but it's not my only body. The dream I just had, the dreams I *always* have, they feel like borrowed memories because that's what they are except they're not borrowed at all. That ghost-limb ache that I get on waking from my dreams, I have it again now and I know what it is: the pain of maintaining two forms, one with blond hair and a human heart and eyes full of stars, and one clawed and winged and ancient—and both of them dying.

I am dying. My dreams are true. The light's countdown is true. But worse than that is the knowledge that *I am a star dragon*, I am one of the creatures who've been unmaking the world, and I know I'm capable of the feat of creation but I think I might have starfire too. I am afraid of knives and guns and bad thoughts...and I've just been handed a nuclear bomb.

I've been leaping through the air toward the dragon but the ground finally catches up with me, and I twist my knee and go sprawling. I fling my hands out to catch myself. My fingers brush against jeweled scales, a sharp claw. The starfire tightens around me, intensifies, lays thick on my skin like a syrup. The dragon's sense of wonder and purpose intensify, too, building toward something that I can't quite grasp—until the scales and claw beneath my fingers suddenly disappear in a brilliant spark of amber light, and the sense of joy and wonder vanish along with them. The starfire coating my skin jolts *into* me, sinking toward my bones, and I can feel something deep within me reaching toward it in return like a drowning man flailing for a lifeboat. And somehow, I know this is what I've been searching for: the energy of stars that can save my life. But even as that energy spirals into the depths of me, I recoil.

I don't want to be this. I am *Peregrine*, a person, not a destroyer, not an unmaker. I reject the energy and my identity together. With everything in me, I shove the starfire's energy away. I tear it from my bones, peel it off my skin, fling it out and up.

The starfire surrounding me begins to dissipate. I see wisps of the world through it like a clearing fog: a knifelike emerald shard lodged in midair where the dragon's back leg was a moment ago. A dark bronze hand outstretched, fingers slick with red blood. My sister's eyes widening with an impossible alchemy of relief and horror as her gaze meets mine.

The shard falls to the ground with a delicate tinkling sound.

I understand then what's happened: she saw me enveloped by starfire and she leapt to my defense, as she always does. The Star Slayer had killed a dragon with a piece of shale and now so has she.

The Star Slayer has slain one of my kin, and now so has she.

A terrible sound claws its way out of my throat. *My kin.* It was my kin that uncreated Z's mother. My kin that erased the Albergian town. My kin that tore through the sky three days ago and waged war on humankind.

An immense *BOOM* shreds the air: two falling slabs of shale, colliding with each other and splintering into a billion billion pieces. I crane my neck and watch them start to fall toward me. *I should do something*, I think distantly, but my mind feels like it's being torn apart by a hurricane and it's all I can do to hold it together.

A hand closes over my arm. I look up. Anthem's eyes—blank with horror, dark with shock—meet mine. "*Run!*" she screams, and drags me toward the embassy. I stumble to my feet. I'm disoriented, dizzy, weak. I'm no longer glowing, which is a good thing, because there are dozens of other people also running for the embassy, one of the few solid structures in the settlement that can protect us from the falling shale. We pass Chessie, still splayed against the wall, eyes closed even as her fingers twitch weakly.

I skid to a stop. *Leave her, leave her,* clamors a voice deep within me, and I know it could be a forgivable sin, leaving her behind as I sprint with my sister toward safety. If I try to drag her inside too, it could mean the death of us both. And...she's seen what I am. She saw me glow. Once she wakes up, she'll say so to anyone who'll listen, and there are a lot of people—including the military—who will listen.

But I have just found out I was born—hatched? Oh, gods—a dragon and I need to prove to myself that that's not what I am. I'm not a killer. I don't leave people behind, not even when it would benefit me. *Especially* when it would benefit me.

I tear myself away from Anthem and lunge toward Chessie. I yank her up by the arms, shove my shoulder into her chest, and pull back. Her weight slouches awkwardly over my shoulder. Crashing sounds around us like the world's loudest hailstorm as more shards begin to hit the ground. One aquamarine-shaded piece slices across my arm, and another bites into my forehead. I stagger toward the entry. People jostle me from all sides, pushing and shoving and screaming as they all try to fit through the doorway at once. This place was designed to be a shelter in case of emergency, but emergencies always have casualties, and several people in the crowd fall beneath the increasing rain of shards before they can squeeze inside. Several more massive booms rend the settlement: shale towers crashing into each other in midair and fracturing into deadly pieces.

Chessie's weight starts to slide off. I grapple awkwardly to try to keep ahold of her. Someone—Anthem—grabs her slouching torso and heaves it up. "Go, go!" she shouts at me, and together we hobble-run toward the entry.

Five steps away. Four. Three. Someone elbows me hard in the side. Someone else punches me in the ear. Daggers of shale crash to the earth all around me. Lines of pain open on my back, my arms, my shoulders.

Two steps. One. Then we're in the doorway—just as the bulk of the shards rain down like hellfire. We tumble together deeper into the entry and then curl up, plastering our hands to our ears to block out the thunder of it. It lasts maybe a minute, coming in surges and lags as more of the towers crash and break, until at last it's quiet.

I slowly lower my hands from my ears. I'm still breathing. I genuinely have no idea how I'm still breathing. Anthem is huddled next to me, her own hands still clapped over her ears, eyes tightly shut and tears leaking steadily down her cheeks, her lips moving as she whispers something over and over that I can't make out.

I push myself to my feet. People are milling around the large waiting area, crying and frantically stabbing at their watches, trying to get a call out to loved ones. Several of them head for the door to join the rescue effort or check if their homes survived. Officials in the blue-and-green uniforms of the Ancient Isle are moving through the crowd with lightspeed efficiency, toting boxes full of equipment—flat slabs of plastic with simple straps screwed to them, I see when they get closer. The people nearest the door snatch them up and strap them on their feet like snowshoes. One of the officials thrusts a pair at me and another at Anthem, who finally opens her eyes. "Rescue protocols are being enacted," the official shouts. "Military relief hovercraft are on their way. Anyone who's dead or injured too badly to survive, leave them. Wounded can be taken to the overflow tents on the west side for triage. The worldwide shelter-in-place order is still active and the soldiers will be imposing it with force if necessary once they arrive. So *do not* head for the docks." Then the woman moves on, shouting the same information to the next group.

Her words ring in my ears. *Military hovercraft.* I can't get caught by them here. Even if no one other than Chessie saw me glow, saw me survive starfire, I'll still be trapped once the soldiers reach the docks and enforce the shutdown. I will either be found out—which means I'll be killed or experimented on or imprisoned—or I'll die starving for starlight far from the hole in the sky. And what if they find out Anthem killed the dragon? She'll have a warrant out on her the same as Rick does. What would they be willing to do to her, to get the intel they need to save the world from dragons?

"We have to go," I tell Anthem, and she just nods mutely. I don't mention *where* we will go, because there is only one option that doesn't equal certain death, but it still means being trapped in a tin can underwater with an acting captain who wants me dead—and, because of course I can't leave Chessie behind for the military to find either, I'll also be trapped with a girl who can tell him exactly what I am as soon as she regains consciousness.

All of those will have to be worries for later. For now, I need to focus on immediate needs, both for the sake of survival and to keep my mind from absolutely imploding. I spot rows of canvas-and-plastic gurneys being brought out from supply closets for the wounded, and grab one. We quickly strap Chessie on it and step out into the settlement. I don't think about how dull and bland it looks now without the amber light of the dragon, don't think about the hateful sky staring blankly down, don't think about the low buzz of the hovercraft in the distance. I push away images the starfire trying to sink into me as Anthem killed the dragon. I keep my focus on sliding the plastic slabs strapped to my feet across the heaps of knifelike shale that have covered everything here in deadly, jeweled debris.

Our earlier spying trip didn't take us too far into the settlement, and even though Anthem and I are both injured and carrying an unconscious girl, we make it to the docks just as the first hovercraft buzzes to a landing at the special pad next to where the market used to be. Panting with effort and panic, I scan the docks for *The Shitty Clunker.* There—its hatch is closed, its rope untied from the pier, and it's starting to pull away toward deeper waters where it can dive.

"Damn it," Anthem shouts. She drops her end of the gurney and hurtles down the dock, leaping the widening gap to the ladder and scrambling up it. She pounds on the hatch. "LET US IN!" she bellows. She waves frantically at me. Dragging the gurney like a sledge, I hurry down the dock as fast as I can toward her. The sub has paused, the ladder not getting any further away but not returning either. As I near, the hatch cracks open.

"Is Dad with you?" Lexie shouts out at us. She looks *livid*. If she's already onboard, she must've taken off for the sub—and, she'd probably hoped, for her father—the second she saw the dragon. Which means she definitely didn't see what happened to me. I won't have to worry about her, then, at least.

"No, but we've got Chessie and she's hurt bad, we have to take her with us," Anthem pants back. "Come help us."

Lexie is already shaking her head. "Drop her and get up here. Z says we've got thirty seconds before he seals the hatch remotely and leaves everyone behind even though Dad's still out there somewhere. Z won't wait even for him, and I can't go back because they'll arrest me on sight as Dad's 'accomplice'." She stabs a finger at the hovercraft that are now spewing out soldiers and rescue workers.

I reach the end of the dock. "Lexie, please, help us." I unstrap Chessie from the gurney as I eye the dozen more hovercrafts that are descending now. "We can't just leave her."

"When she wakes up she can send that vid out to her military contacts and get your dad off the hook," Anthem adds. "But only if she's safe and alive."

My gaze jolts to my sister. Alarm and betrayal clench a fist around me. We *cannot* let that vid get out. We can't let Chessie tell everyone how to kill star dragons. My dismay is just as immediate and visceral as it was when Lexie first told me there was a way to slay them, but this time it's quickly following by a surge of nausea as I realize what the feeling is: my instinct to protect my own kind.

Anthem is looking back at me, her jaw clenched, her brow furrowed, her eyes tight. *Play along,* her expression says. But something fractured inside me when I saw that emerald shard and her hand bleeding from throwing it, and even though I don't blame her for what she did—I *don't*, I can't, it would be so wrong of me to blame her—I still can't quite summon that instinctive, unquestioning faith in her that used to feel so natural. But regardless, we have to deal with the most immediate concern of getting Chessie onboard, and that means playing along for now. I nod tightly.

Lexie grimaces and curses a few more times but jumps down to help me finagle Chessie toward Anthem, who is waiting a few steps up the ladder. Together we awkwardly shove the unconscious girl up to the tower deck, dangle her even more awkwardly through the hatch, and finally lower her to the floor inside the sub. The second we do, the hatch above us snaps closed with a foreboding *clunk*. "Diving in approximately two minutes, the second we're in deep enough waters," snaps Z's sharp voice over the speakers—and suddenly, everything in me is ignited. A jumble of emotion roars through me, too tangled up to name. I was helpless when Lexie revealed who the real Star Slayer was. I was helpless when I dove into starfire to save my sister, helpless when she killed the dragon for my sake. But I'm not helpless now.

Without a word, I bend down and strip Chessie's watch off her wrist, then turn and stride through the corridor toward the control room.

Z owes me answers, and I will get them from him one way or another.

Chapter Eleven

My steps snap against the metal grating of the floor. My fingers leave bloodstains on the watch as I open the message screen and locate the Star Slayer recording. When I yank open the hatch to the control room, Indy bounds out to greet me and then skids to a stop when she notices my injuries and my attitude. I wordlessly point her down the hall to where Anthem and the other two girls are and then step over the threshold, yanking the porthole door shut behind me.

Z is sitting in his hoverchair in front of a panel of screens, sliding his fingers deftly over them. He turns his head when he sees me and then his eyes widen and he whirls his hoverchair all the way around. "Holy hell," he says, "you look like utter shit."

I'm too angry to register the alarm and concern in his voice or the haggard lines at the corners of his eyes. I feel like a bottle of pop that's been shaken too hard and now all that ugliness is bursting out of me. I want to punch him. I want to haul him up and shake him and make him answer for what he's done, for *everything* that's happened to me, even though I know he's not responsible for most of it. The anger churning within me trips an alarm in my mind—I have a genuine desire to commit violence, and if I carry it out surely it will mean I'm capable of carrying out all the terrible violent thoughts I've ever had—and I force myself to stop, keeping a few feet of distance between the two of us. I fling the watch at him. Surprised, he doesn't raise his hands in time to catch it and it thunks into his chest, leaving a bloody smear on his shirt from the stains on the screen.

"Is it true?" I demand, arms taut at my sides, hands fisted and shaking.

He narrows his eyes and carefully picks up the watch. "You'll have to be more specific."

"The video," I snarl.

He glances at the screen. It's paused on the shot of him, hollow eyes and outstretched arm, hand bleeding from the gash where he gripped the shale. That same hand is still bandaged now, cupping the watch as he registers what he's looking at. His features go still. His eyes go blank. Then, inch by inch, that haunted look drags itself back over his expression. He glances up at me, his gaze hard and guarded now. "Seems like the video speaks for itself."

"*Don't play games with me!*" I bellow. "Is it true, or not? Are you the real Star Slayer? Did you—did you—" I gesture sharply at the watch and manage to finish, "do that?"

He snaps the watch back at me and it thumps into my breastbone hard. I don't catch it. It falls to the floor with a tinny *clink*. "I am the Star Slayer and I killed the Starfall dragon," he says flatly: a statement of fact, a recitation. "It murdered my mother. I returned the favor. If you want to thank me for it, now would be the time."

"Thank you?" I say, incredulous. "*Thank you?*"

One corner of his mouth turns up in his typical smirk, but it's humorless, empty. "You're welcome."

It's too much. I lunge forward and punch him. He's expecting it, though, and ducks his head out of the way at the same time that he grabs me by the shirt collar and flings me sideways. My fist lands hard on the side of the hoverchair with a metallic ringing noise and a burst of pain. Instinctively, I jerk my elbow back as I fall and feel it crunch into Z's jaw.

I tumble into the side of a desk full of screens. Before I can get up, a screwdriver whizzes inches past my ear and impales itself in the panel. Sparks fly and the screens buzz and blink off.

"Stay down," Z snarls. The storage compartment in his chair is hanging open and he's already got another tool—a heavy wrench—in his hand.

"What are you going to do?" I demand. "Kill me?" My voice breaks then, though, and I duck my head before he can see the emotion playing across my face.

There's a long silence. "If you're pissed that I haven't told the military how to kill the other dragons yet, you can shove your righteous indignation right up your ass," he snarls at last. "I have a mission to finish and neither you nor the military is going to stop me. Do you think I'm playing around? Did you think we were friends, that I would tell you all my secrets and we'd sail off into the coral together?" He's shouting now. "I've got news for you, Peregrine goddamned Kent: you are worth absolutely *nothing* to me, and if you get between me and what I'm trying to do, I won't hesitate to remove you in whatever way is necessary. Now. Get the hell out of my control room."

I look up. I'm expecting to see anger on his face, but it's not rage that's twisting his features. It's pain. His mouth is heavy with it, his eyes tight, every feature limned with grief. And there, at the corner of his mouth, is a trickle of blood where I hit him. He doesn't seem to notice it, but suddenly I can't notice anything *else*.

I hit him. I made him bleed. Never mind that he clearly won the fight—what there was of it—and could easily bash me upside the head with that wrench right now if he wanted to. I still did what I did, and

I can't take it back, and now I will know forever exactly what I am capable of. Shame is a bitter syrup seeping down my throat.

I grab the watch. I stand up. And I get the hell out of his control room.

"Where do you think you're going?" he demands when I'm halfway out the door.

I pause and glance back. "Away," I say shortly, but he shakes his head—a single jerk of a motion that speaks of anger on a tight leash.

"What you heard me say was 'get the hell out of my control room.' What I meant was 'get the hell to the brig.' You're a mutineer now, jackass." He slings a forearm over his mouth and it comes away smeared with blood. "And I don't have time for that sort of shit at the moment."

The brig. I absolutely cannot go to the brig. Even if he only intends to let me stew there overnight, Chessie could wake up at any moment and spill everything she saw. Z could deliver me straight to the military wrapped up in a nice little bow or just skewer me with one of his precious screwdrivers then and there without me having any chance to run or hide or fight back, if I could even bring myself to fight him again.

I raise my hands and back away, alarmed. "I'm not a mutineer, I'm not trying to take over the ship," I start, but he cuts me off.

"I'm the captain now—" He chokes off, then inhales tightly and goes on more firmly, the edges of each word sharp enough to cut. "I am the captain now, which means I decide what is and isn't mutiny. You're lucky I'm in a hurry, else I'd toss you off at the nearest glacier and leave you to freeze to death. Now, move."

I scramble backwards through the door, turning to search wildly for Anthem or even Lexie, but everyone must've gone to the bunkroom or the med bay because there's no one in sight. The sub shudders and groans as it begins the dive that Z must've already pro-grammed in. I couldn't get off the sub now even if I wanted to.

"Are you gonna make this harder than it has to be?" Z demands from behind me.

I hesitate, jaw clenched, blood oozing in slow rivulets over one eye from the injury on my forehead. I swipe it away with the back of my hand as I try to think. My choices are few. I can go to the brig quietly and pray that Z lets me go—and that we make landfall—before Chessie wakes up. Or I can shout for Anthem and let this situation potentially escalate even further out of control, because my sister has already proven what she's willing to do for my sake. The whole ugly scene plays out in my head: a confrontation, more violence, and then either Anthem and I will both end up in the brig, or else Anthem will incapacitate Z—the only person who knows how to operate *The Shitty Clunker* and get us to Albergia.

An exhale shudders out of me and my shoulders slump. "Okay," I say. "Okay. I'll go."

He gestures down an adjacent hall with the wrench that's still in his hand, and I move through it with him following silently behind me. I realize I'm limping about two minutes into the trip but it's not until I reach the brig—a single cell containing nothing but a cot and a toilet behind a screen—that I discover I have bits of shale embedded in my shoes and probably my feet. I can feel the pain in a distant way but it has yet to break past the layers of shock that are preventing me from feeling it fully. I'm numb when I step into the cell and the door clanks shut behind me. Z presses his thumb to a pad next to the door and the lock engages with a *snick*. And then I am officially trapped.

He sticks his hand through the bars. "Watch," he snaps out.

I look at him blankly. "Watch what?"

He gestures impatiently at my wrist. "Give me your watch, asshole," he says, enunciating each word clearly.

I clap a hand over it protectively. "No, you can't—I have to contact my parents, I have to—" *see if Chessie's video has already gone live,* I almost say, but manage to cut off the words before I blurt them out. Any information I have that he doesn't is potential leverage now.

He gives me a long once-over and his harsh expression wavers just a touch. I wonder how pitiful and strung-out I must look, that he feels sorry for me even as he tosses me in ship-jail. "There's no signal while we're down here anyway," he says, still impatient, "and I'll give it back once I'm sure you're not going to do anything stupid."

"Like what? What could I possibly do?" I demand, stepping forward and wrapping my hands around the bars. "I'm not going to tell anyone who you are, I swear it. All I want is to get to Albergia."

He doesn't answer, just reaches up and unbuckles my watch with efficient movements and then turns back toward the door. "I've got to go deal with the brand-new stowaway you decided to haul aboard without my permission *yet again*," he says over his shoulder, "but when I'm done with that, I'll be back, and then you and I are going to have a conversation."

There is nothing about that sentence that doesn't sound ominous, and I have plenty of time to mentally dissect it—and everything else that's happened to me—once he's gone and there's nothing to do but panic.

I sink onto the cot and into my compulsions. Like a doomed mouse in a booby-trapped maze, I hunt frantically for any tidbit or detail that might reassure me, might prove that I'm still a good person, that I'm not capable of violence. But any way I look at it, I am one of the creatures that have been destroying the planet city by city, and that smear of blood on Z's face? *I* put it there, because I was angry and *I wanted to.* I inhale a shuddering breath as my vision blurs. I know logically that punching one jerk does not make me a raving murderer, but it doesn't matter. Anger is anger. Violence is violence. If I'm capable of a little I must be capable of more.

And now I might have starfire. A weapon I can never disarm. A force of destruction I can never, ever make safe.

Images flood in, one after the other, queued up by my burgeoning panic attack. Indy looking at me with terror rather than devotion. Anthem impaled on shale, a sapphire blade hatching from her chest. Chessie's head split open like a ripe melon. I wanted to hurt Z, so I did, and I want Chessie gone now, and there is one sure way to make her disappear. I don't *think* I could ever do such a thing, but I'm suddenly, fiercely glad for the bars separating me from the rest of the crew. I remember thinking that people might lock me away if they could see what was in my head, and now I *am* locked away, and maybe...maybe it's the best thing for everyone after all. The thought should be comforting but it's wrenching instead.

A loud huffing noise snaps me out of my thoughts, and then something warm and wet enthusiastically snuffles my arm through the bars. I jump and make an undignified sound and whirl around to see Indy. Her muzzle is pressed through the bars as far as she can push it and her eyes are bright, excited. The image from a moment ago blinks through my mind again—her looking at me in terror—and sickness lurches through me. "Hey, girl," I manage anyway, because I can't bear to ignore her. I can't make myself pet her either, though.

Something clinks outside and then Anthem turns the corner, glances into the brig, and spots me and Indy. Her whole body seems to go loose and taut all at once, like a puppet held up by only a few tight strings. She presses a hand to her face. "Oh, thank the gods," she says shakily. "Good girl, Indy. You found him." She drops her hand, glances around to make sure we're alone, and then strides over to my cell. I back up a few feet, out of reach, but her arm snakes through the bars and she grabs my sleeve and reels me back in.

I try to disentangle myself from her grip as my panic starts to intensify again. I can't be near her. I can't be near anyone. I can't control my glow—what if I can't control my starfire, either? What if I accidentally blast her out of existence? "Anthem, wait, you don't understand—" I try, but she's merciless, grabbing my collar with her other hand now and yanking harder.

"Shut up," she hisses. "Come here so we can talk. I don't know if there are any recording devices in here so be quiet, would you?"

But I can't bear it. I'm so glad she's here, and so terrified she's here, and it's just too much. I tear myself free—leaving a shred of my shirt sleeve dangling from her hand in the process—and fling myself to the far end of the cell. "You have to go," I tell her. "You have to leave me."

A sudden fury lights her expression from the inside out like a bonfire roaring to life. "*Stop telling me to leave you,*" she says through gritted teeth, every word seething like it wants to personally reach out and strangle me.

"I'm trying to protect you!" I must be shouting now; my throat is raw. I'm too upset to register volume.

She wads up the bit of shirt sleeve in her hand and hurls it at me. It flutters to the floor next to my foot. "Stop trying to protect me and listen to me!" she says. "*It's you!*"

With a jolt, I recognize the words, the way her mouth frames them, the terrible, lost look in her eyes when she says them. This is what she was whispering when we were taking shelter in the embassy. *It's you.* A creeping sense of premonition crawls up my spine. "What?" I say cautiously.

She swallows. Her hands fist. When she speaks again, her voice wavers. "I killed the dragon."

I wince. "I know—" I start, not wanting to relive the moment again, but she slashes a hand through the air to shut me up.

"I killed the dragon," she repeats, "and when I did, I was...I was *connected* to it for a moment. In the second it took to die, I sensed everything it was feeling, everything it was thinking." Her voice cracks and she shudders but then goes on, wrapping anger and urgency around her words like plaster to hold them together. "I didn't understand a lot of it—it was so alien—but I saw why they're here on this planet, why they're uncreating everything. Per, it's you. I don't know why but they're all searching for *you*."

The air around me congeals. I struggle to breathe through it. "What?" I say, but the word doesn't make it out, just the ghost of a shape in my mouth.

Anthem wraps her hands around the bars. Her knuckles pale with her grip. "They're not here to kill humans," she says. "Or at least, that's just collateral damage. This isn't a war—it's a rescue mission. They came here to save you."

I stare at her. The pieces of the story come together in my mind. A dragon trapped beneath a sealed sky, the survivor of an ancient war. A millennium later, the Barrier finally starts to weaken—or maybe the dragons have been out there on the other side all this time, clawing at it, blasting it, tearing at it until it wears thin. They break through. They land on the planet. They search for me—for my dragon self—and uncreate anything that gets in their way.

My kin are literally tearing apart the world to save me.

Chapter Twelve

I choke in a breath. Bile rises in my throat and I spin around, tearing across the cell just in time to make it to the little toilet behind the screen and throw up everything in my stomach.

It's all my fault. All the deaths, all the people and families and whole damn cities wiped out of existence, it's because of me. And yeah, there's vindication in knowing that I was right—that the star dragons aren't naturally violent, that they've got a reason for what they're doing—but the horror of it looms so much larger. If I wasn't here, they wouldn't be either. I remember the terrified looks on my parents' faces when they saw the massive blue dragon arcing beneath the Barrier, remember the look on Z's face when he asked what his mother's name was. I throw up again.

Anthem is saying something. I don't listen, because it takes every bit of my energy to keep myself from spiraling up out of my body, just completely disconnecting and losing control. I know that can't actually happen but what I know has absolutely no bearing on what I feel in this moment—or most moments for that matter—and it seems like a very long time before I manage to get myself under control enough to tune in to what Anthem is saying.

"—stop freaking out and *get over here* and tell me *why* they're trying to rescue you! I only have a few more minutes before Lexie gets suspicious, I told her Indy needed to stretch her legs, but pretty soon she'll figure out I was tracking you down and then Z might figure it out too, and I don't know if he's cool with you having visitors—"

I wipe off my mouth and step shakily out from behind the screen that shields the bathroom area. "Why are you still here?" I croak. "You have to go. Talk Z into surfacing wherever we are and get off. Paddle back to the shales if you have to, wait for Mom and Dad there." Earlier, I couldn't imagine leaving her in such a dangerous place. Now it seems like the safest place in the world compared to anywhere near me.

She gives me a look. It's not an angry look this time, just a long-suffering, annoyed one that does its damnedest to communicate how very stupid I am for asking such an obvious question. She doesn't understand. I don't want to make her understand, but I have to. Before I can chicken out, I face her and speak all in a rush.

"I'm a dragon. Okay? That's why they're looking for me. That's why I have the dreams, that's why I have the light." I wave a hand in front of myself and make it shine, and Anthem inhales sharply and winces away. I'm grateful and miserable all at once. "I am a dragon," I tell her, "and they want to rescue me before I die of starlight starvation."

I can't look at her right now so I look down at my hand instead. At the thin blue glow that threads through my skin, through my identity, through this body that is mine and was never mine, and shows me for what I am: otherworldly.

Anthem has been silent for too long. I dare to glance up. Her face is very still; she's trying very hard not to show an emotion on it. "You saw something when the dragon died too," she guesses, her voice level but also frayed ever so slightly with the strain of being level.

"Not when it died. When I was in the starfire." I curl my fingers in over my palm. "The dragon was trying to give me its energy. That's why it breathed starfire at me—not to uncreate me, but to lend me some of its light. And in the process it...I don't know, unlocked the rest of my dream. It showed me who I was. What I am. I was a dragon trapped down here when the Barrier was created and I've been slowly dying ever since. Then a decade ago I used the last of my energy to make...me. This body. My seven-year-old self. Because apparently some dragons can create stuff, not just destroy it. And then I stuck my own soul into this human body like—like filling in a donut. I'm a dragon-filled donut, Anthem." A hysterical laugh bubbles up and tears blur my vision at the same time. I have never felt so utterly hopeless, so completely lost. My whole life long I never knew myself at all.

Anthem stares at me. She swallows once, then again. She tilts her head back and stares up at the ceiling.

"What are you doing?" I ask, my voice quavering.

"Giving myself a moment to freak out in semi-privacy."

My misery deepens. Anthem is scared of me again. "I can...I can go back over..." I motion at the toilet area behind the screen.

"Do not move," she orders me. "I'll be with you in a sec."

Several long minutes pass in silence. Indy, who has been trying to pounce on the shadows cast by my light, gives up when I extinguish it and flops down to pant. I do my best to not think about anything at all, which works about as well as it ever does, which is to say it doesn't.

Finally, Anthem tilts her head back down. Her expression is triumphant, which is so jarring it takes me a long second to hear what she's saying: "You're not a dragon."

I inhale sharply, hope struggling to rise within me. Has she figured something out? Uncovered some clue I missed? "What do you mean?"

"The dragons are tricking you. Or infecting you. That's what's happening here."

I want her to be right so badly, but I know, I *know*, she's wrong. I shake my head wordlessly.

"No, I'm right," she insists, even as her voice wobbles on the verge of something that sounds an awful lot like panic. She lifts her chin, squaring herself against the emotion, and speaks more firmly: "You're my brother. Not a dragon. Them tricking you, infecting you somehow with the light and dreams, it makes sense."

My vision goes blurry. I realize belatedly that I'm crying, unable to hold back all my gut-wrenching, identity-shattering emotions any longer. "No," I say, my voice warped and cracked like a piece of old wood. The hope that was struggling in my chest dies stillborn, and when I speak again, my voice is thick and toneless. "Me being a dragon makes sense. It's the only thing that makes sense. I don't have memories from before the glint mine because I didn't exist as a human before the glint mine. I shine like a dragon and have memories of being a dragon because I am a dragon. What's that old saying—the simplest answer is usually the right one? This is the simplest answer, Anthem."

"That is NOT a simple answer!" The volume of her voice goes up with every word, her emotional control visibly fraying.

"You have to see me for what I am." I'm begging her now, and gods, it hurts—but she's got to understand, got to accept this so she knows what's at risk.

She's shaking her head again but it's more vehement now, a motion so sharp it's almost violent. "I do see you for what you are! YOU. ARE. MY. BROTHER."

I cover my face with my hands. "I never was," I say. "I never was."

There's silence for a long moment with only the sound of Indy's panting to fill the quiet. Then Anthem breaks. She does it without any noise, no fanfare, no crying or fleeing. I sense it even though my eyes are covered, feel the truth swallowing her up the same way it did me.

Now she'll go. She has to.

But when I finally drop my hands, she's still standing there. Her gaze is distant, her face is wan and pale and tear-streaked, but she hasn't moved. After a second she blinks and her eyes focus on mine. We look at each other like we've never met before, which is a brand-new and horrible thing that feels like a railroad spike being driven through my heart. I open my mouth.

"I'm not leaving you," she says, beating me to the punch. Her voice is as thick and toneless and certain as mine was a moment ago.

"I'm not—"

Her voice goes from toneless to heated in a snap. "Don't you dare say you're not my brother. Don't you ever say that again. I don't care if you really are a goddamned glowing space lizard, you're still my brother, and I'm *not* going to abandon you."

My heart stutters with an impossible relief. I fend the feeling off. "Anthem. You can't fix this. Please—you have to go, you have to be safe. I'm *not safe.*"

The last traces of her thousand-mile gaze flake away like a shed skin. Her lips peel back, a frightening and feral expression I've never seen on her before. "Stop that!" she says in a voice that's almost a physical blow. "Just *stop it,* Per. What exactly is it you think of me? That I'm a helpless little girl who needs protecting? Because I wasn't that even when we *were* kids. Who punched the bullies when they threatened you? Who covered for you when you skipped class to run off to that planetarium every week? Who *stole a car* and drove into a mob to rescue you at Starfall? If you care about me at all, if you still think of me as your sister, then *goddamn it,* stop trying to protect me and let me help you!"

She's breathing hard by the time she's done, eyes alight with fury, hands fisted—and I realize that the pressure behind these words has been building up for a long time now. She's thought of saying this, or something like this, to me before. When I kept my dreams a secret from her. When I begged her to go along with my compulsions even though I knew they made things worse. I've been protecting her for so long, and I never once realized that it made her feel small, not safe. I was too wrapped up in how *I* felt, what *I* feared, to even notice things like that.

I inhale shakily and rub my face. My hands come away wet. I blow out a long breath, gathering both my thoughts and my courage for what I've got to say next. It's hard, so hard—not because I don't want to trust Anthem, but because I don't trust *myself*. But she's asking for me to take a leap of faith anyway, and for her, I have to do it. Even if it means risking her safety. Even if it means I might hurt her. Because if this has come down to a gamble between Anthem's capability and my own fears, I will put my money on her every time even though it absolutely terrifies me.

"I'm sorry," I tell her. "You are..." I shake my head, still trying to gather the right words, the words I truly mean. They come to me: "The most capable, intimidating, badass sister in the history of sisters, and I'm sorry I made you feel like anything less than that. So." I swallow hard and force the words out even though they feel unnatural, even though I'm scared as hell. "Help me. Please stay with me, and please help me."

I expect to feel cowardly for asking such a thing of her, but I don't. This does not feel like an act of cowardice. It feels like...trust. It feels like faith.

She nods, takes a breath, and some of her ferocity fades. "Apology accepted. Now. Stop being an absolute dumbass, if you can manage that, and tell me what we're going to do next—because I need a plan, Per. Something to do. If you don't give me something to do I'm going to absolutely fall apart in like the next twenty seconds."

I rub my forehead and wipe my face off, trying to think clearly. "I need...I need to get to the sky. I need to get in the starlight before my dragon body dies."

"Yep, got it, check." She nods and then pauses, her eyes slowly narrowing. "But then what?"

"Then...I don't die?"

"But which one of your bodies lives? Dragon Per, or human Per? Or will you be able to, like, switch between them at will? How does that work?"

I stare at her wordlessly.

"You don't know," she surmises.

"I don't know."

"So you might absorb starlight and then your human body will drop dead while your soul goes back into...into..." She can't quite say it.

And there is a brand-new nightmare I hadn't even considered yet: that I, Peregrine Kent, human, will vanish entirely and whatever creature I was before will subsume me. I don't want that. Oh, I do not want that. But I don't think I have a choice either way. "I have to get to the sky." I force the words out. "I have to communicate with the dragons, and I think I have to be a dragon myself to do that. I tried to talk to the one back in the shales but I couldn't get through to it, couldn't understand it."

"Why in the name of the gods do you care whether you can talk to the dragons?" Anthem demands.

The answer seems obvious. "So I can tell them to stop attacking us. So I can save everyone."

She scoffs loudly, angrily. "Jumping straight to saving the world, of course. You've got a real savior complex, you know that? You always talk about me not being able to fix everything, and here you are—"

"Anthem," I say, my voice mangled by emotion. "This isn't what I want. I want to stay me. Desperately. But I can't let everyone else die for what I want."

She takes one deep breath and then another. Her shoulders hunch. "I know. I know. I'm sorry. I just—I can't imagine you…" She shudders and looks away.

"Maybe there's a way for me to stay—stay human," I tell her, stumbling over the words but putting every ounce of hope I still possess into them. "If there is, I swear to you, I will do everything in my power to find it. But I *have* to get the dragons to stop, Anthem. They're killing people trying to find me, and now with Chessie's video maybe going live soon, people will know how to kill dragons too—it's going to be all-out war, and both sides are going to lose. I think I'm the only one who might be able to stop it."

Her jaw works but she doesn't respond for a long moment. Finally, she takes a deep breath. "Yeah," she says at last. "Okay. I get that. So for now at least, our plan is to get you to the sky. We can do that. We just have to break it down into smaller goals, right? So the first goal would be getting you out of that cell, then getting us off the sub before Chessie wakes up." She pauses then and squints at me. "Why are you even in here, by the way? When I asked Z what happened to you all he would say was that 'mutineers get locked in the brig.' I had to search nearly the entire sub to figure out where the brig even was."

I remember the smear of blood on Z's face and wince, covering my eyes with my hands. "I punched him," I confess, my voice muffled and my heart twisting at the memory. "Well, I tried to punch him, and then I actually elbowed him in the jaw, then he threw me on the floor and nearly stabbed me with a screwdriver and threatened to bludgeon me with a wrench."

Anthem makes a noise. It takes me a moment to realize it's choked-off laughter.

I lower my hands and stare at her, incredulous. "I made him bleed," I say, in case I wasn't clear enough earlier, but she only snorts messily and coughs on another laugh.

"Good for you," she says after a second, her expression a tiny bit lighter than before.

"You know what I mean," I bite out. "You know how I feel."

"Yeah, I do. Are you afraid that because you punched Z, you might what, go around murdering everyone else now? Per, don't take this the wrong way, but you're a giant helpless marshmallow. That light freaks me out and I'm still trying to process the whole dragon thing, but I know you, and you wouldn't truly hurt—" She cuts off then, swallowing the end of her sentence as her shoulders go rigid. "Wait. Wait. You think you have starfire. Don't you? That's why you're so freaked out."

I laugh, hearing the note of hysteria in my own voice. "I am freaked out for many, many reasons, but yeah. Yeah, I think I have starfire."

"Why?" she challenges, her voice like a bulldozer, barreling right over the end of my own sentence—but she's a little bit more worried now, I can see it in the way she holds herself. "Because you 'sensed it' in your dream, or whatever? Come on, Per, you can't possibly put so much weight on—"

"I saw it, okay?" I say loudly, before I can chicken out. "In my dream, I saw what would happen if my dragon body dies. It'll explode into starfire, just like every other dragon when they die. Which means I must have the capability to make starfire. To uncreate as well as create. If that's true, that's a deadly weapon I can never disarm."

Her eyebrows slam down into their attack positions, but then she pauses and her expression slowly turns speculative. "Wait. If that's true...maybe that could actually be helpful."

I throw my arms up, exasperated now. "In what way is a deadly dragon power that I may not be able to control *helpful*?"

"Well," she says, "it could get you out of that cell."

I curl my hands up and then stuff them under my arms for good measure. "I am not going to try summoning starfire on purpose." I feel panicky just thinking about it. Some childish part of me stubbornly believes that as long as I don't see any physical proof of what I am, I can still pretend I'm just me, no more dangerous than I ever was. But if I summon a weapon like that and actually *use* it...I will never be me again. Just like I would never be me again if I pulled the trigger on a gun or programmed *The Shitty Clunker* to shoot a torpedo or touched a knife while intentionally thinking about the color red. *None of those things makes you inherently evil,* whispers the logical part of my mind, but it's been drowned out long since.

Agitated, Anthem tugs at her hair, shaking out the dust and coiling it a messy knot at the back of her head. "Fine. Then we've got to figure out some other way to get Z to let you out of there before Chessie wakes up. He seems to like you, maybe you could just sweet-talk him into letting you go?"

I roll my eyes. "Yes, throwing someone in ship-jail is always a declaration of affection."

"You didn't see him afterwards," Anthem says. "He's upset. I think he genuinely likes you. He wouldn't get so worked up about it if he didn't." She steps over to the lock on the cell door and prods at it, scowling when it beeps recalcitrantly at her.

"Even if that's true, it's still not going to be easy. He said he won't let me get between him and his mission in Albergia, which has to be—what, killing more dragons? Guarding the breach? Finding a way to *seal* the breach?"

A bit of her old fire snaps into her eyes. "I won't let you die," she says. "And I won't let him kill any more dragons." That's not really a thing she can promise at this point, but something loosens in my chest just a little anyway at her declaration, at her willingness to defend the dragons for my sake.

"What about Chessie?" I dare to ask, trying to make sure I'm feeling the appropriate amount of concern for her well-being and not just hoping she may have conveniently gone fully comatose while I've been locked up. "What's...her status?"

"Still unconscious but Lexie thinks she's stable and should wake up soon." My anxiety burrows deeper. The lock buzzes at Anthem and she growls back at it before throwing her hands up with a huff. "There's no way I can get this thing open. As far as I can tell it's keyed to Z's prints."

I start to pace, remember with a jolt of pain that I still have sharp bits of shale in my feet, and sit down on the cot. "Do you think you might be able to talk him into letting me go?"

She twists her mouth into a skeptical shape. "Doubt it. We're not super fond of each other."

"What about Lexie, then? Her dad is still out there and I know she wants to help him. Maybe we could try to strike some sort of deal with her. She helps me get out, and we could...I don't know, help her find Rick?"

"We don't know how long that would take or if it's even possible, and we can't delay getting you to the breach," Anthem argues. "We don't know how much time you have left. And anyway, I doubt Z would listen to Lexie any more than he'd listen to me or you. Indy probably has the best shot of us all at softening him up, and *she* can be bought off with bacon grease." Indy's tail whaps faintly against the floor as she hears her name before she dozes back off.

"So basically, there's nothing we can do to spring me until Z feels like letting me loose?"

Anthem bites her lip. "I know you don't want to try it, but starfire might really be our only option," she says hesitantly.

An instant shock of fear jolts through me. "No."

"Do you want to get out of there and save the world, or not?" she argues. "I'm not suggesting you hurt anyone. Just try to uncreate the lock. The worst thing that can happen is you fail because you don't have starfire after all, in which case you'd at least be able to stop freaking out about it."

I gape at her. "Anthem, we're on a submarine. A literal metal can submerged thousands of feet below the ocean surface, with several atmospheres' worth of pressure waiting to rip us apart and/or drown us if it cracks. And you want me to try summoning starfire for the first time ever onboard? Failing is *not* the worst thing that can happen here."

"But what if it does work?" she demands. "What if it's the only way to get you out of that cell safely?"

"It wouldn't matter anyway!" I shoot back. "We're still trapped down here, whether I'm in a cell or not." I ease off my shoes and start examining my injured feet, mostly to distract myself so I don't spiral into another panic attack.

"Maybe we could sabotage the sub, then? Not so badly that anyone gets hurt," she hastens to add, "just enough to force Z to surface for repairs or something. Then he'd probably be happy to toss us off at whatever port is nearest, and we can figure out how to get the rest of the way to Albergia from there."

I pause and reluctantly let myself turn the idea over in my head. "The glint tank," I say slowly. "I helped Z fix it last night. I could try to figure out how to sabotage it—maybe disconnect it or have it spring an internal leak. Z would have to stop off somewhere to get more fuel."

"Isn't glint corrosive? We don't want it eating a hole through the hull."

"It is, but I don't think it's as bad as like, straight acid or anything," I say, recalling the speckled chemical burns across Z's shoulder. "As far as I can tell I don't think it'll burn through metal. And *The Shitty Clunker* is made of Pioneer Ship metal, which has to be even stronger than regular submarine materials."

Anthem nods, looking more herself with every passing moment now that she's got a plan to focus her. "Okay, that could work. Where would Z be likely to stop though? Where does he buy his glint?"

Remembering, I wince. "He doesn't buy it. He steals it from military facilities."

"What?" she yelps, and I have to shush her in case Z might be on his way back to interrogate me already. "Per, that is literally *the last place* we want you to be," she hisses, slightly more quietly.

"Didn't you say that no one would suspect me as long as I act chill?"

"That was before I found out you were *a literal human-shaped dragon*," she snaps back through gritted teeth, but then hesitates. "It's not a good plan, but it might be our only option. Unless you want me to see if I can figure out how to drug Chessie to stay asleep, or something?"

I shake my head quickly. Anthem has no medical knowledge of the sort that would help her drug a person, and that sort of thing is way too easy to mess up in a potentially fatal way. Plus they may not even have that kind of medical supplies on board anyway.

Her eyebrows scrunch together. "You could just tell me about the glint tank and I could try to sabotage it myself? That way you wouldn't have to try using starfire to escape first."

I rub my forehead, trying to convince myself that that's an option, but it's just not. Oh, gods, how did I get myself into this mess? "That's not a good idea," I say, having to force the words out. "You've never even seen the glint tank before and if you do something wrong, it could leak glint *outside* the sub instead of *inside*, and that'll attract the eels."

She gives me a sympathetic look. I pretend not to see it, hunching my shoulders in like I'm a turtle trying to retreat into its shell.

"Okay," she says. "You escape, do the sabotage, then hide till we surface. Then you, me, and Indy all get off together and slink out of whatever military facility Z is stealing from. Then we figure out how to get the rest of the way to Albergia."

I try to think of any other option, anything at all that doesn't involve me using starfire, but come up empty. This feels like the only available option and I can't just sit around and do nothing while the world gets uncreated and more dragons get slain. "Okay," I agree at last, even though Anthem's idea is less of a plan and more a set of aspirational goals.

"I'll go keep an eye on Chessie in the meantime. If she wakes up, I'll try to distract her or strike a deal with her or something."

I inhale deeply. "I'll have to wait till tonight to try...I'll have to wait till tonight." I tear off a piece of my shirt to wrap around one of the worst gashes on my foot, mostly to have something to occupy myself with. "That way the control room is more likely to be empty." Unless Z has trouble sleeping again and finds some other unnecessary repair work to do. But I'll have to cross that bridge when and if I come to it.

Anthem nods and turns toward the door. "Love you, big bro," she says after a moment's hesitation. It's not something we usually say out loud to each other—at least, not in any language that isn't shoves and insults—and the words hit me like a sucker punch. It feels like she's saying goodbye just in case something goes wrong, which is pretty likely.

I swallow down my dread and manage to say, "Love you too, little sis," before she exits and leaves me alone again.

Exhaustion hits me then, less like a wave and more like I've been dunked into a washing machine intent on not only drowning me but making it as tumultuous an experience as possible. Sleep is a vicious current dragging me under. I manage to stagger to my cot and think, *I'm probably going into some sort of shock*—and then I blink into sudden and complete unconsciousness.

Chapter Thirteen

Waking up is much harder than falling asleep. My dream clings to me and tries to pull me back under, and it's a slow, groggy, hand-over-hand slog toward wakefulness before I finally drag my eyelids open and sit up. *Clunk.* Something slides off my chest and hits the floor with a solid, sullen noise. I have to stare at it for a few seconds before I realize it's a first aid kit. I have to stare a few more seconds after that before I realize that the weird square of green that's blocking part of my vision is in fact a sticky note that's been plastered to my forehead. I peel it off—it takes a few eyebrow hairs with it in the process—and squint at the messily scrawled words: *Be back later for that conversation.*

Z was here. He unlocked my cell, came inside while I was asleep and vulnerable, and...stuck a note on my forehead. And left a med kit. I spend the next minute or so trying to ascertain what that might mean before I think to get up and check the lock just in case he's decided to let me out, but no such luck. It's still shut fast. I return to the cot, open the med kit, and start patching up my many luckily-mostly-minor injuries, moving slowly due to the phantom-limb ache that feels like it's hollowing out all my bones. I have to tear the medical tape with my teeth since Z apparently removed the scissors and the multi-use nail clippers from the kit, a fact which is somehow both comforting and annoying. What did he think I was going to do, file down the bars? Scissor my way to freedom? At the same time, I'm glad I don't have to deal with the extra anxiety of deciding whether or not medical scissors meet my potentially-weaponizable criteria.

When I'm done seeing to my injuries, I have nothing else to delay me from uncreating the lock.

I don't have my watch to tell me the time—and even if I did, I don't have the power to spare for turning it on—but my own bone-deep grogginess tells me it's somewhere around the middle of the night. I told Anthem I would have to wait till tonight and now it's tonight. I hoped our circumstances might've changed by now, that Chessie might've woke up with amnesia or Z would turn out not to be immune to Anthem's sweet-talk after all, but nothing appears to have changed. Time is still running out and I am still my own best option at escape.

I approach the lock with trepidation. I shake my hands out and roll my shoulders like attempting to summon a quasi-magical death ray is something I have to warm up for. I pace—carefully, since my feet are bandaged inside my sliced-up shoes—and try to talk myself into just *doing the thing.* I don't have time to analyze this, to play out every step, to make a thousand Plan Bs. There's barely a Plan A, and this is it. Either I summon starfire and learn once and for all that I'm basically a living weapon, or I find out I can't summon it, in which case I'll be relieved but doomed. Along with the entire rest of the planet.

I stop pacing and hold my hands out in front of me, fingers fully spread, though I've got my back to the door and my upper body hunched over my hands out of habit just in case. *Shine,* I think. The dim glow takes a heartbeat longer than last time to appear and when it does it's a slow fade-up rather than immediate. Somewhere out there, my original body is a few hours closer to death.

Grimly, I let the glow fade and step over to the cell door. I reach through the bars and cup them over the lock, and then pause. I don't want to do this. I cannot even express how much I don't want to do this. My brain already plays host to a full-time horror show; it doesn't need any extra ammunition to fuel my nightmares or intrusive thoughts or even my regular old normal-person fears. Right now I can pretend that hiding knives and avoiding the word "murder" makes me safe for everyone around me, but if I succeed in doing this that's all gone.

My hands are still cupped around the lock, though right now I'm not doing anything to it. I close my eyes and grit my teeth. I try to summon up all my courage, try to scrape together the bits of bravery hiding in the corners of my soul. It feels like pulling teeth. Every bit of me says that doing this crosses a line—that there'll be no going back from it, that it will end catastrophically somehow, that I will be helpless against the urge to use my powers for evil. This choice feels like inviting disaster, like willingly picking up a meat cleaver and tucking it into my pocket. I can't do this. *I can't do this.*

A spark of anger flares then. This is likely the only way to save myself, and probably Anthem by extension too—not to mention all of humanity, if I really can get the dragons to stop attacking. I have to do this. I *will* do this, even if it means never knowing for sure that the people I care about are safe from me. The thought carries with it a sudden, utterly unexpected surge of relief. I've been fighting my fears for so long, spending so much energy trying to prove them completely and definitely false, that to acknowledge them and then blow right past them anyway like this makes me feel oddly...powerful.

Okay. I'm gonna do it. I blow out a long, slow breath and open my eyes, about to try to will starfire into my hands—when I realize that the brig has gone dark. I blink a few times, thinking something's clouding my vision, but then realize that a faint blue light is emanating from the corridor. I inhale sharply. Blue light—that means an eel. I shudder. I don't think starfire makes a sound, but I should probably wait till it's gone to try it just in case.

Then I remember that the monster protocol automatically shuts off power to everything in the sub. Lights, computers...and locks. Experimentally, I withdraw my hands and nudge the cell door with my foot.

It opens.

Disbelieving, I edge out into the main part of the brig. Nothing happens. I shut the door behind me. The lock doesn't click. I'm free. I'm free, and I didn't even have to use starfire.

Thank you, I pray fervently to any deity that might be listening, and then I quietly hurry into the corridor toward the control room to commit some sabotage.

I tiptoe down the sub's halls but it's hardly necessary; there's no signs of wakefulness or even life anywhere nearby. At that realization, I have the sudden jarring thought that maybe it's finally happened; maybe I somehow sleep-walked through *The Shitty Clunker* and killed everyone without even being conscious of it. My heart rate accelerates and I pause right there in the junction that leads to the control room, glancing carefully over myself for signs of blood or struggle—of which, of course, there are *many*, seeing as I recently survived a catastrophe in the settlement. The blood on me is all dried but that's not comforting, because I have no idea either how long blood takes to dry or how long I've been asleep. Maybe I should stop by the bunkroom and stick my head in and check to make sure everyone is still breathing. Or go to the med bay—though I have no idea where that is, but if Anthem found one map of the sub, surely there must be another one posted somewhere—and check on Chessie and Anthem.

I try to tell myself that I'm being ridiculous, but it doesn't help. I know all too well how ridiculous my fears are. That only makes things worse, because I know I should be able to quash the clamor in my head like it's nothing, and the fact that I can't means there must be something fundamentally wrong with me. And what if that fundamental screwed-up something also makes me more prone to violence than regular people? And round and round it goes.

That snap of anger kindles in me again—I will not let my OCD mess this up—and gives me just enough juice to force my feet onward toward the control room rather than turning toward the bunkroom. I pin my thoughts in place and focus all my effort on remembering what the readout screen on the glint tank looked like and where the pipe Z had been messing with was beneath it. I think I know where I could unscrew it to get it to leak the way I want it to, and once all the ship's fuel is a puddle on the floor, I'm betting it'll be too contaminated to use again without some sort of purification process *The Shitty Clunker* likely won't have onboard. The trick now is I'll have to do it all in complete silence lest I accidentally alert whatever monster is near. Maybe, I reflect, I should wait until the lights come back on to start my work, just to be safe.

Anxiety dogs me with every step. It takes everything I've got to keep going. When I reach the control room and find it dark and silent, I don't even have the brain space to breathe out another thankful prayer as I hurry over to the glint tank's closet and very quietly ease its door open—nor do I have the clarity of mind to realize there's an oddly-shaped shadow in the far corner until Z's chair slides smoothly out from behind a desk and he says, "Nice night for a little light sabotage," in a hard, tight voice.

I whirl around and leap backwards at the same time. The door to the glint tank clangs loudly against the wall at the movement and I suck in a breath, my gaze jerking to the giant window, waiting to see a vast sleek shape outlined in veins of electricity.

"Oh, that," Z says, jutting his chin at the window. "Don't worry about that."

I jerk my gaze back to him. "*Don't worry about it?*" I hiss as quietly as I can, and make frantic motions toward the dangling blue lightbulb and then the window that hopefully communicate how very, very much we should be worried. But he just smiles—a thin, gleaming line of teeth that's all challenge and no mirth—and raises a hand to his armrest and snaps a tiny lever on its side. The main lights in the control room flick on, nearly blinding me. I flinch and the door at my back clangs again. I curse under my breath, looking from the window to the hallway to the lever on Z's chair that controls the power. If the monster out there is as attracted to noise and light as the last one, his actions are as good as putting out a flashing neon *restaurant open now* sign. What is he playing at? Would he really gamble with all our lives like this? And if he is, what could he possibly hope to gain from this little confrontation that could outweigh the risk of getting zapped or eaten?

But he just looks back at me coolly, his eyes an odd mixture of hollow and challenging and cautious, and that's when I realize that there is no eel, and this isn't a confrontation.

It's an ambush.

Heat rises through me, anger and fear braided together. I edge forward across the room toward him. He tracks me, turns his head to keep me in his sights, but he doesn't move when I stop in front of him and reach toward his armrest and flick that little lever he snapped a minute ago.

The main lights go out. The single blue light flicks back on

"You bastard," I say, with great feeling.

He raises that eyebrow, mocking as always, but there's something darker behind it now. He's stiller than he usually is. "I wanted to see what you'd do," he says. "Lights go out, monster alert comes on, lock opens. You can learn a lot about a guy from what he does with an opportunity like that."

My breath shudders in my chest as my mind begins to spiral. I'm caught—*again*—with no good options. "And what is it you've learned about me?" I ask, hoping to buy time. Maybe Anthem heard the clang of the door, and if she did, then she's already on her way. Maybe she'll have ideas better than what I've got, which is nothing. I can't—won't—hurt Z again. I have nowhere to run, and he knows the hiding places in this sub better than me. Without the head start I'd planned for, he'll find me easily, stick me right back in the brig with a better lock this time—or do something even worse.

"I learned that your first move was to attempt to sabotage my boat," Z says, tilting his head ever so slightly, his gaze still locked on mine, "and also, that you glow."

He says it in the same tone he used when he said *I am the Star Slayer and I killed the Starfall dragon*: matter-of-fact, a dare thrown in my face. Except this is a dare I have no way to answer. Gravity strips itself out from under me. Panic is a drumbeat beneath my skin. "What," I manage to rasp out as I take a long, slow step backwards.

He holds up something. A watch with its rubber strap half disintegrated. *My* watch. He swipes his thumb across the screen then double-taps it. "After I got back from tossing you in the brig," he says, "I talked to your sister about what happened when you were all ashore. She was unsurprisingly evasive. Well, I say evasive—I suppose a better descriptor might be 'actively confrontational', or perhaps 'a heartbeat away from kicking me in the balls.' Naturally I wondered what had her so worked up. I tried talking to Lexie but she only saw the dragon for a second before she took off—smart girl—and of course I can't interrogate Chessie in her current condition. But then I realized I didn't have to interrogate her. An enterprising girl like Chessie, there's no way her first thought wasn't getting footage of the event for her cast. So I tinkered around with her watch a little to see what she might've recorded."

I take another step backwards. I drag in a breath of air that feels too heavy for my lungs. My skin feels too tight, like something is clawing at it from the inside. I need to run. I need to *run*.

But Z is still talking, and his voice makes it too hard for me to think, to plan my escape. "She keeps most of her stuff locked away behind an automatic firewall, so that was a bust," he shrugs one shoulder and I manage to exhale, "but I *was* able to access the recording function and sync it to the screens in here. I thought, hey, let's see what sort of subterfuge bird boy gets up to when he's all on his lonesome. So when I came into the brig and found you asleep, I left her watch hidden there and set to record. Want to see what happened next?"

Without waiting for an answer, he double-taps the watch again and one of the large screens mounted on the walls blinks on. It shows a still shot of me from an extreme low angle. It's just my torso and the lower half of my face in the picture, but that's more than enough to condemn me, because in the shot I'm hunched over my hands and they're glowing with a dim but undeniably otherworldly blue light.

My gaze crashes back to Z's. There's a fire in his eyes now, an anger that sparks electric and tries to lock me in place with its current, but I tear myself free and spin away. I'm halfway across the room and headed toward the door when Z careens forward and cuts off my escape. I skid to a stop and pivot, searching wildly for any other exit. He knows what I am. The Star Slayer knows what I am. I'm as good as dead and what'll happen to Anthem then? What'll happen to the whole damn *world*, if I really am the only shot at both the humans' and dragons' survival?

The glint tank. It's the only way. I have no chance at stealth now, but maybe I can still sabotage the sub enough to force it to surface. It'll disrupt whatever Z's plans for me are, in any case. I scramble backwards toward the closet. He follows, implacable. My back slams into the tank and the readout monitor digs into my spine. Before I can try to reach for any pipes, though, Z leans forward and grabs my hand, slams it into his armrest, and pins it there with an iron grip on my wrist.

"How did you do it?" he demands, and his voice is ice and steel and shale, all brittle edges that crack further with each word. "Did you get ahold of a scale or a fang or something? Are you some military lackey sent along to insinuate yourself into my crew, to get intel from me on how to kill dragons?" He's examining my hand as he speaks, shoving up what's left of my sleeve to check my wrist for—what? Then I process his words and realize that he thinks I'm a *spy*. I laugh out loud, the sound wild and high in my own ears. He hears it and lifts his head again, his eyes narrow now. I snap my mouth shut but it's too late. "Not a spy," he realizes, still keeping my hand pinned. "And you're not carrying any sort of device that could make..." He makes a sharp gesture at the screen and finishes, "That. So how the hell did you do it? And why are you really trying to get to Albergia? Who are you?"

He's got me backed into a literal corner. The glint tank is uncomfortably warm against my back and the hinges of the closet door scrape against my arm. There's nowhere I can go without having to leap over him. My only slim shot at survival is sabotaging the tank—and potentially burning us both, since I can't even see what I'm doing—and keeping him distracted enough that he can't tell what's happening until it's too late.

I angle myself so that the opening along the side of the glint tank is behind me. I feel something poking me in the shoulder—a rusty knob next to a sheared-off elbow pipe. That's how I was planning to do my sabotage, by messing with that. Maybe I can still manage it. I keep my eyes on Z. If glint sprays out now, I should take the brunt of the damage, but at least I'll be ready for it. Once he sees the leak he'll move, either to get out of the way or to try and stop me, and that's when I can run.

His eyebrows furrow as he follows my movement and I can see him starting to form a question about what I think I'm doing, so to distract him I speak the question that's been digging barbs into me ever since I learned who he was.

"Did you like it?" I ask. My voice is frayed, cracking. "When you killed it. Did you think you were a hero? Did you enjoy watching it die?"

His expression goes blank. His shoulders stiffen. His grip on my wrist tightens painfully, the small bones there grinding against each other. "You're not angry because I haven't told everyone how to kill the other dragons, are you?" he asks. "You're angry that *I* killed a dragon."

My free hand is sliding around the side of the tank. I find the knob.

"Yeah," I say recklessly. "I am angry. I'm angry that you killed a dragon. I'm angry that you lied to me. I'm angry that I *like* you, that I ever liked you, that I ever thought we could be allies. You think you killed a monster and maybe you're right, but you're a monster too, Z."

His eyes are wide now and his lips are parted like he's going to say something, but he doesn't say a word, just sits there and stares at me. He's still got me pinned but from the look on his face he's pinned too. It makes something in me go suddenly uncertain, hesitant.

This isn't how I thought the Star Slayer would look when I accused him of monstrosity for being true to his name. My fingers are still wrapped tight around the knob but I don't try to turn it yet. I wonder suddenly exactly what Z did feel when he killed the dragon. It didn't look like joy or triumph on his face in the recording when he did it. It looked like shock, and grief, and horror. When I first saw it I thought those emotions were for his mother—but he was *avenging* his mother. Wouldn't he have been relieved, at the very least?

My hesitation stretches into one second and then another. "Z?" I dare to say finally.

He doesn't get a chance to answer, because at that very moment the lights all go out again and the dangling monster-alert bulb washes the room in grim blue hues.

I don't look at the window. A moment ago I thought to distract him, and not it seems he's trying to do the same to me—but that won't work twice. "Stop messing around," I say sharply.

His gaze cuts to the window and then back at me. "That's not me," he says, his whisper so quiet I practically have to read his lips.

Deep in the curtains of dark water beyond the sub something flickers purple, like jagged heat lightning in the desert. The floor shivers beneath us, sending the dangling bulb swaying, and it fizzes and brightens with a sudden burst of extra power. Swinging shadows streak Z's face with shades of steel and cobalt. He slides a hand over his armrest and nudges the switch that powers his chair off. It settles quietly to the floor.

He's mouthing something. I squint, and this time I do have to read his lips to make out the words: *shit, shit, shit.* He's looking at the window again, and I realize this is my chance. He's distracted. His hoverchair is off. If I cause the leak now—and shove him out of range of the glint before I run—then he won't be able to chase me for at least a minute or two, and the lead time might be enough to make the difference between survival and capture. I can't hesitate any longer. I try to turn the knob.

Nothing happens.

I apply more force. Still nothing. It's rusted shut all the way, completely useless. Panic starts to rise in my gut, high and cold and achingly bright like I've swallowed a winter sunrise. The sensation crawls upward until it eddies into my shoulder and then careens, all at once, down my arm and into my hand—

And I am holding starfire.

I jerk my gaze over my shoulder and see that my hand is wreathed with beautiful pearlescent flames that hum like a heartbeat. There was something digging into my palm a moment ago. I can still feel the echoes of the feeling but I can't remember what it was, what the shape of the pipe was that I was trying to sabotage. It's gone now. It never existed.

Because I have used starfire on it.

Terror rings in my head like deafness, so great a sensation that it omits absolutely everything else. Something sickeningly warm and wet like blood washes over my wrist in a torrent. Glint. I yank my arm away and throw it out to catch myself against the door. When I plant my hand on it, it evaporates beneath my touch and I can no longer remember what it looked like, what color it was or if it was rough or smooth under my touch.

I did it. I have uncreated something. I have starfire. And it feels *wrong*. The certainty of it, the knowledge that this is not what I'm meant for, slips into my marrow and hardens there. It doesn't feel like fear. Or rather, I am definitely still very terrified of what I've just done, but there's also this—a quiet stillness from deep in my soul that whispers, *no.*

The pressure around my other wrist releases. Z has let me go. I look up, afraid to see myself reflected in his eyes, but he's not looking at me in fear. He's staring at the starfire in my hand like he's hypnotized, like a deer caught in headlights, and then he leans forward and lifts his fingers toward my palm. He's going to touch me. Touch the starfire. And the second he does, he'll be obliterated, wiped from existence just like the door and the pipe, just like his mother. And me...I'll be a murderer. I will be everything I ever feared.

A wave of nausea hits me and I clench my hands. *No,* I think to myself, agreeing with that whisper from the deepest part of me, *I'm not this,* and the starfire dissipates. When it vanishes, so does my strength. My vision goes spotty and my knees give out and I hit the ground. Turning on my glow doesn't sap my energy but apparently using starfire does. Something warm soaks through at my knees: the whitish gleam of glint spreading in a puddle. And now that I've stopped blocking the torrential leak from the pipe with my back, it's spraying like a firehose straight at Z.

His expression snaps instantly from hypnosis to awareness. He grabs ahold of the armrests and uses that leverage to throw himself forward and sideways, out of the hoverchair and at me, grabbing me by my arm—which is still wet with glint—and toppling us both away from the closet. In the same movement he rolls back up to sitting with his back pressed against the wall. His head snaps into the panel behind him, his skull cracking against the metal. His legs are scraping weakly against the floor and his head is thrown back and his expression is screwed up with agony and the effort of staying silent in the midst of it. He's gripping one hand with the other. In the wildly-swinging blue light I make out the glint that's coating his hand and arm from where he grabbed me to shove me out of the way, and I also see the hissing trail of smoke wisping up from it where it's eating through his skin. The smell of burning flesh clogs my nostrils.

I am on the floor a foot or so away from him. The back and side of my shirt is covered in glint and so is the hand and arm I used to uncreate the pipe. But there's no smoke wisping up from my injuries, no injuries for them to wisp up from in the first place. The glint isn't burning me.

The sub shudders again, harder this time. The lightbulb fizzes brighter and then pops. Glass shards tinkle across the floor. The only illumination now are the zips of purple lightning drawing slowly closer. There are at least two monsters out there: whichever one is nudging us, and the purple one that's headed our way now. But I can't keep my focus on the window because Z is right next to me with his eyes screwed tightly shut, the tendons in his neck painfully taut as he writhes against the wall, biting back a scream—and it's my fault.

He knocked me out of the way. He thought I was going to be burned by the glint and he took me with him when he rolled away, to save me. Even though he saw the starfire. Even though he has to at least have some idea of what I am now.

I don't bother looking at the door. I already know I'm not going that way, not now. As the sub shudders and jolts again—harder this time, enough to knock me sideways—I start to move toward Z. My arm is still coated in glint like a second skin and I start to wipe it off on my shirt but as soon as I think of doing that, the glint all streams down to my hand at once and puddles beneath my fingers on the floor. I stare at it, then experimentally touch it again. It moves back up my hand and coats it. The glint is...responding to me?

A high metallic shrieking scrapes across the hull, sending me and Z both sliding sideways. He's in too much pain to catch himself so I reach out and grab his arm to keep him from skidding into a desk. I don't realize that I've grabbed his injured hand until he makes a sharp, cut-off noise of pain and flinches away from me. Hurriedly, I snatch my hand back—and all of the glint that was eating its way through his arm goes with it.

He inhales and blinks his eyes open. Violet lightning flashes outside, close enough now for me to make out the long, dark shape of the second, closer eel. The strobing light illuminates the shock on Z's face as he stares down at his hand. It's red and raw and pocked with bloody blisters, and his sleeve is nothing but a ragged, crispy lace, but the glint is gone. Or more accurately, it's coating *my* hand now, a shining white gauntlet of acid that should be eating through my skin but is instead not doing anything at all.

Z looks up. His gaze lands first on my left hand, which is coated with glint, then my right, which was holding starfire a moment ago and now is splayed empty on the floor. Then he looks at me. Just like the dragon did back in the settlement, just like Chessie when she caught a glimpse of my shine, Z looks at me and he *sees me*. I can't make out his expression in the dim, distant flares of lightning and I wish I could. I want to know if he's looking at me in horror. If he's scrambling to think of any nearby weapons he can use against me.

The sub jerks again, but this time the power flickers and then returns fully, dousing the room in bright light. Some automatic mechanism in the porthole door whirs to life, pulling the door shut with a loud clunk and turning the wheel to engage the lock. I'm now officially trapped in the control room. Multiple flashing lights strobe urgently across the many screens in the nearby panels. The closest one has an error dialog box open that reads *Automatic emergency override activated.* Another one says *Hull contact in sector two.*

The dark shape of the nearest eel moves sinuously, starting to flicker with zips of yellow lightning. Its scales and slick black skin flash past the window and then slow. An eye the size of my torso slides into view. It's black from edge to edge, tiny bolts of electricity darting across it like blood veins. There's no intelligence in it like I saw in the dragon's eyes. This is a creature of hunger, a mindless monster. And if I don't do something right now it's going to kill us all.

Very slowly, I stand up. I edge over to the light switches on the wall and flick them. Nothing happens. The power is stuck on.

The eye outside twitches slightly with the eel's movement. The hull of the sub clanks and groans and everything inside starts to list sideways, more slowly this time, as if *The Shitty Clunker* no longer has the power to right itself after a blow. Which it probably doesn't. Because I drained all its fuel.

I look at the liquid on the floor. The firehose spray has lessened to a dribble now. The pearlescent liquid is spreading over the floor like oil in a hot pan, smoke and a terrible smell rising up wherever it touches the metal. It apparently won't burn me, but I don't truly know what damage it might do to the metal, and it will definitely hurt Z when it reaches him. He's dragging himself up to sit in a chair that's anchored in front of one of the panels right now, stabbing at the screen with his good hand, his expression tight with pain and emotion. He doesn't look at me when he says, "We're in lockdown. Automatic emergency feature. I can't turn the power off without killing the life support and ballast system too."

I have to try twice before I can respond. "And…if that happens we'll sink?"

"Like a rock. Straight to the sea floor, where the eel nests are."

I try to breathe normally, but I'm close to hyperventilating at this point for so many reasons. "What about the others? Anthem?"

He waves a hand, still busy jabbing at the screen in front of him. "They're as safe as we are. Meaning not safe at all. They'll be trapped in whatever section of the sub they were in when the emergency protocols went online. If one sector floods, the others will stay intact for at least a few minutes, but the more water we take on the faster we sink."

"How much water have we taken on so far?"

"None, but that won't last long," he replies grimly.

The yellow-lightning eel vanishes from the window and the violet one swims closer. The sub jerks again, much more violently this time, and a loud metallic screech deafens me. I stumble hard as *The Shitty Clunker* rolls fully on its side, sending anything not bolted down flying toward the walls. Including the glint. It splashes and laps across the floor, sizzling loudly. Z is holding on tight to the panel in front of him even though he's being slung sideways by the force of the roll, and glint hisses and smokes where it splashes on his pants' hem.

"Do something!" I shout.

He frees one hand long enough to slam it against the screen in front of him, which fizzes and flickers uselessly at the impact. "*You* do something," he shouts back at me, his voice strained over the groan of metal and the clanging of all the loose objects hitting the wall. "You're the one with starfire!"

I freeze. Our eyes connect for the barest jolt of a moment. That look is in his eyes again—the *seeing me*. There's something else too, though, a dare or maybe a question, something I can't read.

"I won't use it," I say, my voice hoarse and barely audible. "Never again."

"Oh, *now* you're back to being a pacifist?" he yells. The sub slowly rolls back upright and he stops stabbing at the screen, instead yanking his hands through his hair. He flinches and gasps in pain then as he remembers his injured arm. He pulls it away from his head and looks down at it: streaked with rivulets of blood, pocked with painful-looking blisters. He grimaces and drops it back to his lap, then reaches over to another nearby screen with his good hand and jabs at that a few times. Whatever he sees there must not be good news, because the fight goes out of him all at once. He slumps forward and closes his eyes for a second and a terrible despair slackens his features. Then he reaches beneath the panel in front of him and pulls something loose—an ancient handheld radio. He presses the button on its side.

"Mayday," he says into it, his voice toneless and cracking. "Mayday, mayday. This is *The Shitty Clunker* requesting assistance. We are being attacked by two eels and we're under emergency power. We've got maybe twenty minutes of life support left. Please assist. Repeat, please assist." He waits, staring fixedly down at the little device in his hand. I don't understand the despair on his face until the radio crackles to life.

"*Shitty Clunker, this is Corporal Nguyen of Albergian mining fa-cility number five-oh-one. We acknowledge your mayday but cannot respond.*"

My breath catches. I'm hanging on to the porthole door's wheel now to anchor myself in place, and at the realization that the Albergian military are the ones who'll decide all our fates, my grip tightens to the point of pain.

Z grits his teeth and holds down the button to speak again. "We have five souls onboard including several minors. Please assist, dammit!"

Five souls? I'm surprised at the low number for a moment before I remember that almost the entire crew disembarked at the shales. The only people left now are him, Anthem, Chessie, Lexie, and...me. He's still counting me as a soul. I don't have time to register my reaction to that before Corporal Nguyen responds again. "*We cannot assist. With the fuel rationing in place we are currently only responding to military emergencies. May the gods save you."*

Z swears vigorously and colorfully, though he doesn't hold down the button to broadcast that. When he's done, he takes a breath and closes his eyes again, then says: "I am..." He exhales jaggedly. "I am Captain Zeus Colton, AWOL navy student."

Silence for a moment, then the voice speaks again, less detached now: *"And you think that makes us want to rescue you?"*

With the fatalistic grimace of a man using his last Hail-Mary, Z replies, "How about this, then? The Star Slayer is onboard."

The radio crackles. *"Verify,"* the corporal orders in a sharp voice.

Z lets out a sharp whip-crack of a laugh and then swipes at the screen in front of him. The video that Chessie had downloaded appears on the large screens around the room. He taps at his panel and the video loops through at a fast speed and then zooms backwards, dialog boxes and command screens blipping up and then away quicker than I'm able to make out what he's doing. Another swipe of Z's hand and the video vanishes with a chirp, uploaded to the military to prove Z's identity. "Verified," Z snaps into the radio, adding "you bastards" in a vicious tone, this time before he lifts his finger off the button.

There's eight long seconds of silence, during which one of the eels brushes against the sub again, making the lights brighten and buzz. Several bulbs pop from the sudden influx of power and two more screens hatch dialog boxes with dire warnings of hull contacts and weakened junctures. Then Corporal Nguyen's staticky voice comes over the radio again. *"An escort is on its way."*

Z doesn't respond, only gently slides the radio back into its holder beneath the panel. Then he just sits and stares down at the screen without focusing on it. After another long moment, he finally lifts his good hand and flips a switch on the panel. The intercom overhead crackles to life, broadcasting his voice throughout the sub.

"This is Z," he says tonelessly. "Everyone, prepare to be boarded."

Chapter Fourteen

I stare at Z across the widening slick of glint. Slate-gray tendrils of foul smoke rise from it and puddle over the ceiling until the light turns hazy and brown.

"How long do we have?" I ask hoarsely. My mind feels sticky and slow. I can't think of anything except what the Albergian military—the people who saw their comrades wiped from existence by dragons—will do once they realize what I am. I don't even bother trying to think of arguments to make to them. There's no way I'll ever be able to convince them to let me go. They'll never believe that I want to save the world as much as they do. And Anthem. What will they do to someone who they've got to see as my accomplice? Our only shot is if I can manage to mislead them—convince them that my light and starfire is some sort of weird effect of being close to a dragon attack, or something. They'll probably still detain me and/or experiment on me, but maybe they'll let the others walk.

"A few minutes," Z says flatly, and even as he speaks I see a distant white light through the window and beyond the eels. The light splits into four pieces like a dividing cell, diverging further from each other in a diamond-point pattern until I realize they're all the lights of separate subs. The military has sent *four* subs to apprehend us. No—to apprehend the Star Slayer, because he knows how to kill dragons.

My chest feels heavy. It's hard to breathe. It's even harder to speak, but I push words out anyway. "Look. Anthem isn't guilty of anything. She didn't know about—she doesn't know anything." I fumble. "Don't implicate her in this. Please. I'll—I'll do anything. I'll help you with your mission in Albergia." Even saying the words makes me feel sick, but my sister is my first priority, and if I have to help him close the sky back up to keep her safe then so be it.

He still won't look at me, staring down at the panel in front of him. "If they get me back to their base they'll dose me with interrogation drugs and then I'll answer anything at all they feel like asking me."

My breath catches. "*If* they get you back to their base? Do we—is there another option?"

He smiles humorlessly, a sliver of teeth and resolve. "Yep. But it's not a good one."

Outside, the eels lurch away from *The Shitty Clunker*, setting us rocking in their wake as they shoot toward the other, more aggressive-looking vessels. Something launches from one of the subs and blasts through the water: a torpedo. It explodes into the violet eel's side. The creature thrashes, sending water and dark debris roiling all around it until it's no longer visible as anything but an inky cloud suspended in the water. The other eel doesn't waste a second in lunging toward the sub that shot the torpedo, crunching it between its jaws and thrashing it back and forth like a bulldog with a bone. The sub suddenly detonates then—a catastrophic hull breach, or a last-ditch self-destruct? More debris shoots through the water. I flinch as some of it dings off the hull and window. The second eel is limp now, and both it and the wreckage of the sub drift toward the seafloor somewhere far below.

And then all three of the remaining subs' lights turn directly toward us. Without wasting a second, without even bothering to try to retrieve any of the debris or investigate if there might be any survivors, they advance on us.

I turn back to Z. "Whatever the other plan is, I vote for it."

"You don't get a vote, but yes, we're doing that plan," he says, then braces his hands on the panel before him and leans forward. "Earlier, the glint responded to you, and it's not burning you now. Can you control it?"

Caught off-balance by the change in subject but eager to help him avoid the coming disaster, I nod. "I...think so?"

He waves at his hoverchair, which is being steadily eaten through by glint spatter. "Then get it off my chair so I can use it. Oh, and also, that glowing thing you did in the brig, can you do it any brighter than that?"

I hesitate for a little longer this time—he's asking me to make myself wholly vulnerable to him, to tell him the darkest secrets about me that I've only just learned myself—and he snaps his fingers with impatience. "Yes," I answer at last. "But only for a second. Bright enough to temporarily blind people." I start to feel a trickle of optimism. Maybe his plan involves neutralizing the soldiers, which is a step in the right direction, unless of course this is some sort of con to get me to out myself to the military with no interrogations needed.

Z nods, then turns on the intercom again and speaks into it as I head toward the hoverchair. "Okay, folks," he says, "this isn't gonna be fun and it's likely at least one of us is going to die violently, but we're not ending the day in the belly of a giant eel *or* with our veins pumped full of interrogation drugs, so I'm still leaning toward calling it a win. In about thirty seconds, you're gonna hear a lot of clanking when these goddamned soulless military subs latch onto us. Our system is currently in emergency lockdown so we need them to pry open our main hatch for us. Then I'm gonna do a thing, and *then* we're all going to commandeer ourselves a brand-new, ass-ugly but fully functional Albergian military submarine. Anyone got any questions?"

I'm halfway to the hoverchair at this point but stop to spin back around and stare at him. "Uh, I have *many* questions," I say, raising my hand like we're in class.

"No? Good," he says, ignoring me completely. "Then everyone, get to your battle stations. By which I mean grab the nearest pointy or blunt object and prepare to wield it at anyone who isn't us."

Outside the window, the seafloor is rising up from the murky darkness to form a sudden jutting cliff. Lights are spangled across its surface, illuminating a series of structures jutting out from the cliff's side. They're not elegant at all, the way the coral was—they look more like splinters in a wound than anything natural. The towers, or pumps, or whatever they are, are driven down into cracks in the cliff and joined together by long cables and tubes.

Z sees me looking. "Glint mining facility," he explains. "Also, probably a military base of operations. One that's full of nasty question-answering drugs and people happy to kill us all. Aren't you supposed to be cleaning my chair?"

A loud clank reverberates through the ship. Cursing, I hurriedly splash through the glint to the hoverchair and stick my hand onto it. All the glint flows toward me like a river running downstream, and my arm is coated once again. I shake it off onto the floor and then flip the switch to power the chair up so that the glint on the floor will stop eating away at it from the bottom. Z pulls a necklace out from under his shirt—some sort of small device like a key fob. He presses it and the hoverchair glides silently over to him. He slings himself out of the panel's chair and into his own seat.

"Are we going to talk about this?" I demand as I get to a spot of relatively dry floor and pull glint off my shoes before the rubber gets eaten through.

"Not if I can help it," Z says flippantly, steering over to a panel on the far wall and flicking several of its switches before swiping and tapping at the screens. He seems to be writing some sort of code or program, maybe, based on the glimpses I manage to catch.

"Z!" I shout, desperate now as a louder clanking noise makes the whole sub shiver.

He lifts his head and looks at me. His eyes are dark and grim, all traces of gallows humor wiped away. "I told you I wouldn't let anything get between me and my mission," he says, "and it turns out you, Peregrine-goddamned-Kent, *are* my mission."

I freeze in the middle of shaking glint off my hand. He's still staring at me and I'm pinned in place by that gaze, by the sudden, utter unfathomableness of him. The harsh lights gleam on his cheekbones and paint the hollows beneath his eyes in shadow. He is, all at once, an entirely alien creature. We both are.

"Z..." I manage to grate out, not sure what I'll say next, but he holds up a finger to cut me off.

He cocks his head like he's listening, and as if on cue, there's a loud groaning noise and then an echoing snap. "That'll be them forcing the main hatch. If emergency protocols still have any juice left at all, they should..." A chorus of beeping alarms erupt from his panel and he pumps a fist in triumph. A whirring noise and a soft *schnick* pulls my gaze to the porthole door, which has just unlocked itself. "The control room is now open, thanks to safety protocols for the unlikely event of an underwater rescue," he says. "I've manually set the other doors to stay locked for now. I don't think it's wise to let the others—well, mainly your sister—out just yet."

"You're going to keep her trapped?" I demand, tensing.

"I didn't say that."

"You didn't *not* say that!"

Shouting and running footsteps echo faintly from the other side of the porthole. Z doesn't look away from me. "Decision time, bird boy," he says. "Do you think you can trust me?"

I scoff, incredulous. "*No,* of course I don't trust you, but I don't exactly have another choice at the moment since you're the only one offering an option that isn't imminent death or dissection, and also if you call me 'bird boy' one more time I swear to the gods I will tell Anthem your real name is Zeus!"

He blinks and then laughs—a shockingly genuine chuckle that I've definitely never heard from him before. "He bites back again," he says in an echo of the first time we met. And then the porthole door is bursting open and five soldiers in stark white-and-gray uniforms surge into the room one after another, and the time for talking is done. The men and women don't seem to have weapons but they don't look like they need them. I'm swept off my feet by one soldier while another efficiently yanks my arms behind my back and cuffs them. I barely pay attention, craning my neck and trying to peer out the open door for any sign of Anthem. I hear barking. "Indy!" I shout, my pulse thudding as I search for her. She's a big dog and intimidating-looking, a lot like one of those old Shepherd breeds—if someone didn't know her they might think she was attacking instead of afraid. "Down! Take it easy, girl!"

"Quiet," orders one of the soldiers, a tall brown-skinned woman with a fuzz of super-short black hair. She has a thick northern Albergian accent that drags out the consonants and gives her vowels sharp corners. She glances at Z's chair and then pulls something out of the bag at her waist. A roll of some sort of thick silvery tape. She tosses it to the soldier standing next to Z. "Block those controls off," she tells him.

Indy gives a muffled howl. "That's my dog." I keep twisting, searching for her. "She won't hurt anyone, please don't—"

The soldier next to me cuffs me on the ear hard enough to knock me sideways. I hit the ground right next to Z's chair. His storage compartment is open. He flicks a gaze down to me, sees me looking at the tools inside, and mouths a word that looks an awful lot like *multitool*. Then he bellows out, "Anyone hurts that dog and I'll gut you bow to stern!"

The two nearest soldiers look at him, skepticism and then amusement twitching over their features before the professional, emotionless expressions slide back into place. While they're distracted, I struggle up to sitting and reach my shaking, bound hands into the storage compartment at my back. I have no idea why he wants the multitool, and I have no real reason to trust him, but if it's a choice between him and the military I'm gonna go with the devil I know.

I am getting a tool, not a weapon, I chant in my head as I run my hands through the mess of equipment and oddities in the compartment. By sheer luck my thumb snags on the folded shape of the multitool, which I recall with painful clarity from when I was holding it through a piece of magazine paper. Normally I wouldn't be able to touch it without panicking, but that's the beauty of being in a life-or-death catastrophe; I'm *already* panicking so hard that it doesn't make much of a difference to add a little extra anxiety. A semi-hysterical laugh bubbles up in my throat. Look at me, making therapeutic progress at the bottom of the ocean surrounded by people who want me dead. I manage to tuck the multitool into the back of my waistband and pull my shirt down over it just as the short-haired soldier yanks me back up.

An authoritative voice with a less-noticeable northern Albergian accent snaps out from the doorway. "Keep working at the interior hatches and arrest anyone you find. Ignore the dog for now, it's trapped in one of the rooms anyway." The owner of the voice, a woman with graying hair pulled back in a neat bun and a don't-screw-with-me expression plastered clearly across her face, takes in the scene with a quick and expert glance. "Jacobs, Olafdottir—you're standing in glint, make sure you stop at supply to get new boots when you're done. Ramirez, search that hoverchair. Huong and Lee, check the rest of the vessel for targets." She raps out the orders without looking to make sure they're followed, and then she levels a look at Z. "And you must be *Captain* Zeus Colton," she says, raising one eyebrow. "AKA the Star Slayer. Tell us how you killed the Starfall dragon."

I blink and tear my gaze away from the door, where I was trying to catch any sign of Anthem, and frown at the woman. Didn't Z send in that video as verification of his identity? Judging from it, they should already know how he killed it. Unless...all of that zooming and editing he did was to cut out the bit with the shale. But why would he do that?

Z tilts his head and raises one eyebrow too, a perfect mockery of her expression. "Go to hell," he says pleasantly.

The woman's expression clouds over. "Most of Albergia—your own nation, correct?—has been uncreated thanks to those creatures. We can help you make it right if you'll only tell us how."

His mocking expression collapses, replaced by something raw and genuine for just a moment. "I will make it right myself, and I don't need your help to do it."

She shakes her head, a single impatient, sharp movement. "Trust me, young Mr. Colton, having a nice, civil conversation with me right now is the easy way, and there's a very, very hard way waiting in the wings if you refuse it."

"That's *Captain* Colton to you," Z says, baring his teeth, "and I've never been big on the easy way."

One of the soldiers who'd been crouched next to the hoverchair stands up. Z's magpie-nest of tools and odds and ends are heaped in a pile on the ground and the soldier is holding the magazine article about his mom. Wordlessly, he hands it to the commanding officer. She scans it over and then glances up. "So you're not faking, you really are disabled," she says casually, though a muscle in Z's jaw tightens at the suggestion. She shrugs. "Should make it easier to detain you, at least."

"Another day, another ableist asshole," he tosses back. Then, to the soldier who's taping over the controls on the armrest: "Watch it, that one activates the torpedoes." The soldier stops what he's doing and looks up at the commander, alarmed, but she just rolls her eyes and motions at him to continue.

One of the soldiers that the commander had sent into the rest of the sub reappears. "Done surveying the vessel, ma'am. Still working on the hatches; they're all shut and locked, we can't tell how many crew are aboard. Might take us a bit to get the lay of the control room to unlock everything. None of this stuff looks standard." He sweeps the control room with a faintly disgusted look.

Z scoffs. "Damn straight it's not standard."

A frown tugs at the commanding officer's face. "See if you can find the manual overrides for the doors. I'll signal the rest of our crew to come help with the search. And pat these two down," she says as she motions to me and Z. Then she turns on her heel and strides toward the tower exit, leaving the others behind in the control room to fulfill her orders.

My shoulders tense. As much as I've been telling myself the multitool doesn't count as a weapon, they'll definitely take it away from me if they find it. Before I can do anything about it, though, Z shoves himself up to standing, his knuckles white as he grips the top of the hoverchair to hold himself steady. "Me first, bitches," he says cheerfully. "I am both disabled *and* thoroughly capable of shanking you all." His legs are even more unsteady than usual, though, and he staggers to the side, causing one soldier to swiftly reach out and grab him to hold him in place—in case he was actually going for his hypothetical shiv, I guess?—while the other roughly pats him down. While they're focused on him, I quickly slide the multitool out of my waistband and tuck it into the small hollow space between his armrest and seat cushion. They've already searched the chair, so hopefully they won't feel a need to do it again, meaning the multitool will be safe.

The soldiers finish their pat-down and shove Z back in the chair, then give me the same treatment. When they're finished one of them grabs onto the bar behind Z's shoulders—it doesn't have handles like a regular wheelchair—and pushes him forward while the other one propels me with an iron grip on my shoulder. I twist my neck around when we get to the main corridor but don't see anyone other than soldiers streaming through the halls. I can hear Indy howling frantically somewhere down the corridor to the left, though, and breathe a sigh of relief that she's okay. For now, at least.

"Hey, bird boy," Z calls to me.

"Yes, *Zeus*?" I say through gritted teeth, internally praying that whatever plan he's got, it's one that will save us before we're forced onto an enemy ship.

"How many soldiers do you count? My view's a bit obstructed."

The soldier pushing his chair forward growls, "Quiet."

I quickly scan the soldiers around me and try to tally up the ones I can hear down the other corridors. "Maybe...ten, fifteen total?" I estimate.

"Any more coming down the ladder?"

"I said quiet!" the guard snaps, louder this time, and lifts his fist but then hesitates and drops it without hitting Z.

Three soldiers are walking away from the ladder like they just came down it but no one else is behind them, so I say, "No."

"Excellent!" Z says. "In that case, do the thing now, please."

The thing—he means the glowing. He wants me to glow right now in front of half a dozen soldiers, with twice that many more waiting safely out of blinding distance down various corridors. I twist around and meet Z's gaze. His expression is serious, grave. *Do you think you can trust me?* he asked earlier, and somehow, impossibly...I think I do.

I slam my eyes shut and think, *shine.*

The blast of light is bright enough to dazzle me even with my eyes closed, and judging by the startled shouts from the soldiers around me, it's plenty bright enough to temporarily blind them too. I hear a jagged ripping noise and when I turn off the light and look up, Z has the multitool out and the plastic hand bindings are dangling from each wrist, their link sliced through. He's cut through the tape on his armrest too and peeled it back so he can access the controls again, and now his fingers are flashing across the screen there.

"What in frozen hells—" snaps out a female voice as footsteps stomp toward us from a nearby corridor. The commander's head pops into view. She takes the scene in quickly—soldiers on their knees and leaned against the walls, their eyes running with helpless tears as they rub at their faces, and Z frantically working on his screen. Then she lunges the last few steps out into our corridor and pulls something out from her vest's inside pocket.

A gun. It's small, some sort of snub-nosed, matte black pistol, and I start to fling myself away from it before I realize that if I do that, she'll have a perfect bead on Z. I freeze. Do I stay here while she runs toward me with one of the weapons I fear most, or do I distance myself from the gun and the danger I might pose if I get ahold of it and in the process leave Z unshielded?

There's no time for debate. I come to a compromise and whirl around, putting my back to the gun but staying between the commander and Z. "Whatever you're doing, finish it before I catch a bullet in the back," I say through gritted teeth.

"This is your only warning, kid, get out of the way!" the officer shouts. I grit my teeth harder and don't move.

Z presses his thumb to the screen. It chirps. He nods in satisfaction and then lifts the multitool, twirls it around his hand, and stabs its bladed end deep into the screen.

Sparks hiss out from his armrest. All the lights in the corridor blink out, and the whole sub groans and shudders. "Self-destruct armed," says a guttural and deeply scary voice from the intercom. "Torpedoes armed; kill box includes all vessels within one nautical mile. Protocol Z set for action in three minutes."

"Tell me," Z says from the darkness somewhere in front of me, "do you think you can get all your people aboard your ship, retract the underwater dock, and get one nautical mile away within the next three minutes? No? Then I should probably tell you that there's only two ways to shut down Protocol Z, and the only one that I didn't just stab is in the control room."

A moment of silence. Then, from out of the pitch blackness somewhere to our right: "You wouldn't do such a thing." But the words are threaded with an undercurrent of uncertainty.

I can't see Z's wolfish smile, but it comes through clearly in his tone when he speaks again. "I would, I assure you. I'm not going down unless I take you with me." There is absolutely zero uncertainty in his voice, and apparently the officer hears it too, because she swears and shouts for her crew and starts stumbling her way through the darkness toward the control room.

Z's chair buzzes and then a tinny thunk sounds, and he curses. "Turn the glow thing on again," he says to me, "but dim this time, just enough that I don't run into my own damn walls."

I do as ordered. "Tell me you didn't actually arm a self-destruct and torpedoes," I hiss at him in the mercurial silver-blue glow, quietly enough that the nearest still-blinded soldiers don't overhear.

He tears his gaze away from my hand—his eyes are wide, his pupils dilated, but he seems to have an iron grip on whatever reaction he has to my light now—and zips past me down the corridor. "Okay," he says flippantly, "then I didn't."

I hesitate, looking between him and the control room, where dim light from the mining facility outside is leeching in and illuminating the officer and several of her soldiers frantically messing with various panels. Then I hear Anthem shouting and a bark from Indy that sounds downright joyful, which must mean Z has opened the med bay. I hurry down the corridor and follow the sounds until I run headlong into my sister, sending us both staggering.

"Per!" she shouts, relief resonant in her voice even though her whole frame locks up for a second when she sees my glow. "Are you—what happened—Z said—" She can't seem to decide which line of interrogation to take first. Then she dares to glance down at my shining hand again and makes the connection that if she can see it then Z can too, and she moves to try to block me from his view.

"He already knows. Questions later," I say, grabbing her by the arm and taking long strides toward the tower exit, wielding my light ahead of me. "Right now we've apparently got two minutes until everything within one nautical mile of us explodes."

"*What?*"

"Torpedoes, self-destruct," I explain as quickly as possible. Z emerges from a room that must be the med bay, trying to fend off a gleeful Indy, who is dead set on climbing in his lap and licking every part of him that she can reach. Behind him is Lexie, who is yelling questions as she follows him into the corridor—until she spots my light.

A jolt of sick horror rips through me when I see the visceral terror on her face. She scrambles backward into the med bay. I lean forward to follow her, to try to reassure her, but stop myself when I realize it'll look like I'm chasing her. "Lexie, I—I can explain, I won't hurt you, I swear..."

"Jesus Christ," she breathes, and I can't tell if she's cursing or praying. "Oh, saints. Shit. Stay away!" She bumps into a table at her back and fumbles her hand across it while keeping her gaze glued on me, and comes up with what looks like a set of large tweezers.

Z pushes past me into the corridor. "Let's go," he raps out. "Lexie, you can come with us or you can stay here and try to tweeze Peregrine to death, but we're leaving right now."

"Wait," I say, turning toward the rest of the med bay, shining my weak light over the gurneys lined up against the walls. "Chessie, we have to take Chessie with us."

"She's still unconscious and we don't have time to haul her up the ladder and across an underwater docking bridge before our time runs out," Z replies, already halfway to the ladder.

I hesitate, torn. I have to get away from the military, but I need to get Chessie away from them as well, and now Lexie has seen what I can do and she could tell the officers about me, too. Unless Z wasn't bluffing and they're all about to explode. Either way, this is a nightmare. "Lexie," I try, "please, come with us, help me bring Chessie—"

"What the hell are you even talking about?" She laughs, a harsh, tearing sound, and with her skin pulled taut and bloodless over her cheekbones in the flickering, ever-weakening blue glow, she looks almost hollow. "Look, man, I have no idea what you are or—or how you're doing that, but if the military is taking this ship then I'm sticking with them. I can clear my dad's name, no thanks to any of you."

I hate the fear in her eyes when she looks at me. It's a thing with claws, with fangs, and it bites a little deeper into me with every second. I back away a step even as I try pleading with her. "You won't have any *time* to clear Rick's name! Z set the self-destruct and the torpedoes are—"

She laughs again, louder this time, almost hysterical. "There's no torpedoes! And why in the gods' names would a research vessel have a self-destruct? He's bluffing, you moron!"

I hesitate, leaning back to peer at Z, who is in the puddled darkness at the far reach of my light, near the ladder's base with Anthem and Indy. He glances back at me as the magnets on the back of his chair engage against the ladder, his expression shadowed. "And that's why I kept her locked up," he confirms. "She never did go along with my bluffs. I estimate that officer will figure out the same thing in less than thirty seconds now when the self-destruct turns out to be the dancing devil emoji I programmed a few minutes ago, so if you still feel like not getting dissected today, I recommend following me quick-like."

Of course he was bluffing. Does he ever say anything true? It doesn't matter right now, though—my choices are still him or imminent death. I step backwards into the hall and cast one last pleading look at Lexie, who glares back at me and starts feeling around on the table again, probably for a better weapon.

I don't have any other options. I have to leave her and Chessie with the officers and discover the consequences later. With an agonized curse, I turn and run toward the ladder.

Chapter Fifteen

Z is already atop the tower when Anthem and I reach it, Indy hitching a ride on his lap. His chair's magnets are moving from the tower deck to the somewhat flimsier-looking tunnel that leads straight up to the military sub that's hovering above us. The tube is jointed with accordion folds every few feet, probably so that it can extend a variety of distances for underwater rescue, and fluorescent lights are tacked onto the metal to illuminate a pair of ladders stretching upward. The whole thing is creaking and groaning like there's a gale outside.

Anthem and I hurry up the rungs. Z lingers for a moment even after his magnets are ready, one of his hands resting on the open hatch where the name signifier is painted in sloppy all-capital letters: *THE SHITTY CLUNKER.* I can't see his face from this angle but I remember his expression from the first eel attack, when he realized his ship could've been damaged. I recall the magazine article I found that night: he'd built this vessel with his mother, a woman whose name he can no longer remember. This is all he has left of her. And he's abandoning ship—why, exactly? To avoid being questioned by the military? I'm grateful he's apparently set on not telling them how to kill all my kin, and that he hasn't outed me, but I don't understand why that's worth giving up the only thing he has left of his mom.

An angry shout drifts up from the open hatch. Time is up. Z withdraws his hand and toggles a lever on his chair that makes it rise swiftly enough to pass me and Anthem on the ladders. "Get a move on!" he shouts as he whizzes by, and the grief in his voice is almost obscured.

The docking tube's metal groans and crackles even more ominously as we scramble upwards and I wonder what depth it's rated for, and whether we're past that. Between that and the shouting that boils over onto the tower deck below me when I'm about halfway up, I've got a lot of motivation to get to the military sub as fast as a person is capable of climbing a ladder. Even though I'm pretty sure none of the soldiers have guns and they wouldn't risk shooting in here even if they did, the back of my neck still prickles, waiting for a bullet to burrow between my shoulder blades. I am officially committing treason right now. Or, wait, is it still treason if the crime you're committing isn't against your own country? What would this be, then, an international incident? A crime against humanity? Unless it's only humans who can commit crimes against humanity, in which case, I probably won't qualify. I clamp down on a hysterical laugh and climb faster.

Z is waiting at the top of the ladder. Once Anthem and I haul ourselves over the edge into the new sub, he shouts down the tube, "I'll give you ten seconds to seal up before I tear this tunnel loose!" and then slams the hatch and wheels the lock shut. "One, two, three," he mutters under his breath.

Indy jumps at me and snuffles curiously at my hand, which is still glowing. I realize that the entry we're in is fully lit by fluorescents and douse my shine.

"Nine, ten," Z finishes, and fiddles with the control panel next to the hatch for a second before a loud screeching noise makes the hull shudder.

"Subaquatic dock retracted," says a smooth, pleasant feminine voice from the panel.

"Ugh," Z says, shaking his head at the panel and its voice. "Soulless. I told you."

"Better than the creepy demon-robot voice in your ship," I pant back.

"That was *my* voice, thank you very much. Modified quite thoroughly one night when I was a little too bored writing code, but still. Mine." He wheels around and zips up the corridor. Unlike *The Shitty Clunker*, this vessel is clearly not designed to be accessible, and the sides of his chair scrape and spark against the narrow walls. I have no idea where he's going but he looks like he does, and he's gotten me this far, so I follow him.

"Someone tell me what is going on or I swear I will punch one of you at random," Anthem threatens as she jogs after us. Fear saturates her expression, belying her angry tone.

"Uh," I manage as I come up behind Z, who is stuck trying to navigate his hoverchair through a small porthole, quite literally attempting to shove a square peg through a round hole. "Well, I escaped—actually it turns out Z let me escape to see what I would do? And then an eel attacked and I thought it might be my only opportunity to sabotage the ship so I did it. With...with...the only tool at my disposal." I can't make myself say it.

Z has no such problem. "With starfire," he calls over his shoulder. "He broke my goddamn glint tank *and* its goddamn door with goddamn starfire. Give me a shove, would you?"

Anthem's gaze is locked on mine. The fear is sliding from her expression into the rest of her, tightening her shoulders, curling her hands into fists. I don't know if she's afraid of me or for me or both. She cuts her gaze away from mine, pushes past, and shoves the back of Z's chair as requested. With a groan and a few sparks, it skids through to the other side, which turns out to be a control room. It's much smaller than *The Shitty Clunker's* and also much, much nicer. Everything is sleek and gleaming and understated, from the gentle curves of the black metal chairs to the grand sweep of the panoramic panel in the middle of the room.

Z breaks the moment of quiet with, "I hereby christen this vessel *The Soulless Monstrosity.*"

Anthem's brow wrinkles. She points at a plaque above her head, over the door, which reads *Albergian Navy Vessel Commodore Beta.* "I think it already has a name."

"That's a terrible name. Mine suits it much better." Z careens his chair straight into the seat in the middle of the panoramic panel, knocking it aside with a clatter. He spends a moment glancing over the controls before he finds whatever he's looking for on one of the screens and starts tapping and swiping. "Ugh, always hated these things," he mutters.

"What are you doing?" I ask.

"I can't activate any actual weapons without the commanding officer's strike code," he says shortly, "but there's usually one emergency measure that anyone can...aha!" He swipes the screen one last time with a grand gesture. A high-pitched, whirring whine—much quieter than *The Shitty Clunker's* engines—starts up, and I put out a hand to steady myself as the floor rolls gently sideways. "Lady and gentleman, and also dog, we are now leaving the vicinity. Please strap in. That's metaphorical, you can't strap in because there are no seatbelts, because this is a boring ship that never does anything but shoot the occasional torpedo at a curious eel."

I peer sideways at him. Z usually has a quick wit and a healthy appreciation for banter, but his comments over the last few minutes have felt almost sharp, quick and snapping like a whip. Like a weapon. Or maybe a distraction. Soon the three of us are going to have to have a capital-C Conversation, and if he's trying to avoid that for a while longer, I'm all for it. "That doesn't sound boring," I tell him, "and also your boat doesn't have any seatbelts either."

He points a finger at me without looking. "Shut up, you're ruining my vibe." He spins sideways and examines a few more screens before sitting back with another flourish. "As for the emergency measure I mentioned, I've left behind a present for the other two navy subs—an EMP to remember us by. Their electronics should be shot for, oh, half an hour or so before the mining facility realizes something is up and sends out a repair-and-rescue."

"What about *The Shitty Clunker?*" I ask, alarmed. "Lexie and Chessie and a bunch of other people are still onboard, and you said life support wouldn't last much longer—"

"Wouldn't it be better if they all just went away?" Z asks pointedly, finally locking eyes with me.

"*No*," I say, putting everything I've got into the word. "No one else gets hurt."

He cocks an eyebrow at me, mocking again. "Too late for that, I think. But don't worry about them. *The Shitty Clunker* isn't affected by the latest EMPs because I've installed workarounds for that. Plus they've got a whole crew of engineers and officers down there now. With luck, they'll fix my ship for me without even bothering to faint from oxygen deprivation first." He leans down and feels around beneath the console, then slides out of his chair and underneath the desk. He taps around for a second and then calls, "Look for a toolkit. I need to disable the onboard tracker. Also, there's some primo equipment in here that I am definitely going to appropriate."

Anthem and I glance at each other. A silent conversation passes between us: *What are we doing here? This is crazy,* says her wrinkled brow. *Yep,* agrees my strained smile. *But what other choice do we have?*

Her eyes narrow and she starts to lean toward Z, one hand curling into a fist. I reach out and grab her arm, shaking my head. *No one else gets hurt.* She makes a violent pointing gesture at him and then me and then slides her thumb across her throat, meaning...I'm not sure, actually. We should kill him? He'll kill *me* if we do nothing? Either way, I shake my head again, more firmly this time.

Her shoulders somehow manage to get even tenser. Her gaze darts from me to Z and then she rubs her brow and lets out a long breath. She shrugs one shoulder, a quick, blunt jerk of a movement, then grimaces. *I don't like this.*

I spread my hands, indicating once again our total lack of other choices.

Her expression slowly shifts from reactive anger to something more considering. She sucks in one of her cheeks—Anthem's thinking face. Her gaze slides back down to where Z is flat on his back, tinkering with the underside of the panel, completely vulnerable and just as completely ignoring us. Anthem's gaze finds mine again and the stiffness starts to leech out of her spine, just a little. Both her shoulders lift a fraction and then drop with a silent sigh. Her mouth twists. *I still don't like it. But I guess it's up to you.*

I give her a weak thumbs up. She rolls her eyes. We split up to search for a toolkit.

I find it in a very obvious bright orange box hanging on the wall near the entry and carry it over to Z. "Hand me the flathead," he says. I pry open the box, gingerly extract the tool without touching any of the weapony-looking ones, and slide it over to him.

"Thanks," he says, then, "Here, take this." He hands something to me. I nearly take it automatically before I realize it's the multitool. I inhale sharply and flinch away. He lifts his head and peers out at me with a frown.

"I, um. I don't like weapons."

"So I gathered," he says evenly, but doesn't press the issue, just tosses the multitool to Anthem instead. "There's a panel beneath my chair's seat cushion. It's secured with number-four bolts. You can unscrew them with the third flip-up tool from the left," he tells her, and then goes back to disabling the tracker. He's got a square-shaped chunk of metal taken off the bottom of the desk now, and wires dangle down from it. He motions for the toolbox and I hand the whole thing to him so he can dig out wire cutters himself.

Anthem steps around to his hoverchair and kneels down beside it to get to work. A minute later there's a quiet squeak of hinges and the hidden, bolted-in little door in the seat of his chair swings open. I edge around to her side so I can see whatever vital tool or bit of tech he's got hidden in there.

Anthem pulls out a small, flat canteen-shaped thing. She unscrews the lid and sniffs it, then rears back in surprise. "It smells like a flask of whiskey."

Z finishes his job with one last turn of the screwdriver and then sits up. "It is exactly a flask of whiskey. We're gonna need it." He reaches out and tugs his legs beneath him so he's sitting cross-legged on the floor and then holds out his hand. As soon as Anthem gives him the flask he passes it to me. "Now, bird boy," he says, all traces of banter suddenly gone from his tone, "are you or are you not a dragon?"

I stare at him, fear burning low in my throat. He looks back steadily. Slowly, I sit down and tip the flask against my lips. I've never drank anything alcoholic before so I have no frame of reference, but the stuff feels like a wildfire slipping smoothly over my tongue and into my chest. I barely manage not to cough. "I am," I say hoarsely, and hand the flask to Z. Anthem is still standing next to me and I can feel the tension radiating off her, but this is a risk I need to take—and, I realize, one I *want* to take. I want to trust Z. I want to believe that somehow, despite everything, he could be on my side.

Z lets out a long exhale, tips his head back, and swallows a good third of the whiskey in one gulp. Then he lowers the flask but keeps his head tipped back against the frame of the desk and closes his eyes like he's resting. Under the unflattering fluorescents, the gauntness in his face returns, casting brittle shadows over his features and making him look hollowed out. "I killed a dragon," he says at last, roughly.

The fire in my chest spreads. Unlike the pure burn of starfire, it feels ragged and dirty, an oil slick someone threw a match into. I don't like whiskey, I decide. "I know."

"So did I," Anthem says out of nowhere, still standing, shoulders squared and eyes sheened with guilt and bravado.

Z picks his head up at that. A cautious surprise lights his features as he looks up at her. "The one in the settlement?"

She nods sharply, not looking at me.

His gaze goes unfocused. "Then you know. You've felt it too. When you kill one of them, you're connected to them for a second. You get a look inside their minds."

Anthem's gaze jolts to mine, a spark of shock travelling between us.

I look back to Z. "You were connected to the Starfall dragon when you killed it?"

He nods, looking suddenly exhausted. "I didn't mean to kill it. Not at first. I just wanted to see it. Maybe find a way to communicate with it." His voice holds a mirror to my longing, and I remember what it was like to get a glimpse of that beautiful melted-ruby dragon on the screen for the first time. The otherworldliness, the sense of seeing through a window to the whole wide universe beyond our sealed-off sky.

Z drops his head. "But then when I was on my way to the town, my—my mom—all the details that made her who she was, they just...evaporated. Snatched right out of my mind like they never existed. That's how I found out she was gone." He swallows hard and blinks, then angrily swipes the back of his wrist over his eyes. "And that's when I decided I was going to slay the monster who ended her, even if it killed me."

My gaze slides away from the ache that's clear in his expression. I don't want to think about this. I don't want to picture the ruby dragon vanishing in a burst of starfire, don't want to know if it felt afraid as it died. I don't want to feel Z's ache resonating in my own chest. But I need to know whatever it is he's trying to tell me, so I don't interrupt.

"The only thing that can kill a dragon is another dragon," Z says. His voice goes dark and bitter and self-mocking. "Lucky for me, I had a piece of one. A scale. I wasn't sure if it would do the trick, but I was set on finding out, even if it got me uncreated."

Slowly, Anthem sits down next to us. Z doesn't look up. I try to recall the video I saw, the gleam of amethyst he threw at the Starfall dragon. Earlier I mistook it for a piece of shale rock, but I watched the recording on a tiny watch screen and I was emotionally compromised at the time, so it makes sense that I could have misinterpreted it.

"I charted the Starfall dragon's course," Z goes on. "I saw that it was going in a straight line, so I set up an ambush point for it. I waited a few hours, not long. And then it came closer, breathing that starfire that wiped out my mom, and...I killed it. And then I *felt* it." He shudders and hunches inward. "I understood then why it broke through the sky. I saw what it was trying to do."

"They're on a rescue mission," Anthem says softly.

He nods, his eyes tight at the corners. "They're trying to save one of their own—a dragon who's been trapped down here alone, slowly dying for a millennium. And I killed one of them for it."

Anthem looks away. "I think…it's more complicated than that," she offers.

She's right, but I can't make myself agree with her out loud, because it feels too much like acquittal. Complicated does not mean just. Instead I say, "What about afterwards? You told me you had a mission in Albergia, one you wouldn't let anyone get in the way of. What's the mission?"

He lifts the flask like he's toasting me. "I told you, *you're* my mission. Not that I knew that before today, obviously."

Anthem narrows her eyes at him and leans forward a little like she wants to insert herself between the two of us. "In what way is my brother your mission?" she challenges, hackles up.

"Well, obviously, he's the dragon they were here to rescue," Z answers flippantly.

"And what's it to you?" She's almost snarling now.

I hold up my hands to intervene. "Just tell us the rest of the story," I say to Z, then to Anthem: "He wouldn't have given up his boat to get me away from the military if he wanted to hurt me." I desperately hope that's the case, anyway.

Z lifts one shoulder in a half-hearted attempt at a lazy shrug, though his eyes darken at the mention of *The Shitty Clunker*. Anthem's mouth twists but she sits back again and crosses her arms. "Fine," she says. "Get on with it, then. What happened after you killed the dragon and figured out why they're here?"

"I decided to help them," he answers, like it's the only obvious conclusion, like it's the choice anyone would make. My breath stutters and I stare at him as he continues. "But I had to figure out how. So while I did my civic duty and transported a shipload of refugees to safety, I started charting out the paths of all the dragons who came through the breach. I figured they must know better than anyone how to rescue one of their own kind; maybe if I mapped out where they landed it would help me figure out how I could assist. But when I plugged all the details into the software I wrote especially for this case, guess what it said? The only thing the dragons' landing locations had in common was that they were all spots where the planet's crust is thinnest. The dragons have been systematically flying to calderas and valleys and ocean trenches and blasting them with starfire."

Brow furrowed as I try to process this, I shake my head. "That doesn't make sense. Do you mean the dragons are—what, trying to uncreate the planet?"

He tries for a smirk, but it falls flat before it's even fully formed. "No. They're trying to wake up the planet." He goes in for another swallow of the whiskey, but Anthem snatches it out of his hand, takes a quick, expert swig, then screws the cap back on and slides it out of reach across the floor. Indy gets up from where she's been laying to sniff at it curiously.

"No more drinking," Anthem says, businesslike and stern even as she laces her fingers together with a strong enough grip to make her knuckles whiten. "Get to the point. What do you mean, 'wake up' the planet?"

He narrows his eyes at her but doesn't argue. "Remember what I said about only dragons being able to kill other dragons?"

"Yeah," I answer before Anthem can snap at him again.

He levels his index finger at Anthem. "Except I'm betting she used shale to kill her dragon. And guess what, so did I."

I pull up short with a frown. "But you said...you said you used a scale."

His eyes go unfocused. "I did. The shale rock formations, those *are* scales."

My breath stills in my throat. The wildfire that the whiskey started in my chest sends tendrils of heat into my gut, into my arms and legs—or maybe that's the beginning of a panic attack. "*What?*"

Z lets out a breath that's almost a laugh but is also nothing at all like a laugh. "Yep. They're dead scales starved of starlight, gone brittle and crooked over the centuries, pushed up through the layers of sediment as they die off. Glint? That's dragon blood. The shortage now is because we've been bleeding it dry for a millennium. And the eels? Those are part of a dragon's immune system. Like white blood cells. Giant, angry, electric white blood cells."

Anthem is shaking her head, her eyes wide with denial. "That's impossible. They're *eels*, not cells. What are you even trying to say—that some gigantic dragon is buried underground?"

"No," Z replies, looking at me. His expression is a graveyard: full of echoes and haunted things. "I'm saying the *entire goddamned planet is a dragon.*"

Chapter Sixteen

Usually, panic feels like heat to me: the roar of a bonfire, the blinding intensity of a flash of lightning, the slow ache of a bad sunburn. Now is the first time it's ever felt cold. Like frost crackling over a windowpane, the panic creeps into my veins and crystallizes there, metastasizing out into my muscles and down into my bones until I'm locked in place.

Z is still talking. "We've been living here on its back for generations, literally infesting a living, sentient creature like some kind of parasite, and only a handful of the world's government higher-ups even know about it."

I am a rabbit in a snare. I'm caught, helpless, forced to hear what he's saying even though absolutely everything in me wants to flee—but I can't flee from him, and I can't flee from myself either, no more than I ever could. Because in the back of my mind my dreams are stirring again: the sense of being buried, entombed, sealed away from the stars. The knowledge that I'm dying and have been for a thousand years. The weakness that came from my blood being drained, so that I barely had enough energy left to create this body. I remember the sense of connectedness I had back at the settlement when I touched the shale. And the glint, the way it responded to me rather than burning me.

The panic breathes ice over my neck. Frost feathers up my spine.

Anthem is still protesting, nearly shouting now. She's stood back up at some point. "—be real!" she's yelling. Indy whines and slinks to hide behind the knocked-over chair. "You can't possibly saying that Per—that he's—"

The panic has reached my skull now. Wintry tendrils of it slither across my scalp, pull taut the skin on my face, stretching my expression into something I probably wouldn't even recognize. The fear wants me paralyzed. It wants me helpless, broken.

That's the realization that finally lets me break through.

"How?" I say. It sounds more like a croak than a word, but it's enough to spiderweb the ice with cracks. I manage to shake off my paralysis enough to stumble to my feet. "How could you know all of this?"

Z is still sitting against the bottom of the desk, his posture loose, his gaze empty and haunted once again. After a second he looks up at me. There's no pity in his gaze, no sympathy, and I am pathetically grateful because I don't think I could bear pity from him right now. "Remember that magazine article? The one that said we—" His voice cracks on the *we* but he rolls right over it, "bought the scrap from the Pioneer Ship a few years back? Well, its flight recorder was in there too, the black box that recorded all the data from when it first landed here. It was the whole reason we wanted to buy the scrap in the first place—to unearth the recorder from the wreckage, to decipher it and uncover all the history that was lost during the first dragon attacks before the sky was closed."

Anthem tries to move toward me, tries to say something. I can't look at her. "What did you find out?" I manage instead, speaking to Z. A roar like the end of the world is building in my head, ratcheting up pressure behind my eyes, beneath my ribs. I fear I am going to explode.

"That the story of the last human survivors nobly fending off vicious star dragons from their new colony world is a damned lie," Z says. "Want to know what actually happened? The Pioneer Ship crash-landed on a star dragon the size of a large moon and didn't have enough fuel to lift back off again. They knew that a dragon's wings power its faster-than-light travel, and they also knew that if the dragon went to lightspeed with them on it, it would rip the ship apart and kill everyone onboard. So, of course," he says, his tone dark and mocking, "they decided to do the logical thing, and used the last of their energy to slice off the dragon's wings."

The words are visceral, a hand reaching inside me and twisting, pulling free a fragment of memory: a violent spatter of massive pearlescent droplets spinning off into space like new stars, a tangle of pain so sudden and shocking that it feels more like betrayal than agony. The phantom-limb ache fills me again, centering this time on my back—the place where wings would be, if either of my bodies still had them.

The ice trying to entomb me shatters a little more. I take a long, slow backwards step, not even feeling my foot connecting with the floor, like I'm gliding just above it: disconnected, ghostly.

"Some of the blood splashed back onto the ship," Z goes on, still in that bitter tone, "and that's when they realized just how powerful glint is. It stores all the solar energy a dragon absorbs. They could've just used it to power the ship and fly on their merry way to find Earth 2.0."

"I'm guessing that's not what they did," Anthem says. Her tone is even but one of her hands is outstretched and gripping the corner of the desk like she can't bear her own weight.

"You'd be right. They'd already searched for a new planet for nearly two full generations with no luck. They thought rather than keeping up a fruitless search, they could make a home right there. They'd have all the glint they'd ever need to build their new society. All they had to do was finish subduing a star dragon who had already proven reluctant to harm them, even when they cut off its wings."

A keen sense of nausea—something like double vision mixed with vertigo—sweeps over me. I'm going to throw up, or come undone, or I don't even know what, but I have to get out of here. The door is behind me. A few steps. I can't make myself move.

"The dragon tried to shake them loose," Z says. "That's when all its kin came to its aid. They uncreated a good half of the humans—and in the process, wiped out a hell of a lot of memories having to do with the ship's initial landing and the truth of what the 'planet' was—and ruined the first terraforming efforts. That's when the ship's leaders decided to seal off the sky."

Anthem swipes a shaking hand across her face. She's crying. When did she start crying? Her other hand is splayed across her stomach like one of those soldiers in an old vid who's been mortally injured but is still trying to hold their insides together.

Z goes on, relentless. "They used the last of their old-world force-field technology—powered by the world-dragon's own blood—to erect a Barrier. It blocked the starlight that the big dragon needed to stay conscious and fight back, along with all the other dragons that were fighting to free it. It forced the big one to curl up, go into a long sleep to conserve energy, as we buried it in layers of terraformed sediment and built our society on its back." He waves a hand, looking disgusted. "And thus began a thousand years of peace for humankind."

Until the world-dragon got closer and closer to death as more of its blood drained to power the Barrier, to firm up the bars of its own cage, to fuel the parasites who had infested its body.

I lift a shaking hand to my mouth. *Parasites,* I'd just thought, and the pressure that's been building beneath my ribs and behind my eyes surged at the word—and now I understand what that pressure is. Anger. *Rage.* A rage that's bleeding into the storm that's screaming around me: my entire life, uprooted and torn apart. I realize now that I never understood wrath before, but now I am made of it. I can't identify where the emotion stems from, whether it's a reaction to humanity's sins or dismay at being forced to remember them, but it's all-encompassing. I am going to shake loose from myself. Crack apart like shale in an earthquake and leave nothing but a thousand deadly shards behind.

And then...what will I do? When there's nothing of me left except this terrible anger, this shock, this realization that my whole life long I've never known any part of the truth at all? I might hurt someone. I might *want* to hurt someone.

The ice around me shatters wholly. I wheel around, find the door, and flee through it.

Anthem and Z shout after me, probably. I can't hear anything past the roaring in my ears. I can barely see where I'm going, because the entirety of my mind is filled up with a sudden memory: the creak of a bookcase door, a yellowed page from an ancient fable, the smell of glue from my scrapbook. *Come close, and I will show you the heart of a dragon.* How comforted I'd felt by that tale. Anytime I read it, the idea of a creation dragon existing soothed my anxieties, because if a dragon could be good then maybe I could too.

But what use was being good? Look where it had got the dragon. Look where it had got *me,* I realize with a sudden, sickening lurch. *I* must have been the one trying to make a home for the humans in that story—and look what they did to me for it.

There are bright spots in my vision. It probably means I'm about to pass out, but all I can see is pearled blood floating in space, obscuring the gleam of stars.

The hallway ends. I thrust myself through a door and find myself in some sort of game room. Ping-pong table bolted to the floor, magnetic chess board in the corner, abandoned deck of cards splayed across a chair. The ping-pong table is shoved up against a wall, creating a dark nook. I cram myself beneath it and try to fold myself up into the shadows. I realize too late that I didn't close the door. They could follow me. I could harm them.

I pull up my knees and wrap my arms tightly around them. I will make myself safe. Somehow. I have to. But with all the knowledge I have now about who I am, *what* I am, what I can do—and what's been done to me—how can I ever make myself safe again? Despair unspools within me, braiding with my rage until I can barely breathe. I try to make my anger smaller because it feels like such a dangerous emotion, but my attempts only make it greater. And lying below all of that like a sludge of toxic waste on the ocean floor is a terrible sense of loss.

I am Peregrine Kent. I thought I was Peregrine Kent. I could hold onto that when I found out I was a dragon, because I thought maybe I could still choose—but *this*, it's too big and too awful. It will swallow me up and then there will be nothing left of me but rage.

Something nudges me in the knee. It's as good as a bomb going off in my current state; I startle so violently I knock my head against the table and my elbow on the wall. Barely managing to cut off my shout, I look down at what's nudging me.

It's a plate. Holding...a sandwich? I blink and then examine it more closely: a slice of stale-looking bread painted with some sort of thin brown goop that seems unidentifiable until I get a whiff of it. Peanut butter. And the second slice of bread, which is sitting off-kilter halfway atop the first, is slathered with what looks like an entire jar's worth of bluish jelly. It's perhaps the messiest sandwich I've ever seen, which means I have a pretty good guess at who's assembled it.

I follow the plate to an outstretched arm and the arm to a person. Yep. Z. He's sitting on the floor in front of the ping-pong table, leaning against his powered-off hoverchair. I must've been utterly lost in my own head to not even hear him enter.

"Go away," I say weakly, wishing I could make myself mean it. Truth is, I want him to stay. I care about him despite my best efforts and it's agonizing. More people to care about, more people to worry about.

"Shut up and eat the sandwich," he says, tapping the plate none-too-gently against my knee again.

The anger from a moment ago was temporarily muted by surprise, but at this it surges again. "How the hell is a sandwich supposed to help?" I demand, hating the way my voice frays, hating how terrified and helpless I sound.

He scoots forward and shoves the plate at my chest until I'm forced to take it lest the messy sandwich fall onto my lap. "Three things that help manage a crisis," he says, holding up his fingers. "A snack, a nap, and a breakdown, always in that order. You can't skip steps, bird boy. Eat your peanut butter sandwich."

"Then what?" I scoff, a last-ditch effort to shake him off. "Are you gonna chloroform me into napping?"

He snorts. "Nah. That's what the whiskey's for."

Something like a surprised smile tries to twitch across my face and I look down to smother it before it can be born. This isn't going to work. He wants to, what, nurse me back to health? Take care of me, the way he fed me a banana muffin back on *The Shitty Clunker*? It won't do any good. This situation is pretty damn unfixable. I am a dragon who is also a planet. He is a boy who lost everything to the dragons who were trying to save me. We can never be whatever it is we might like to be.

But still, as I bow my head, the storm inside me eases a little. He knows me, knows who and what I am and what's been done in my name, and how does he respond?

He makes me a sandwich.

I look up again. He's right in front of me now, head tilted forward, mouth tense like there's more he wants to say, and all of the sudden I see the truth of him: the terrible hurt and buoyant hope warring at the core of him, the vulnerability of his pose, the wanting in his eyes when he looks at me. Suddenly there's wanting inside me, too, though it should be impossible in the midst of all this.

Recklessly, fatalistically, I raise a hand. His gaze flicks from it to me and his expression opens, the tension in his mouth easing. He doesn't move as I dare to softly touch just the tips of my fingers to his cheek, skimming over his jawline. In the silence I hear his breath hitch.

I want to kiss him.

I cannot kiss him.

"Z," I say, my voice sounding less like a noise and more like a deepening of the hush that surrounds us.

He swallows. His own hand is half-raised toward me like he's not sure what he wants to do with it yet, or maybe like he's not sure if he's brave enough to do what he wants to. "Yeah?" he asks, his voice low and a little hoarse now too.

"This is not," I say, lifting the plate between us, "a peanut butter sandwich."

He stares at me for a second longer, then peers down at the plate, looking completely taken aback and befuddled and also adorable, which is not a word I ever thought I would apply to him.

"This sandwich is at least eighty percent jelly," I go on, my hand still on his face because I can't make myself move it just yet. "Making it, at best, a jelly sandwich with a brief guest appearance by peanut butter."

He blinks a few times and then his eyes narrow. "Are you...insulting my sandwich?"

"I am not insulting your sandwich. I am giving your sandwich a factually correct moniker."

Eyes still latched on mine, he lowers the hand he'd been holding in the air and uses it to pick up the top piece of bread. Then, as gently as I'd touched his jaw a moment ago, he places it jelly-side-down on my own cheek. Blueberry-scented jam oozes down my ear and plops onto my shirt.

"There," Z says. "Now it's only sixty percent jelly."

I lower my hand from his face. I peel the bread off my cheek. And then I laugh—the sort of laugh that lasts way too long, that makes your stomach hurt when it's over, that feels as much like relief as humor—while Z sits there, looking smug, until I pick up the other side of the sandwich and shove it peanut-butter-side down right smack on one of his glorious cheekbones.

We briefly scuffle, both of us aware of how absolutely ridiculous we look but not caring at all, because for this moment we're just Peregrine and Z and nothing more. Then the moment ends and I'm smeared with jelly and he's speckled with peanut butter and reality settles back onto us, but not quite as heavily as before.

"Did I win?" Z asks, lifting up his shirt hem to wipe the peanut butter off his face, which ends up just smearing it around. "I'm pretty sure I won."

I'm briefly distracted by the sight of his abs, which is probably what he intended, the smug jerk, and he grins in triumph when I don't protest his victory quickly enough. Then he sighs and pulls his shirt back down and looks at me, his expression turning grim. "You didn't know, did you?" he asks.

I don't question what he means. We've had our moment of reprieve and now we have to capital-T Talk. "No," I answer, my voice only a little rough now. "I didn't know. A decade I've been—been *this*," I wave a hand over myself, "and I didn't know anything."

Z scoots out from under the ping-pong table and leverages himself back into his hoverchair. "*How* are you this?" he asks, waving his own hand at me. "I've spent most of the last decade trying to figure out how the hell I'm supposed to help free an entire planet without killing everyone on it, and you turn up as…" He frowns at me, searching for words. "As that," he says at last, stabbing a finger at me like that explains exactly what he means.

"As a fake human?" I say, using my sleeve to wipe off my own face, mainly so I don't have to look at him when I say it. My voice feels thicker than it should be, layered with too many echoes.

He doesn't let that answer stand even for a second. "As Peregrine Kent," he says instead, throwing it out like a dare, "the guy I've been trying my damnedest to not fall for."

My gaze shoots to his. He doesn't look away. The *seeing me* is all over him now, in his eyes, in the feathering of a muscle in his jaw, in the way his hands curl tight around his armrests. Suddenly I want him to know me. The real me. Everything.

"I created this body," I tell him as I stand up. "That's what I am—a creator. I think I might be the only dragon with that ability. Ten years ago when I realized how close I was to dying, I made a human body and put my soul into it. But human brains can't hold dragon memories and I forgot everything, thought I was just a regular human, until a few months ago when I started having dreams about flying through space and being close to death. That's why I sought you out. I thought if you could take me to find a real dragon, I might be able to figure out what was happening to me and whether I was truly dying. Then I started glowing during Starfall, and then at the settlement, the dragon breathed starfire over me and it unlocked the memory of what I was. What I am." I venture a step closer to him. "I thought you were my enemy. I thought you would kill me."

The lingering hollowness in his expression sharpens to knife edges. "Never," he says with a ferocity I haven't seen in him before.

I spread my hands. "Why not?" My voice sounds almost plaintive. I don't understand why he would want to free me, or help me—dragon-me, anyway.

He rakes his good hand through his hair, looking like he's trying to remember something or trying to string together the right words. "Per, I just told you that I've known the planet was a trapped dragon for the last nine-ish years. What do you think I've been doing all that time?"

"Researching dragons," I answer, but it's half a question, because...what does anyone really know about the Star Slayer? Most of what I knew about him when I met him was conjecture, and a good amount of what I learned after that was a lie.

"Yeah," he answers me. "I was researching dragons, so I could *figure out how to save you*. I joined the navy university so I could figure out how to save you. I went AWOL because I found out I was the *only* one there interested in saving you. They've been exploiting the hell out of you for ages, and I couldn't be a part of it."

I stare at him. He looks back, earnestness and unease tightening his jaw and drawing his brow down. He looks so unguarded. "But," I stutter, "you're the Star Slayer."

He winces. "Yeah, I picked that callsign when I was fifteen. It sounded like a cool nickname at the time, plus it helped establish a decent cover story so the government wouldn't get too curious. But I never intended to actually kill dragons, I swear. We were always only trying to help you. It was our project."

"We," I say, frowning at him. "Our. That's what you just said. Who else is in on this?"

He blinks in confusion for a second and then a wall slams down over his expression, and I remember.

"Your mom." Dread and regret wash over me. "It was you and your mom's project. She was the captain, wasn't she?"

Z's jaw works. His hand fists. The wall over his expression slowly crumbles, brick by brick, and I can see the effort it takes him to dismantle it and be honest with me and himself. "Yeah," he says roughly. "I think it was her. Even when a memory is gone you can still see the hole it left behind, and there are holes all over *The Shitty Clunker*."

"I'm sorry," I say quietly, uselessly, and he gives a sharp nod. "I just...I still don't get it. I don't get *why*. Why would you try to help me, Z? You didn't even know me."

He presses his hand flat on the ping-pong table in front of him, leaning toward me. "Because it's *wrong*," he says fiercely. "You're a sentient being. A person. And humans cut off your wings, they sealed you off from the sky and *used you*, all because they were greedy and afraid. Even now, the world's governments are draining your blood dry to seal the breach back up."

"What?" cries out a voice from the doorway. We both jump and twist around to spot Anthem. She's holding Indy by the collar but as she stares at us in shock, her fingers go slack. Indy bounds free, pauses a moment to sniff the air, then shoves herself into Z's lap to lick a clump of peanut butter off his ear. He tries to fend her off while I address my sister.

"Where have you been? Are you okay?" I ask, not quite able to meet her eyes. I tell myself I want to give her time to adjust to what she knows about me now but the truth is I'm a coward. I don't want to see how she's looking at me.

But she just waves me off. "I'm fine. I mean, I'm obviously super not fine, but you know. Fine. I thought I'd give you two a minute to do...whatever you were doing," here her voice gets arch as she gestures at our peanut-butter-and-jelly-stained clothing, "but then I decided to check on you, and good thing I did, because *Z, what in the name of all the gods did you just say?*"

At her exclamation, Z's earlier words rush back to me too, and I whirl toward him. "Wait—did you say they're...draining my blood? To keep the Barrier powered?"

He grimaces and finally manages to push Indy off his lap. "That mining facility back there, it was way over capacity. Last time I stole fuel from there it wasn't nearly that active. It's the same every-where—heightened activity near every mining facility I've passed since Starfall. Even though there's a glint shortage, even though they know you can't survive much more blood loss, they're pumping it all out to reseal the Barrier so they can keep the rest of the dragons out."

"What do you mean, *even though* they know he can't survive more blood loss?" Anthem asks, voice thick and shaking with anger. "Don't they want him dead? Isn't that the whole damn point?"

Z avoids my gaze. "No," he says shortly. "They don't want him dead. They want him inert. Big difference."

Anthem responds, every inch of her seething with righteous fury, but I can't quite make out her words. My vision has gone foggy, my hearing full of echoes. I'm thinking about why humanity would want me inert. I'm realizing I've been so preoccupied with fearing my past that I forgot to fear my future. I forgot a key part of my dreams—the part where I create a human body in the Hail-Mary hope of finding starlight, because if I didn't find it then I would die, and if I die...

I'll explode into starfire. Just like the Starfall dragon, just like the one Anthem killed. Except unlike them, I've got *an entire world* on my back.

Which means if I die...so does everyone else on the planet.

Chapter Seventeen

"P er?" Anthem says, her voice a thin and cautious thing, a pane of ice tested with gentle footsteps.

I don't need gentle. That is not what I need right now. What I need is a plan. Which is why I'm yanking open drawers and pulling out their contents, tossing things with no regard for where they land until I find what I'm looking for: a marker and the deck of cards. Paper would be better but I don't have the patience to keep searching any longer. Exhaling shakily, I fan out the cards, grab an ace of spades from the deck, and lift the marker.

Options, I scrawl across the top. Just writing the word makes the noose around my chest loosen a fraction. Yes. I have options. I can decide things. I start a numbered list.

Number one, I write. *Everyone dies.*

Z peers around my waist. "Grim," he comments.

"It's my system," I say roughly. "Get the worst possible option out of the way first. Then any ideas other than that don't sound nearly so bad in comparison."

Number two. I pause, marker hovering in the air. What are my other options? For this system to work, I have to write down everything I think of, even if it terrifies me, even if I think it's an awful idea. I usually use this method for brainstorming homework essays, though, not life-or-death situations, and my OCD is already screaming at me to scribble out that first sentence, tear it right off the card, shred it into confetti and then jettison it into the sea just to make it absolutely clear to myself that it's not an option. Especially because there's also a small but very real part of me that feels a surge of ugly validation at the thought of taking my parasites—my *abusers*—down with me. What if that's what I truly want, deep down? What if I somehow sabotage any other plan we might come up with, fail intentionally, because of that little urge for revenge? I press against that emotion like I'm testing a bruise, trying to judge my reaction to it, feeling sicker with every passing second.

Humans might be my abusers, I reason, but the vast majority of them don't even know what they're doing, and no one alive now had anything to do with the decision to cut off my wings and infest me. And there are some humans that I care about very, very much. Surely I would never let them die. Even when I was fully dragon I wanted to save them, not hurt them. Surely that means my urge to protect, and not my desire for vengeance, is the truer emotion.

I can almost hear Anthem's voice in my head: *or maybe they're both as true and real as any emotions ever are, and you are as capable as anyone else of acknowledging them, stepping back from them, and making your own damn decisions.*

I press my fist to my forehead. "What's wrong?" says the real Anthem from over my shoulder.

"I'm arguing with you in my head," I mutter.

"Oh." A pause. "I'm winning, right?"

I sigh deeply, but feel marginally better. "You always win."

I put the marker back to the card and draw a little arrow branching off from option number one and write in parentheses, *this is not an option.* That doesn't exactly shut my OCD up, but it's a compromise that lets me focus enough to move on to the rest of the list.

I go back to option number two and write, *We find a dragon and let it give me energy via starfire.*

"And then what?" Z demands sharply, reading what I've written as soon as I lift the marker. "You get enough energy to live and then...you just stay curled up, slightly less dead than before, and let humans keep hurting you for another millennium?"

"What else am I supposed to do?" I demand, my voice tight. "I can't die, and I can't let everyone else die either."

His answer is quick and brutal. "Kick them out. They're squatters; you're the landlord. Give them, like, a year or two to pack their bags and move on. I can show them the Pioneer Ship's blueprints, they can build other spaceships and go find some other actual non-living planet to screw up."

"And *then* what?" Anthem says. "Play it out. He's a dragon who can't fly."

Z levels a glare at her. "And I'm a human who can't walk. What are you trying to say, that a disabled life is automatically inferior? Because that would be a pretty shitty thing to think, Anthem."

She inhales sharply and flushes. "I would *never*—that's not what I—" She stops herself and takes a longer, slower breath. "You're right," she says, her tone more measured now. "I was careless with my words. I'm sorry."

Z squints at her, suspicious. "Did you just apologize?"

"I apologize when I'm wrong," she says in a defensive tone.

"Hmmm," is all Z replies with.

I cut them both off. "I don't *want* to be a dragon, wings or no wings."

That pulls their attention straight back to me. "What?" Anthem says, leaning closer to me. "I thought...I thought it was what you wanted. To get to the stars, to be free."

"It was. It is," I tell her, even though when I daydream lately, it's not the stars I'm flying through but coral formations and curtains of plankton motes. "But I don't want to be a dragon."

"Because you're afraid you might turn into a starfire-wielding serial killer?" she asks, exasperated, then winces and glances sideways at Z when she realizes she's come close to outing my harm OCD. My pulse jumps. Letting Z in on that detail is the last thing I should be worried about, but somehow, him knowing about my mental illness feels even more intimate than him knowing I'm a planet-dragon.

I give my sister a look. "I would be an *apocalypse,* Anthem, so yes, I am worried about my ability to control myself. More than that, though...I like being me."

Even though there are some parts of being human that are a struggle. Even though sometimes I wish I could be someone, anyone, else. Even with all that—I still think being human is worth the cost.

My eyes burn. Damn. What a time to have an epiphany.

"Is that possible? For you to stay you, I mean?" Anthem asks, eagerness winding through her voice. And of course she's eager. With a guilty jolt, I realize that it can't be fun for her, thinking that her brother would just keel over and be essentially gone as soon as our mission succeeded. I mean, I'd still be alive as a dragon, but my whole consciousness, my entire sense of self, would be different. Vast and ancient and far less human.

"I hope so," I say, finally daring to meet her gaze. I exhale sharply when I do. She looks *wrecked.* Her eyes are puffy and rimmed in red. Her hair is pulled into a tight, merciless bun that still sparkles with jewel-toned shale dust. She's got both arms braced on the card table like she can't hold up her own weight otherwise, and her fingers are white where she's splayed them over the cheap laminate surface.

I'm fine, she said earlier. And like an idiot, I let myself believe her. My little sister has always been a juggernaut of a human being, unstoppable, an iron-willed force of nature. I have never seen her broken. And she's still not broken—there's defiance in the set of her jaw and anger smoking in her dark gaze—but even so, I have never seen her look quite so shockingly...human.

I've been so selfish. So focused on what's happening to me that I barely considered how it could affect her. A bolt of anger and frustration shoots through me and the card wrinkles in my grip. She deserves better than that.

"If there is a way for me to stay myself, I swear I will do everything I can to find it," I promise her. She nods once, solemnly, like we're sealing a blood pact.

Z clears his throat. "We don't have time to track down a dragon in any case," he says. "We're on the clock now. When that Albergian commander is done getting *The Shitty Clunker* back online, she's going to talk to her people about what happened in that corridor, and she'll find out about your glowing trick. Then she'll find out the glint leak was caused by an uncreated pipe—no other tool can cut that cleanly, down to the molecule—and she'll put two and two together and call all her superiors. Then *they'll* put two and two together and guess what you are."

"Surely they won't guess that Per is the world-dragon," Anthem says, her tone half skeptical and half desperate. "There's no precedent for a dragon going human. Is there?"

"There's a few ancient myths about creation dragons," Z answers, and I remember the fable from my scrapbook. "Enough for them to at least put it out there as a hypothesis. Enough for them to put a kill order on Per, just in case they're right. You really think they'd do anything else, with a hundred thousand people already killed and more getting wiped out of existence every day? They'll do whatever they think they have to do to save their species, and murdering a minor would be the least of it."

The acrid smell of the marker is flooding my senses, but I can't make myself pull my gaze away from Z long enough to re-cap it. "How long do we have before they catch up to us?"

"I disabled the onboard tracker, but one of their radar stations will ping us soon enough. Wherever we're going, we need to get there quick."

I swallow, then cross out option number two. "Okay. How far are we from the breach?"

We're all quiet for a second. "A day or so," Z says at last.

"I don't think just standing beneath it will be enough," I confess. "It's only a pinprick in the sky, comparatively—it'll barely be letting any starlight through, especially if the governments have already started re-sealing it. I think I might need to get *out* in order to absorb enough energy."

I don't want to get just barely enough starlight to survive for another decade or two before I explode into starfire. If there's a chance I'll have to give up this life, *my* life, then I want it to be worth more than that.

I look down at the list. I'm trying to force myself to be pragmatic about this, and it's working for now, but I can sense a keen-edged grief just out of sight.

"How exactly would you 'get out'?" Anthem asks. "All the hovercrafts are grounded like everything else, and they aren't made to fly that high anyway."

Z taps his fingers on his armrest. "Unless...could you use creation magic to make a spaceship or something?"

I shake my head. "I'm not sure. From what I saw in my dream-memory thing, it takes way more energy to create than to it does to destroy stuff with starfire, and I was already down to almost nothing when I created this body a decade ago." Wow, that is a weird sentence to say out loud. "I think creating anything else would probably kill me."

Z clears his throat, a particular look on his face—hesitation or reluctance, I think. "There may be one other option."

Oof, I know that tone. "But it's not a good one?" I guess.

"You learn fast," he says with a snort. "And yes. It's a bad one. But...if we can't get you to the sky, maybe we could bring the sky to you."

"Cryptic and foreboding," I note. "Go on."

"We could turn the Barrier off."

I'm so stunned by this statement I physically rock back for a second and nearly lose my balance. The ace of spades I've been clutching flutters out of my grip and drifts to the floor. "What? The Barrier's been up for a thousand years. Presumably that's how long it took the dragons to claw a relatively small hole through it. We can't just shut it off. Can we?"

Z spreads his hands. "The Barrier is powered by your blood, and your blood is down here, not up there in the sky. Meaning somewhere, there has to be a pipe or a converter or some kind of connector that we could blow up to decommission the whole thing."

I flatten my hand against the card table. "We are *not* blowing anything up."

Anthem looks thoughtful, though. "We'd have to find it first."

"I could narrow it down to three or four locations," Z says. "It'd have to be somewhere heavily guarded and fortified, probably somewhere high up, most likely in the Conglom—"

"Did you hear the part where I said we're not blowing anything up?" I demand loudly, my heart starting to pound.

"This sub is equipped with warheads," Z says, which successfully shuts me up but only because horror has wrapped itself around my throat and squeezed tight. "I might be able to find a workaround to launch them, or hack into the personnel files and get the authorization codes. You wouldn't even have to use starfire if you don't want to."

My hand is still flat on the table. A dim glow is starting to tumble through the veins there, a lace of blood and stars. "I am not reluctant to blow people up because I would have to use starfire to do it," I say in as measured a voice as I can manage. "I am reluctant to blow people up because it is *murder.*"

"We're not talking about blowing *people* up," Anthem protests, "just a generator or something—"

I whirl around to glare at her. "Do you think the generator that powers the Barrier would be unguarded? Z just said it would be somewhere heavily fortified! That means if you shoot a torpedo at whatever bunker or secret base houses it, you'd also be killing a lot of people."

The set of Z's mouth is rigid. "They started killing you first," he says, vicious.

My glow brightens. Anthem makes a noise that isn't quite a word but I keep my gaze on Z. "I don't care."

"You don't care that they're killing you?" His voice ratchets a few notches louder. His pupils contract in the light but his expression might as well be carved in steel.

"Who do you even think you're talking about?" I shout. My shine casts spinning shadows around the control room as I slice a hand through the air. "Soldiers? They're just following orders. They had nothing to do with the decision to cut my wings off and trap me here."

"The 'following orders' defense has been bullshit since old-Earth wars and you know it," he shouts back.

"*I. Don't. Care!*" I yell, and my light flares so brightly it burns spots into my vision. "No one else gets hurt!"

A hand fumbles into mine. Anthem. She squeezes, her other hand held up to shield her eyes. "Per," she says quietly. "Per."

I inhale deeply through my nose. I smother my light. I don't speak.

Z is breathing hard and glaring at me, unrepentant. Anthem looks conflicted. "We might have to be logical about this," she says after a second. "Even if we have to...even if hundreds of soldiers die—isn't that better than *everyone* dying?"

I turn and look at her. "Is it 'everyone' that you're worried about?" I ask, because I know her too well to think this is a simple math equation for her, or that she's thinking only of the greater good.

Her expression cracks and something unapologetic shimmers behind it like a mirage. Her fingers tighten around my hand. "No," she says, voice flat and hard. "It's you I'm worried about. I don't care about hundreds of faceless soldiers, and I definitely don't give a damn about the asshole Council members who must know exactly what the cost of our society is and make you pay for it anyway. I care about *you*. I want you to live, and Mom and Dad, and the good people who I care about. Everyone else can go to hell."

I withdraw my hand from hers and cover my face. "That's the problem," I say. "They're *all* good people."

"How the—" Z starts angrily, even as Anthem snaps, "Like hell they are—" but I interrupt them both.

"What is it you're always trying to tell me, Anthem? When I ask you if a person can have awful thoughts and still be good, when I ask you if *I'm* good? You tell me that no one is really good or evil. You tell me I'm capable of stepping back and acknowledging my fears and my thoughts and my questionable motivations, and making whatever choice I *want* to make anyway. The 'they' you're talking about, the soldiers and leaders and whoever else, they're capable of that too. If they knew the truth, if they knew they had a choice, they would choose to do the right thing."

And as I say it, I suddenly believe it. That they would make the right choice, and that I would, too. It's not certainty. It's not foolproof. I've made bad decisions in the past and I will again—but I can feel the small, fragile shoots of a brand-new faith growing within me. That maybe I will never be able to prove to myself that I am wholly and definitely good...but that I don't have to be that to be a good person. I am good enough. And *that's* good enough. Even if I have starfire, even if I have scary thoughts, even if I'm angry, I still get to choose who I want to be. And in any case, the stakes are too high now for me to spend my time being terrified of myself rather than doing whatever I can to save the world.

Funny—I guess an impending apocalypse is all it takes for me to finally be willing to face down my OCD.

"You can't be serious," Z is saying now, incredulous. "There are people out there, people on the Council and military officers, who *do* know the truth, who *do* have a choice, and they've chosen to keep on killing you anyway."

I shake my head slowly. "They don't have all the facts," I tell them. "They don't know that I want to save them. They don't know that my kin are only trying to save *me*, that I would call them off if I was in my original body, if I could communicate with them."

"So, what," Z says, his eyes bright with anger, "you think you could just call up the Conglom Council and the Albergian president and the Ancient Isles Waymaker and all the rest of the world leaders and tell them 'oh hey, I'm the planet dragon, please drop the Barrier and I pinky swear you'll be totally safe from the hundreds of dragons waiting out there to eat you afterwards'?"

I ignore his sarcasm, knowing he's upset for my sake. "They need to know there's no way to win this war. If they keep trying, humans and the dragons will destroy each other, and then I'll die and uncreate anyone who's left in the process." Even though it's a simple statement of fact and not anything I actually want to happen, I still have to say that bit through gritted teeth, and afterward quickly think a good thought—*everyone lives, everyone lives*—to cancel it out. "We have to get the people in charge to understand that this isn't a choice between them winning and the dragons winning. Either *everyone* wins, or everyone dies."

"Knowing the truth and believing it are two different things," Anthem points out. "Like Z said—you can tell them all of this all day long, and there's no way they'll believe you. Or even if they do believe you, they still won't be willing to stake their lives on just your word."

I rake a hand through my hair, feeling like I'm at the end of my rope. At the end of my options. I pick up the ace of spades but then crumple it in my hand because it still only has two ideas on it, and neither one will work. I'm worried this won't either, and then what'll be left? I'm not willing to kill anyone no matter what, but I just can't figure out anything else we can do. "I could go to them in person," I try, and I can hear the desperation in my own voice. "Give myself up as a sign of good faith."

"They'll kill you," Z says, his good hand curling into a fist. "They won't take any chances."

"They might not kill you," Anthem says, and I feel the slightest grain of hope until she adds, "They might just toss you in a dark cell somewhere and interrogate you or experiment on you. *Then* kill you."

Something feels stretched thin inside me, like a bow strung too tight. "Maybe only this body would die," I say recklessly, gesturing at myself. "I bet my consciousness, my soul or whatever, would just go back into my dragon body if they kill me."

"After which you'd continue dying of starlight starvation and explode into starfire, like you were going to originally," Z snaps back, raising his voice again. "Do me a favor and stop trying to martyr yourself."

I blink at him. The plan that started to form in my mind earlier suddenly snaps together like fate falling into place, and the pit of my stomach drops out.

"I know that face," Anthem says, eyes narrowing as she peers at me. "That's not a good face."

I lick my lips. "Maybe I could...create a shield. Over my dragon body."

Z gives me a suspicious look. "How would a shield help? Did you hear me just say that you'd be exploding into starfire? *Nothing* can withstand starfire."

I take a breath and lift a finger, pointing straight up. "Except the Barrier. Dragons have been out there since the sky was first sealed off, and there's no way they weren't trying to uncreate it the whole time. It took them a millennium before it worked. I could try to create a new Barrier right over my dragon body. If the worst happens, it would hold down the starfire and keep the shape of the planet intact." Probably not for very long, since I have barely any energy left to put into it, but just maybe it might buy humanity a few years to get safely off-world.

Anthem peers at me, looking just as suspicious as Z. "I intend to find a solution that ends with you not exploding, but creating a Barrier to shield the planet could be a nice show of good faith for the Council. Although...judging from the look on your face I'm guessing there's a catch. Spit it out." But before I can speak again, her eyes snap open wide—probably because she's remembering what I said earlier. *I think creating anything else would probably kill me.*

"Hell no." She says it flatly, but her spine is stiff and her eyes are bright with a scrabbling sort of fear. "We are not even considering that."

I want to agree with her, but deep down inside me, that thing that felt like fate still feels like fate. "I'm not sure if using that much energy will kill me or not, but...I have to try, don't I?"

"No," Z and Anthem both growl at the same time. Their gazes flick to each other, surprised to be in agreement, then Z juts his chin in acknowledgement and Anthem tilts her head like a queen accepting tribute. I would roll my eyes if the situation wasn't so serious.

"Look," I tell them, "I want to live. Everyone else living and me living too is the ultimate best outcome here. This isn't about me trying to martyr myself, or—"

"Or trying to prove you're good?" Anthem says, cutting to the quick of the matter as always.

I wince. "I can't help how I feel about that," I admit, "but this isn't me saying I want to end my life, or that death is somehow a noble choice, or anything like that. This is me saying...I think I need to try a risky thing in order to achieve a potentially huge gain."

Anthem crosses her arms tightly against her chest. "The gain isn't worth the risk," she contends, but she can't meet my eye as she says it.

"Even if the gain is in lives?" I ask softly. "Mom and Dad's lives? The lives of your friends from school? The lives of all the little kids in the whole world?"

She shakes her head mutely.

I press on. "If I can create this new Barrier to protect everyone, then I can talk to the Council afterward and they'll listen, because I will have proven my good intentions." Of course, that part of the plan will only work if I survive, but I'm trying not to focus on that. "But if I'm going to try this then we need to move quick. If the military really is mining the glint at an accelerated rate, then soon I might not have enough energy left to create the new Barrier. The longer I wait, the less likely it is I'll be able to do this and survive."

Z glares at me. "I think we should go back to you creating the spaceship or something to get you through the breach. If you've got energy to shield the planet, you've got energy to get yourself to the stars."

"Saving the world—or, well, the people who live on it—is the priority here," I tell him, my voice firm despite the turmoil inside me. "If I make the Barrier and I have enough energy leftover, and talking to the world leaders afterward doesn't work, *then* I can try creating a spaceship."

Anthem and Z both grit their teeth and grimace, and I can tell they're trying to think of more arguments to stop me from trying this, so I cut them off.

"I need to do this, guys," I tell them. "I appreciate that you want to keep me safe. But I want to keep *everyone* safe. I promise I won't do anything reckless."

"Everything about this is reckless," Anthem says, but her voice is strained.

My heart goes heavy and aching. "I have to at least try. You can help me or not—that's your choice. This, though...this is mine."

Anthem's shoulders snap back like she's been punched. Her eyes flash with emotion. Without another word, she turns and strides out of the room, every footfall an indictment. I droop. I'll have to track her down and talk to her more soon. If this plan goes south, this isn't how I want to leave things with her.

Z bows his head, his hair falling over his eyes. He's quiet for a long moment. Finally, he says, "I've been trying to save you for so long. This isn't how that story's meant to end."

I let out a breath. "Maybe I'm supposed to save you."

He shakes his head, denying that, but has no answer. At last, he sighs. "Apparently I can't talk you out of trying, anyway. Where do you want to do this?"

The dropping-stone feeling in my heart keeps going, and I wonder if I'll be falling forever. I think of all the things I want to do in my life: travel the world, see the stars, fall in love, see my parents again. The last one, at least, I can do something about. I don't have a watch to call them on anymore...but I do have a submarine. And Mom and Dad are headed to the Conglom port.

"Home," I tell Z. "Take me home."

Chapter Eighteen

Z programs in the course. Military subs are wicked fast—"almost as fast as *The Shitty Clunker*," Z claims—and the shales weren't that far from the Conglom to begin with; he reports it'll take less than a day to make the trip back. There are no windows to watch the sea slip past, no Pioneer Ship metal to calm me—even though it shouldn't calm me anyway, now that I know the truth of what it's done. It doesn't matter. It's still seen the stars, and I don't know if I ever will now.

I avoid Anthem. I linger in the sterile control room to watch Z when he's not looking and see the haunted expression slowly taking him over again. After an hour or two, I can't stand the roiling silence between us any longer, so I go to hunt through the halls for the bunkroom. When I find it, I tear a bedsheet into strips and use it to make a toy for Indy, then occupy myself playing fetch with her until we're both exhausted enough to sleep.

I dream. The light of faraway suns on my wings, the birth of galaxies in my wake. The weight of the earth bearing down on me. The waning starlight in my blood. I wake up, and the ache of dying is worse than ever. I lay in a borrowed bunk, muscles locked, vision blurry, no longer able to keep my grief at bay as tears trail slowly across my temples to dip behind my ears and soak into my hair. Indy tries to lick them away and whines when I don't respond, stretching herself out next to me and tucking her head beneath my hand. When I can finally sit up, I pet her and tell her she's a good girl and thank her for always being there for me.

Then I go and look for Anthem.

I find her in the weapons room, sitting cross-legged facing the wall and tapping away on her watch, surrounded by torpedoes. The long, slender, deadly cylinders are secured to the wall with clamps and there's no way I could launch any of them from here without authorization from the control room, but I stand carefully in the exact center of the room and interlace my fingers behind my back anyway. And then I wait.

Anthem has never been good at silence. She told me once that for her the quiet feels like drops in a bucket, and when it gets too full, she can't restrain her urge to knock it over with as much clatter as possible. True to form, it's only about thirty seconds before she says loudly, "I've decided I'm not going to be a therapist after all."

It's a gut punch, squarely aimed and deliberately delivered. She doesn't want to be a therapist anymore because of me. She's abandoning her future career because I proved too hard for her to deal with. But before the thought can drag me too deep into the mire of self-blame, I notice her posture: she's sitting up straight but her shoulders aren't as tight as they were before, and when she turns her head slightly I see she's wearing an expression that looks...rueful? "Why do you say that?" I dare to ask cautiously.

She tips her head forward. Her hair is loose now and it careens in wild waves around her face. Bits of jewel-toned dust fall out of it and drift to the floor. "Because you were right, you terrible jackass," she says, with only a little sharpness behind the words. We're back to insults, which in Anthem-speak means we're okay, or at least moving in that direction. My relief is so strong it nearly whites out my vision for a second. Still, though, I don't understand what she means or what her aim is now.

"What exactly was I right about?" I ask.

She lifts one shoulder, taps on her watch a few more times, then speaks again. "Back there, what you said—that this was your choice, and that I had to make my own. When you said that, I had this incredibly strong gut reaction, this deep-down urge to try to fix the whole situation anyway even if it meant doing it against your will. And I realized...that's a part of me. That need to fix people and things. And I'm not saying that it's a bad thing, because being a natural fixer has definitely come in handy for me loads of times, but as far as administering therapy goes..." She shakes her head. "It's not an asset. By trying to bully people into solving their situations the way I think they should solve them, I'd be taking away their right to choose—I'd be stealing from them. I don't want to be the person who does that to a patient who's already in a vulnerable state." She grimaces, an expression I only see slivers of through her chaotic hair. "You know what's worse? I think Dr. Hernandez extended my internship to give me the chance to realize on my own that it's not the right career for me."

I peer at her. She doesn't sound too upset, but this is a big change, and she's making it in the middle of a crisis. "Are you sure? Couldn't you just...try not browbeating people anymore?"

She snorts. "Oh, I'm way too good at browbeating to give it up. I just need to find a career where it is an asset. Life coach, maybe. Or probation officer. Something like that." She lifts one shoulder in a shrug.

With a furtive glance at the torpedoes lining the walls, I edge forward and sit next to her, tightly balling up my hands and tucking them in my pockets for good measure. "I thought your watch was dead," I say after a second, nodding at it.

"It was. This is a military sub; apparently they get specially-requisitioned recharging stations and three times the energy allotment of civilians. I'm back to one hundred percent now."

"Oh," I say, then, because I can't hold it back any longer: "I'm sorry."

"There you go again," she says, tension resurfacing in her tone. "Apologizing to me for gods-know-what when everyone in the whole world should be apologizing to you."

"You've never done anything but try to protect me. Out of every good thing my life has been for the last seven years, you may be the one I'm most grateful for."

"Shut up," she snaps, her tone thickening. "Don't you dare say goodbye."

"I'm not saying goodbye. I'm saying thank you."

"Well, it sounds too much like goodbye, so quit it."

I lift my shoulders helplessly. "I just mean...I'm sorry that things happened this way. Both with your career and...everything else." I pause for a moment, and when she says nothing else, I add, "Thank you for letting me make my own choice. You can still browbeat me a little bit if you want."

She side-eyes me. "Are you going to tell Mom and Dad what you're doing?"

"I don't know." I want to see them before I do anything, but a big part of me is afraid that if I explain all the details—particularly the part where I'm not sure if my idea is survivable—they'll find a way to talk me out of it. I can't let them do that. This is the only plan that stands even a chance of protecting everyone I care about.

Anthem reads my thoughts as always. "Find another way, Per. Or else I swear I'll make you regret it even if you're already dead."

"I thought you said you weren't going to try to steal my choice."

"No," she says, a hint of acid eating through her tone now. "I said I wasn't going to do that to *patients*."

That sounds foreboding, but I don't want to argue with her anymore, so I change the subject. Unfortunately, the only thing I can change it to is something that will aggravate her even further. "When we surface at the port, I think you should—"

"Stay on the sub," she cuts me off. "No way in hell."

"It would be safer. I'm not sure what exactly happens when I create stuff, and I don't want you to get caught in any kind of crossfire."

"If your plan doesn't work, no one will be safe anywhere. If it does work, then—" She balls up a fist and presses it against the ground. "Then I will be right there with you, waiting to tell you what an idiot you are when you're finished. Just like always. Dumbass."

Something in my heart cracks a little. "Thank you."

She looks back down at her watch and doesn't respond. She must be writing text after text to all of her friends, queuing them up so they send as soon as we get signal. Guilt stirs within me again. Of course I'm not the only person she's worried about. I leave her and head to the base of the tower to wait for us to surface.

Z is there. I slow down, wondering if it's me he's waiting for, and I get my answer when he looks up at me and says, "I'd like to kiss you, you know."

I freeze. I have never kissed anyone before. That's pathetic, I know, but I was busy trying to convince myself I wasn't going to literally stab any potential romantic partners in the back. That being said, I'm about to risk my life, and falling in love is one of the things I wanted to do with that life, and I don't know if I'm in love with Z but I'm pretty sure I could be if we had more time, so yes. Yes, kissing sounds good.

I start to step toward him. He holds up a hand. "Not now," he says, even though his eyes are full of want almost as much as haunting. "I don't know you well enough yet. I'm not the type of guy who kisses someone they just met."

I let out a shaky, disbelieving laugh. "Z, at this point you know me better than almost anyone on this entire planet. You're the only person who even knew I *was* the planet." And that is yet another very weird sentence to say out loud.

He shakes his head. "Not like that. I want to take you out on a date. I want to watch a terrible horror movie with you and laugh at all the scary parts and make you buy me kettle popcorn."

"I don't do horror movies. I do love kettle popcorn though."

"See, there's something I didn't know about you. Who kisses someone without even knowing if they like kettle popcorn?"

"I've wanted to kiss you a little bit even when I thought you wanted to kill me," I confess.

The wanting in his eyes takes up a little more space. "There, that's another thing I didn't know."

"So do we know each other well enough to make out yet?" I ask, feeling reckless.

He smiles, and his whole expression is triumph. "Not even close. Stay alive, bird boy, and take me on that date. Then we'll see."

I shake my head but can't help a grin. "Your pitch is much better than Anthem's."

"What was her pitch?"

"Mostly just threats."

"Sounds about right."

I sit down next to him and we wait together. The silence isn't as loaded between us as it was before, and soon I'm leaning against the side of his hoverchair and his fingers have found their way to my hair—ostensibly to pluck out bits of shale from it but actually because I think both of us need to be touching each other right now. Time passes. I zone out, trying hard not to think about, well, pretty much anything. Usually that doesn't work but sitting here next to Z with his fingers tangled in my hair, it feels the same way being surrounded by Pioneer Ship metal did: not safe, exactly, but less alone. Watched over.

My ears pop as the sub rises. The floor rolls beneath my feet and I grab onto the ladder to steady myself. Z extends his chair's magnets and locks them to the floor. Then the sterile, pleasant computer voice says "Surface protocol completed," and the hatch above us clunks as its automatic lock disengages.

Anthem walks down the corridor to join us in silence. Indy wanders out of the bunkroom to see what's going on and then happily jumps into Z's lap to ride up the ladder. I was planning to leave her here, but she's anxious when she's alone, and to be honest I would feel better having her with me. Having *everyone* with me: Mom and Dad, Anthem, Indy, Z. All the people I care about most. All the biggest reasons I'm doing this.

The hatch is open, a perfectly round window of dim, blank-paper sky. I climb through it first. The deck is wet and a little bit slimy, bits of algae and grayish foam skulking in the corners. The city is a jagged predawn skyline beyond it: half-built skyscrapers with dark broken-window gaps, a few trails of smoke rising up between them, the sound of sirens a distant, discordant melody winding beneath it all. Then the smell of fish, trash, and rot hits me, and my stomach rolls. I swallow a few times, trying to convince myself that I am *not* going to start what might be my last day alive puking my guts up, and focus on climbing down the ladder to the dock. It rocks a bit beneath my feet. When I step from it to the shore, I think there should be a difference in how the earth feels beneath my feet, in how it bears my weight, now that I know it's my own tomb. But when I close my eyes, it's not my potentially looming end that I think of. It's the sound of waves on a different shore, the feel of a different beach beneath my feet. A drop of blood on an oyster shell. A streak of brilliant blue across the horizon, stretching lurid shadows over the sand. A family huddling in a cabin and knowing it wouldn't protect them.

My mind reaches further: a car engine growling to life at midnight. A paltry note left behind, because I was too much of a coward to tell them I was leaving.

No. I hadn't been a coward because I was too afraid to face my family. It was *myself* I couldn't face. Myself I was afraid of. And now, with starlight in my veins and a hole punched through the sky, I'm still afraid, still a coward. But with these people at my back...I think I can move forward anyway.

"I'm going to tell them," I decide, and open my eyes.

Anthem is at my side, looking at her watch. "What?" she says, looking up sharply.

"Mom and Dad. I'm going to tell them the truth. Everything." My OCD, my dragon self, what I need to do next. They might try to stop me or they might support me; I know my own choice either way, and I also know that no matter what, I will be loved. And isn't that a marvelous thing all on its own? How long, I wonder, have I known they would love me even if they knew all my terrible secrets? Maybe that truth was something I was afraid to face, too.

"I'm glad you decided that," Anthem says with a smile that's half a grimace as she holds up her watch. "Because all my texts telling them everything just went through."

I freeze. Then, slowly, I turn to face her. "What. The. Hell?" I ask carefully.

She drops her hand back to her side and lifts her chin, squaring her shoulders: battle pose. "I texted them everything about the dragon stuff—I did it back on the ship, set it all up to send as soon as we got signal—because I didn't think you would tell them. They deserve to know. They deserve the chance to talk you out of...of what you think you have to do."

Frustration and betrayal churn through me. I take a step toward her. "Are you serious right now?"

"Yes, I am! Someone has to look out for you."

I fling my hands out, exasperated. "Are you going to follow me around my whole life trying to protect me from myself, Anthem?"

She leans forward and shouts right in my face. "I would love that chance, *if your life lasts longer than the next twenty minutes!*"

Z's voice breaks in from the dock behind us. "Guys."

I wave him off, not looking away from Anthem. "Not right now."

"Oh, sure, I can wait for you to finish your little sibling rivalry thing, I just thought you might want to know that *my sub and therefore all the people who probably want us dead are parked three berths to our left.*"

My gaze is still locked on Anthem, so I can see the moment she starts panicking. I do my best to clamp down on my own panic as I look over her shoulder and scan the berths; *The Shitty Clunker* is indeed there, its masthead festooned with algae and a few barnacles. The hatch is open but there are no soldiers in sight. It doesn't make me breathe any easier. If the soldiers aren't there, where are they? What if they already know my identity?

"Mom and Dad," I say, the words barely audible through my dread as I turn to Z. "They wouldn't go after them, would they? To try to get to me? We have to get to them before the soldiers do."

Z is frowning. He starts to say something, but then Anthem lets out an exhalation that's half a relieved laugh. "It's okay!" she says, smiling. She holds up her watch. "Mom just texted back. They're at the port station. They're here, they're fine."

Relief is a flood so strong I am nearly unmoored. I put out a hand to steady myself against Z's armrest even as I stand on my tiptoes to scan the buildings before us. There: the station is a squat, ugly building just a block or two away, right in the middle of the port. I recognize it from when I went to hide in the bathrooms and panic after I first saw Rick's knives. My parents are okay. They're a one-minute walk away.

But if they're a one-minute walk from us...how far are they from the soldiers?

Worry jars me into motion and I set off down the docks at a jog. Z calls something from behind me—a warning to hold on, something's not right—but I ignore him. I'm incapable of doing anything but running to my family right this very second. They know the truth about me now, they know everything, and I need to see them. I need to make sure they're safe.

Indy barks joyfully as she gallops past me, snapping at seagulls as she rushes ahead. Then, just a few meters from where she'd round the corner to the port station entrance, she stops. She backs off the stoop, hackles raised, tail stiff, teeth bared. She *growls*. I have never in my life heard Indy growl before. A premonition opens its wings somewhere in my chest, dread feathering across my ribs and down my spine. Anthem reaches out to try to stop me but I lunge forward too fast, round the last corner, and see who is standing in the doorway.

It's my dad.

With a gun held against his neck.

The world crashes in around me like thunder. Terror clings to my skin like humidity, like a storm about to break. I stride forward with no idea what I'm going to do until a pale soldier with her graying hair pulled into a neat bun and her hand wrapped around the gun's grip edges into the doorway. "Peregrine Kent," she says in a commanding, familiar Albergian accent, "stop right there."

I stop.

Anthem gasps behind me as she comes into view and Z spits out something low and angry. I ignore them both. Everything in me is focused on Dad. His wrists are cuffed in front of him, his gentle book-seller's hands scuffed, one fingernail torn and his knuckles bloody. His gaze is on me, his eyes intent with some unspoken message I don't have the capacity to try to interpret. He's got a scratch on his cheek and his hair is mussed. The pencil that is usually behind his ear is gone, and that's the thing that makes me, all at once, *furious.*

"You're to come with us," the woman—who is, of course, the commanding officer who tried to arrest us on *The Shitty Clunker*—says, her eyes trained carefully on me like I'm the one holding the weapon.

"What are you doing?" I ask her, and I don't recognize my own voice: distant and even and frigid.

Shapes shuffle behind her. More soldiers. I catch a glimpse of Mom's bright red hair from further inside the station as she twists toward me, trying to yell something through the duct tape someone has put over her mouth. An older man in a soldier's uniform is next to her, holding something—her watch, lit up with Anthem's message and the reply that we thought was from Mom. The fury inside me snaps tighter and starts to fray.

"We have you surrounded," the commanding officer says. I glance over my shoulder and see what I didn't think to look for before: men and women in tactical camouflage holding assault rifles and sniper guns, rising from their positions behind docks and atop roofs.

I should feel scared, I realize distantly. And I do, but something bigger and much more dangerous is burgeoning inside me. "You hurt my parents," I say.

"Don't move," she snaps.

"You kidnapped them. You hurt innocent people to get to me. And you don't even know for sure what I am."

I take a step forward. Soldiers shout, Anthem bellows at me, Z is yelling something. I ignore them all. I have become something implacable—a glacier, a landslide.

"Let me show you what I am," I say.

I don't even have to think *shine*. It just blinks on, washing every shadow from existence, a floodlight rolling out over the sand. The storm I was feeling earlier is gone. Now, I'm the storm. The light flickers and intensifies. I can't hold it long, but they don't know that.

"Let them go," I order through gritted teeth.

Inside the port station, radios crackle and several of the soldiers start shouting. The one with the gun held to Dad's neck doesn't move but her pupils contract and her frame goes rigid. Her gaze darts from my hands to my face to Dad and back. Her hand tightens on the gun's grip.

"Let them go!" I repeat more loudly, and now I feel the cold, brilliant flames of starfire rising through my chest. I catch them, hold them down. I am angry, but I'm still not this.

For just a second, a tiny snippet of time, I feel like I'm standing outside myself. I am angry. *Furious.* I have just about lost control completely. And I am still making the choice to not hurt anyone. *So, this is who I am,* I think, and feel a flitting moment of relief.

Then someone screams an order. Mom yells something in protest. Dad starts to turn toward her—too quick, too sharp.

A gunshot.

My shine collapses back in on me. I'm moving forward before I can even see clearly enough to make out the blood spattered on the doorframe, the gun that's swiveling to point at me. Dad is on the ground, splayed across the steps. A smear of red is emblazoned across his chest and down one arm. His eyes are glazed with shock but he sees me, he's reaching for me. I reach back, dropping to my knees at his side. Inside the station, Mom is screaming, choking behind her gag. Two soldiers are trying to subdue her. She catches one in the nose with an elbow, wrestles with the other for a second, and then dives to the ground toward Dad. Anthem is screaming too, lunging at the soldier who has the gun. Something flies through the air past my ear and stabs into the soldier's hand before she can get her weapon turned toward my sister. The pistol flies out of the soldier's grip and bounces to the ground. She yells and yanks the bloodied projectile out of her hand: a shard of emerald shale, thrown by Z, who is already pulling a pair of pliers out of his chair's storage compartment and leaning back to hurl it at one of the snipers atop the roof. But bullets are faster than tools, and the soldiers have been trained for combat and we're just a group of desperate teenagers. The sniper snaps his rifle up and aims at Z.

That's the instant the flames inside me boil up and out. I launch myself to my feet. Starfire slices cleanly through the air in a protective wreath around me, encircling all the people in the world that I care about most. Several gunshots rip through the air in quick succession. The bullets hit the starfire and dissipate into nothingness; they never existed. I can't remember what it sounded like when they were fired. Soldiers scream, more gunshots sound. I flex the starfire outward and it eats the eastern wall of the station.

"NO ONE. ELSE. GETS HURT!" I bellow with every bit of strength I possess—which is less and less with each passing second as the starfire shield swiftly drains what little is left of my energy. Dark

spots start to spread in my vision like ink splatters on canvas. My fingers are claws carving into my palms with the effort of protecting my family, but I won't let go of them, not even if it kills me.

What's left of the station groans and sways and splinters. I hear the loud hum of an approaching hovercraft beneath the gunfire. The medley of sirens grow louder: reinforcements. They'll keep throwing weapons and soldiers at me until something gives, and every bit of starfire I use to protect myself and my family is only bringing everyone, soldiers, civilians, and us, closer to death. I came here to save them. I came here to save them, and they only want to kill me.

Z was right. They will never stop hurting me even if they know the truth. They won't even let me speak. They're too afraid of me.

But I've been afraid too. I have spent my entire damn life afraid, and I'm still afraid now. That doesn't mean I can't make my own choices.

Gritting my teeth, I envision grasping my starfire and holding it tight in place while I let my light dim. My breath shudders and sweat slicks my brow but the shine blinks off and the swirling shield stays in place. My father on the ground, my mother bowed over him, Z tensed in his chair and Anthem on her feet ready to fight: I am surrounded by my people. A slow, whirling wall of flames that are every color and no color bars us from everyone else. I can still hear them, though, and I can't keep them out forever.

I drop to my knees at Dad's side, partly because I'm unable to support my own weight any longer. His cuffed hands are pressed against his injury. I reach for him, even though his fingers are coated in blood, even though a tumble of terrible thoughts flash through my mind one after the other at the sight. The feeling of his blood-slick hand beneath mine makes me want to retch, makes me want to run before I lose control and hurt him in more ways than I have already hurt him.

I don't move.

"I'm sorry," I say one last time, my voice shaking. Dad's eyes are screwed shut with pain and he's shivering violently in shock, but he squeezes my hand and his mouth shapes my name. Indy is pawing at him and howling, frantic, her beautiful black and tan coat smeared with crimson.

Mom's managed to tear the tape off her mouth and then the cardigan off her shoulders, and she's pressing it to his injury even though the fabric is still all tangled up in her cuffs. Her expression is glazed with panic as she looks from him to the starfire to me. Whatever calculation is happening in her mind, it must suddenly reach its conclusion, because the panic dissipates like mist and is replaced by a preternatural calm. She untangles the cardigan, gently eases away from Dad, and turns to face me. She fumbles at something in her hands: her watch. She must've grabbed it back from the soldier she was fighting with a moment ago. She smears blood over it as she slips it off her wrist, grabs my hand, and lays the little device face-up in my palm. I don't understand what she's doing until I catch a glimpse of the long text scrolling down her screen. I only catch a few words: *planet, starfire, Per, shield.* My eyes shoot to the top of the screen where the sender's name is listed: Anthem. It's the text she sent explaining everything. How much of it did Mom get to read, or overhear from the soldiers?

The inkblots in my vision are spreading and my hearing pulses in and out. I don't have the strength to turn away, to run. I can do nothing but raise my eyes and meet my mom's gaze. In them is my answer: everything. She knows everything.

She's crying. Without shame, without even seeming to acknowledge the tears. She raises a bloodied hand and touches my cheek. "You are our son," she tells me. "You were our son when you were an orphan in a glint mine. You were our son when you ran away on a submarine. You are our son now. I would know you in any shape." Her words shake with the cadence of urgency, a poem with serrated edges, and I'm crying now too, grasping her wrist as she cups my face in her hands. Her acceptance feels physical, a thing with mass and volume, a tincture poured into my soul to seal up all its cracks.

"Mom," I tell her, my voice wrenched out of me. "I have to save you. I have to go."

A fresh course of tears tracks through the blood on her face, sticking her ginger curls to her cheeks. "I know," she says, her voice half a sob. "I know."

Anthem's voice rings out, jagged with betrayal. "No!" she shouts, her hands curling in the cardigan's fabric where she's taken over holding it on Dad's wound. "You—you're supposed to stop him, not let him go! How could you? How *could you*?"

Mom drops her hands away from my face. "I love you," she tells me fiercely, even as Anthem rages. "We all love you."

"I love you too," I manage to reply. The starfire shield is starting to flake away like mist in a breeze. Weakness pulls me down, a gravity I can no longer resist—so I don't. I put my hands on the ground. Somewhere down there, beneath a century's worth of earth and bones and the remnants of a war no one remembers, is me.

I turn my head. I find Z. His expression is a graveyard again, full of echoes, full of haunted things, and I am one of them. He shakes his head mutely. He wants to stop me. I can't let him. This is the only end that will save them, so it's the only end I will allow, whether or not I manage to save myself as well.

"I hope you get your ship back," I tell him, trying to put everything in me into the words. "I hope you see the stars."

And then I take every drop of energy that I possess, rip every bit of strength and starlight from this human body, and *shove* it downward.

Deep below the ground, under centuries of terraformed sediment and layers of broken scales, the eyes of a great dragon open. Its mind, which at first seems vast and alien and then, as it adjusts, is neither, clears and wakes. The ridges of scar tissue on its back flex—a body trying to open wings it no longer possesses.

Distantly the dragon feels its much smaller, far more precious body collapse; there's not enough energy to maintain two forms, not when the dragon is gathering the vast amounts of energy it will need for what it has to do. Still, the creatures pauses and listens as its human heart stutters and stops, as its human eyes close beneath a papered-over sky. There's a grief in it, the keen, ravaging sort that is a blend of the most painful parts of both humanity and dragonkind. This dragon is both and neither.

A girl catches the slumping body of her brother. She wails at it, angry words gilded with grief. She starts chest compressions. The body doesn't respond. It needs starlight to flow through its veins along with blood, and there isn't enough of it. Not with the shell of the sky bending close overhead. It's an equation she can't solve, an unfixable problem at last. Her chest compressions slow and stop. She sits back and stares, her breath catching on the jagged edges of her anguish.

Nearby, a boy in a hoverchair closes his eyes, unable to watch. He's lost so much: his mother and all her memories, even the ship that held her ghost, and now he will lose this too. At least, he tells himself, he will remember Peregrine Kent.

It's not enough.

The dragon that is also a world inhales.

Not air. Star dragons have never needed air. It's the stuff of the universe itself the dragon is pulling into its lungs, and as the universe-stuff enters, it goes soft and glowing like iron in a blacksmith's forge. What little starlight there is left in the dragon's blood hums and waits. The dragon remembers seeing all those suns, all the infinite wonders of the universe, and thinking it would be among them forever. It's not them the dragon mourns, though. It's this: a little family kneeling on the ground around a fallen body. A boy who's lost everything, again.

The dragon exhales, and does what it has always done: it creates.

The fire of ancient stars hits the melding universe-stuff and they strike together like flint on steel. Power blooms out from the dragon's maw. The brand-new Barrier starts to slide over it, a second skin.

The energy in its blood drains swiftly. The dragon's body—the only one it has left now—begins to shut down. It's been in the process of doing this for centuries now, vessels dwindling and retreating as systems cut off one by one, but what it's doing now makes it irreversible. There is no way for its dragon body to survive this costly act of creation, and its human body has already given up all the energy it possessed with none left over to sustain itself. But what the dragon is doing will protect everyone else for a year, perhaps two, and there is hope that humanity will find a new home or at least a way off this one before it crumbles and takes what's left of the world with it.

The skin of the new Barrier slips across the dragon's head, closes over its eyes, and seals.

It's done. Except, one last thing: *I'm doing this for them,* the dragon whispers to its kin, who it can sense filling the skies in search of it.

Don't harm them. And—thank you, for coming for me. Thank you for trying to save me. A bit of its old human self slips through then and it adds: *Tell the universe I said hello.*

Its mission is done. It finishes its exhalation and feels its end blooming. It closes its eyes and waits. A minute later, perhaps two, the dragon's body shatters into a supernova of starfire.

A boy's body lies on the dock like discarded clothes. It's surrounded by mourners. Soldiers crowd toward them, all shouts and lifted weapons—until the earth shivers beneath them like a living creature trying to shake them off.

Dragons burst into existence overhead, one after the other, wings flashing with the jewel-bright lightning of lightspeed travel. They fill the sky with the shine of red dwarfs and blue giants and white supergiants. A hovercraft hits a scaled leg, explodes, and spirals down in a trail of smoke until it plunges into the sea. The dragons take no notice. They angle their heads downward and inhale, and starfire begins to spark over their jaws.

Some soldiers lift their weapons and fire into the air. Others flee as the sky fills with more dragons, with *all* of the dragons who have come through the breach. A continent away, the hole in the sky tears a little wider as dragon after dragon shoves through it, sensing the last moments of their kin.

In the middle of it all sits the boy in the hoverchair. As the underside of the Barrier lights up emerald and aquamarine and ruby and bright, gleaming diamond, he reaches a hand up toward it as if the sky were a sheet he could crumple in his fist and pull away. Helplessness is a seed in his chest and its bloom is unbearable. So many times he wished he could tear the sky open to explore beyond it; now he would tear it open and stay grounded forever if it meant getting starlight to the boy at his feet.

A beryl-yellow dragon lands with a *whump* at the entrance of the port, smashing a block's worth of buildings beneath it and sending a cloud of splinters and sand skyward. It is massive, a brand-new mountain range of curved spine, spiked tail, slivered eyes rife with intelligence and a delicate snout that tests the air like a scenthound on the trail. It throws its head back and roars—a sound so deep and alien that it seems to reach inside the boy's chest, grasp his ribs, and rattle them like dice in a cup. More dragons land like disasters: a hulking landslide crashing through a skyscraper, a cresting tsunami just offshore—but the boy's gaze is fixed on the first. An idea forms within him. He doesn't give it time to gestate. He leans down to where Peregrine's body lies and hauls it up into his lap with one great heave. Anthem stares at him blankly, and Peregrine's mother is too busy holding on to his father to do anything else. For long seconds, they only watch as Zeus Colton, son without a mother and captain without a ship, whirls his hoverchair toward the beryl dragon and accelerates.

Peregrine needs starlight. Z will get it for him, even if it means giving himself to the starfire too, even if success means Per won't remember any part of him.

But then Anthem jumps in his path, and he barely manages to decelerate before hitting her. In his lap, Per's body jolts. Z cradles Per's head and shoulders, bending his whole body around the other boy, as he glares up at Anthem.

"Get the hell out of my way," he snarls. "You should want this more than anyone."

"Don't you dare!" she screams, even as the still-shuddering earth makes her stumble to the side. "Don't you dare tell me what I should want!" She gulps in a breath, and when Z tries to go around her, she leans down and clamps her hands on his armrests. "I *do* want this," she manages. "I would let you throw yourself into starfire in a heartbeat if it meant saving Per. I would throw *myself* into starfire. But it's not...it's not what he chose. If you die to save him, he would never forgive you, even if he lives."

Around her waist, Z can see half a dozen dragons on the beach, in the city, offshore. They're all breathing silent, blinding starfire straight down, toward Per's dying dragon body. There's no way they'll reach it in time. The body in Z's arms is the only one that can be revived now, he knows it. Or maybe he's just desperate to have Peregrine back—the pure, kind-hearted, ridiculously optimistic boy who'd helped him face down eels and soldiers and his own ghosts.

"Let me go!" he shouts at last, his voice desperate and ravaged with emotion.

Anthem is weeping again, or maybe she never stopped. "No," she answers. "No. He wouldn't want me to. He told me not to fix this, and I tried anyway, and it didn't do a thing to save him. Let him finish what he started."

The words snap into Z like bullets. He sags back in his chair. Anthem is right. They can't save him. Not like this.

But maybe...maybe there could be another way.

Eyes jolting suddenly wide, he shifts Per's body to the side and scrabbles blindly at the side of his hoverchair. The door to the compartment there swings open. When he was on *The Soulless Monstrosity,* he'd filched a few keepsakes, intending to use them to bolster *The Shitty Clunker's* systems. One of the things he'd stolen was a rare and valuable communicator beacon. It's tuned to the military channel, which is undoubtedly being monitored right at this very second by the Council members and army generals.

What was it Per said? That if people knew the truth, they would do the right thing? Z thought at the time that was bullshit, and a big part of him still does, but maybe Per was right. Maybe there is still a chance to save the world and Peregrine too. It is, at the very least, worth a gamble.

He pulls out the device, a thin, flexible black sheet meant to be installed in a screen panel. He taps it awake and quickly accesses the comms for a system-wide blast—an emergency broadcast similar to the one the Council had sent out at Starfall. Then he pauses. What the hell is he supposed to say? He can think of nothing that sounds plausible, nothing that will jar the Council or even the public into action quickly enough to save Per.

He hesitates too long. The dragon that is also the world has finished its work, and now it is exploding into starfire.

With a hush like sudden death, the ground stops shaking. All of creation seems to go absolutely still and silent for the space of a held breath. There's something reverent about this silence, something waiting.

Z senses the meaning of the hush. He clutches the communicator and bows himself over it. More time. He only needed a little more time.

At his side, Anthem sinks slowly to the ground. Her eyes are glazed, disbelieving. A little distance beyond, her mother bends so low her forehead presses to the ground, tears and rage and insolvent grief leaking into the earth that is also her son's grave. Her father lets out an incoherent moan, a guttural, stricken sound that has nothing to do with his injury. It is the only thing that breaks the reverent quiet, but somehow, it only makes it feel even more sacred.

Then the great quiet ends. Like a bubble rushing toward the surface of the sea, a memory rises from the planet's brand-new core of starfire. It is a shockwave: inevitable, unstoppable. It hits every single person on the planet, seizes their minds and pours them full with the life of a boy who was also a dragon—because when a star dragon dies, it is connected to the mind of whoever kills it, and all of humanity has been killing Peregrine Kent for a thousand years.

The memories feel alien, filtered as they are through the mind of a dragon, but the emotion comes through clearly. Everyone catches glimpses, flashes, of the things Peregrine thought were most important: his family. Z and his mother and their mission. The truth of what the planet is.

The memory clears. Everyone in the whole world knows now exactly what they've built their world on, and exactly what he gave up to save them despite it. Some people drop to their knees in shock. Others weep or scream. Many begin planning an escape, a denial. And a few people—not all of them, but enough—wonder if there is anything they might do to save a creature who has given up so much to save them.

Z's spine hits the back of his hoverchair so hard it bruises. He's trembling, sobbing, gasping for air with the aftereffects of the memories and the borrowed emotions, but he ignores all of that as he fumbles once again with the communicator. He needed more time to know what to say to convince everyone, but now, thanks to Per's dying memory, he doesn't need to say anything at all. He only needs to tell people what to do, and hope that Per was right—that they will do the right thing.

He swipes at the communicator beacon, enters the code he'd hacked earlier, and presses a button: system-wide emergency broadcast. Elsewhere in the Conglom, *everywhere* in the Conglom, screens power up and fill with his face. The communicator beacon doesn't have access to a power source so he's only got enough juice for a few seconds of transmission, but a few seconds is all he needs. He rasps out a single sentence:

"Open the sky."

The fifteen members of the Conglom Council are huddled around a large, ornate table when the planet-dragon's memory crashes into them. Nine of them flee in their hovercrafts, thinking to safeguard their homes and families and squirreled-away wealth. Two huddle in their chairs and weep, insensate, overwhelmed. But four stay. They stare at each other across the slab of a table, the spot where they sat when they ordered the escalation of glint mining, when they listened to the estimates of how many people would be uncreated if the Barrier fell, where a few of them even tried and failed—like a handful of others who came before them—to find a humane solution.

They are still sitting there when the giant screen hovering above their table blinks to life and fills with a boy's face. *Open the sky,* he demands, and then the screen blinks off again.

The Council members stare at each other. None of them budge.

Then someone pounds on the locked door. A security guard. "Open the sky!" he screams, voice muffled by the thick carved wood. "Open the sky!"

Outside, a clamor rises from the base of the building. People flooding into the streets, emerging from the homes and hideouts where they've been sheltering, some of them weeping, others fighting, and a few looting. But above the commotion, a chorus lifts: *Open the sky. Open the sky. OPEN THE SKY.*

The four Councilors look at each other. They consider the crowds below, consider the realization that there will be a riot, that they could be overrun, that even some of their own guards are on the side of the world-dragon. The emotion from the memory is still lingering in their own minds like an aftertaste: sorrow, determination, and an incongruous but bone-deep sense of hope.

The Councilors pick up their consoles, type in brief lines of command, and open the sky.

At the port, as one, the dragons cease breathing their starfire. The dazzling lights cut off. The world seems dull without it, the new gaping chasms in the ground sharply shadowed. The dragons lift their muzzles to the sky and, together with the humans still present, watch motionlessly as the Barrier that has held them out and humankind in for a thousand years peels away like old wallpaper. The universe flares open behind it: the pink edge of dawn at one horizon, gold and silver stars strewn across the navy canvas of the galaxy at the other.

The dragons bend their heads back down to consider the humans at their feet. There are only a few who haven't fled, and they still they aren't fleeing now. One of them holds a boy who smells, very faintly, like starlight. The dragons lean closer, and finally see what the dragon at the shales saw: a boy who was not born but created, an ancient soul clinging to a human body. The soul is almost gone, faded to barely an ember—but the light of a thousand distant suns is a bonfire poured down from the heavens, and there is a chance it could catch.

The dragons watch the boy.

Nothing.

Nothing.

And then—an inhale.

In my oldest memory, I am ancient and endless.

Then, there was this: the glow of wings, the black span of infinite space, the sparks of a thousand suns. Wonder. Freedom. Even then, though, I was dying.

It is my first memory, and now my last thought.

I am a star winking out. An empty night sky, the silence waiting at the end of all things. The universe has closed itself to me and I would like to think I will find my way back to it—dust to dust, ashes to ashes, cosmos to cosmos—but the sky is empty and there is nothing to light my way home. I drift, and sink, and fade.

And then like a scroll rolling back, the universe *opens*.

Starlight hits my veins like adrenaline. It roars into my brain, jump-starts my heart, an electric shock that makes my spine snap into a crescent and my mouth gape as I desperately suck in a breath. My skull knocks into something hard that makes a metallic *clunk* before arms wrap around my shoulders, cradle my head, hold me steady while I spasm and flail. The influx of life is so strong, so painful, that it feels more like death—a pins-and-needles anguish that injects starlight into every cell in my body at once.

It takes what feels like forever before the spasms slow and stop. My ragged gasps start to even out. I remember I have eyes that I can open, and so I do, and the first thing I see is...

The *sunrise.*

One side of the sky is a deep twilight violet spangled with an endless array of stars and planets and the dusty green-and-blue of nebulae clouds. The other side shades from orchid to teal to a thin line of pink heralding the rising sun. Pinpricks of melted-jewel light—dragons?—are spinning through the whole span of the sky in some sort of complex pattern before, one by one, they vanish into space, leaving long tails of color behind like comets. It looks like the whole sky is dancing, and I feel it in my joints, in my marrow: the sky is dancing for *me.* This is my homecoming.

I lift a shaking hand to scrub at my eyes. The hands that have been holding my head steady shift, and there's a trembling exhale somewhere above me. I refocus, turn a little, and see Z. I am sprawled over his lap on the ground next to his hoverchair. He's got one arm tucked behind my neck, holding me steady against his chest, and the other arm braces my torso against my slowly-dwindling spasms. He is staring at me like I am the only thing in the universe, more important than the stars, more wondrous than the sunrise. His hair is even messier than usual and his face is splattered with blood, tear tracks, and a few remnants of machine oil, but he's beaming, and *gods,* suddenly I have never seen anything more beautiful or impossible in my entire life. I can't see anything else. I can't think of anything else.

I lick my dry lips, summon my voice, and manage to croak out, "I would really like to kiss you now."

He laughs, incredulous but delighted. "I—I thought we were waiting until our kettle popcorn date—"

I don't let him finish. Instead, I reach up with my still-quivering hand, grab him by the wrinkled collar of his shirt, and pull him to me. My grasp is about as strong as a newly-hatched chick but Z is more than willing to make up the difference. He lets out a quavering breath before he dips down, angles himself against me, and tenderly, gently, brushes his lips over mine. The kiss lasts a glorious three seconds before memory crashes in: the plan, the gunshot, the blood, the starfire shield…and *my dragon body exploding into starfire.*

I yank back from Z. "What—what happened, did I—did every-one?" I can't cram all my thoughts into words quickly enough, but Z understands anyway.

"You did it," he tells me, still grinning. "The shield worked. It's holding."

His happiness doesn't reach me just yet. I'm shoving myself up and away from him, staggering to my feet and nearly falling again before someone else swoops in to grab my arm and brace me. Anthem. She looks lost, shaken, but physically okay. "Dad," I manage, turning to search for him, my voice loud with fear. "Dad?"

"There," she says quickly, pointing. I follow her gaze. A soldier with a med kit is kneeling over my dad's prone body and spraying his chest with some sort of medical chemical stuff. I panic for a second before I see that his handcuffs are gone and his eyes are open. His face is a rictus of pain and concentration but he's alive and the spray stuff seems to have stopped the bleeding. Mom's sitting next to him and holding his other hand with a white-knuckled grip.

I sag against Anthem. "Okay," I manage. "Okay." Then, a little bit pathetically: "Can someone please tell me what happened?"

But before anyone can answer, the world's loudest, happiest bark sounds about three inches away from my left ear and I barely have time to flinch before Indy's full weight plows into me and sends me sprawling onto my back again.

"Help," I manage between ineffective attempts to shove off my ecstatic dog.

A hand reaches out and shoves her aside and then Anthem is grabbing me and yanking me back up. She looks even more lost than she did a moment ago, her whole self quivering with the aftershocks of whatever's just happened.

"You were dead," Anthem says, her voice hoarse like she's been screaming. Before she can say anything else, Mom's there, alerted by Indy's joyous greeting. She pries Anthem off me and grabs me by the shoulders with a grip that could probably strangle me if her hands were around my neck. She looks down at me intently, like she needs to memorize my face. There's a smear of blood on one of her arms and both her hands. Her eyes are shot through with red and her breaths are shuddering like she doesn't know what to do with the air.

"You," she says, her voice shaking under the weight of too many emotions, "are so grounded." Then she crushes me to her and I have to twist in her grip so I can breathe again.

"Someone tell me what happened!" I demand, my voice cracking.

"I told you. You died," Anthem says to me, staring like she's afraid I'll evaporate into nothingness if she blinks. "And then you died *again* in your other body when you created the second Barrier. And everyone saw into your memories when it happened."

"What?" I say, too loudly.

The soldier who's been tending to my dad—who is also, I realize, the same one that shot him—finishes and stands up. "We all saw...you," she says, not quite meeting my eyes, like I'm either a monster or something too bright to look at. I glance down at that thought to make sure I'm not shining and exhale in relief when I see I'm not.

"What do you mean, you saw me?" I demand. My vision goes blurry and dizzy for a second—I'm probably overexerting myself too soon after, you know, *being dead*—and I reach out to brace myself on the back of Z's hoverchair.

The soldier swallows. "We caught glimpses of your memories. Couldn't understand most of it, but the emotions, and the—the important things, the planet, what you were trying to do, we understood that."

I turn and stare at Anthem, and then when she has nothing to add, at Z. I notice some sort of flexible black device lying in the sand next to him and begin to have a suspicion. "What happened after I died? How am I standing here? Why is the sky..." I glance upward at it and lose my train of thought for a long moment while I stand dazed beneath the stars, beneath the dawn.

Z's voice is rough when he answers me. "You said people would make the right choice if they were given the chance," he says. "If they understood the truth. The sky is open because you were right."

"And," I guess, "because you did something. Didn't you?"

"He was going to drag you into starfire," Anthem says flatly. "And I wanted to let him, but I stopped him instead, because. Because." She has hit some sort of verbal wall but doesn't need to finish. I can imagine the rest. I can imagine how hard it must have been for her, to go against her natural bent like that, to risk letting me stay dead.

"So she didn't let you go through with that very stupid plan," I say with a hard look at Z, who glares unrepentantly back. "What *did* you do, then?"

He scoops up the black device thing and waves it at me. "I used this. Communicator beacon from *The Soulless Monstrosity.* Sent out an emergency broadcast and told everyone how to save you."

I stare at him. "You told them to...open the sky? And they did?"

"They did," he confirms, looking a little incredulous himself.

A buzzing noise interrupts our conversation—hovercrafts cresting the horizon. Mom turns and looks at them and her eyes get beady in a dangerous sort of way. "Who is that?"

"Probably my superiors coming to take us to the Council for debriefing," the commanding officer answers, shifting uncomfortably. It's a very unnatural look on her.

"That's what I thought. Excuse me," Mom says to us, dropping a gentle kiss atop my head and then one on Anthem's. "I have to go have a...conversation...with those people." She says *conversation* like she actually means *murder*. Turning away from us, she plants herself on the docks between us and the hovercraft and puts her hands on her hips with a scowl that would make any wise person tuck tail and run.

My legs finally give out and I sit back down on the ground next to Z. He reaches out without a word and grasps my hand. Anthem sits down at my other side and doesn't say anything either, just stares at the horizon over the sea. I wonder what's going through her mind. I wonder if she feels as lost as she looks. Even if she does I know she'll work through it, come out stronger on the other side of it. She's Anthem; she can't help it.

She sees me watching her. "Did you know it would work?" she asks in a voice that's almost a whisper. "Did you know you'd come out okay?"

I pause, groping for words, and finally say: "I hoped."

Hope. What an odd thing. I'd thought it to be a liability, a danger, an obstacle to trip me up and knock me off guard. Instead, it's bought me this:

My life.

My family.

And the first sunrise in a thousand years.

www.ingramcontent.com/pod-product-compliance
Lightning Source LLC
Chambersburg PA
CBHW061641190726
48289CB00006B/1693